DC THE OFFICIAL DC SUPER HERO JOKE★BOOK

By Sarah Parvis, Michael Robin, and Noah Smith

downtown bookworks

downtown bookworks

Downtown Bookworks Inc.
265 Canal Street
New York, NY 10013
www.downtownbookworks.com

Special thanks: Sara DiSalvo; Sarah Eisler; Althea and Desmond Lasseter;
Julie Merberg and Morris, Nathaneal, Kal, and Maccabee Katz;
Stephen Robin; Miles and Lily Freedman; and Arlo, Gus, Harvey,
and Murphy

Select illustrations © Scott Kolins: Katana (pages 65, 83, 116, 159)
and Bumblebee (40, 121)

Designed by Georgia Rucker

Printed in the United States
January 2017

ISBN: 9781941367339

10 9 8 7 6 5 4 3 2 1

Welcome!

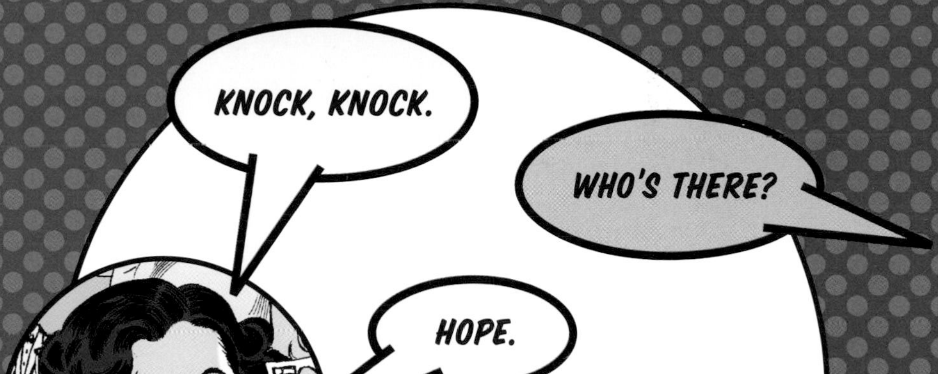
KNOCK, KNOCK.
WHO'S THERE?
HOPE.
HOPE WHO?
HOPE YOU ARE READY TO LAUGH. THESE JOKES SURE ARE FUNNY.

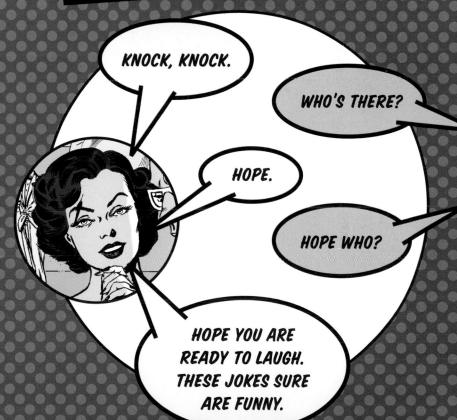

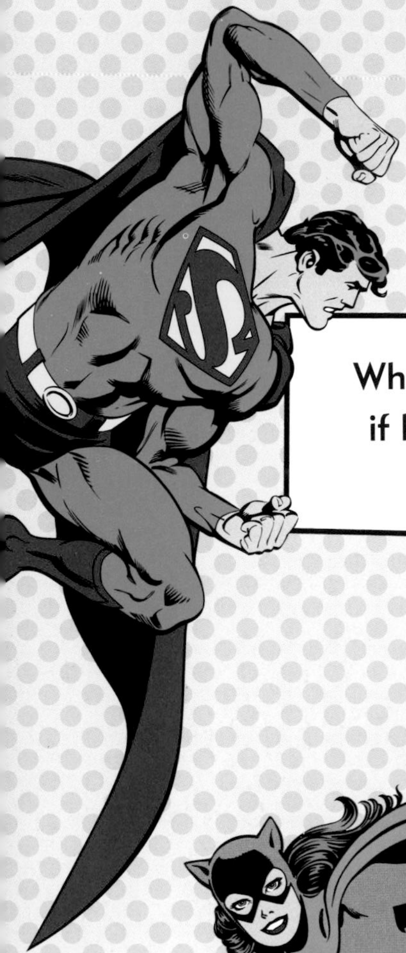

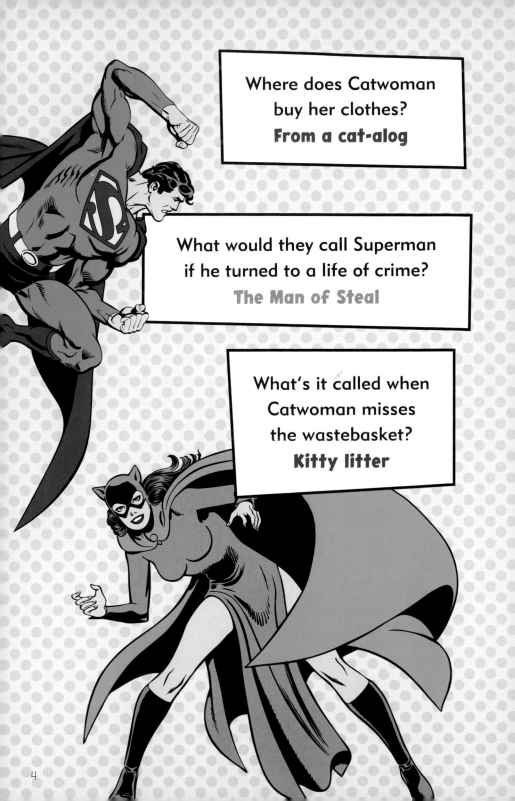

Where does Catwoman buy her clothes?

From a cat-alog

What would they call Superman if he turned to a life of crime?

The Man of Steal

What's it called when Catwoman misses the wastebasket?

Kitty litter

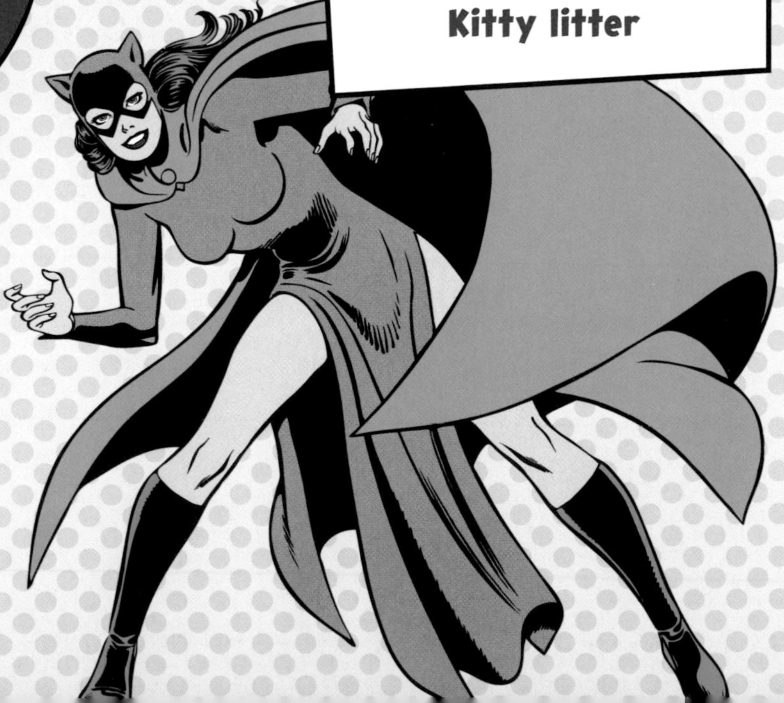

Why did the tiger refuse to eat the Joker?

Because he tasted funny

Why does the Penguin wear white gloves?

It gets chilly in the Iceberg Lounge.

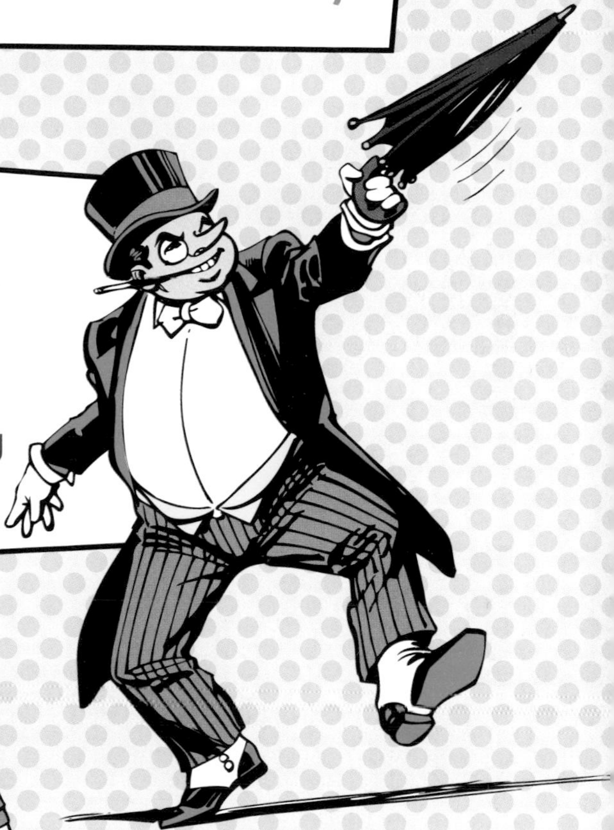

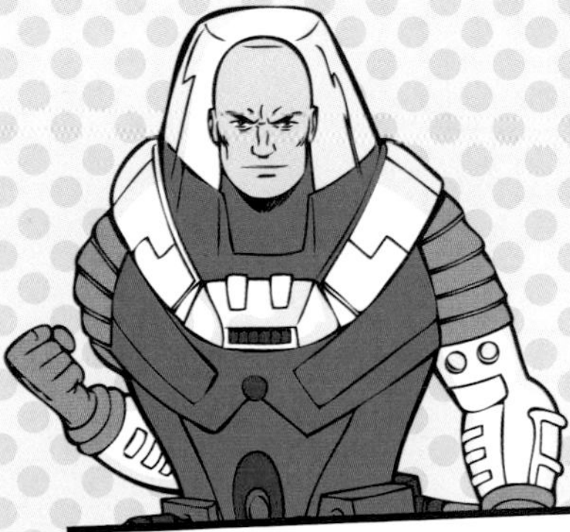

What is Mr. Freeze's favorite food?

Brrrrrrrrrritos

What do you get when you cross Catwoman with a fish?

A purr-anha

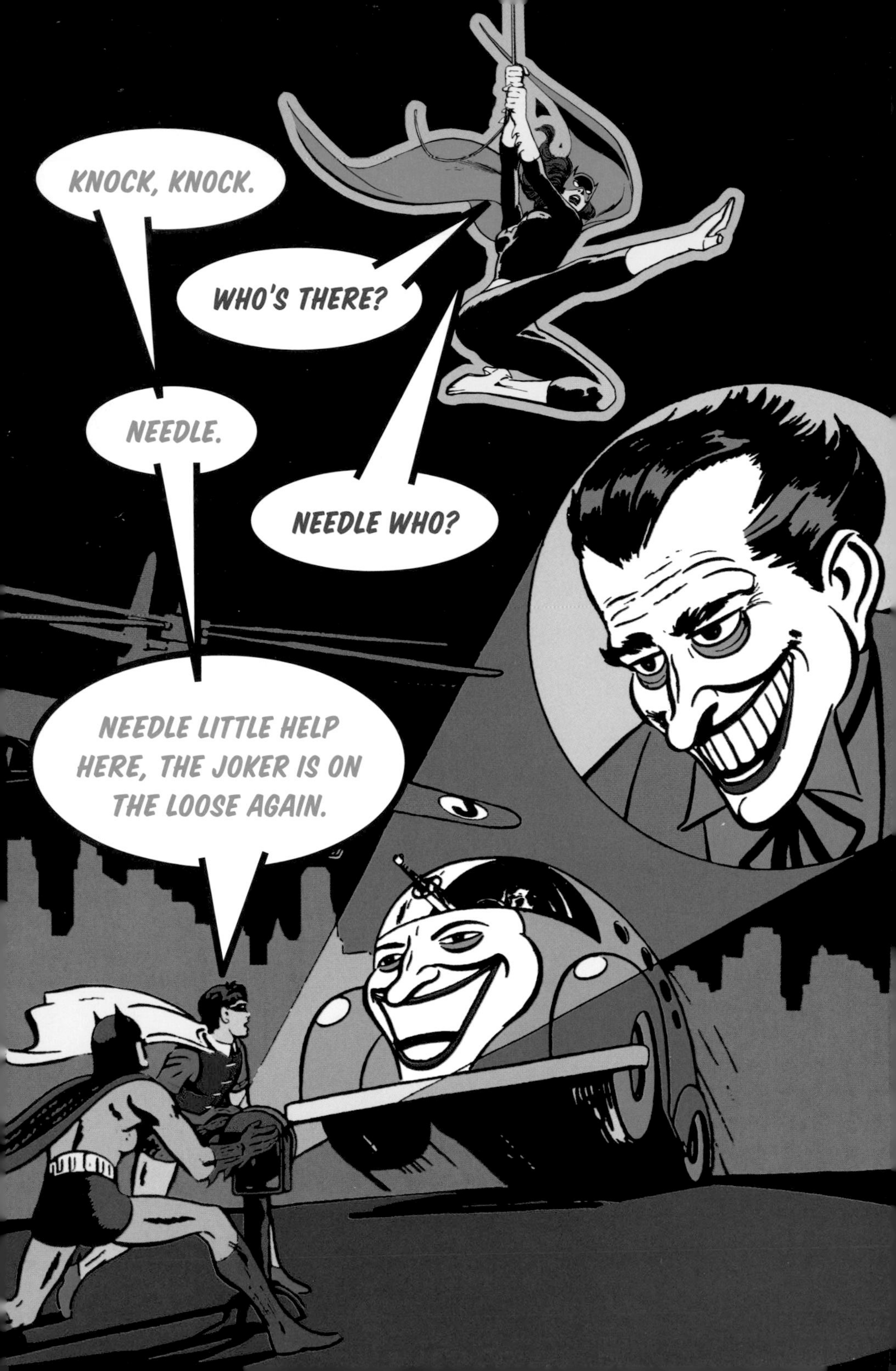
KNOCK, KNOCK.
WHO'S THERE?
NEEDLE.
NEEDLE WHO?
NEEDLE LITTLE HELP HERE, THE JOKER IS ON THE LOOSE AGAIN.

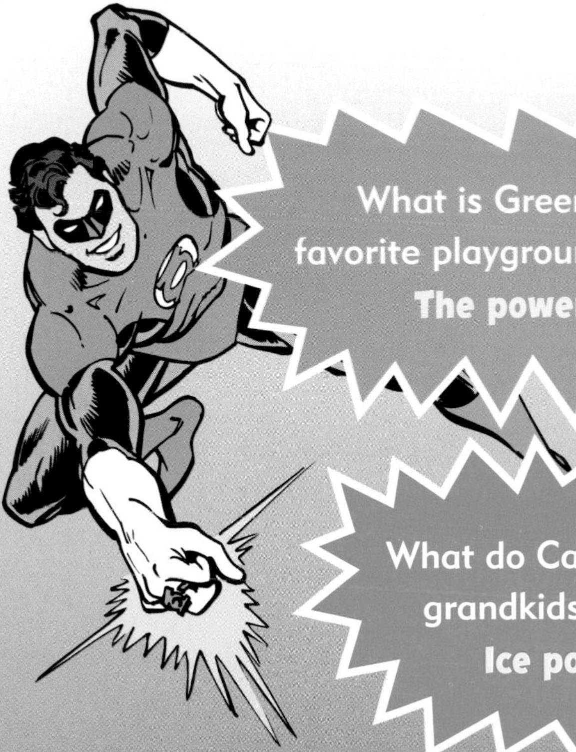

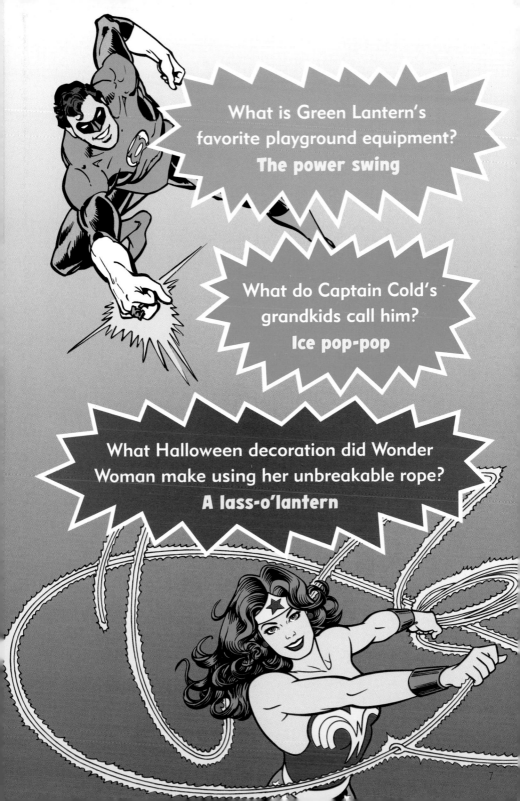

What is Green Lantern's favorite playground equipment?
The power swing

What do Captain Cold's grandkids call him?
Ice pop-pop

What Halloween decoration did Wonder Woman make using her unbreakable rope?
A lass-o'lantern

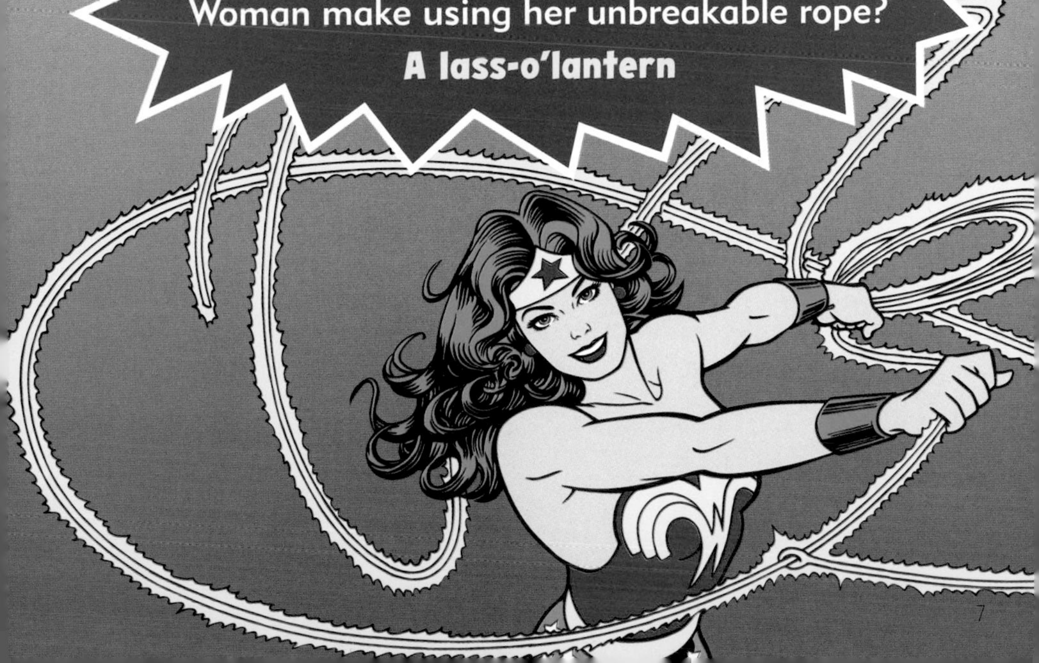

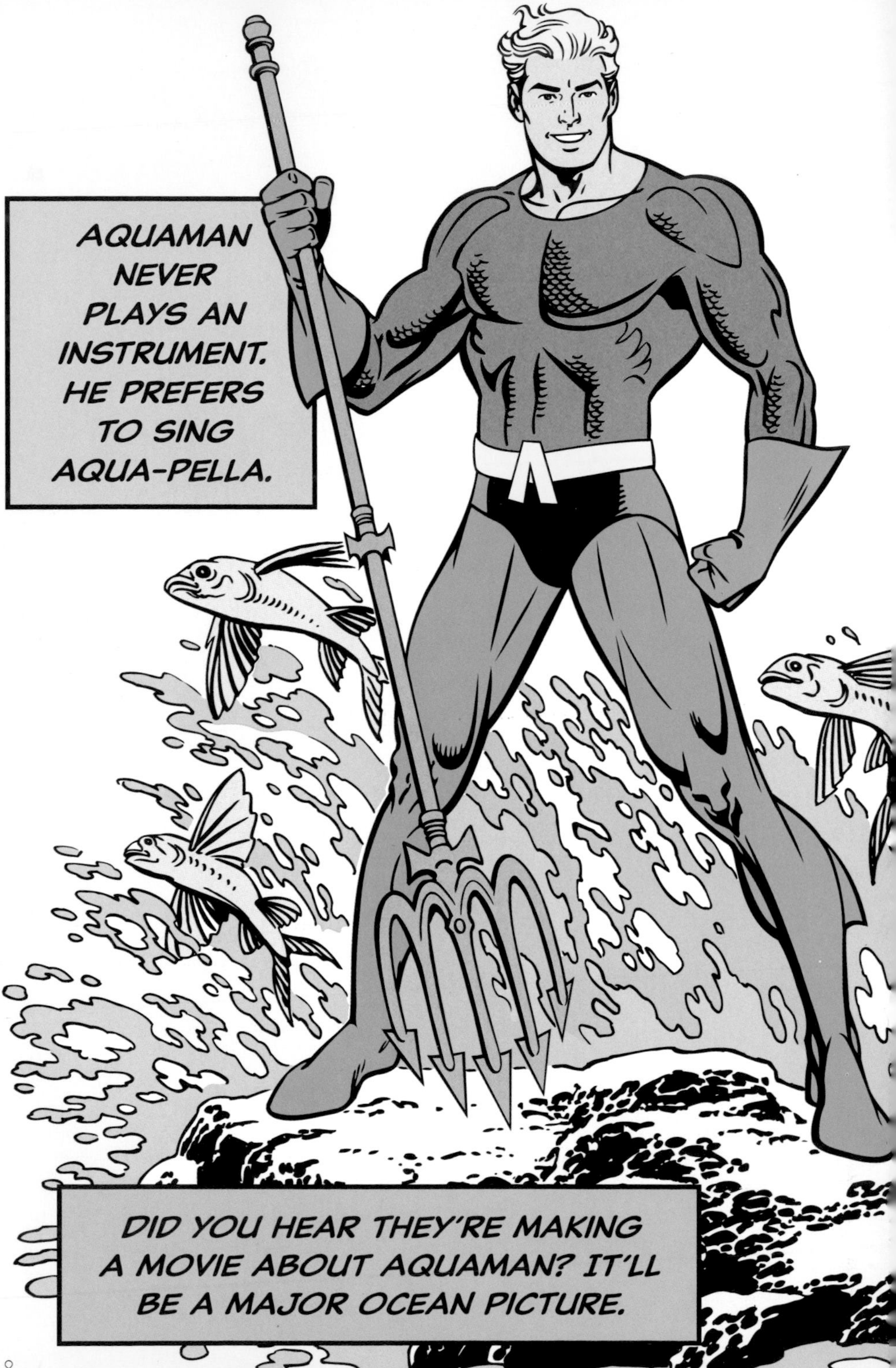
AQUAMAN NEVER PLAYS AN INSTRUMENT. HE PREFERS TO SING AQUA-PELLA.
DID YOU HEAR THEY'RE MAKING A MOVIE ABOUT AQUAMAN? IT'LL BE A MAJOR OCEAN PICTURE.

Why did Aquaman cross the road?
To get to the other tide

Why did Aquaman lose
the spelling bee?
He thought "Earth"
had seven Cs.

Did Aquaman show up
for no reason?
No, he came with a porpoise.

Why did the lobster and the crab refuse when
Aquaman asked them for help?
They were being shellfish.

Why did Aquaman ask an oyster for advice?
He always has a pearl of wisdom.

Why did Aquaman lose
a wrestling match with a seal?
He couldn't flipper.

What do you call Black Canary
when she's wearing earplugs?
Anything you want. She can't hear you.

How did Bumblebee
get to school as a kid?
On the school buzz

What does Aquaman put on his
peanut butter sandwiches?
Jellyfish

Why does Hal Jordan call
himself "Green Lantern"?
**It has a nice
ring to it.**

What does Krypto say before he flies into the air?

PUP, PUP, AND AWAY!

Why can't you believe everything Aquaman says?
His stories are a little fishy.

Why doesn't Batgirl need Batman's help?
She's perfectly cape-able.

What is Aquaman's favorite art supply?
Watercolors

Who's the handsomest super hero?
The Flash. He's always dashing.

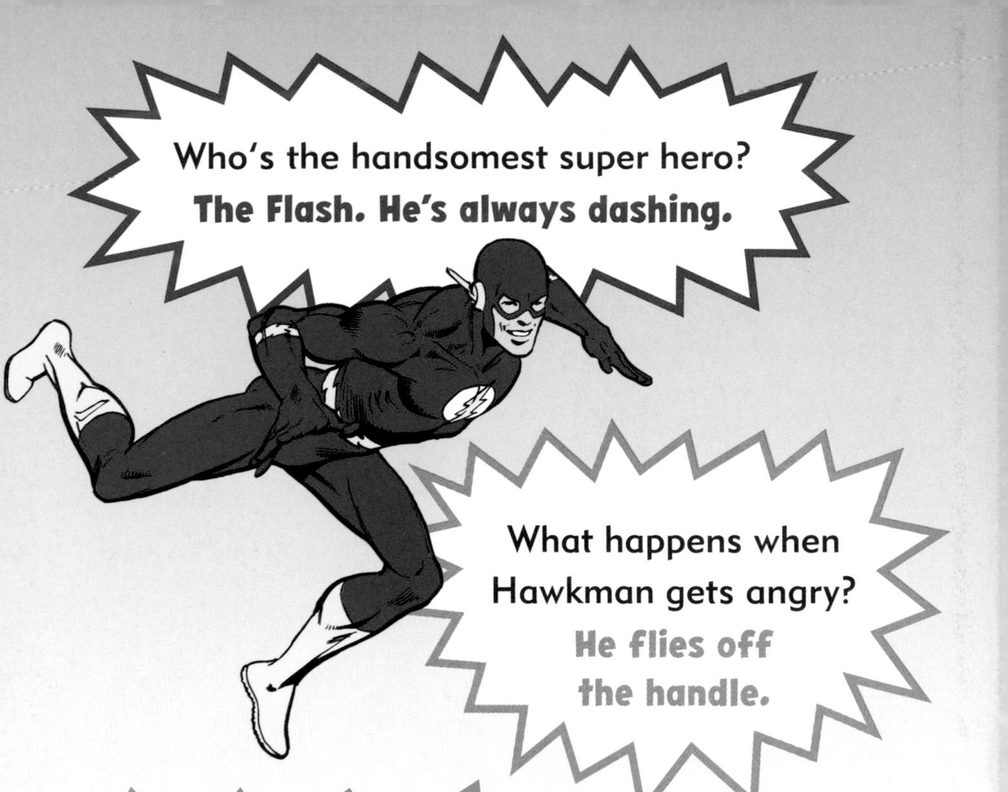

What happens when Hawkman gets angry?
He flies off the handle.

Why is Superman so great at cheering people up?
If you're sad, Superman won't just lift your spirits, he'll lift your whole house.

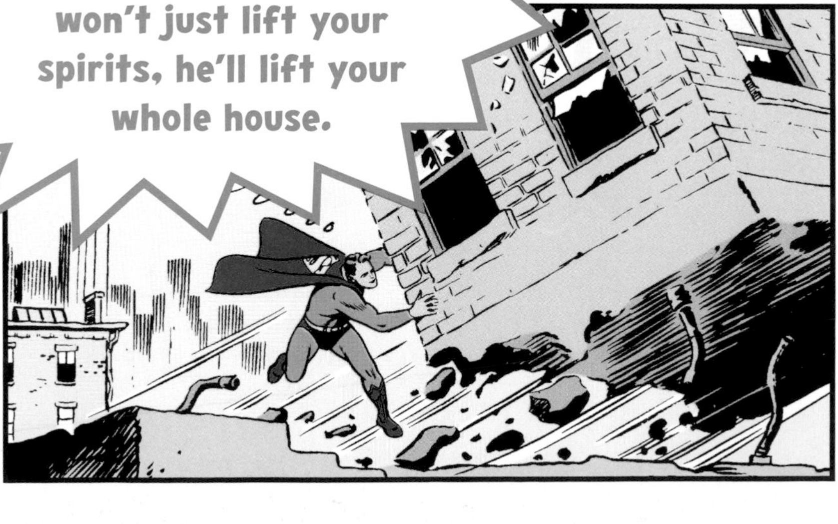

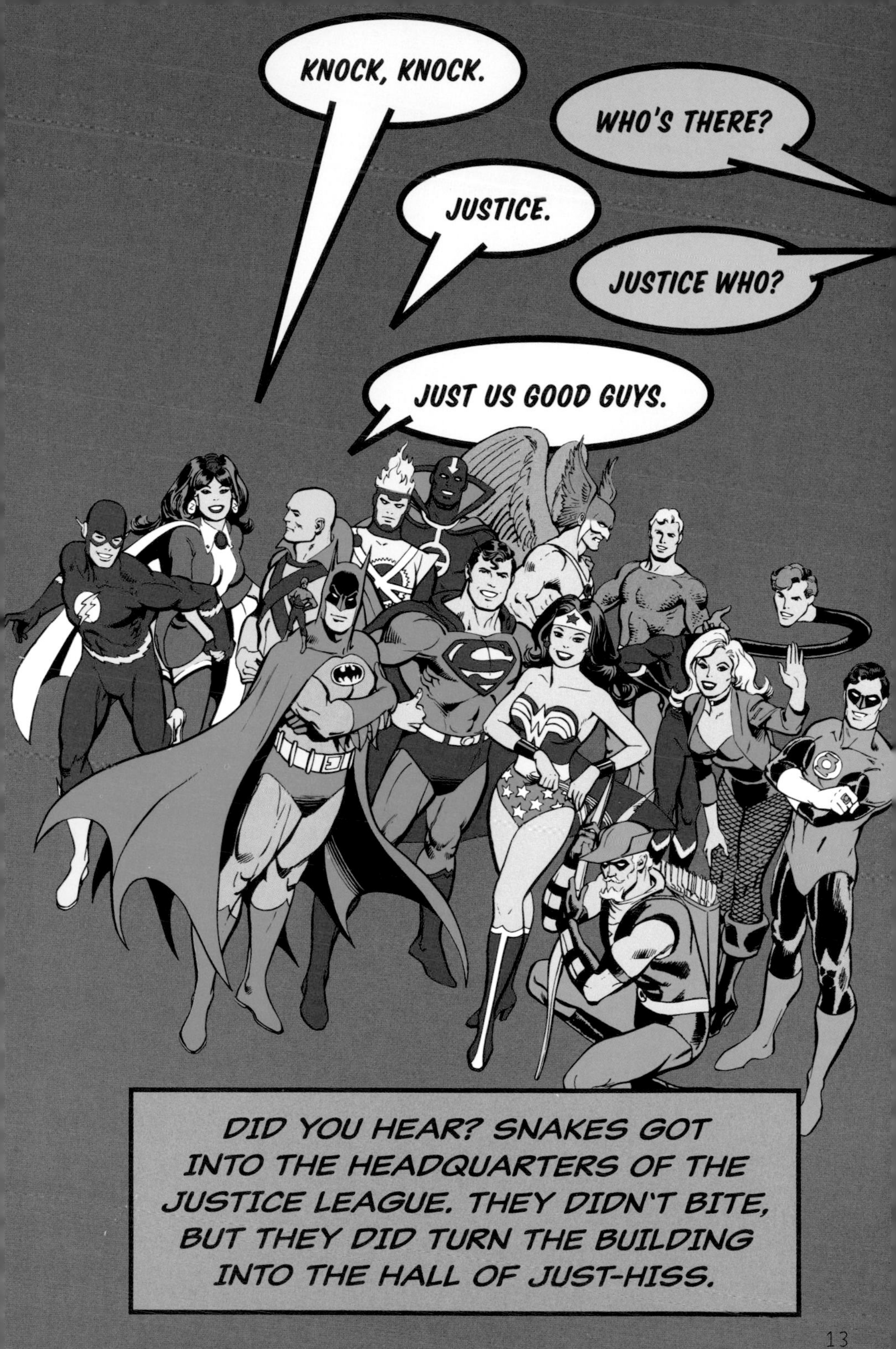
KNOCK, KNOCK.
WHO'S THERE?
JUSTICE.
JUSTICE WHO?
JUST US GOOD GUYS.
DID YOU HEAR? SNAKES GOT INTO THE HEADQUARTERS OF THE JUSTICE LEAGUE. THEY DIDN'T BITE, BUT THEY DID TURN THE BUILDING INTO THE HALL OF JUST-HISS.

What did Batman say when Killer Croc was sentenced to a long prison term?

"See you later, alligator."

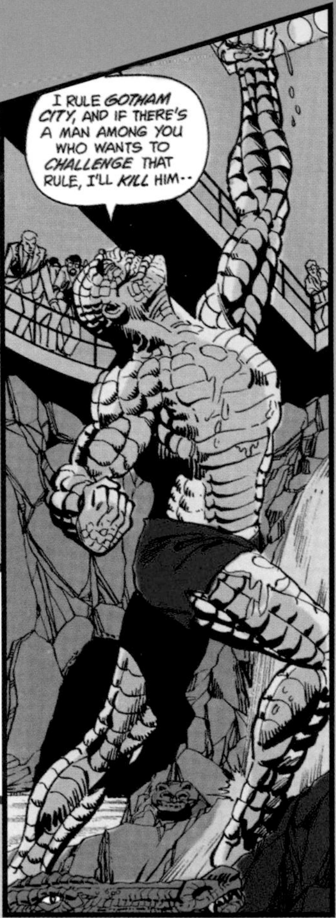
I RULE *GOTHAM CITY*, AND IF THERE'S A MAN AMONG YOU WHO WANTS TO *CHALLENGE* THAT RULE, I'LL *KILL* HIM--

When will Killer Croc get released from prison?

After a while, crocodile.

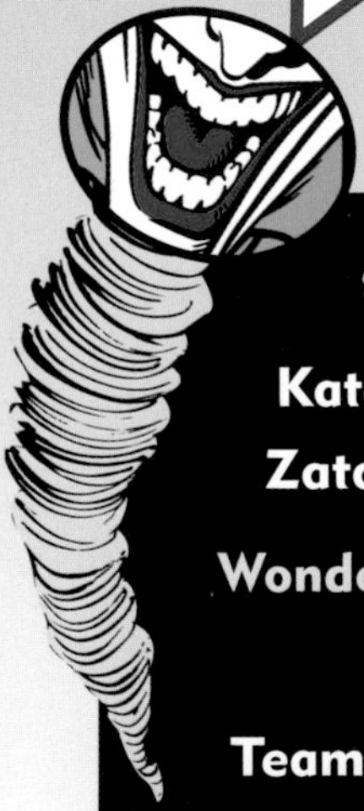

SAY THIS FIVE TIMES FAST!

Katana's cantina contains a banana. But Zatanna's cabana can't stand a bandana.

Wonder Woman wonders when but why would Wonder Woman wander?

Team Teen Titans topples terrors, thankfully thwarting thwacking thugs.

Making messes makes Martian Manhunter mad.

Batman battles baddies into behaving better.

What's the best thing about the Joker's getaway car? **It gets good smile-age.**

Why are farmers happy to see Green Lantern? **No weevil shall escape his sight.**

What's the Joker's favorite thing to do on a Saturday night? **He likes chillin' with the villains.**

HOW TOUGH IS BATMAN?

There are no corkscrews in Gotham City because Batman scared them all straight.

The Bat-Signal doesn't really light up the night sky. It just scares the darkness away.

The Batmobile doesn't get parking tickets. It gets thank-you notes.

If the groundhog sees its shadow, it means six more weeks of winter. If a criminal sees Batman's shadow, it means six to ten more years in jail.

Batman isn't "as tough as nails."
If you hit a nail with a hammer, it stays down.

If Superman were an insect,
who would be his girlfriend?
Locust Lane

If Superman were a plant,
who would be his girlfriend?
Lotus Lane

Why don't they serve chocolate at
Arkham Asylum?
**Because they don't want anyone
to break out**

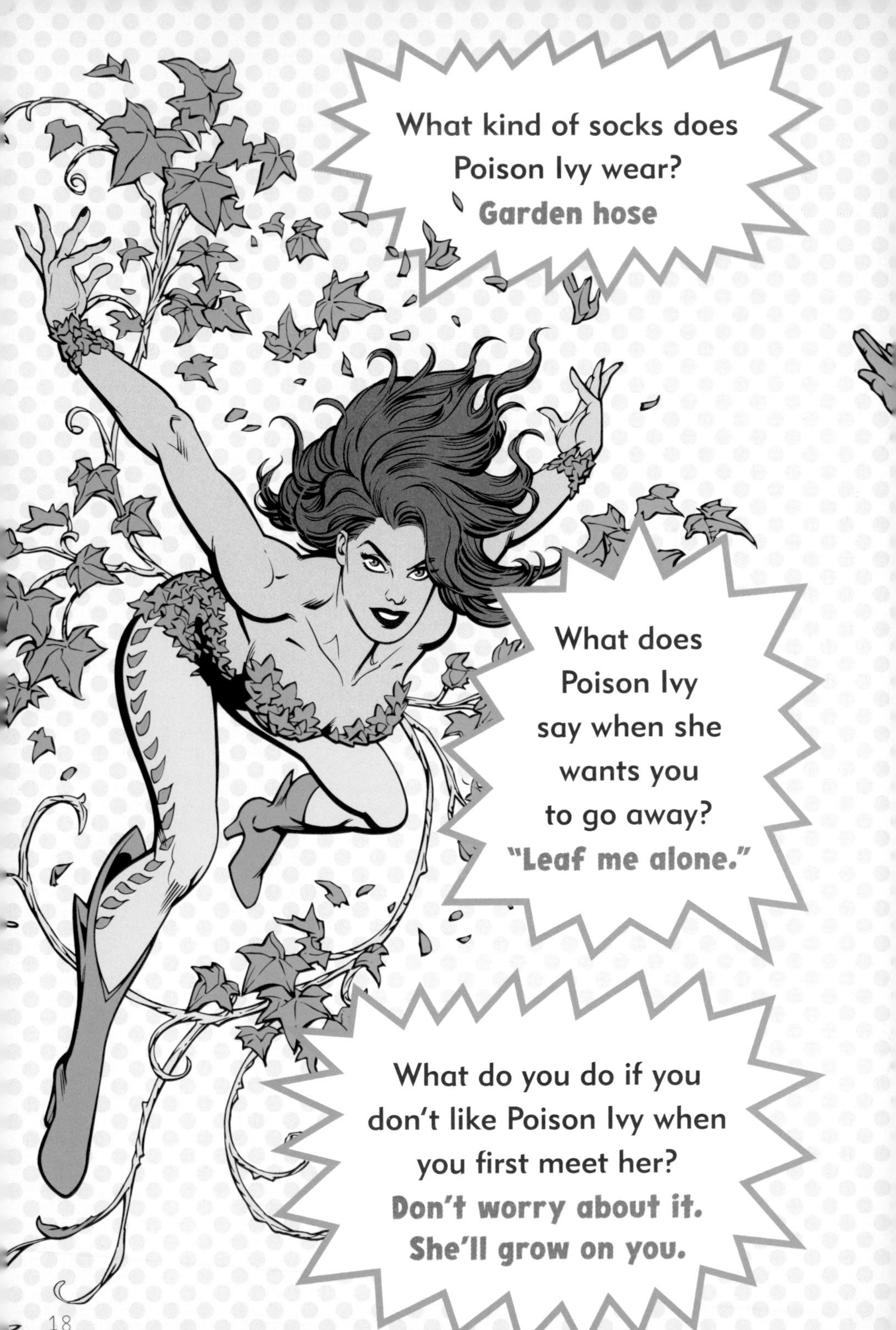
What kind of socks does Poison Ivy wear?
Garden hose
What does Poison Ivy say when she wants you to go away?
"Leaf me alone."
What do you do if you don't like Poison Ivy when you first meet her?
Don't worry about it. She'll grow on you.

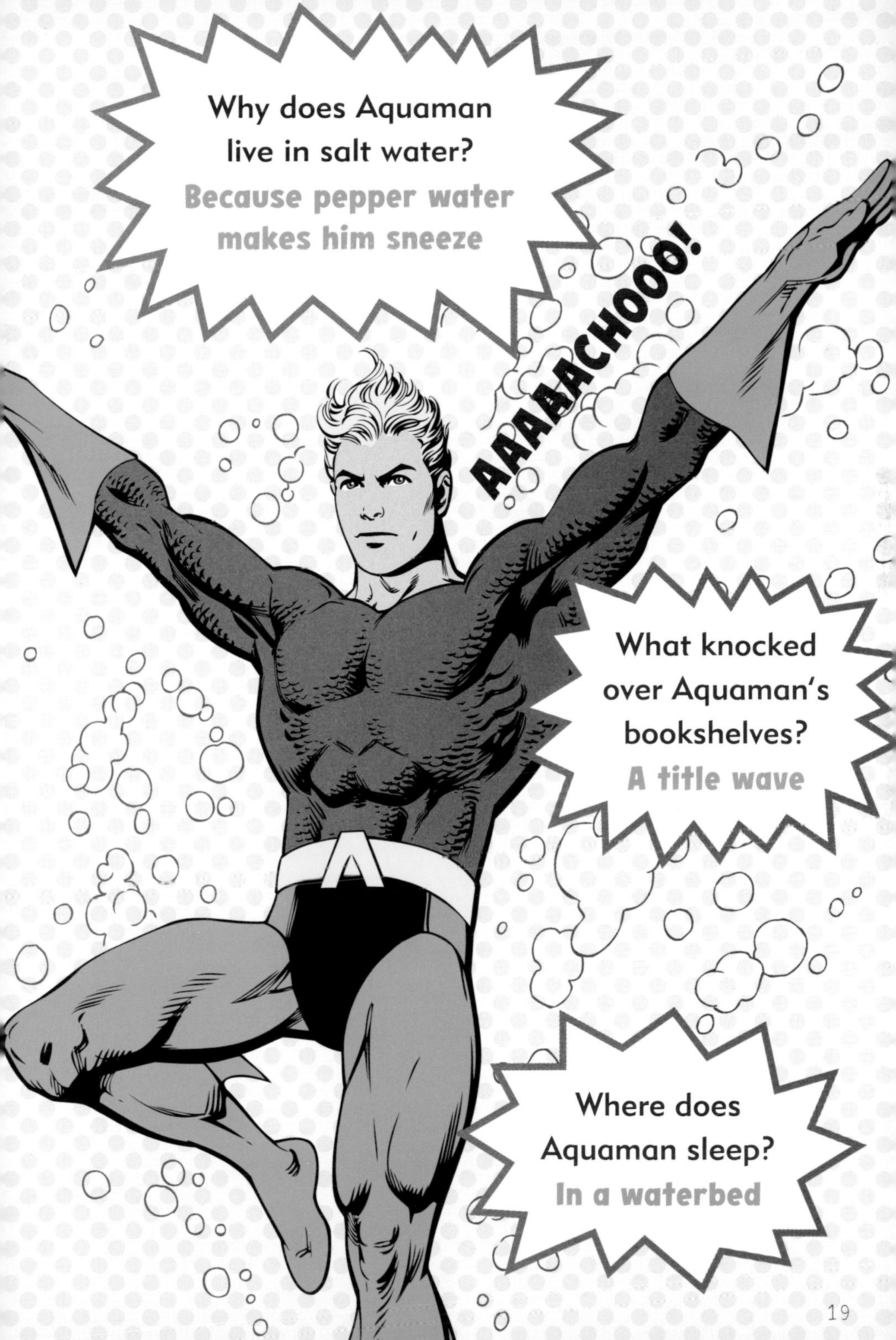
Why does Aquaman live in salt water?
Because pepper water makes him sneeze
AAAAACHOOO!
What knocked over Aquaman's bookshelves?
A title wave
Where does Aquaman sleep?
In a waterbed

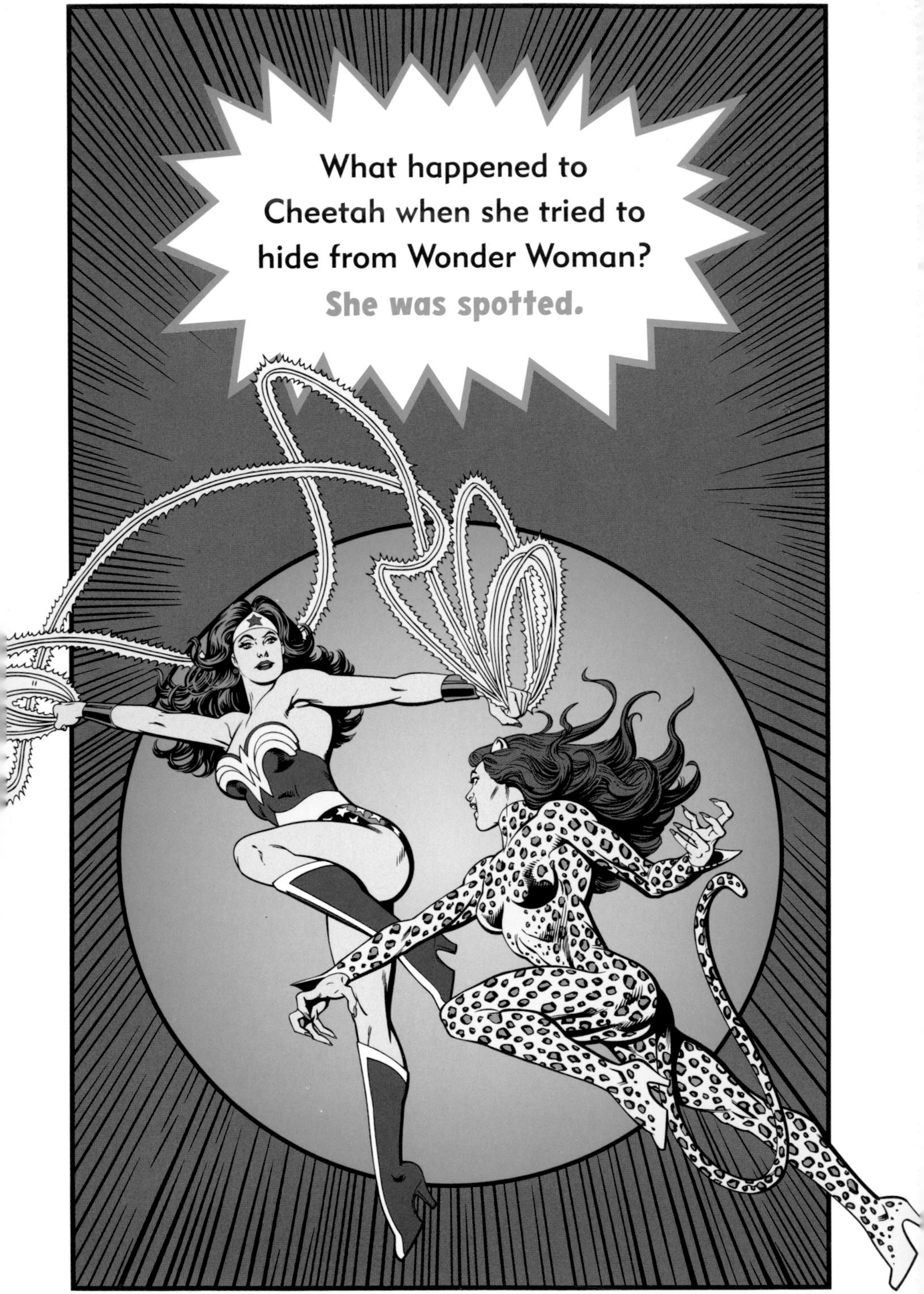
What happened to Cheetah when she tried to hide from Wonder Woman?
She was spotted.

HOW FAST IS THE FLASH?

Even when he's asleep, he's fast asleep.

- — - — - — - — - — - — - — - — - — -

He won the Boston Marathon but, to make
it fair, he started in San Francisco.

- — - — - — - — - — - — - — - — - — -

He calls quicksand just "sand."

- — - — - — - — - — - — - — - — - — -

He got a speeding ticket on a stationary bike.

- — - — - — - — - — - — - — - — - — -

When he ran from Central City to Metropolis,
he arrived three hours before he left.

- — - — - — - — - — - — - — - — - — -

How many Caped Crusaders does it take to change a light bulb?

None. Batman works in the dark.

Did Bruce Wayne ever play Little League?

Yeah, he was the batboy.

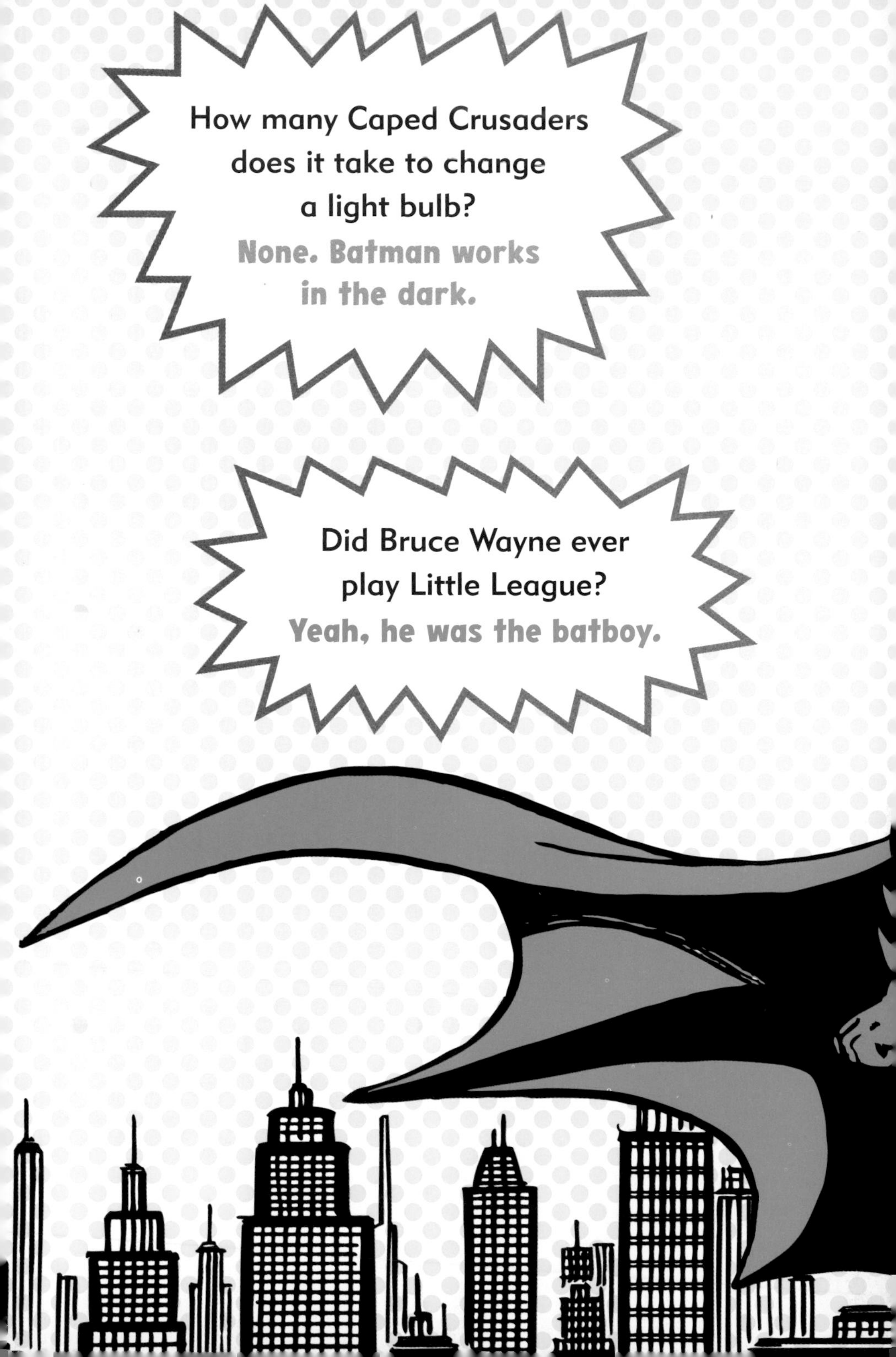

How come no one likes to sit next to Bruce Wayne?

He's got bat breath.

What happened when Batman was late to play baseball with Robin?

There was a Wayne delay.

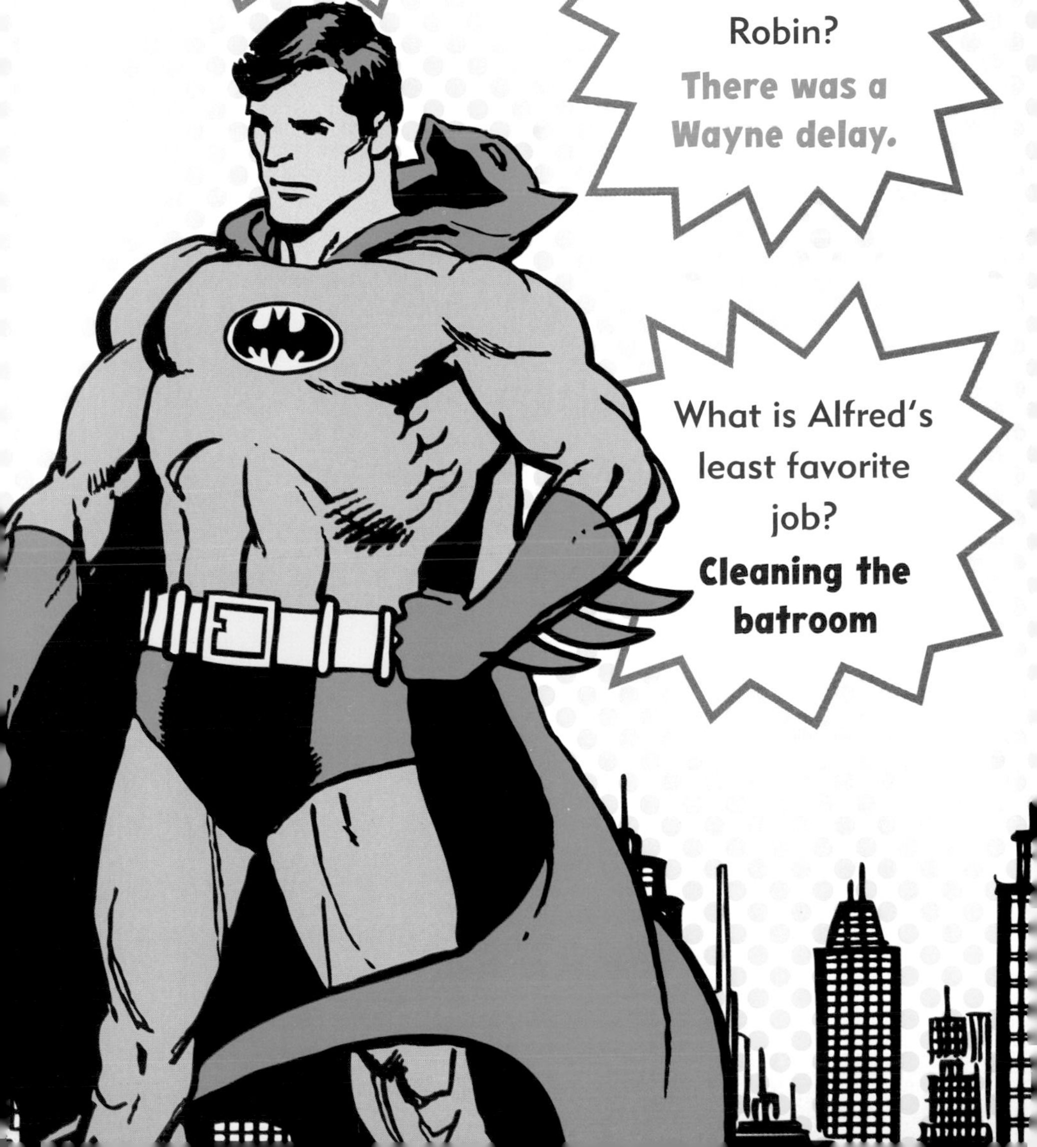

What is Alfred's least favorite job?

Cleaning the batroom

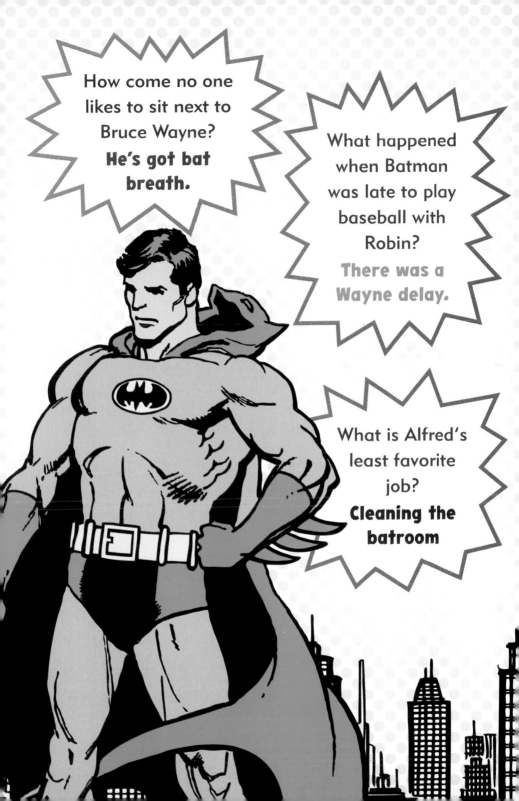

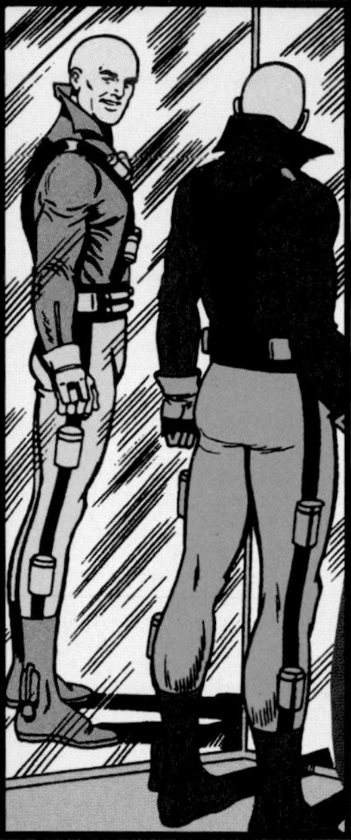

What did Lex Luthor say when Mercy Graves gave him a comb for his birthday?

"Thanks. I'll never part with it."

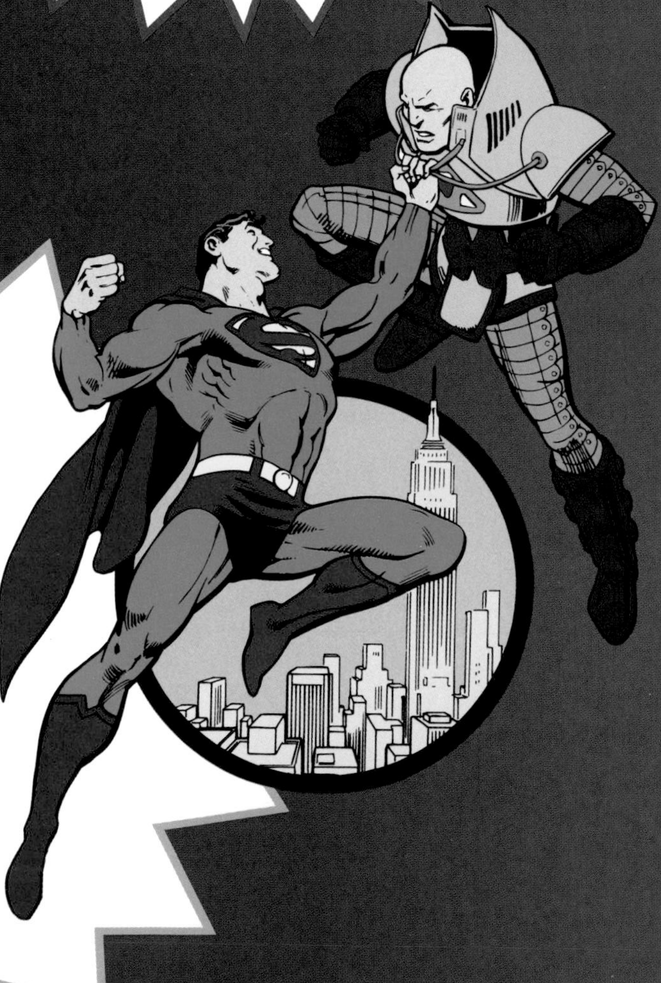

What is Superman's favorite rhyme?

**Eeny meeny miney munch,
catch the bad guys before lunch.
If they holler, I will punch.
Eeny meenie miney munch.**

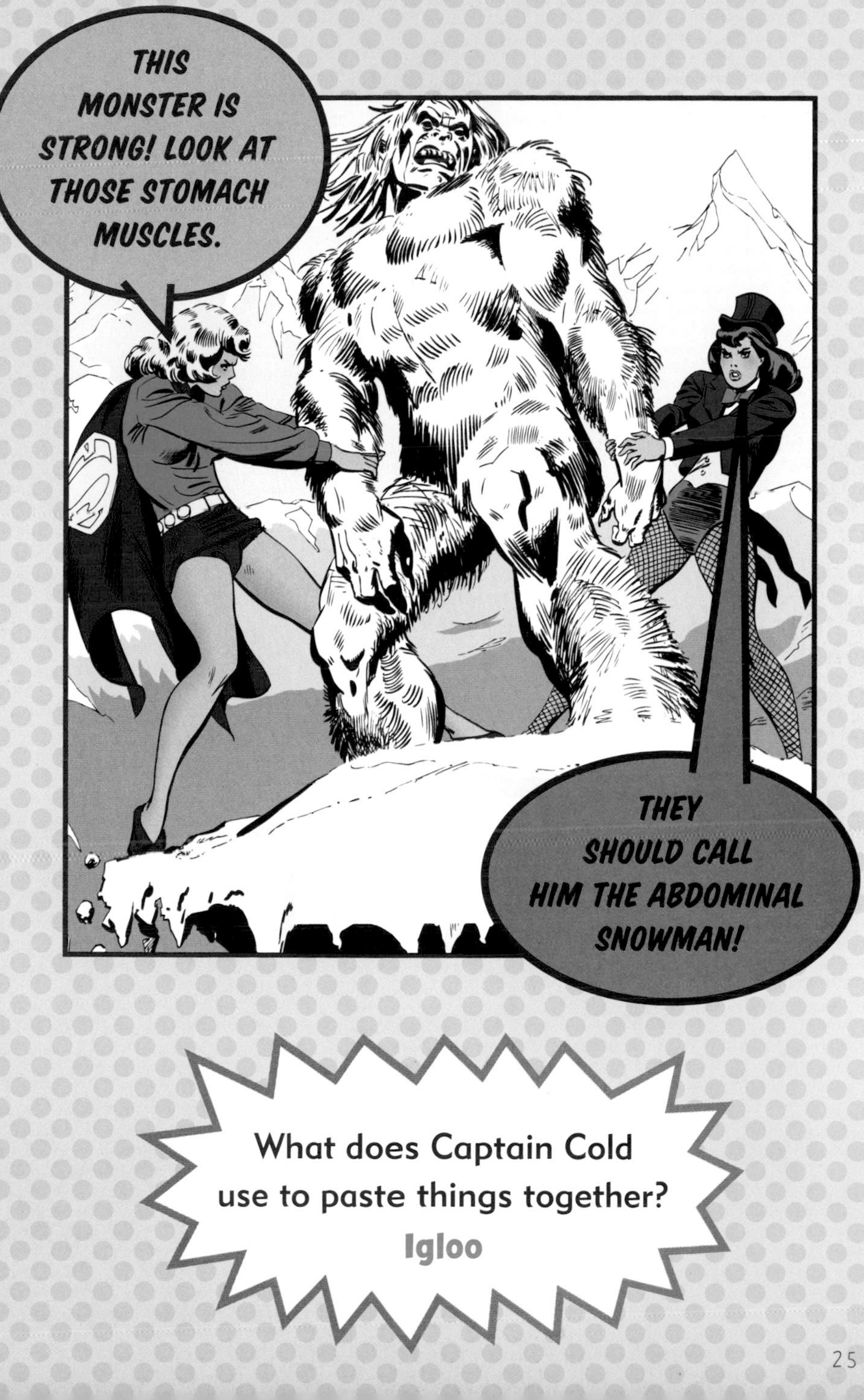
THIS MONSTER IS STRONG! LOOK AT THOSE STOMACH MUSCLES.
THEY SHOULD CALL HIM THE ABDOMINAL SNOWMAN!

What does Captain Cold use to paste things together?

Igloo

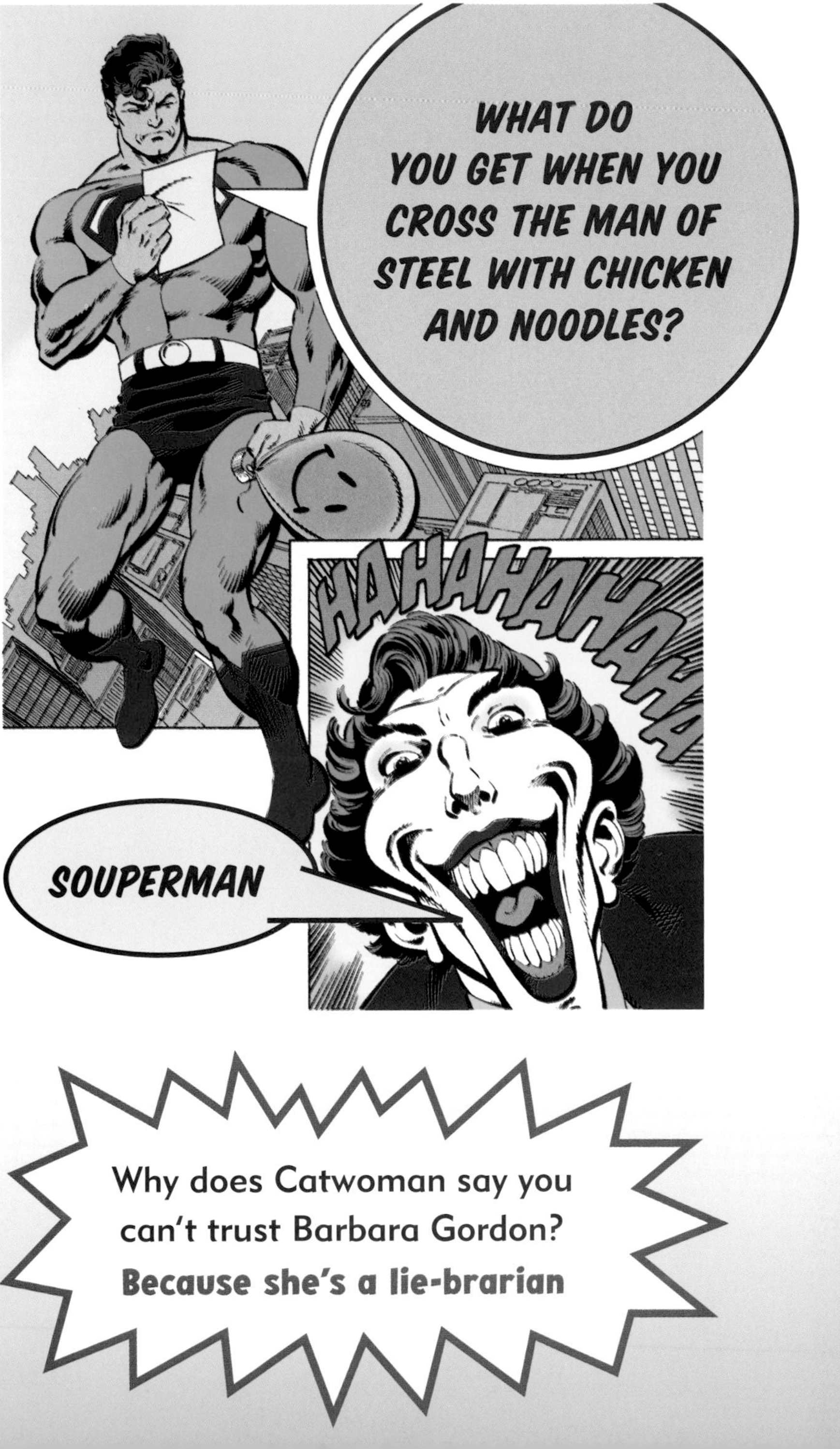
WHAT DO YOU GET WHEN YOU CROSS THE MAN OF STEEL WITH CHICKEN AND NOODLES?
HAHAHAHAHAHA
SOUPERMAN

Why does Catwoman say you can't trust Barbara Gordon?
Because she's a lie-brarian

What does Green Arrow wear when he dresses up?
A bow tie

What is Superman's favorite African city?
Cape Town

What happened when Batgirl left her day job as a librarian and boarded a pirate ship?
Barbara Gordon became Barrrgh-bara Gordon.

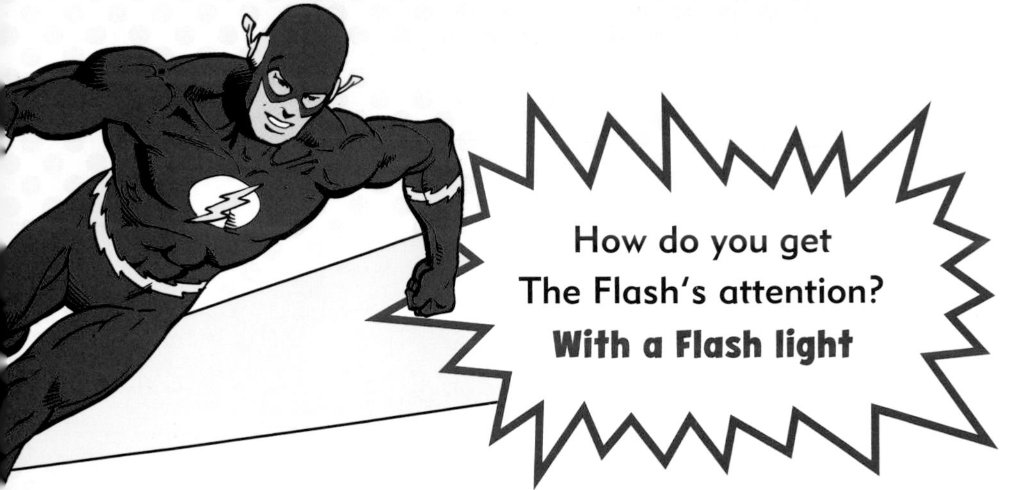

How do you get
The Flash's attention?
With a Flash light

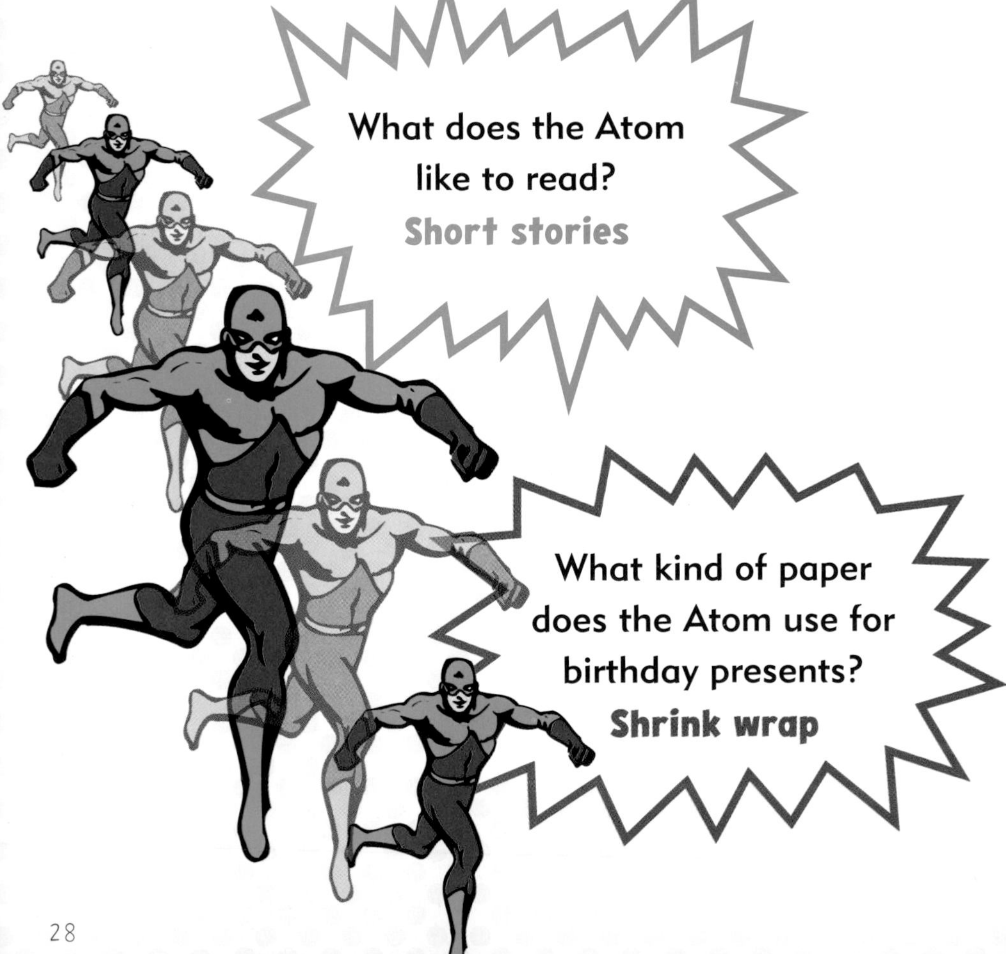

What does the Atom
like to read?
Short stories

What kind of paper
does the Atom use for
birthday presents?
Shrink wrap

HOW DO YOU KNOW WHEN PLASTIC MAN IS UPSET? HE GETS ALL BENT OUT OF SHAPE.

Plastic Man can stretch any part of his body to be any length. Why does he never make his hand 12 inches long?

Because then it would be a foot

Is Plastic Man done writing his memoir?

No, but he's in the homestretch.

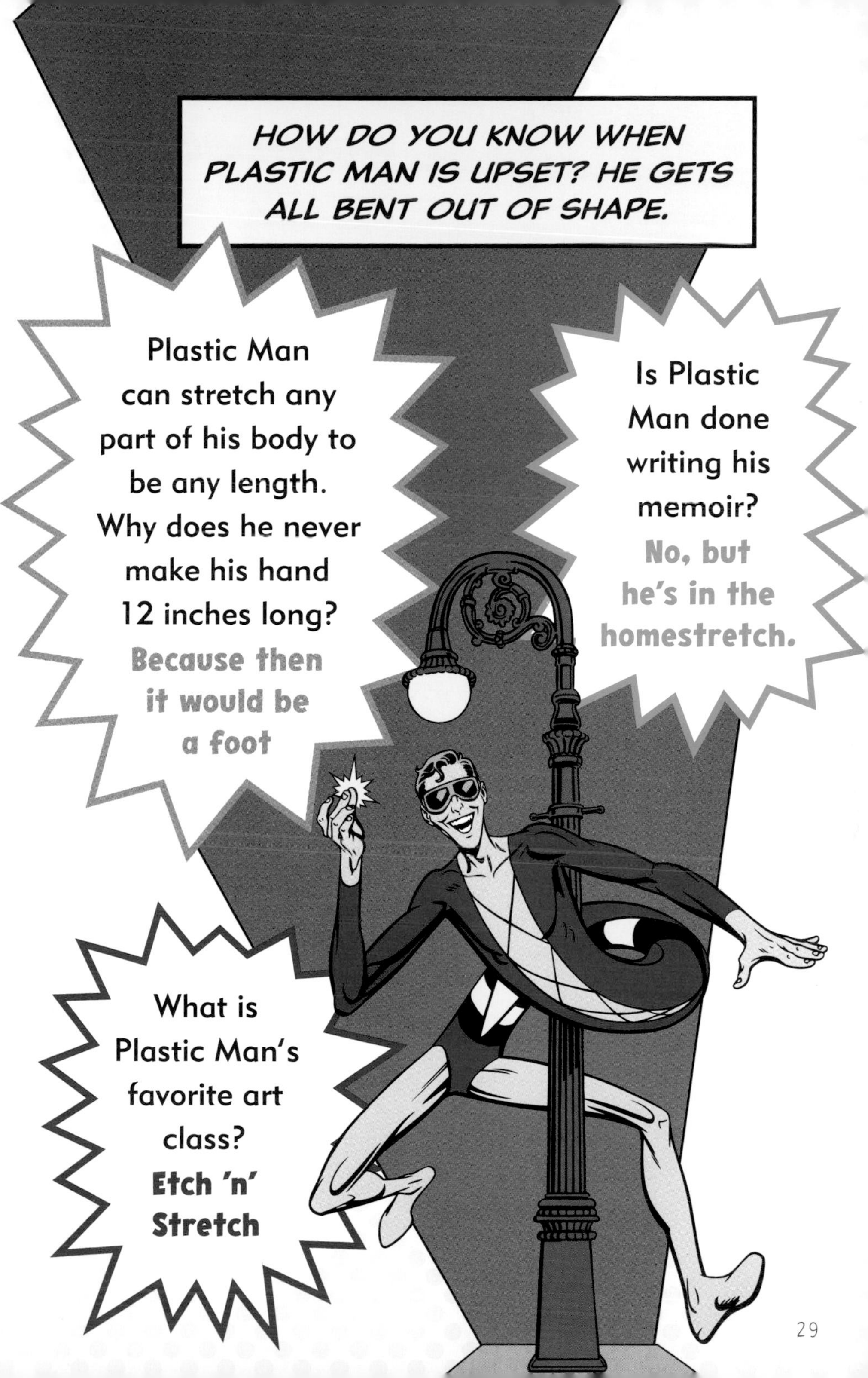

What is Plastic Man's favorite art class?

Etch 'n' Stretch

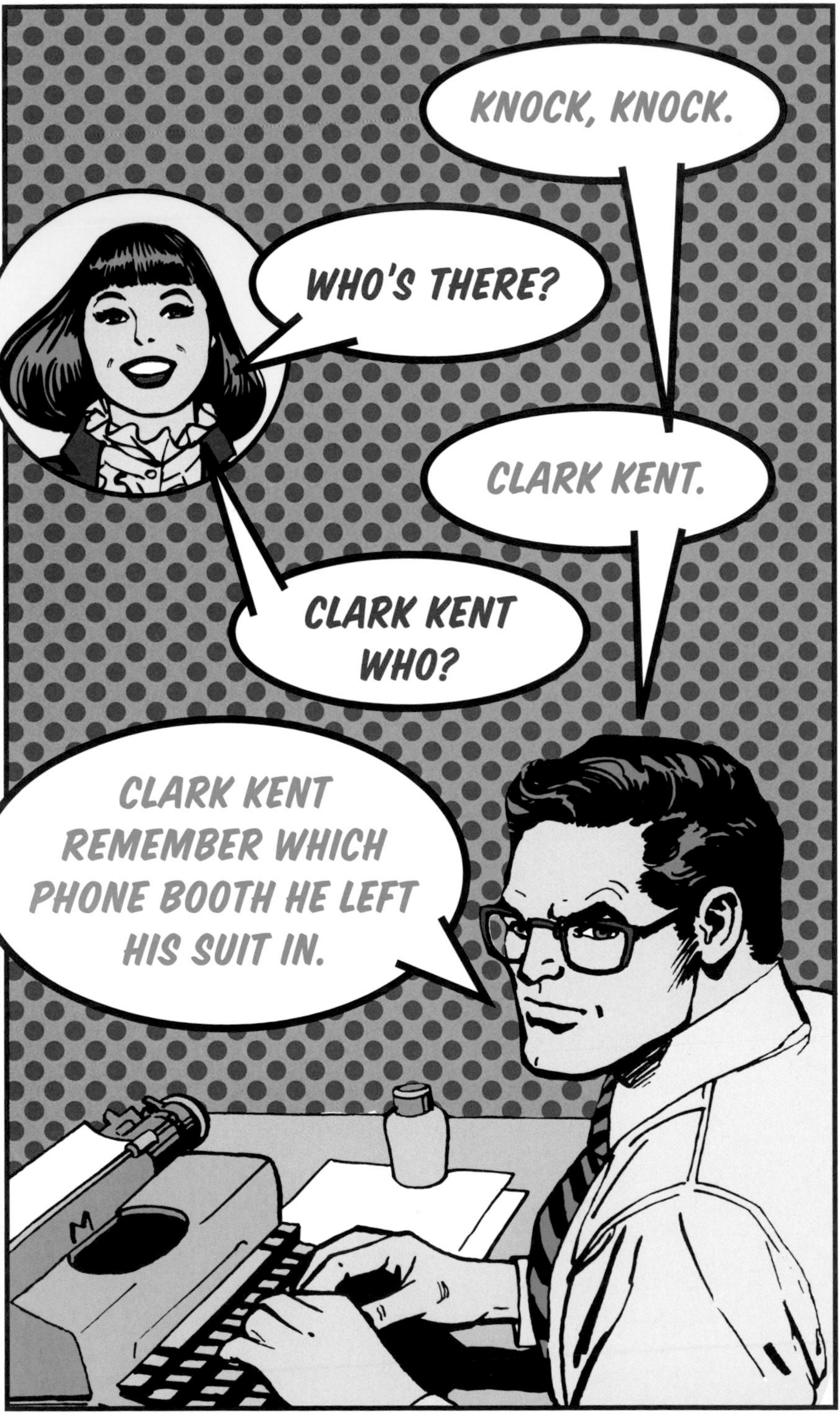
KNOCK, KNOCK.
WHO'S THERE?
CLARK KENT.
CLARK KENT WHO?
CLARK KENT REMEMBER WHICH PHONE BOOTH HE LEFT HIS SUIT IN.

What's the hardest part of riding in Wonder Woman's Invisible Jet?
Buckling your invisible seat belt

What does Batman keep in his bedroom so he doesn't have nightmares?
A Dark Knight-light

What's on the back of Robin's sweatshirt?
Robin's hood

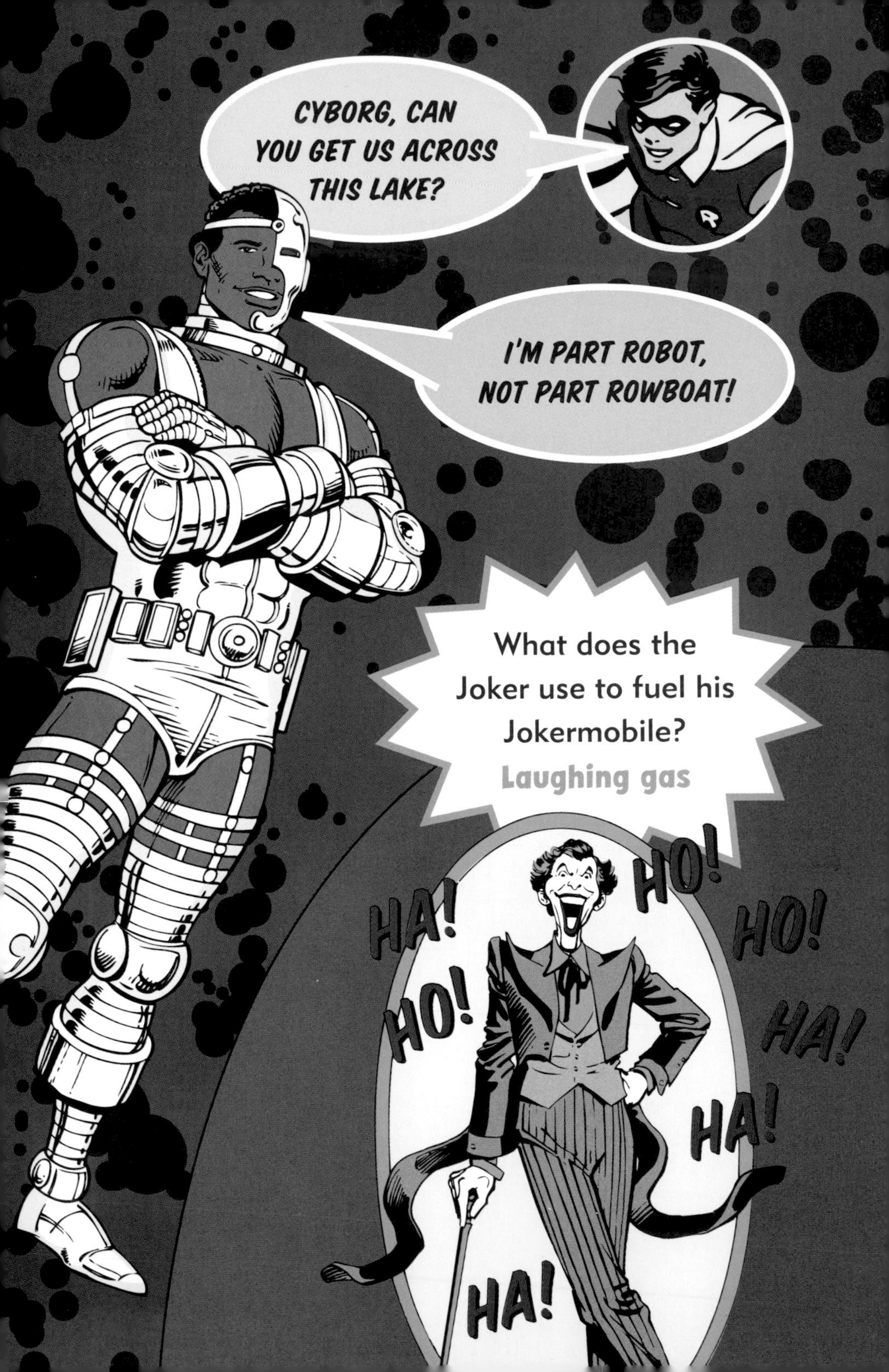
CYBORG, CAN YOU GET US ACROSS THIS LAKE?
I'M PART ROBOT, NOT PART ROWBOAT!
What does the Joker use to fuel his Jokermobile?
Laughing gas
HA!
HO!
HO!
HO!
HA!
HA!
HA!

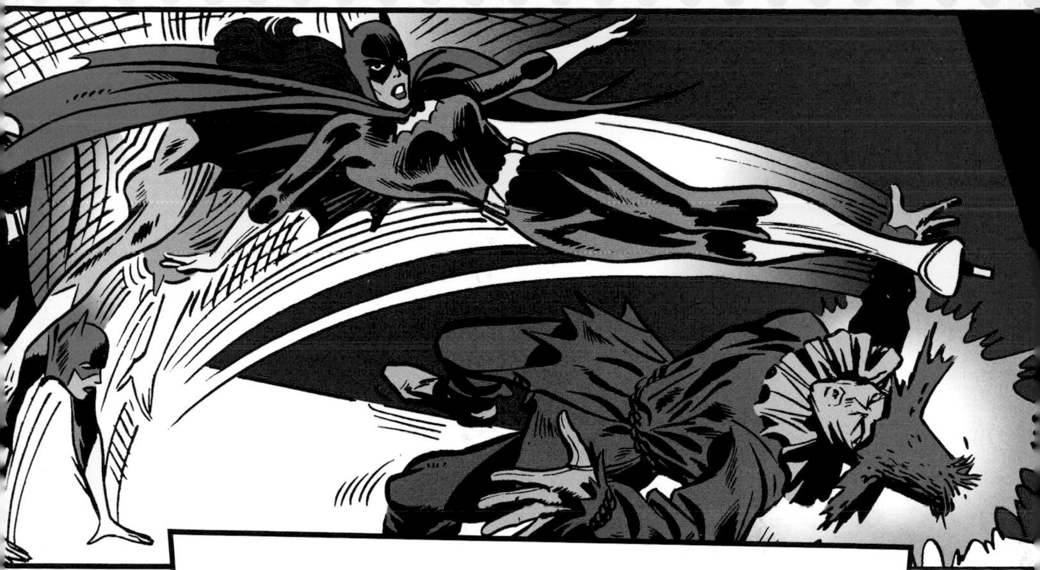

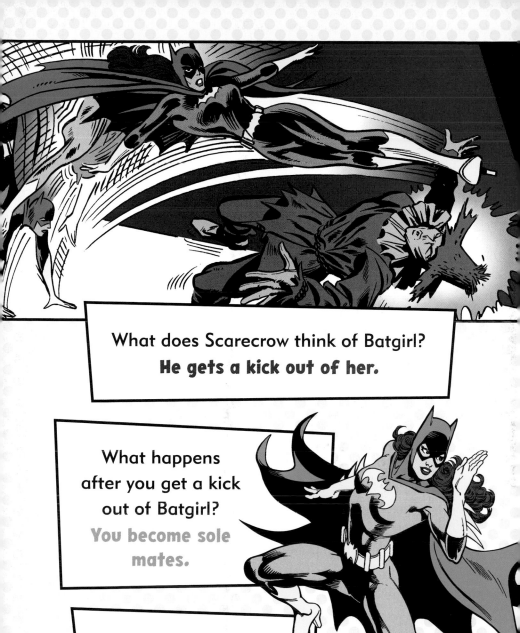

What does Scarecrow think of Batgirl?

He gets a kick out of her.

What happens after you get a kick out of Batgirl?

You become sole mates.

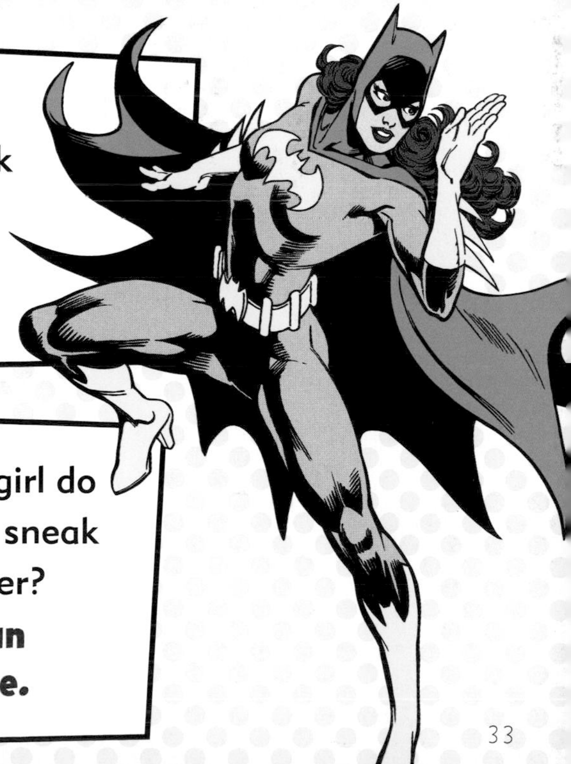

What does Batgirl do when bad guys sneak up behind her?

She does an a-boot-face.

HOW TALL IS GIGANTA?

Her shoe size is "family sedan."

She wears a watch on each wrist because each hand is in a different time zone.

Of all the crimes she has committed, none was more grievous than what she did to the unlimited-refill policy at the cafeteria.

Her shadow has its own zip code.

The Gotham City Candle Company made a year's supply of candles from one blob of her earwax.

She once tried to steal the Washington Monument because she needed a toothpick.

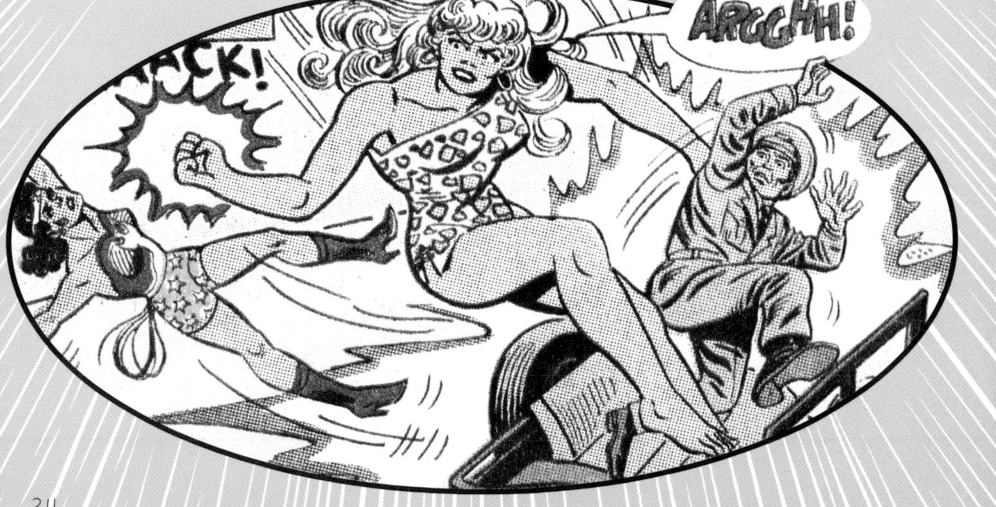
ARGGHH!

What does Bumblebee sound like after a visit to the dentist?

Mumblebee

What did Poison Ivy name the ancient plant species she tried to resurrect?

Tricera-crops

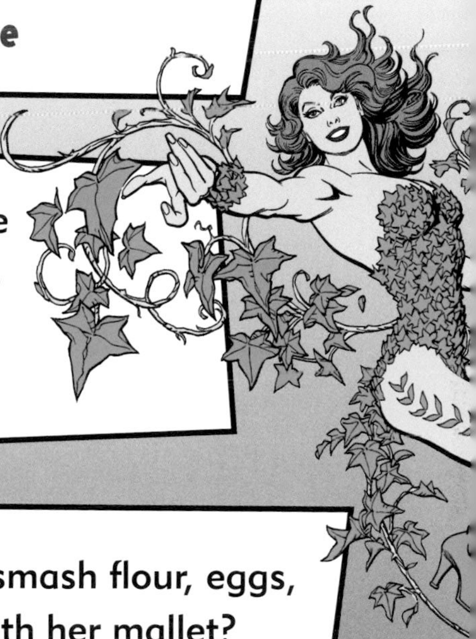

Why did Harley Quinn smash flour, eggs, butter, and sugar with her mallet?

She was making pound cake.

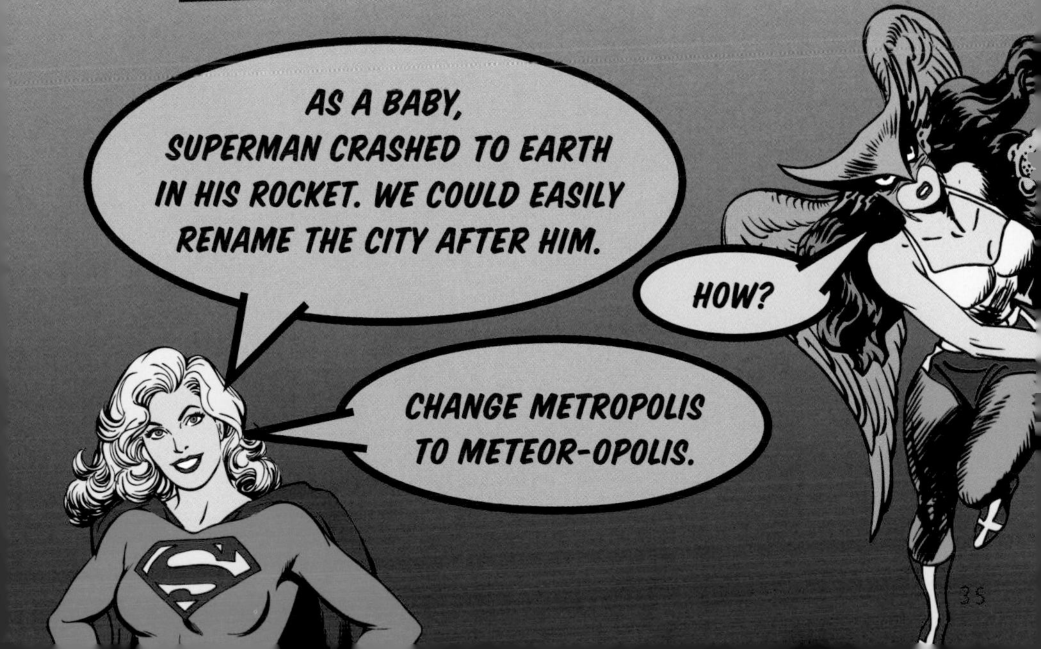
AS A BABY, SUPERMAN CRASHED TO EARTH IN HIS ROCKET. WE COULD EASILY RENAME THE CITY AFTER HIM.
HOW?
CHANGE METROPOLIS TO METEOR-OPOLIS.

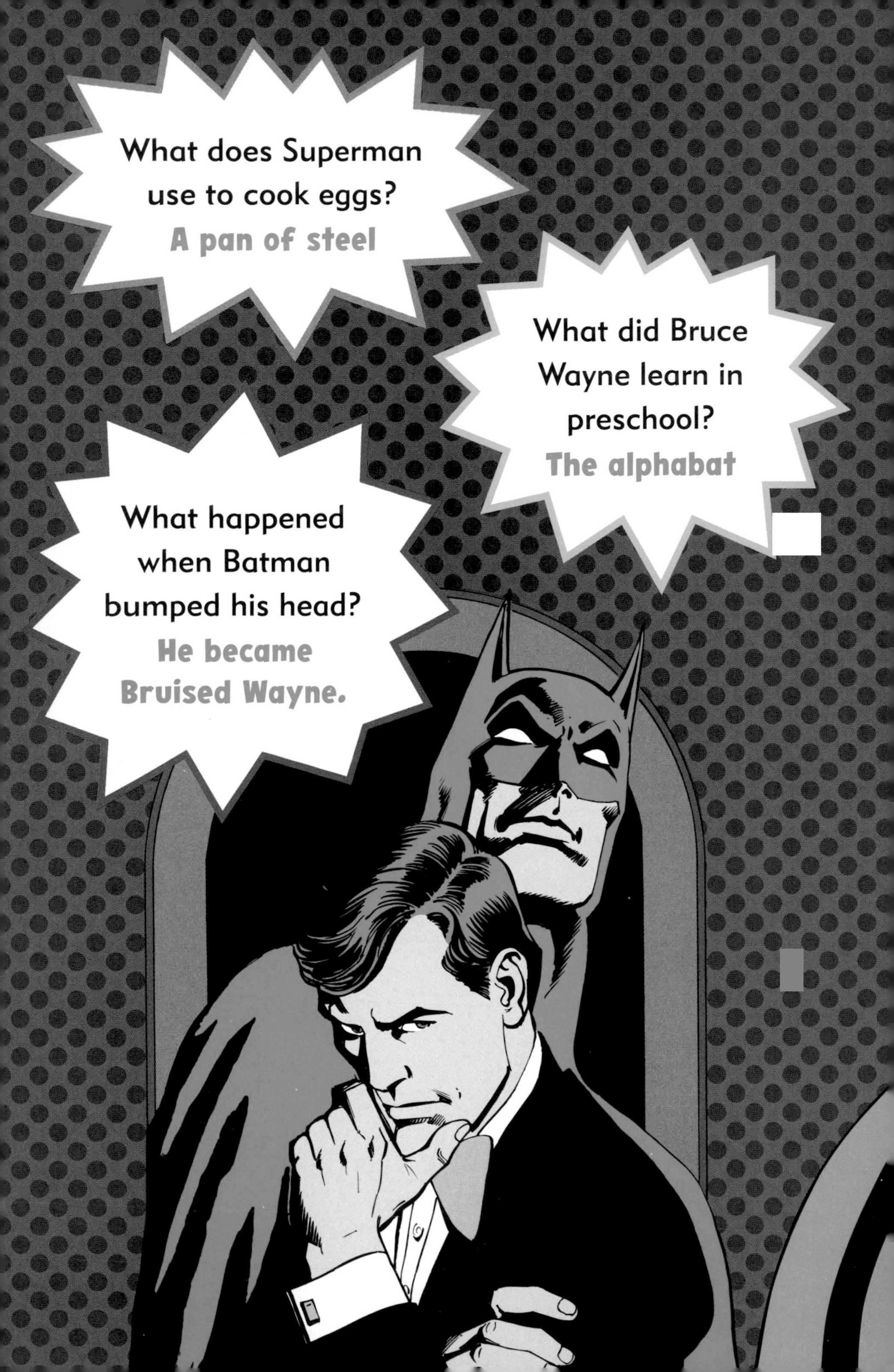
What does Superman use to cook eggs?
A pan of steel
What did Bruce Wayne learn in preschool?
The alphabat
What happened when Batman bumped his head?
He became Bruised Wayne.

Why does it take so long to watch a video with Krypto?

He keeps pressing paws.

Why does Catwoman keep getting caught?

There's no such thing as a purr-fect crime.

Why did Catwoman stay home?

She wasn't feline well.

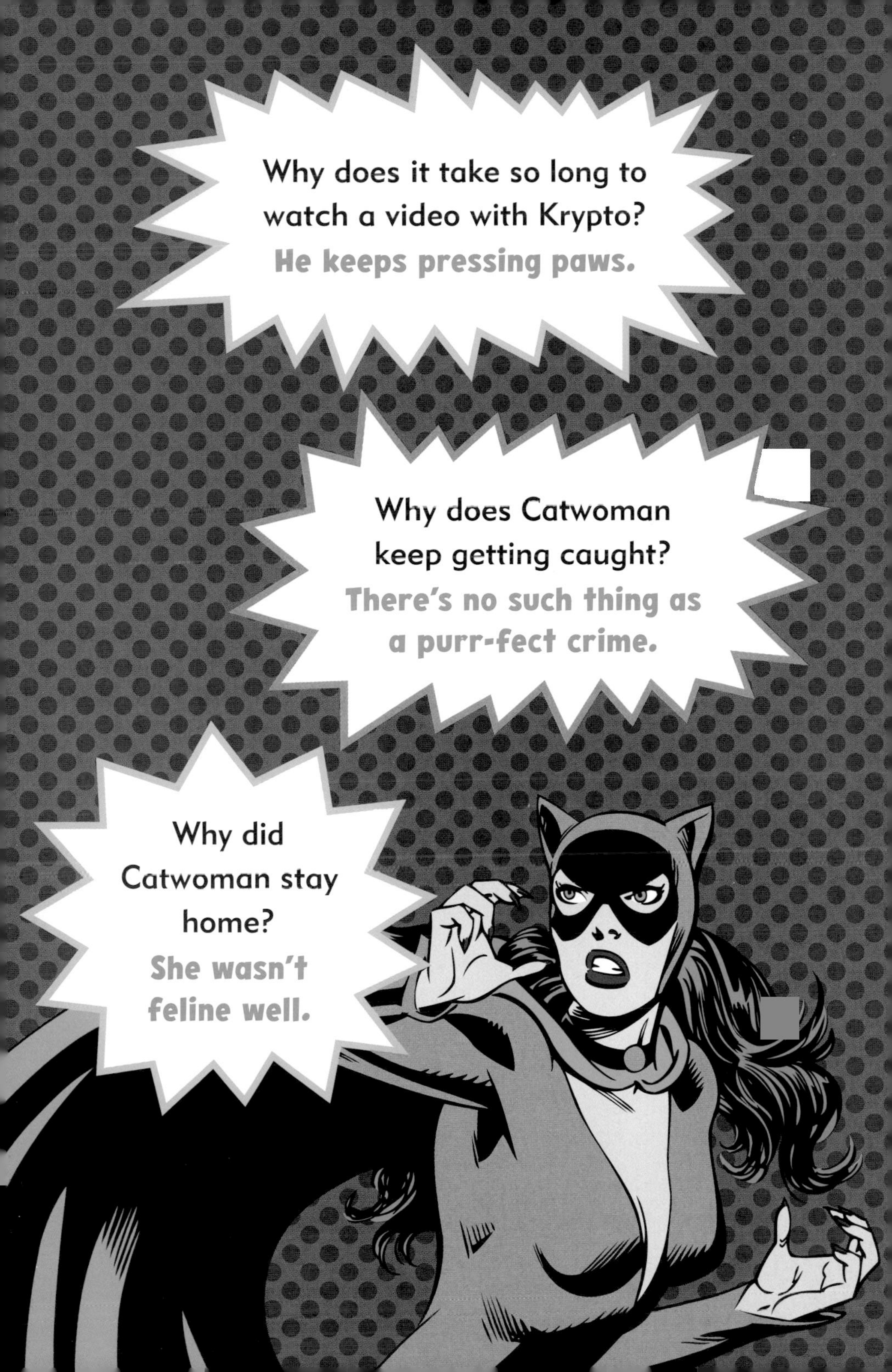

Why does the Penguin wear a top hat?

He can't find one big enough to fit his bottom.

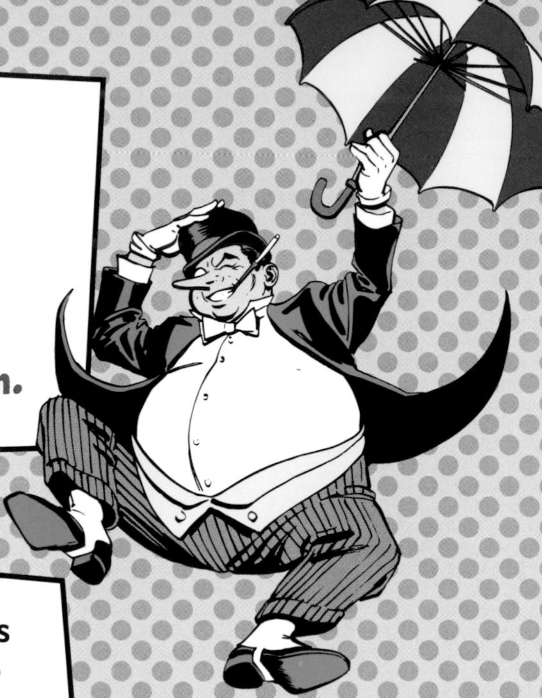

What is Cyborg's favorite cookie?

Oatmeal chocolate micro-chip

Does the Joker like to go boating?

Yes, he likes to go ka-yuck-ing.

What is Batgirl's favorite cookie?

Bat-terscotch

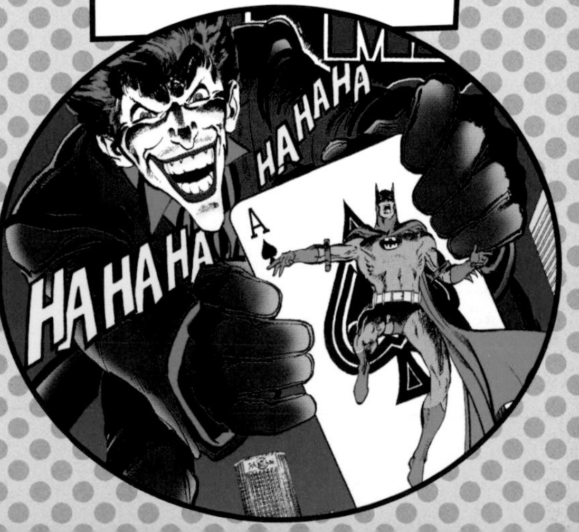
HA HA HA
HA HA HA

What's Krypto's favorite cookie?

Snickerpoodle

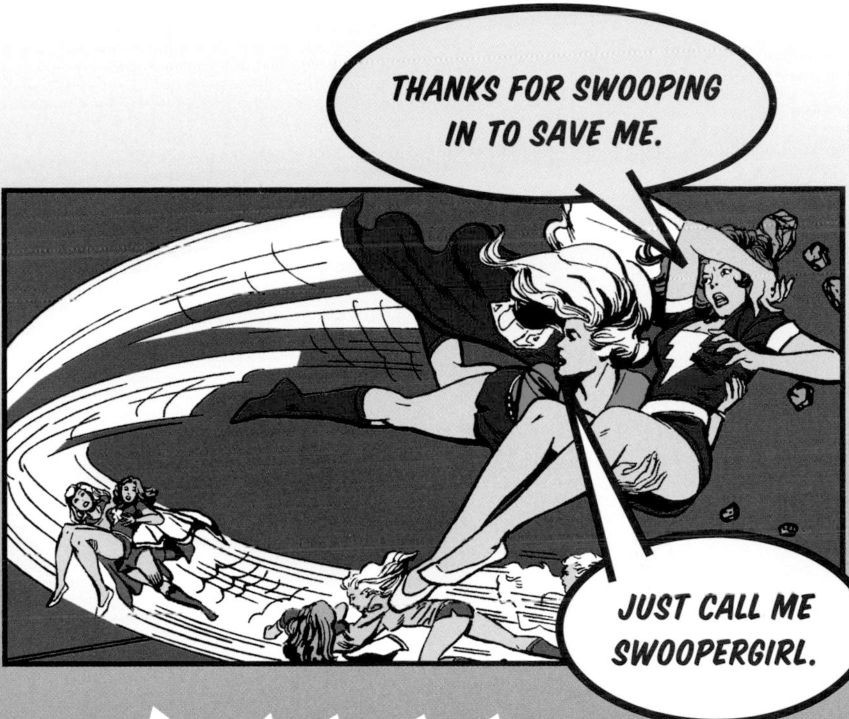
THANKS FOR SWOOPING IN TO SAVE ME.
JUST CALL ME SWOOPERGIRL.

How does Green Lantern spend every December 31?

Ringing in the new year

What name does Green Lantern use when he plays basketball?

Mike-Hal Jordan

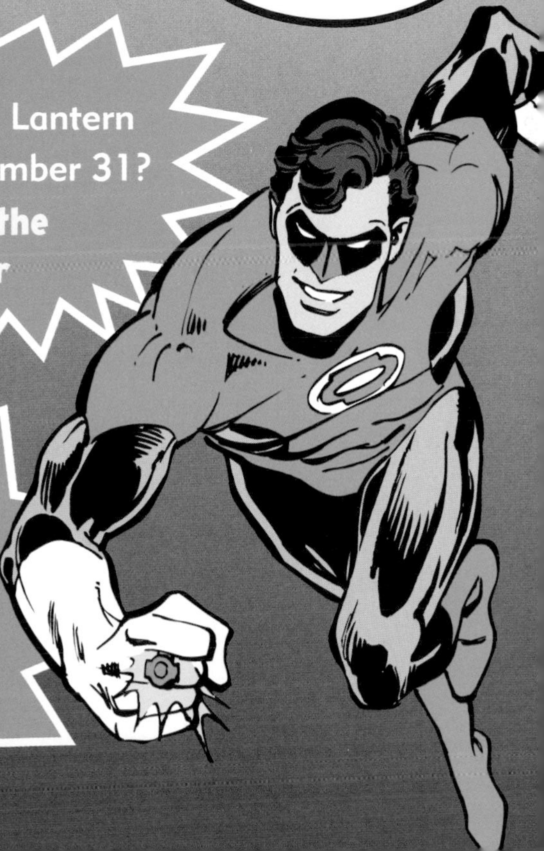

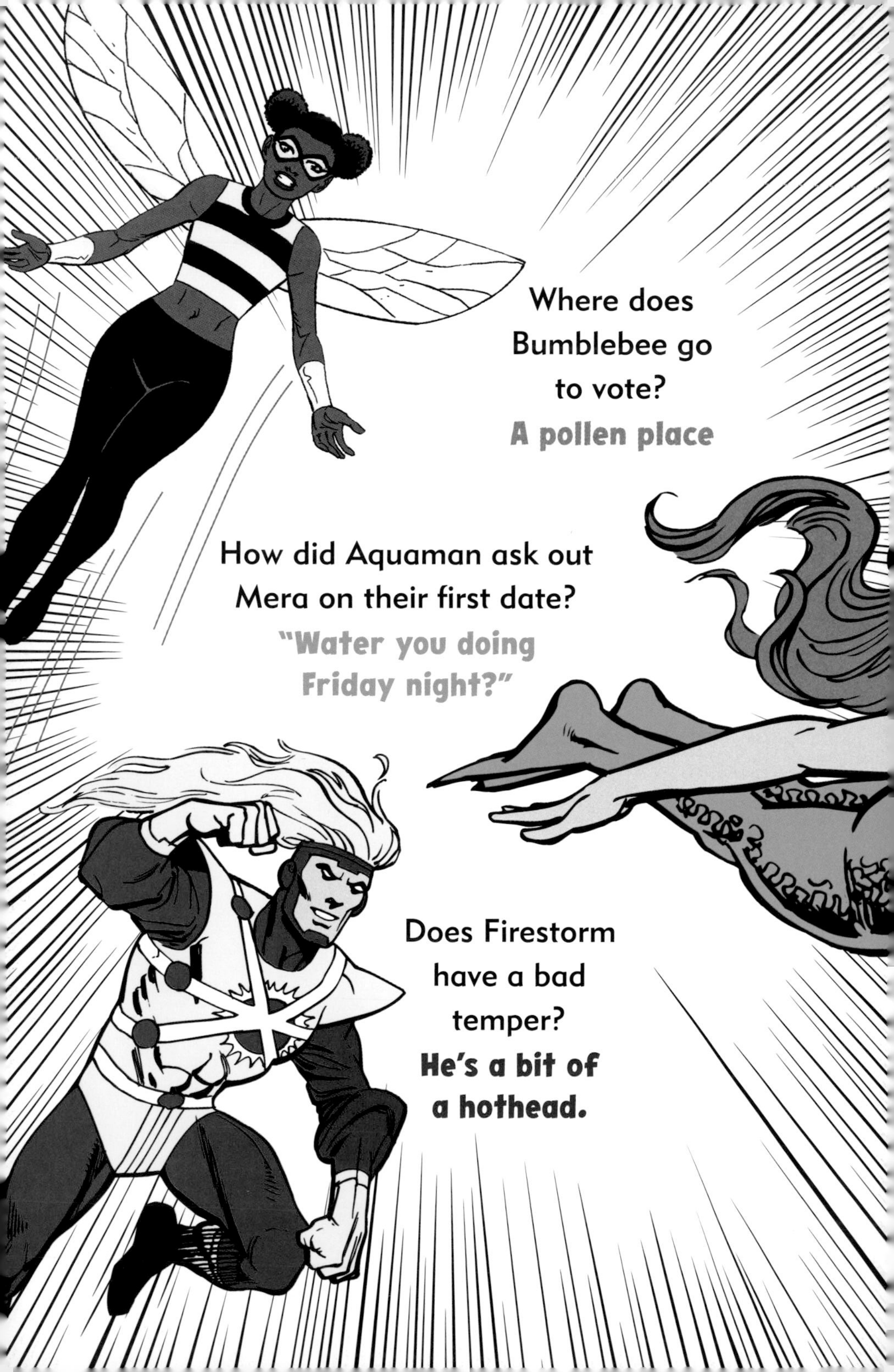

Where does Bumblebee go to vote?
A pollen place

How did Aquaman ask out Mera on their first date?
"Water you doing Friday night?"

Does Firestorm have a bad temper?
He's a bit of a hothead.

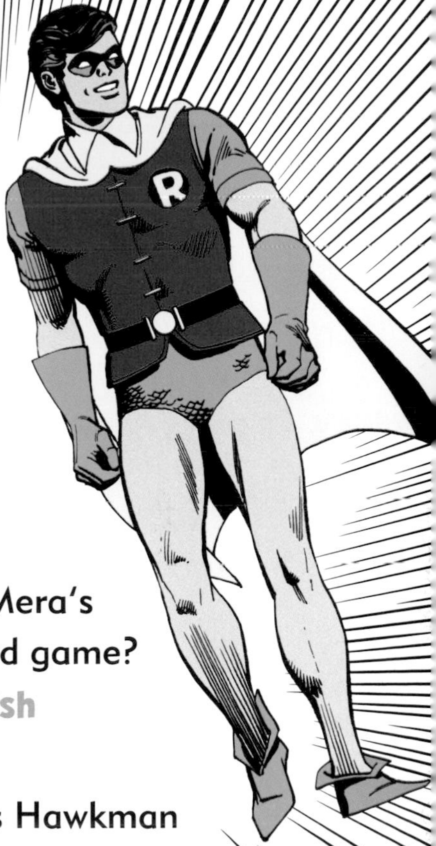

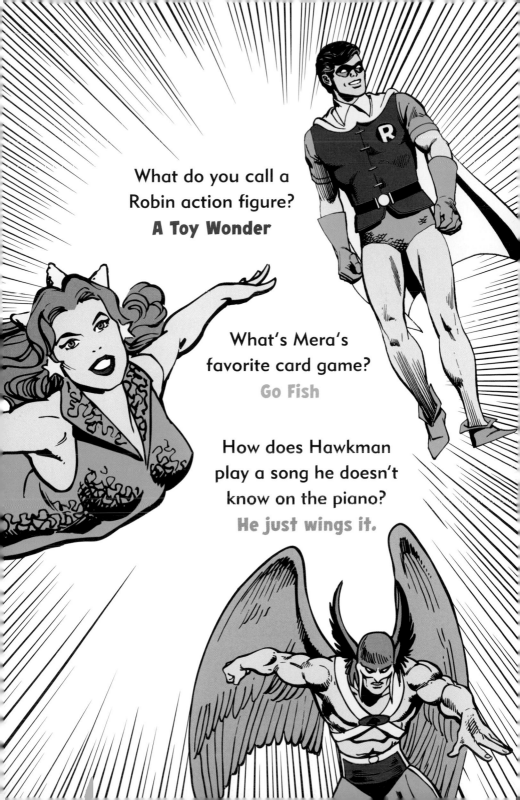

What do you call a
Robin action figure?

A Toy Wonder

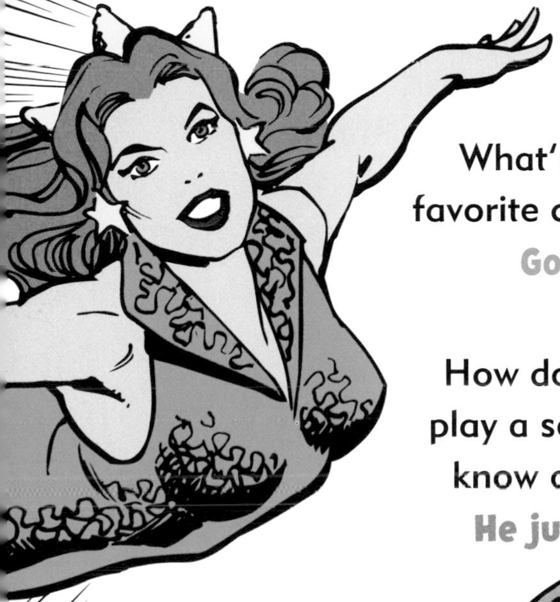

What's Mera's
favorite card game?

Go Fish

How does Hawkman
play a song he doesn't
know on the piano?

He just wings it.

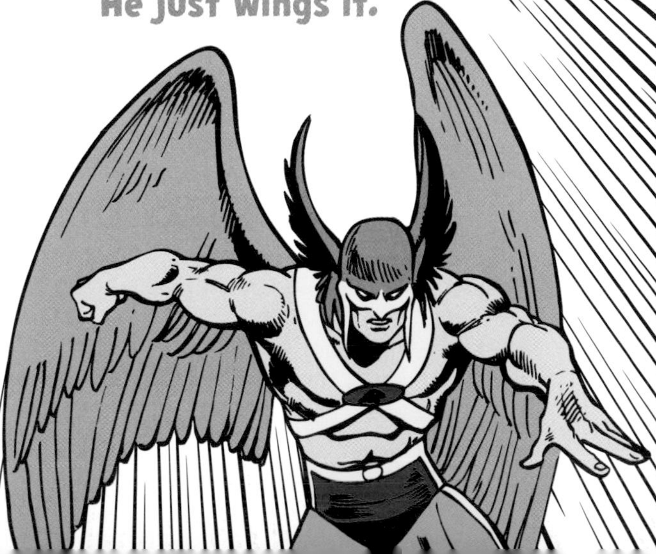

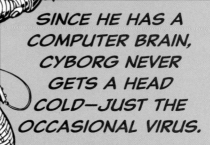

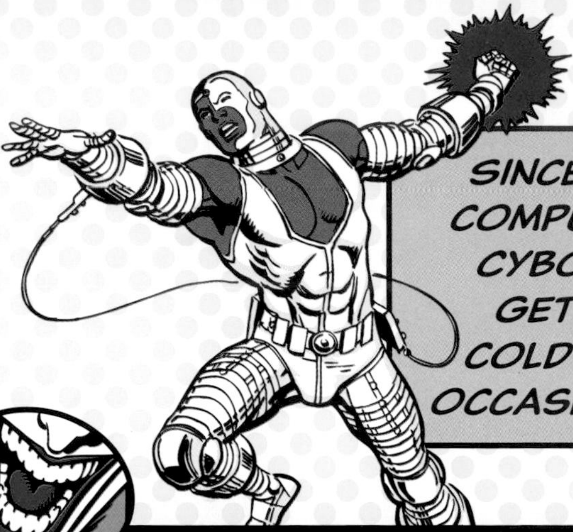

SINCE HE HAS A COMPUTER BRAIN, CYBORG NEVER GETS A HEAD COLD—JUST THE OCCASIONAL VIRUS.

SAY THIS FIVE TIMES FAST!

Selfless Cyborg sees simple solutions.

Captain Cold can't dance the cancan 'cause cancanning causes cancanners to care and kindness could cause Captain Cold's cronies to crush him.

The Flash frantically follows fleeing foes.

Glowing Green Lantern grabs glory galore.

Soaring through the silky sky, stealthy Supergirl scopes sneaky scoundrels.

Why did Plastic Man have to take a break from the Justice League? He was stretching himself too thin.

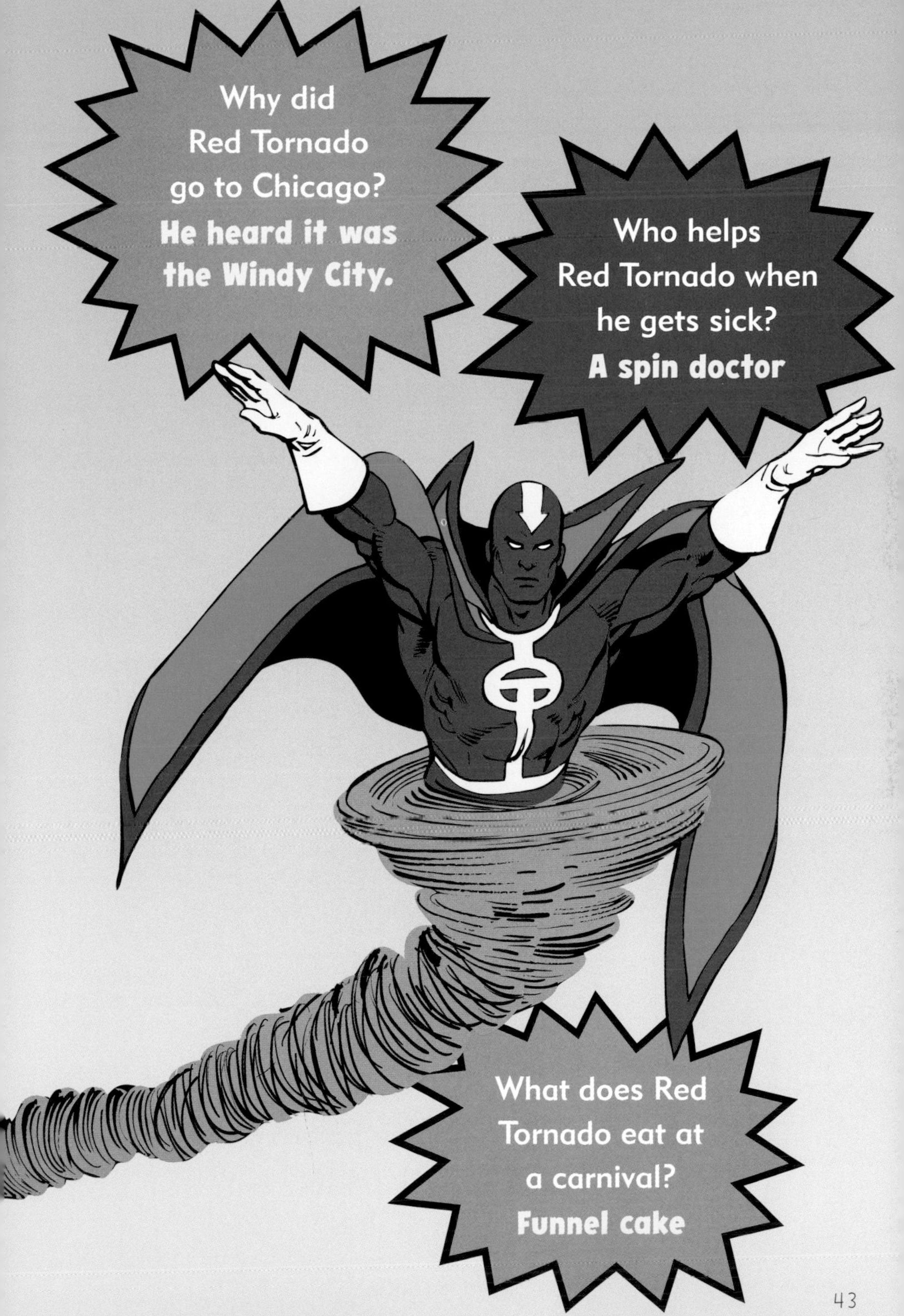

Why did Red Tornado go to Chicago?
He heard it was the Windy City.
Who helps Red Tornado when he gets sick?
A spin doctor
What does Red Tornado eat at a carnival?
Funnel cake

Did Bumblebee do well in school?
She did pretty well. She was a Bee student.

Why is Martian Manhunter such a good gardener?
He has a green thumb.

How does J'onn J'onzz decorate a cake?
With Mars-ipan

What did Superman say when he bumped into Lois Lane just as he was rushing off to catch a bad guy?
"Up, up, and oh, hey!"

What did Poison Ivy say when Batman asked her why she was talking to her plants?

"I don't know what you're talking a-sprout."

Why will Poison Ivy fight for plant life—and for Harley Quinn?

She really cares about her buds.

What are the cleverest crops Poison Ivy can grow?

Smartyplants

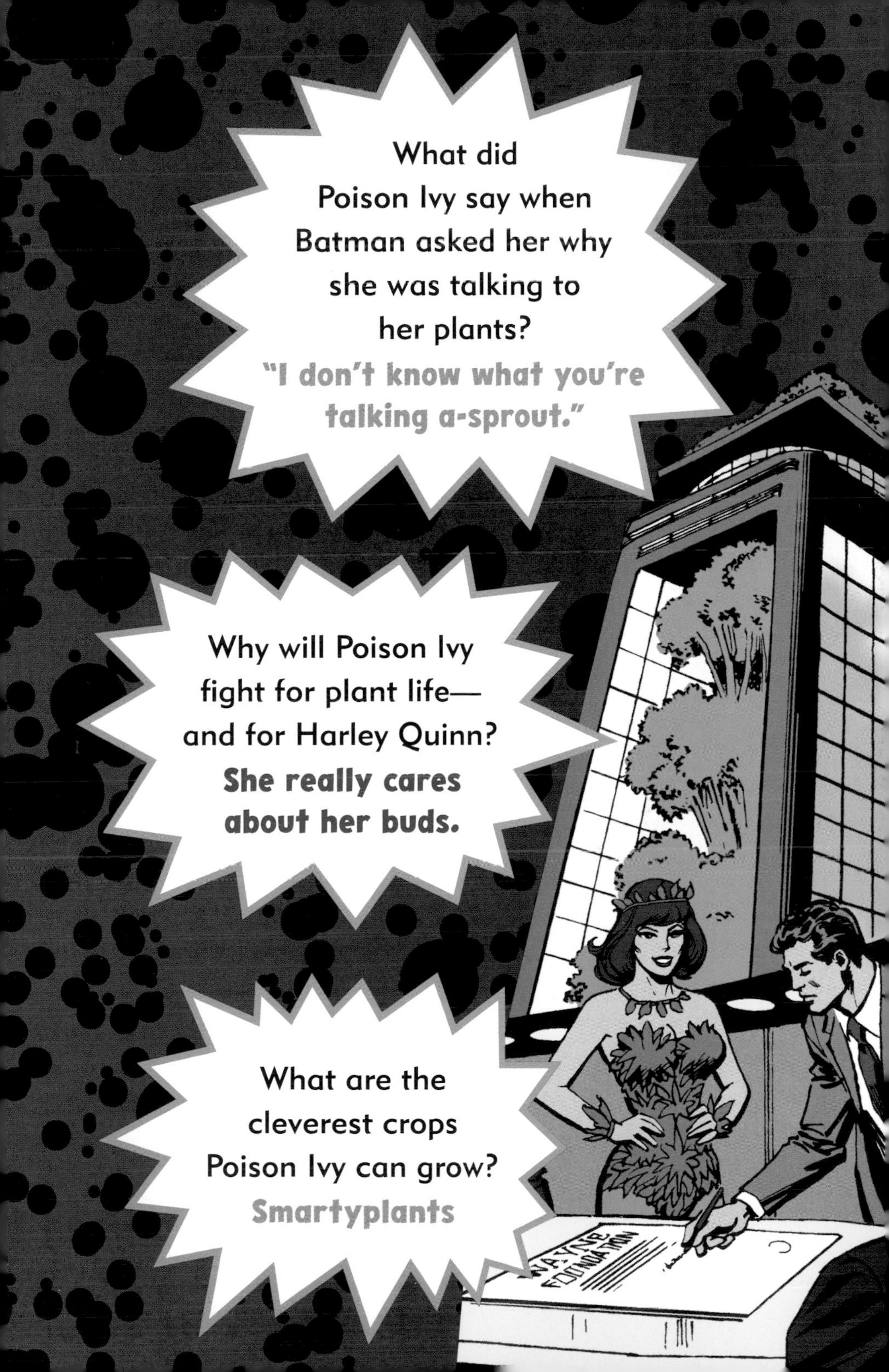
WAYNE FOUNDATION

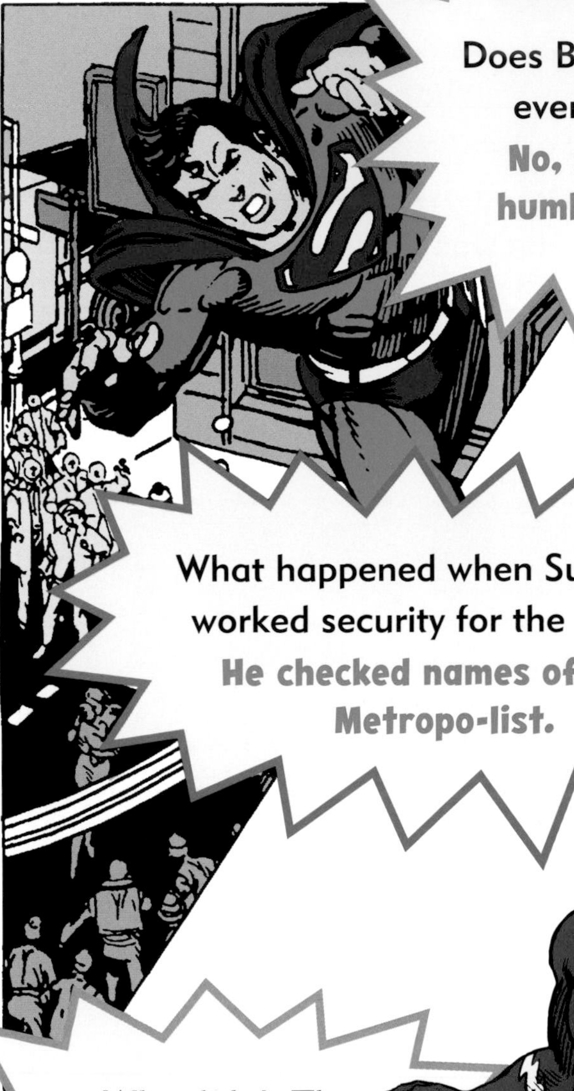

Does Bumblebee ever brag?

No, she's a humble bee.

What happened when Superman worked security for the mayor?

He checked names off the Metropo-list.

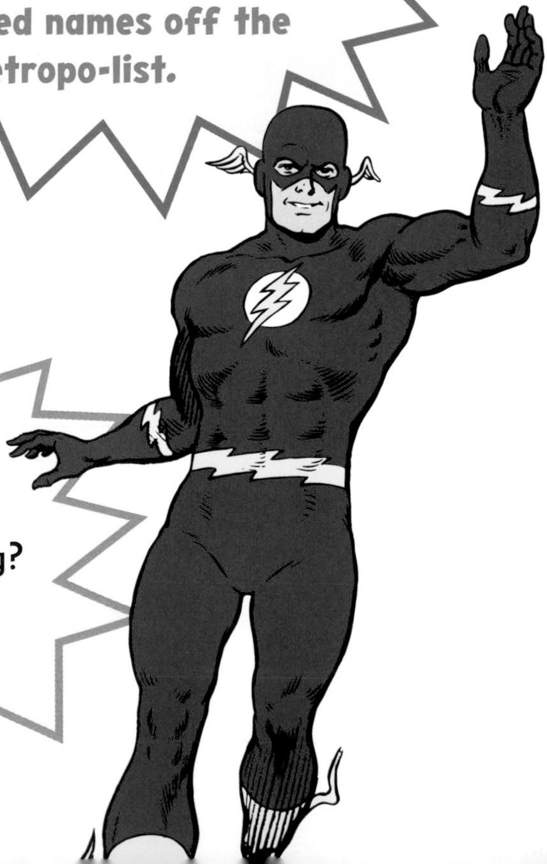

Why didn't The Flash chase after Captain Boomerang?

He knew he'd come back.

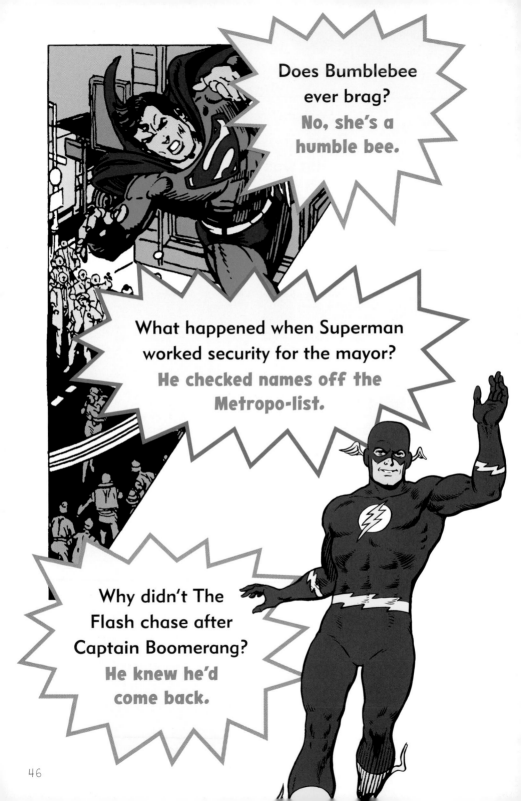

Why did Scarecrow skip dessert?
He was already stuffed.

What happened when Hawkman and Hawkgirl bumped into each other midair?
It was hawkward.

What does Supergirl use to look inside a burrito?
Her Tex-Mex-ray vision

Does Hawkgirl know what she's doing for vacation this year?
No, her plans are up in the air.

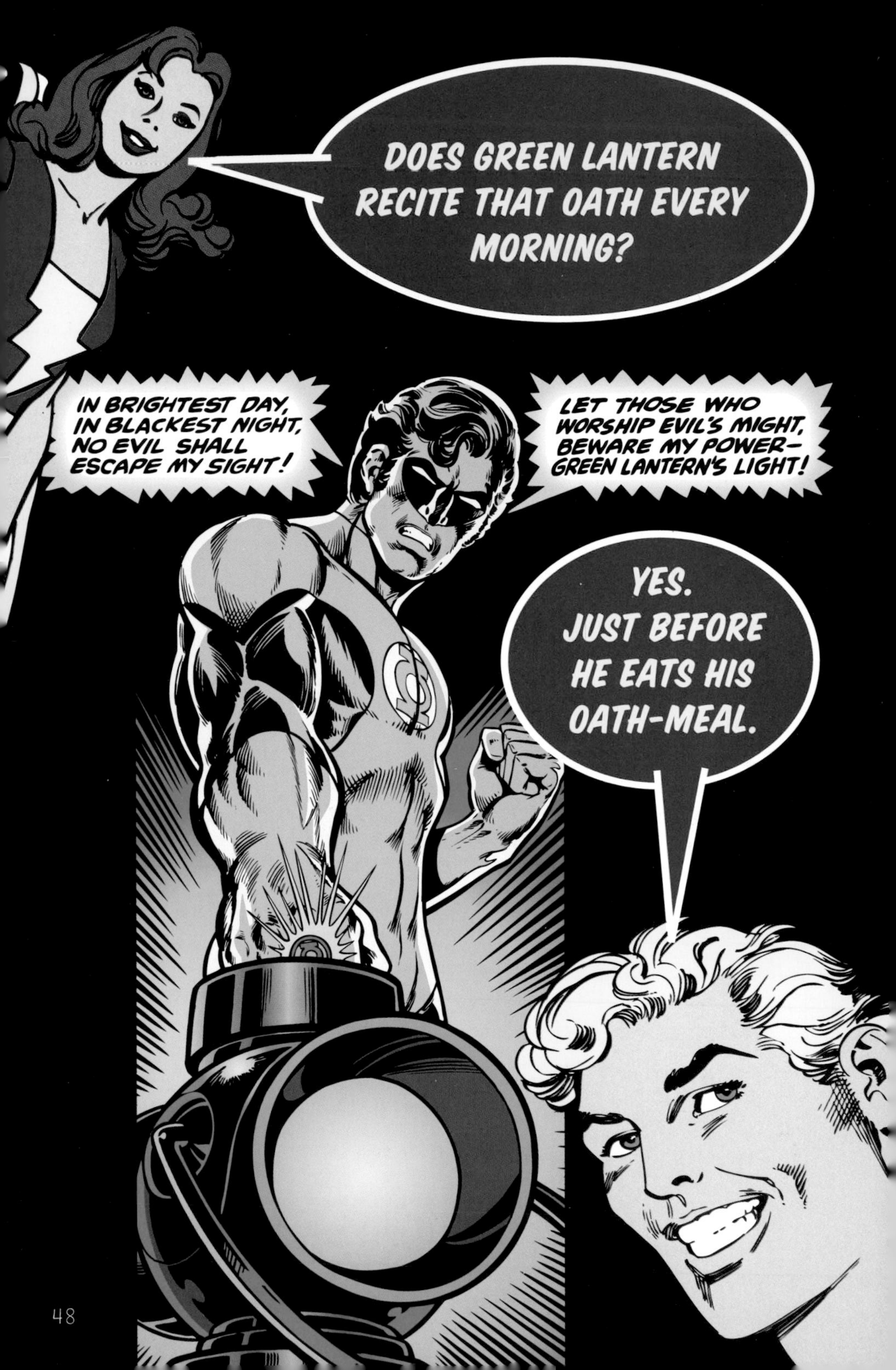
DOES GREEN LANTERN RECITE THAT OATH EVERY MORNING?
IN BRIGHTEST DAY, IN BLACKEST NIGHT, NO EVIL SHALL ESCAPE MY SIGHT!
LET THOSE WHO WORSHIP EVIL'S MIGHT, BEWARE MY POWER— GREEN LANTERN'S LIGHT!
YES. JUST BEFORE HE EATS HIS OATH-MEAL.

If Batman's lunch is in Ohio and Superman's lunch is in Illinois, where is Wonder Woman's lunch?

In Diana

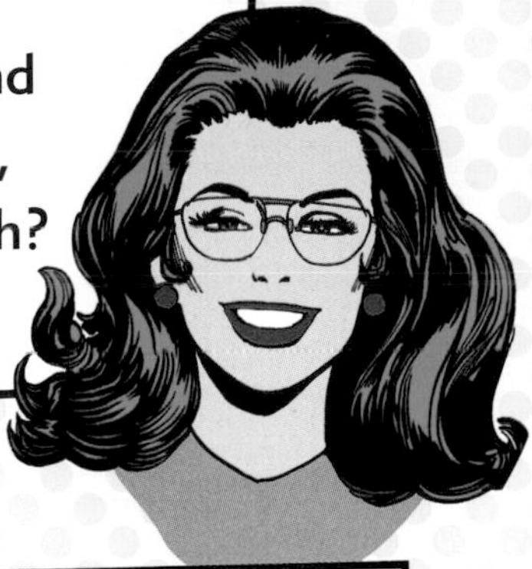

Why does Catwoman have so many birthday parties for herself every year?

You'd have a lot of parties too if you had nine lives.

What did the Penguin find in his stocking on Christmas morning?

A lump of monocole

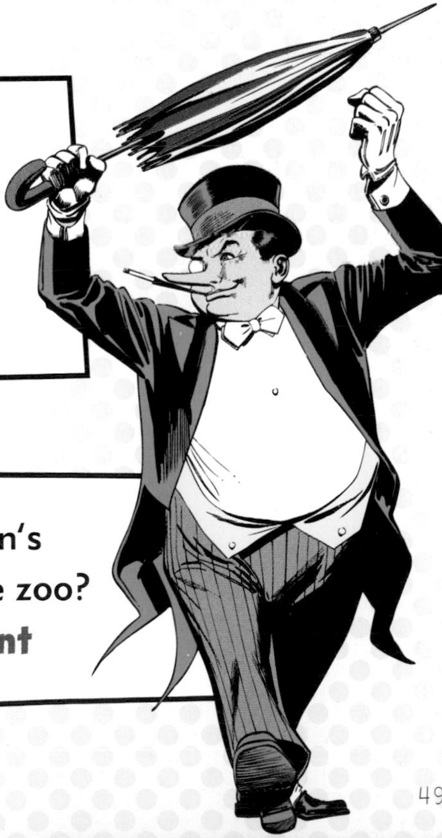

What's the Penguin's favorite animal at the zoo?

The umbrellaphant

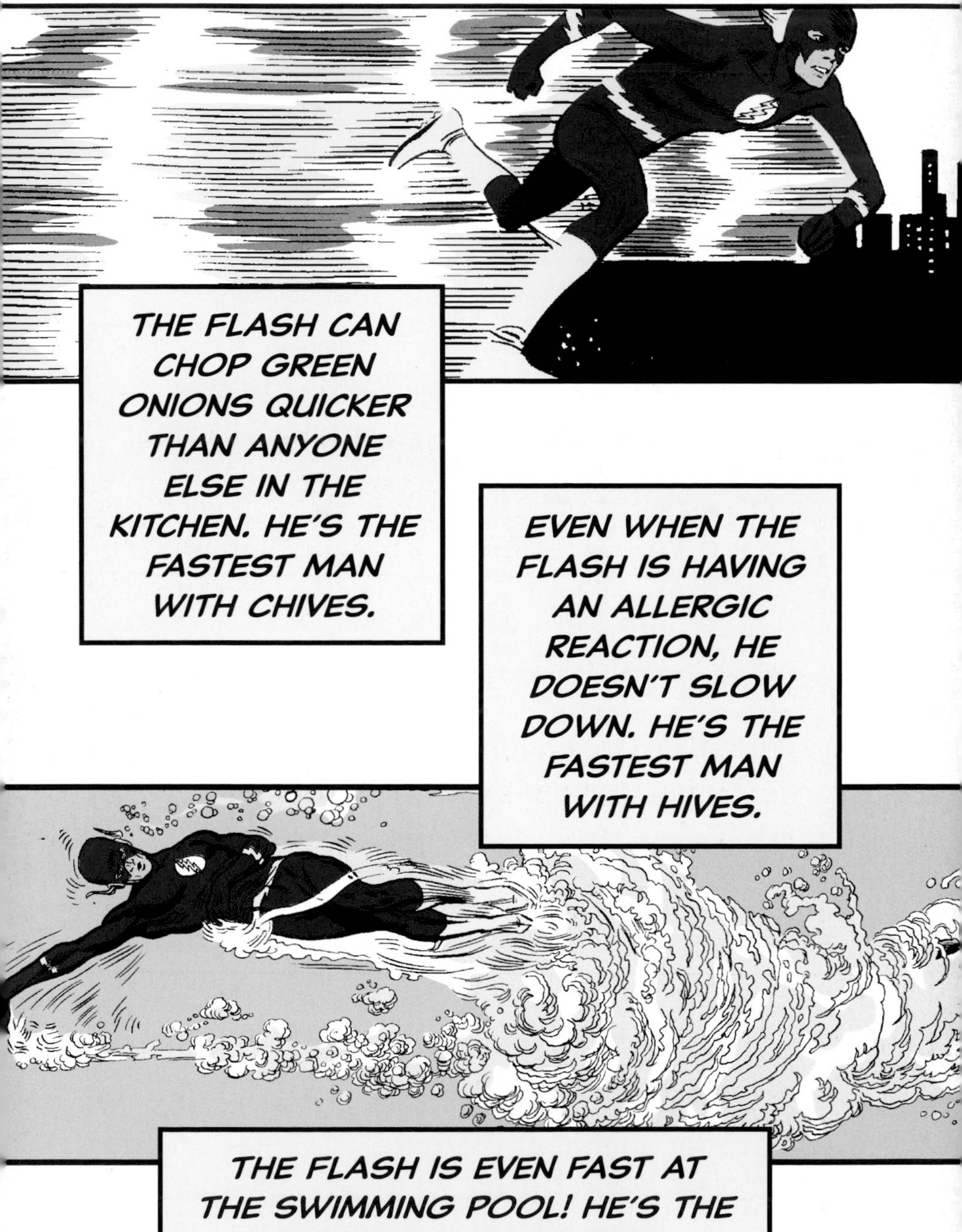
THE FLASH CAN CHOP GREEN ONIONS QUICKER THAN ANYONE ELSE IN THE KITCHEN. HE'S THE FASTEST MAN WITH CHIVES.
EVEN WHEN THE FLASH IS HAVING AN ALLERGIC REACTION, HE DOESN'T SLOW DOWN. HE'S THE FASTEST MAN WITH HIVES.
THE FLASH IS EVEN FAST AT THE SWIMMING POOL! HE'S THE FASTEST MAN TO DIVE.

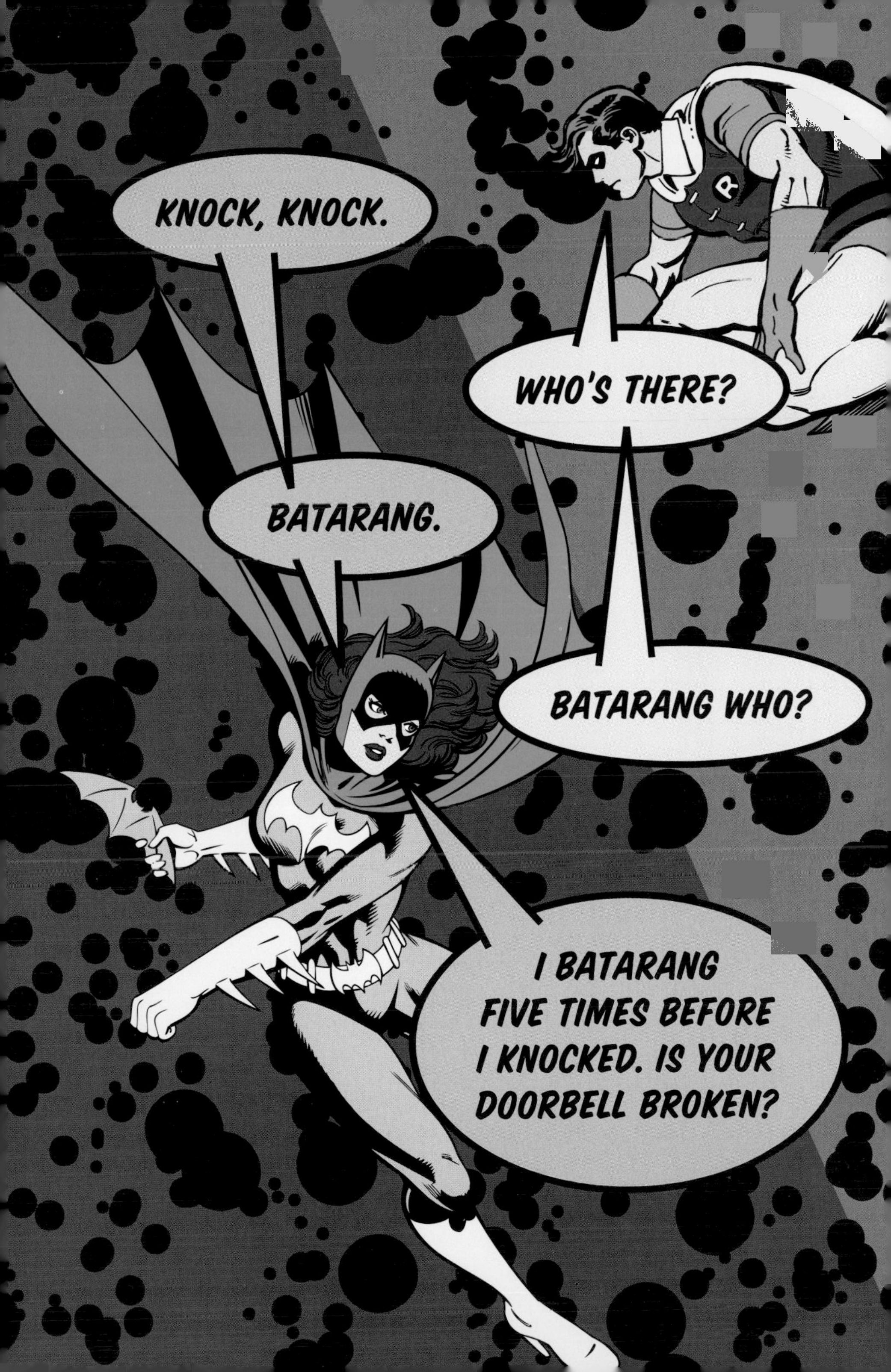
KNOCK, KNOCK.
WHO'S THERE?
BATARANG.
BATARANG WHO?
I BATARANG FIVE TIMES BEFORE I KNOCKED. IS YOUR DOORBELL BROKEN?

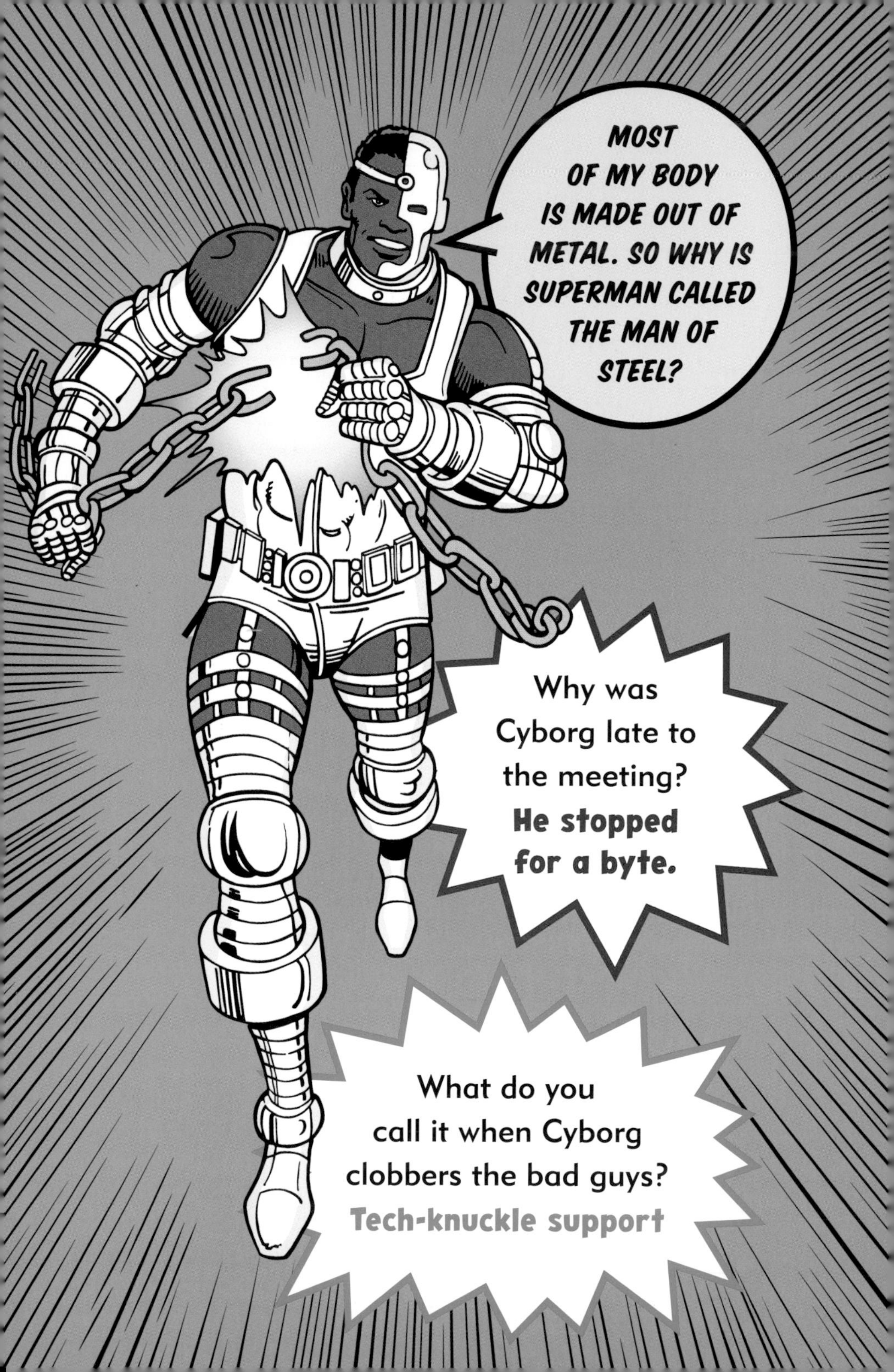
MOST OF MY BODY IS MADE OUT OF METAL. SO WHY IS SUPERMAN CALLED THE MAN OF STEEL?
Why was Cyborg late to the meeting?
He stopped for a byte.
What do you call it when Cyborg clobbers the bad guys?
Tech-knuckle support

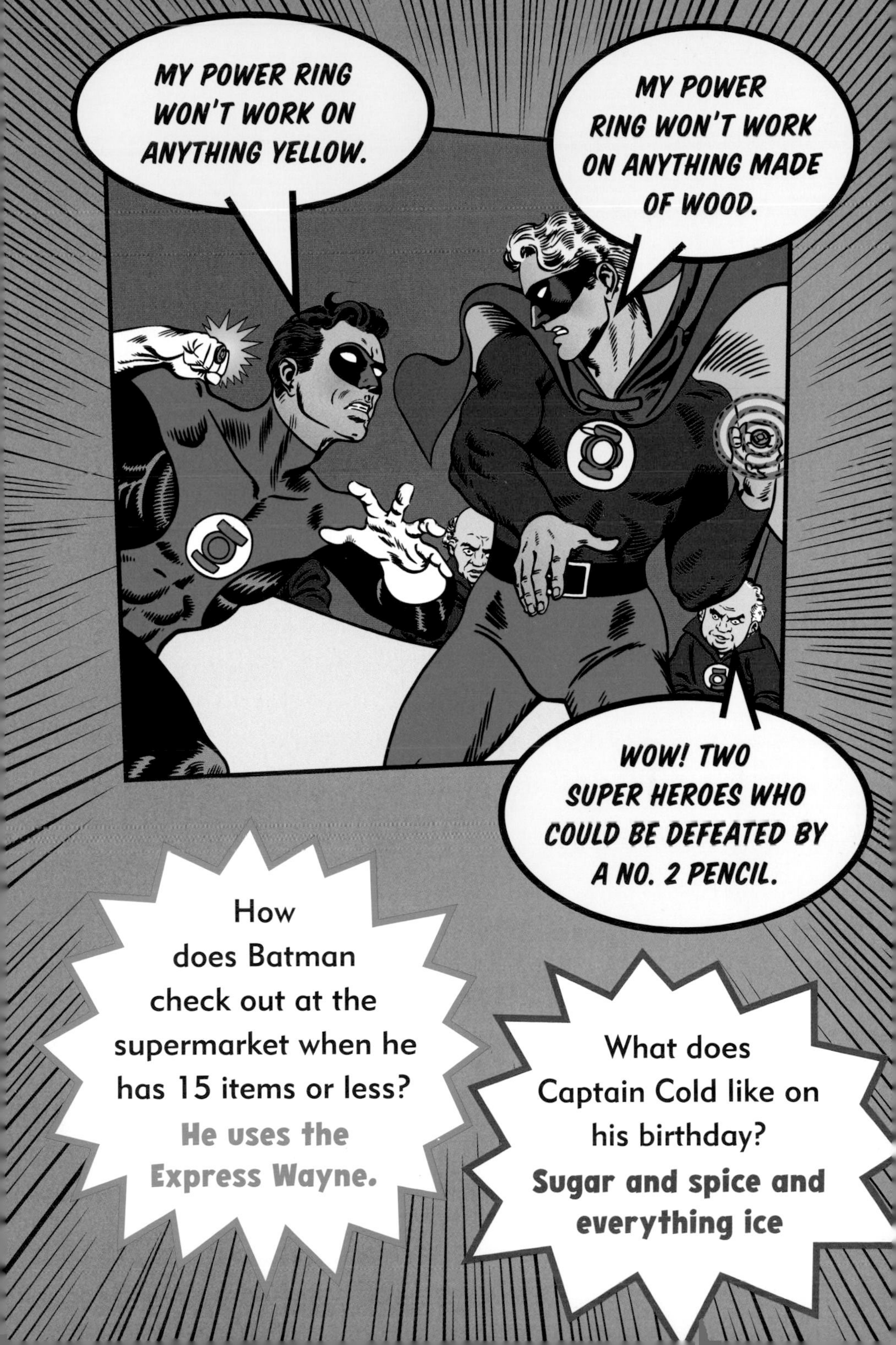
MY POWER RING WON'T WORK ON ANYTHING YELLOW.
MY POWER RING WON'T WORK ON ANYTHING MADE OF WOOD.
WOW! TWO SUPER HEROES WHO COULD BE DEFEATED BY A NO. 2 PENCIL.

How does Batman check out at the supermarket when he has 15 items or less?

He uses the Express Wayne.

What does Captain Cold like on his birthday?

Sugar and spice and everything ice

Beast Boy is a ferocious crime fighter—especially when he morphs into ferocious animals. Here are some of his best changes ever.

BEAST BOY'S BEST TRANSFORMATIONS

When he turned into a lion, it was a roaring success.

When he turned into an octopus, he was well-armed.

He turned into a duck to solve a mystery, and he quacked the case.

Once he turned into a small, red, pointy-eared animal so he could outfox a villain.

He turned into a ram and made
the villains feel sheepish.

He turned into a squirrel and drove the villains nuts.

He turned into an ant and made
the villain cry "uncle."

To listen in on a villain's plans, he turned
into an elephant so he could be all ears.

He turned into a fawn, and Starfire
said he was a little dear.

When he turned into a grizzly, the
villains could bear-ly fight back.

On Thanksgiving, he turned into
a hog, and he really pigged out.

Why did
Beast Boy cross
the road?
He had turned
himself into a
chicken.

What happened
when Beast Boy
went to the
all-you-can-eat buffet?
He earned the
nickname Feast Boy.

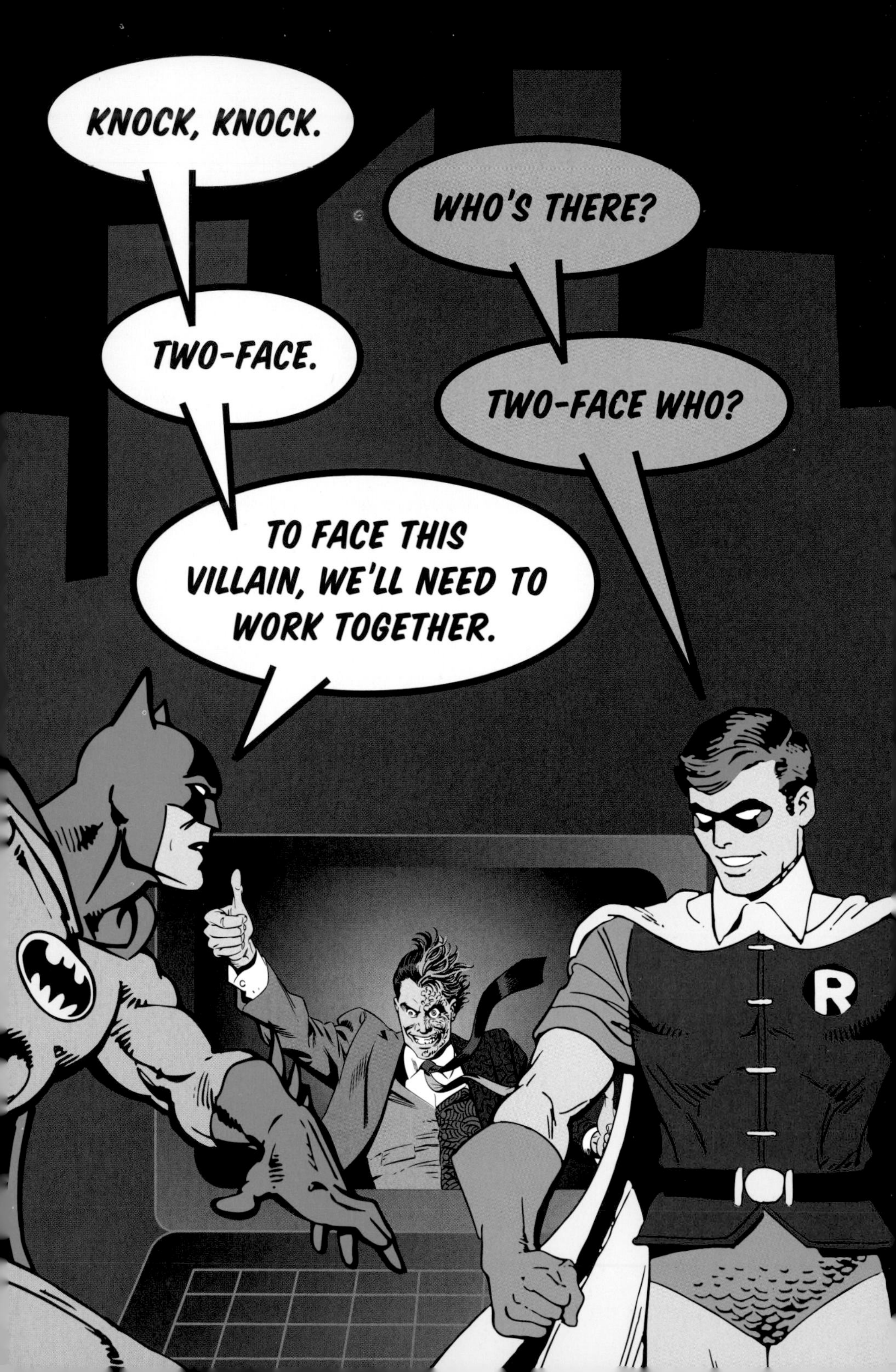
KNOCK, KNOCK.
WHO'S THERE?
TWO-FACE.
TWO-FACE WHO?
TO FACE THIS VILLAIN, WE'LL NEED TO WORK TOGETHER.

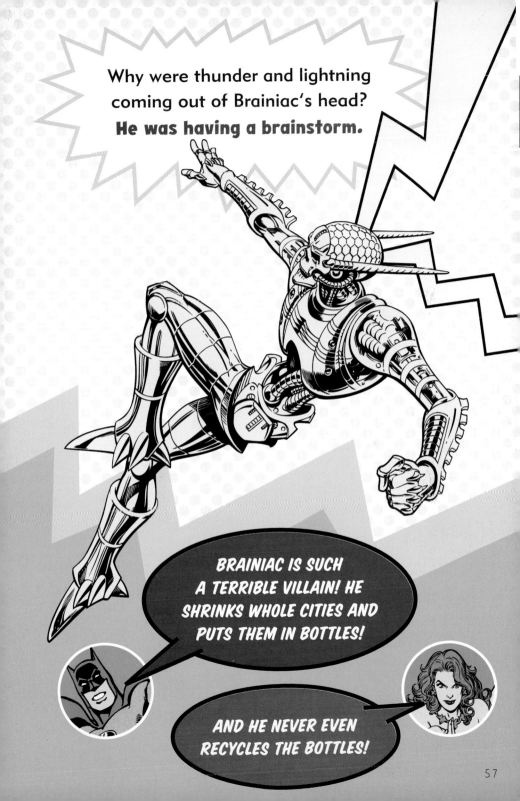

Why were thunder and lightning coming out of Brainiac's head?

He was having a brainstorm.

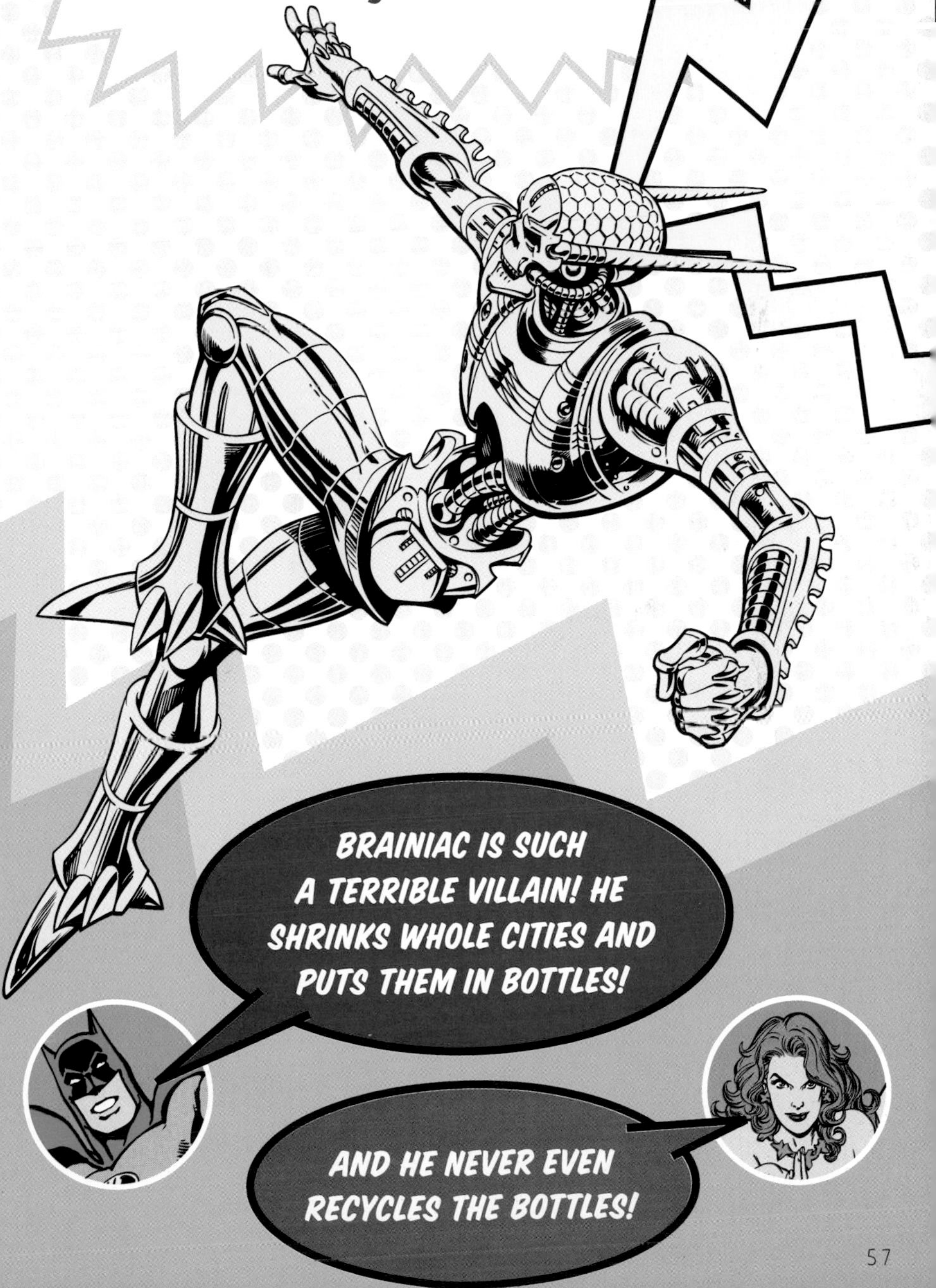
BRAINIAC IS SUCH A TERRIBLE VILLAIN! HE SHRINKS WHOLE CITIES AND PUTS THEM IN BOTTLES!
AND HE NEVER EVEN RECYCLES THE BOTTLES!

What happened when Streaky accidentally distracted Supergirl from catching a super-villain?
It was a cat-astrophe.

What is Streaky when he's imitating Krypto?
A copycat

What did Superman say when Krypto and Streaky started to growl at each other?
"Beware the Krypto-fight."

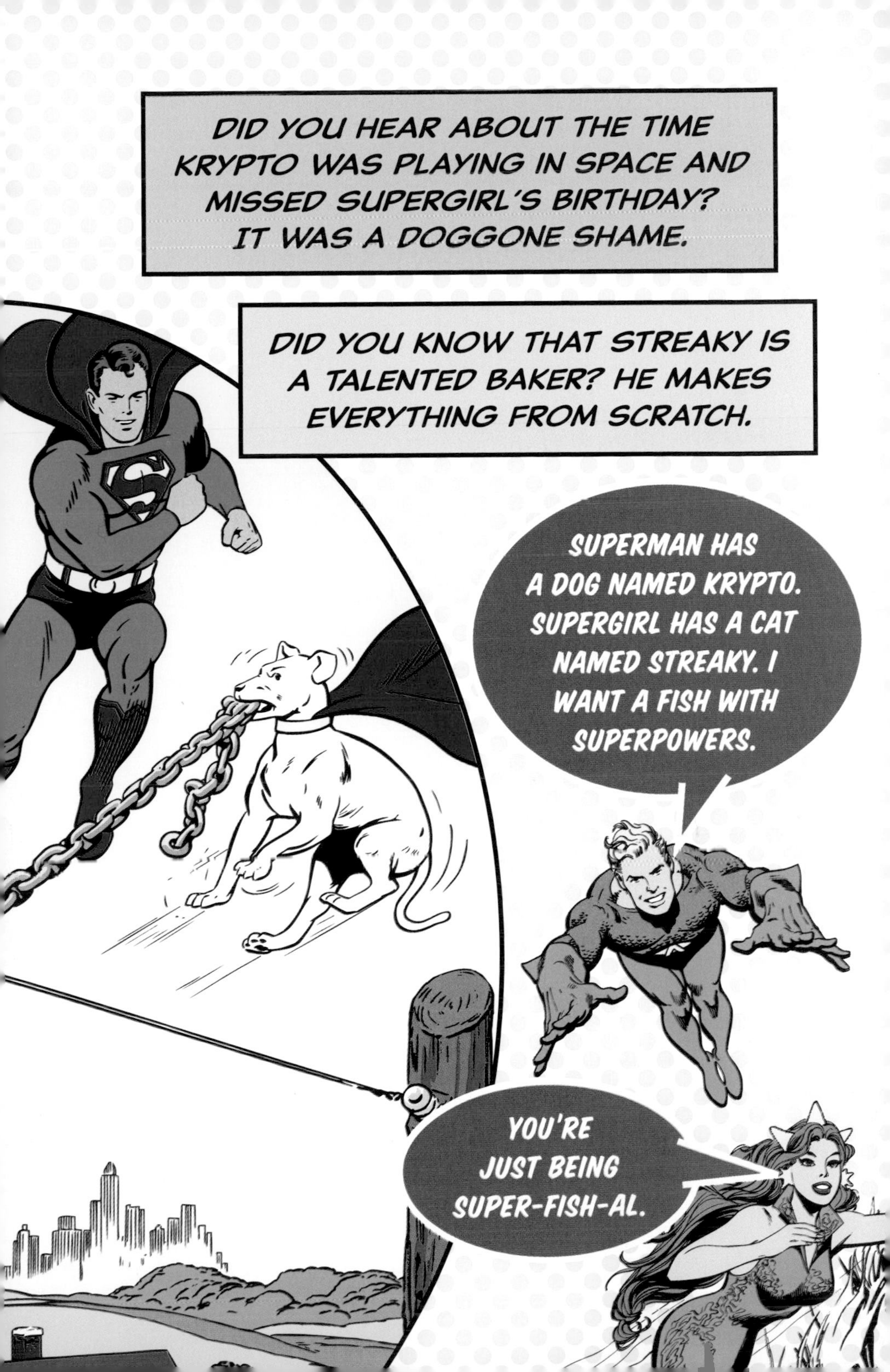
DID YOU HEAR ABOUT THE TIME KRYPTO WAS PLAYING IN SPACE AND MISSED SUPERGIRL'S BIRTHDAY? IT WAS A DOGGONE SHAME.
DID YOU KNOW THAT STREAKY IS A TALENTED BAKER? HE MAKES EVERYTHING FROM SCRATCH.
SUPERMAN HAS A DOG NAMED KRYPTO. SUPERGIRL HAS A CAT NAMED STREAKY. I WANT A FISH WITH SUPERPOWERS.
YOU'RE JUST BEING SUPER-FISH-AL.

GIGANTA LOVES TO TELL STORIES. ESPECIALLY TALL TALES.

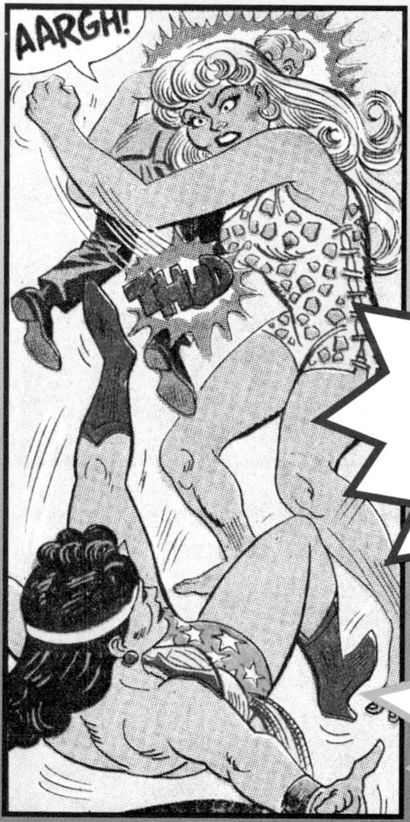
AARGH!
THUD

DID YOU HEAR GIGANTA IS GOING TO BE IN A MOVIE? SHE'LL BE A BIG STAR.

What does Giganta buy at the grocery story?

Fee-Fi-Fo-Food

Do the villains ever get together for a softball game?

No, they prefer bad-minton.

What's Catwoman's favorite playground game?

Hopscratch

What's Darkseid's favorite playground game?

Four Scare

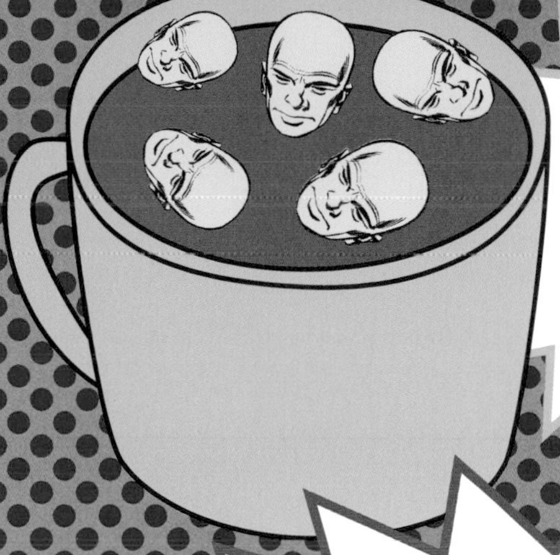

What does J'onn J'onzz put in his hot chocolate?

Martian-mallows

If Martian Manhunter were a principal, what would he do with a student who cut class?

He'd suspender.

Why did Killer Croc try to bite Martian Manhunter?

His mother told him to eat his greens.

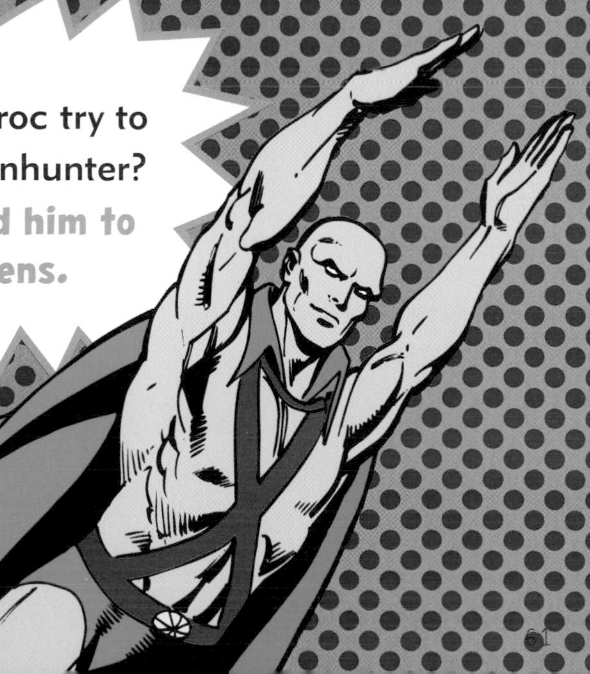

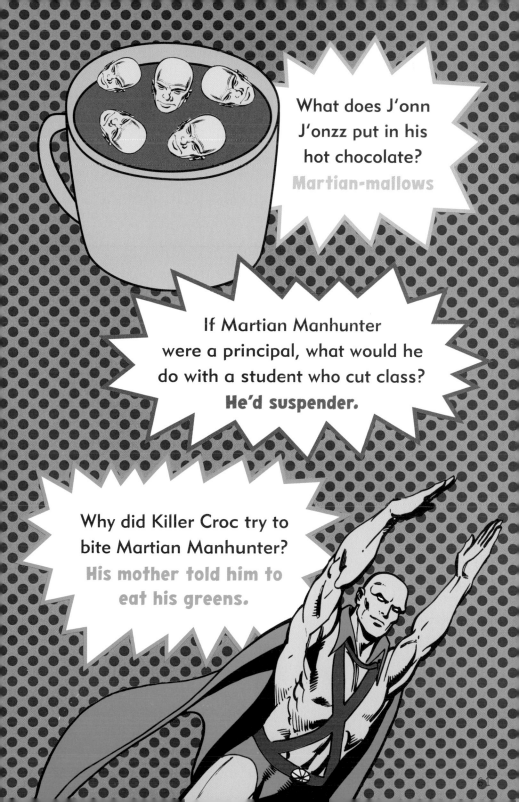

Why did Katana put wheels on her sword?
She wanted to make roller blades.

 *DOES ELONGATED MAN EVER LIE?*

NO, BUT HE MIGHT STRETCH THE TRUTH.

What happened when Batman and Robin made a mistake?
They demanded a Dynamic Do-over.

What does Deadman put on his turkey?
Grave-y

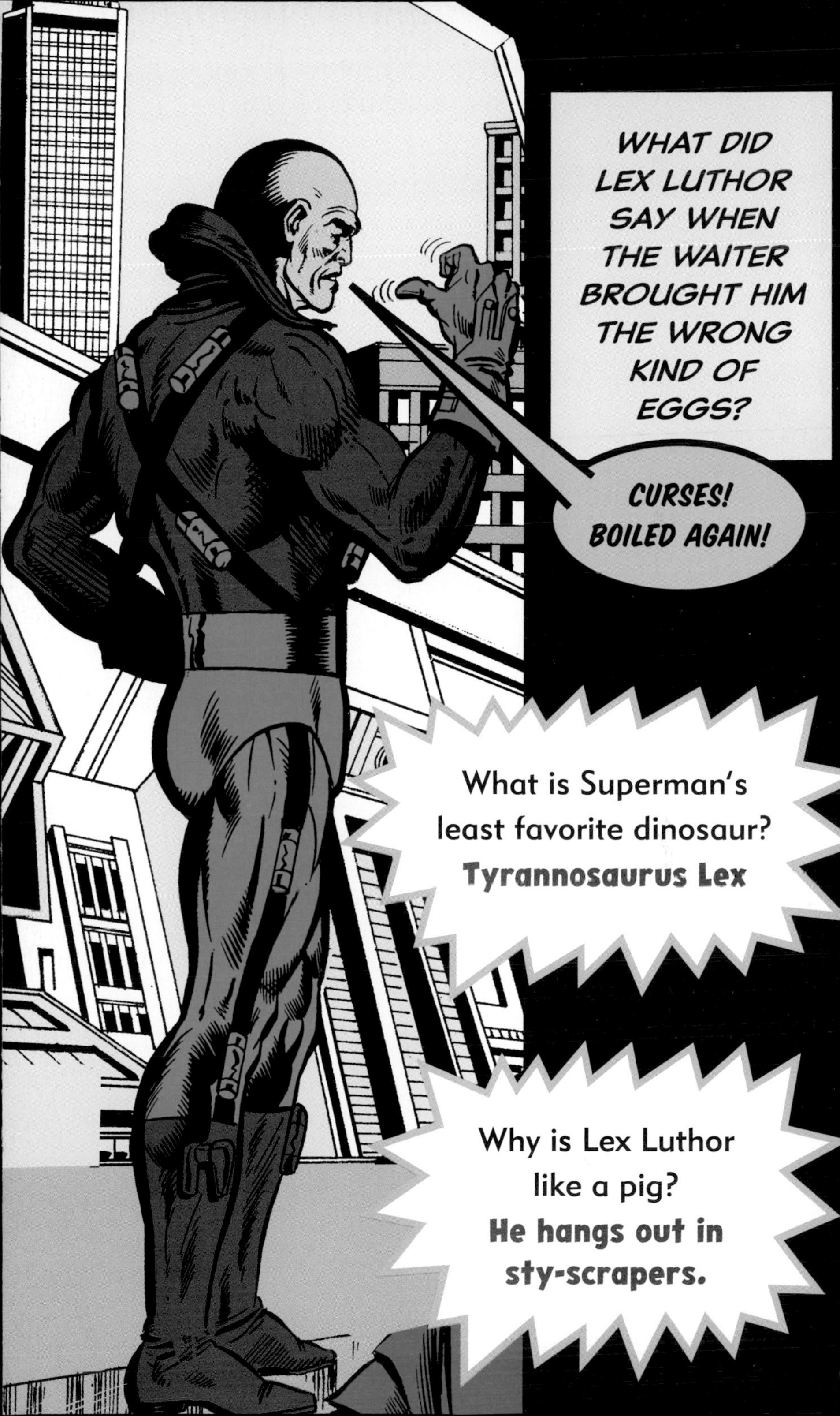
WHAT DID LEX LUTHOR SAY WHEN THE WAITER BROUGHT HIM THE WRONG KIND OF EGGS?
CURSES! BOILED AGAIN!

What is Superman's least favorite dinosaur?
Tyrannosaurus Lex

Why is Lex Luthor like a pig?
He hangs out in sty-scrapers.

HOW STRONG IS SUPERMAN?

When he pitches in baseball, the batter
has to wait for the ball to circle the
Earth a few times before swinging.

- - - - - - - - - - - - - - - -

He has more muscles than the Pacific Ocean.

- - - - - - - - - - - - - - - -

He doesn't have triceps. He has succeedceps.

- - - - - - - - - - - - - - - -

To make a milk shake, he starts
by picking up the cow.

- - - - - - - - - - - - - - - -

Some people have muscles that ripple.
Superman has muscles that tsunami.

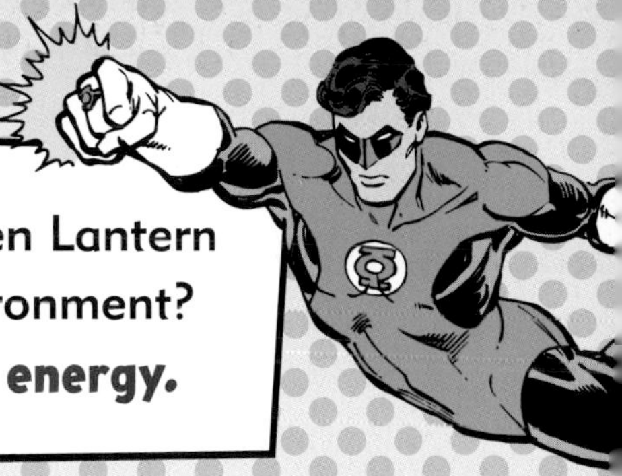

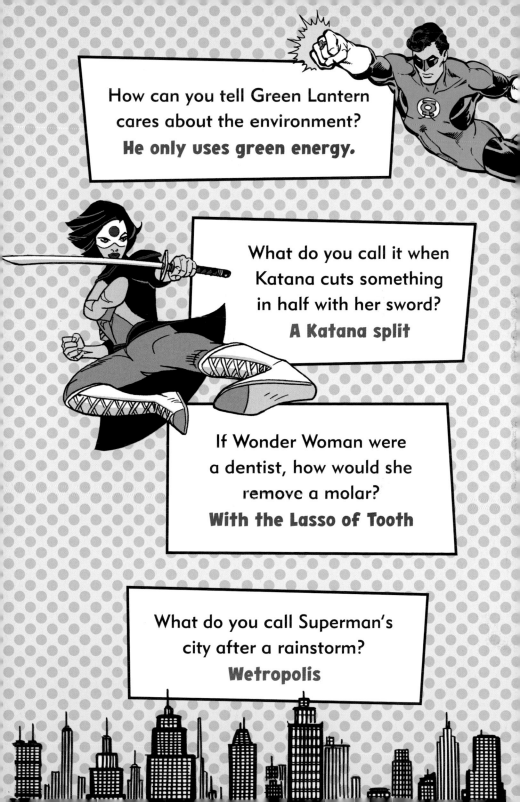

How can you tell Green Lantern
cares about the environment?
He only uses green energy.

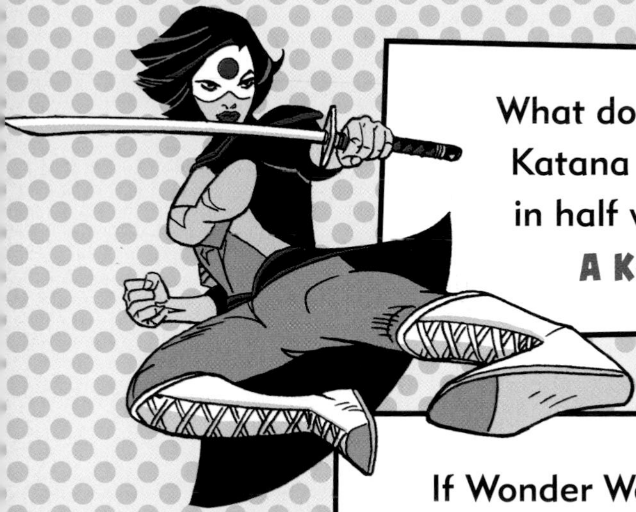

What do you call it when
Katana cuts something
in half with her sword?
A Katana split

If Wonder Woman were
a dentist, how would she
remove a molar?
With the Lasso of Tooth

What do you call Superman's
city after a rainstorm?
Wetropolis

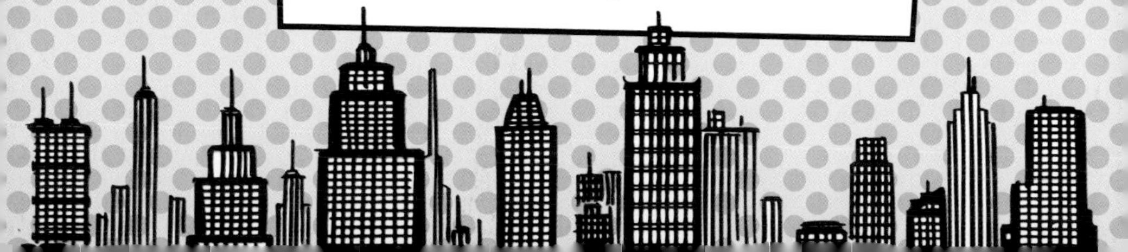

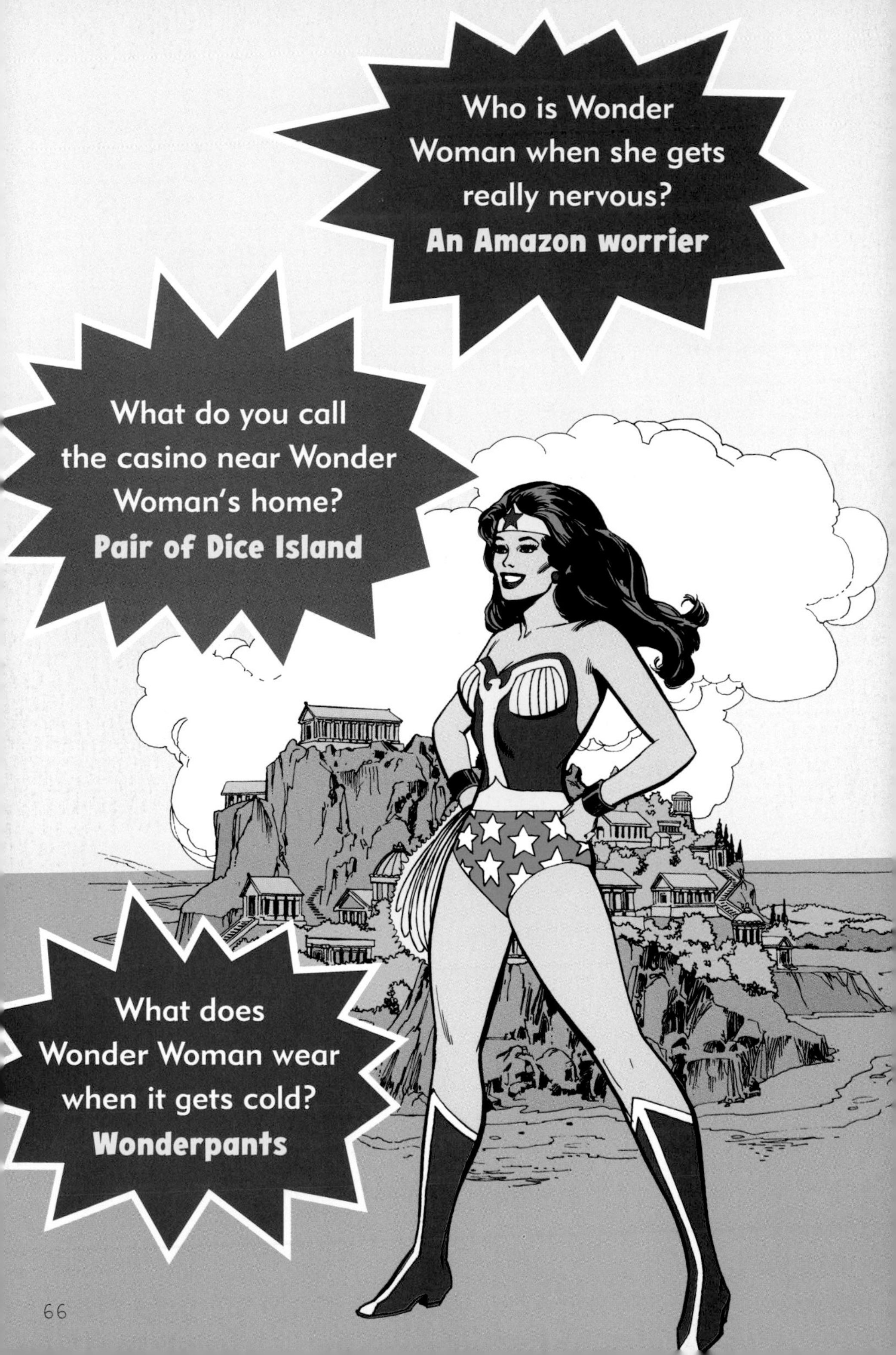
Who is Wonder Woman when she gets really nervous?
An Amazon worrier
What do you call the casino near Wonder Woman's home?
Pair of Dice Island
What does Wonder Woman wear when it gets cold?
Wonderpants

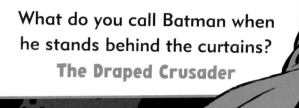

What do you call Batman when he stands behind the curtains?
The Draped Crusader

What do you call Batman when he eats at a French restaurant?
The Creped Crusader

What do you call Batman when he spills his juice?
The Graped Crusader

What do you call Batman after he films a segment for a talk show?
The Taped Crusader

What do you call Batman when he spends all day mowing the lawn and trimming the hedges?
The Landscape Crusader

What vocal part does Barry Allen sing?

He's a Barry-tone.

What's The Flash's favorite hot drink?

Veloci-tea

Why does The Flash smile so much when he travels more than 26 miles?

He's a merry-thon runner.

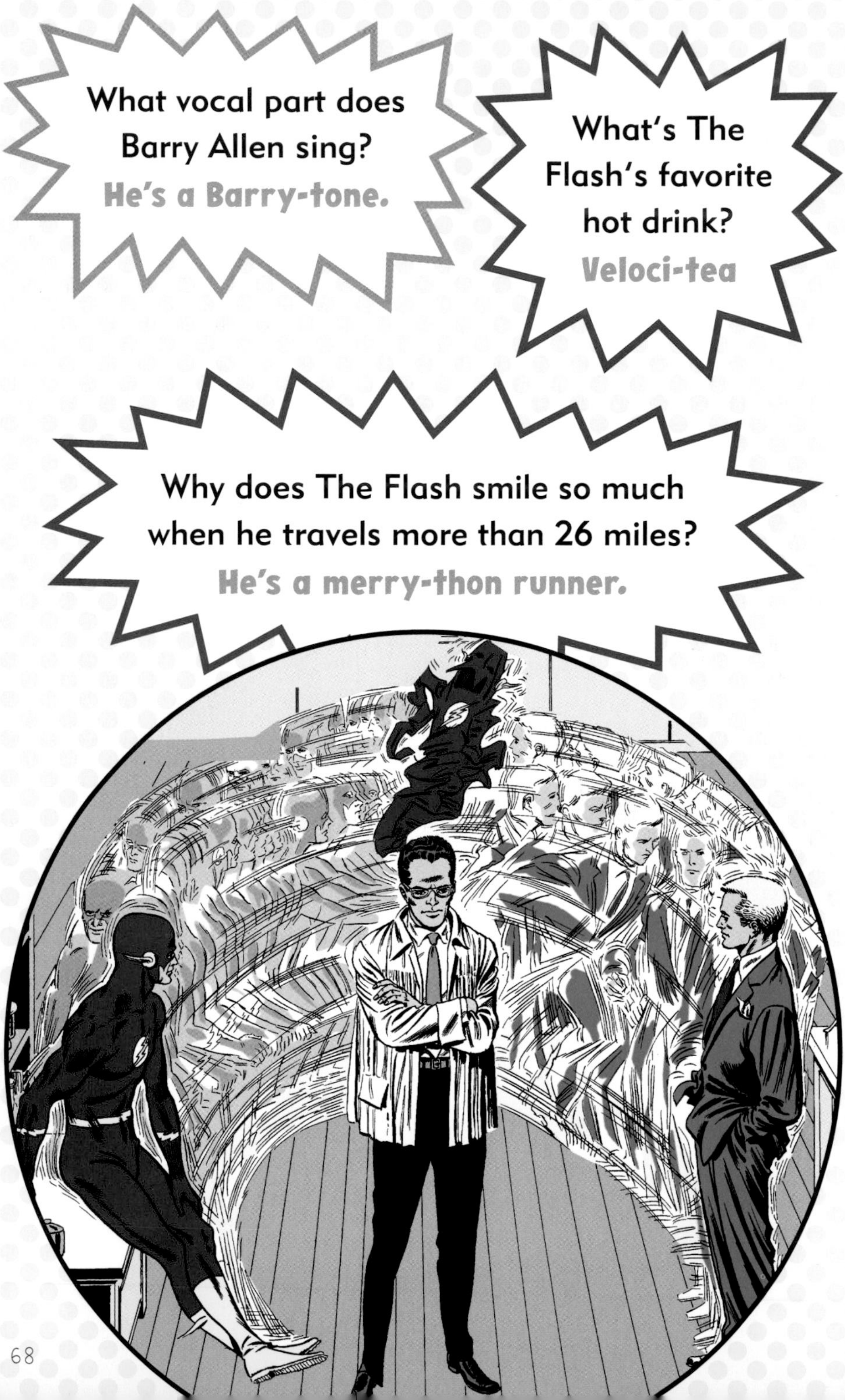

Why does The Flash love watching science documentaries?
He finds them fast-inating.

Why does The Flash hate battling Gorilla Grodd?
Grodd really drives him bananas.

What do you call it when The Flash cooks breakfast?
A Flash 'n' the pan

Why did The Flash's doctor put him on a diet?
He was eating too much fast food.

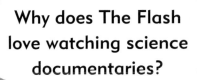

Why does Supergirl wear a watch while soaring through the air?
She likes to see time fly.

Why does Supergirl wear red boots?
To keep her feet dry

When she was younger, why didn't Supergirl like how her name was spelled?
She wished Kara Zor-El was spelled with more Ls.

What's Supergirl's favorite candy?
Kara-mel

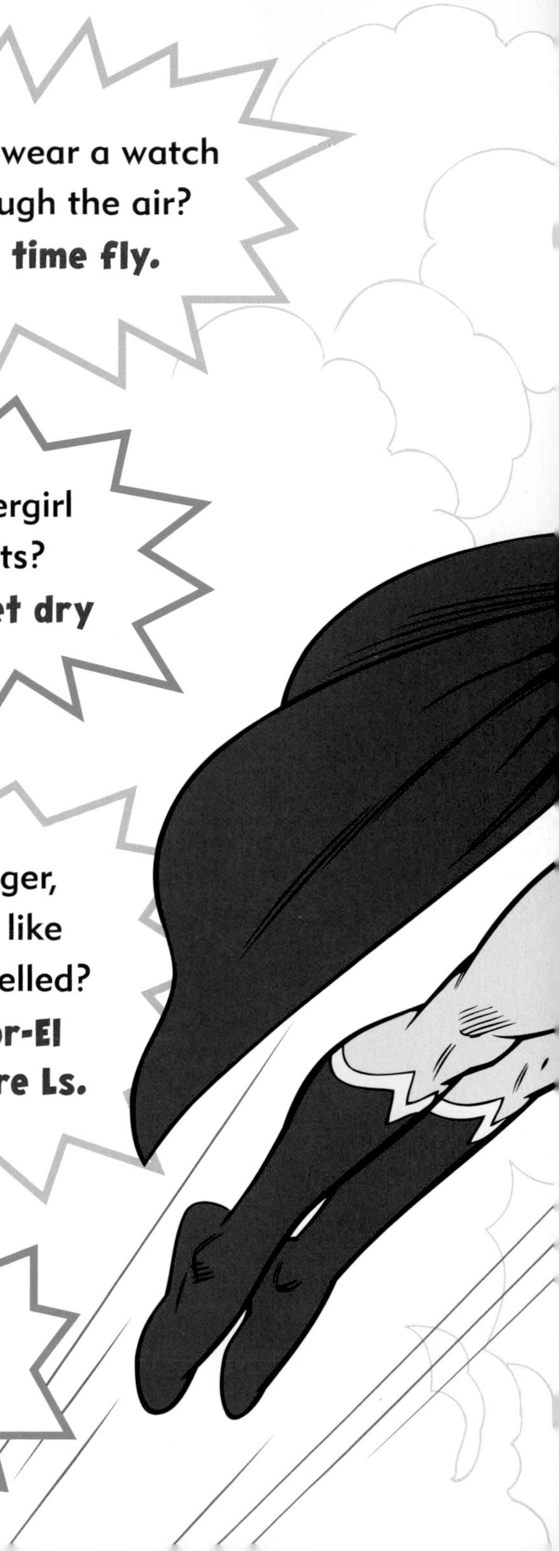

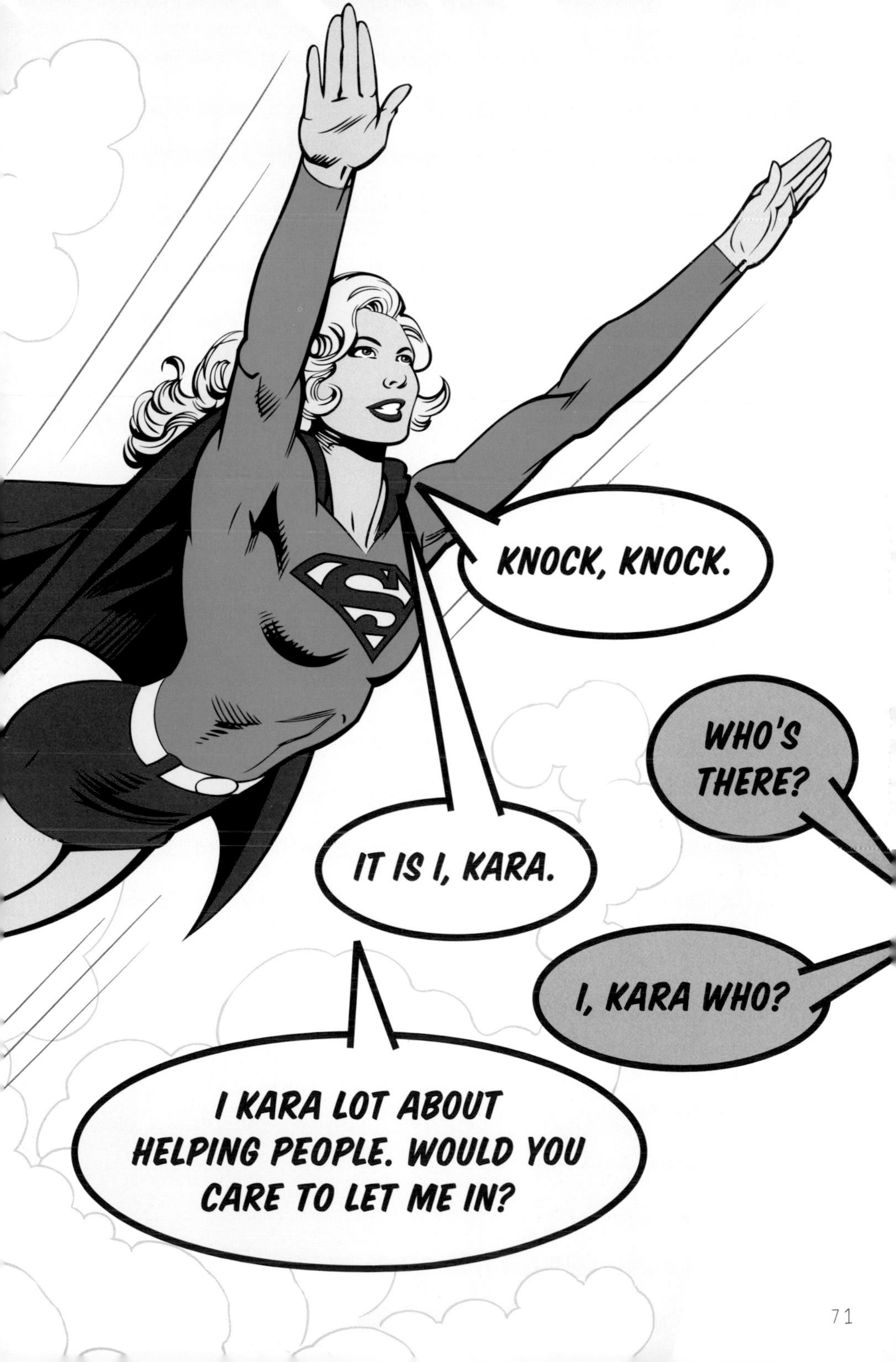
KNOCK, KNOCK.
WHO'S THERE?
IT IS I, KARA.
I, KARA WHO?
I KARA LOT ABOUT HELPING PEOPLE. WOULD YOU CARE TO LET ME IN?

Zatanna casts magic spells by speaking words backward. Sometimes this causes problems . . .

She asked a waitress for some **desserts,** but it made her feel **stressed.**

Then she asked for a straw and gave the waitress warts.

She told Wonder Woman she liked the **star** on her tiara and accidentally turned it into some **rats.**

She offered a man a reward for helping out on a Justice League mission, but all he got was a boring old drawer.

When Batman and Robin were on a spy mission, she called them **snoops** and accidentally turned them into **spoons**.

When a reformed villain was released from jail, she said he had "repaid his debt to society," and he turned into a diaper.

She went to fill her car with **gas,** and it started to **sag**.

She shouted "Stop!" at some villains, and they became pots.

When she said, "I led a mission," she turned the Justice League headquarters into a **deli**.

She complimented Green Arrow's hat and offered to swap, but instead she gave him paws.

She's powerless against villains named **Bob, Hannah,** or **Otto**.

She kept trying to cast a spell on a race car, but nothing happened.

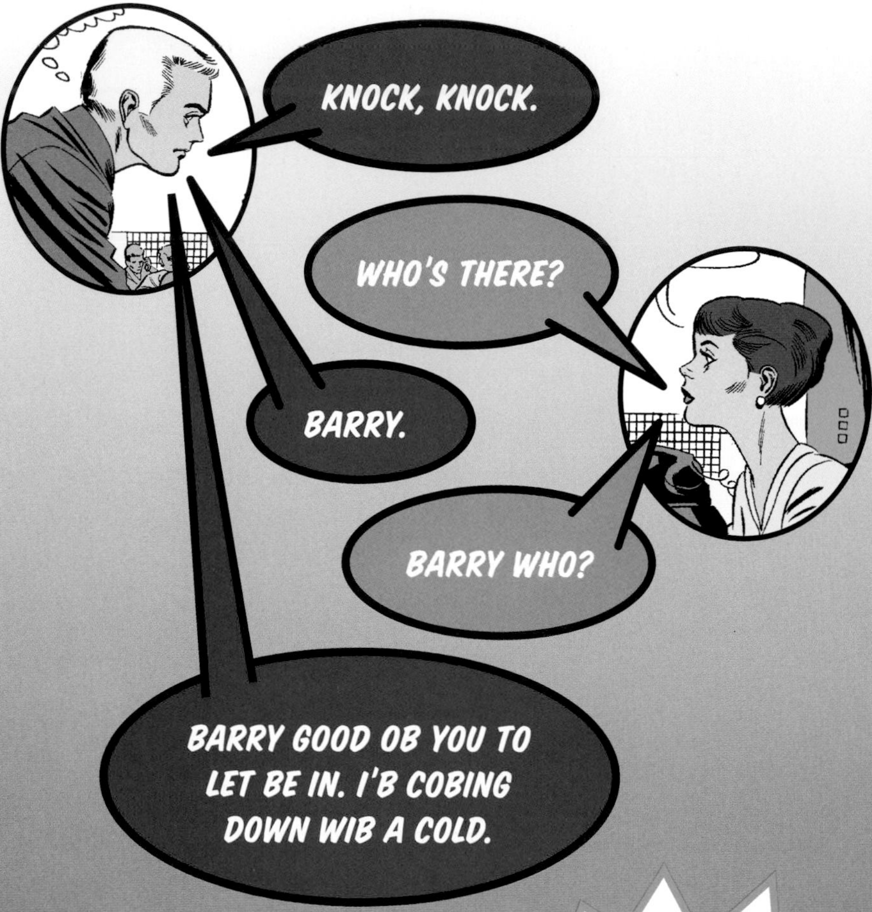
KNOCK, KNOCK.
WHO'S THERE?
BARRY.
BARRY WHO?
BARRY GOOD OB YOU TO LET BE IN. I'B COBING DOWN WIB A COLD.

Where does Hawkman wear his wedding band?

On his wing finger

What does Aquaman say when his fish friends tell jokes?

"Stop it, you're gilling me."

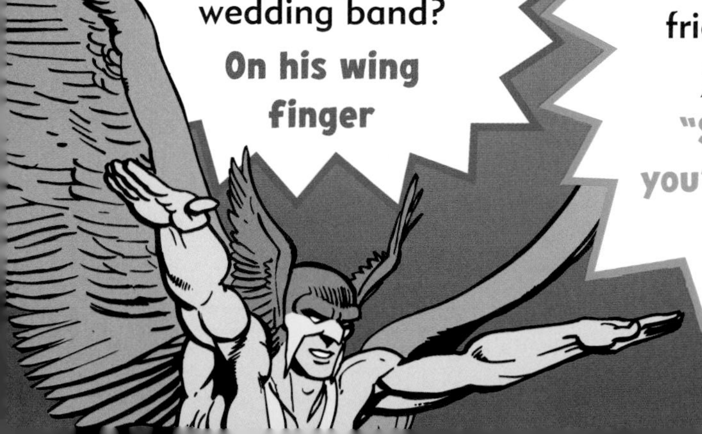

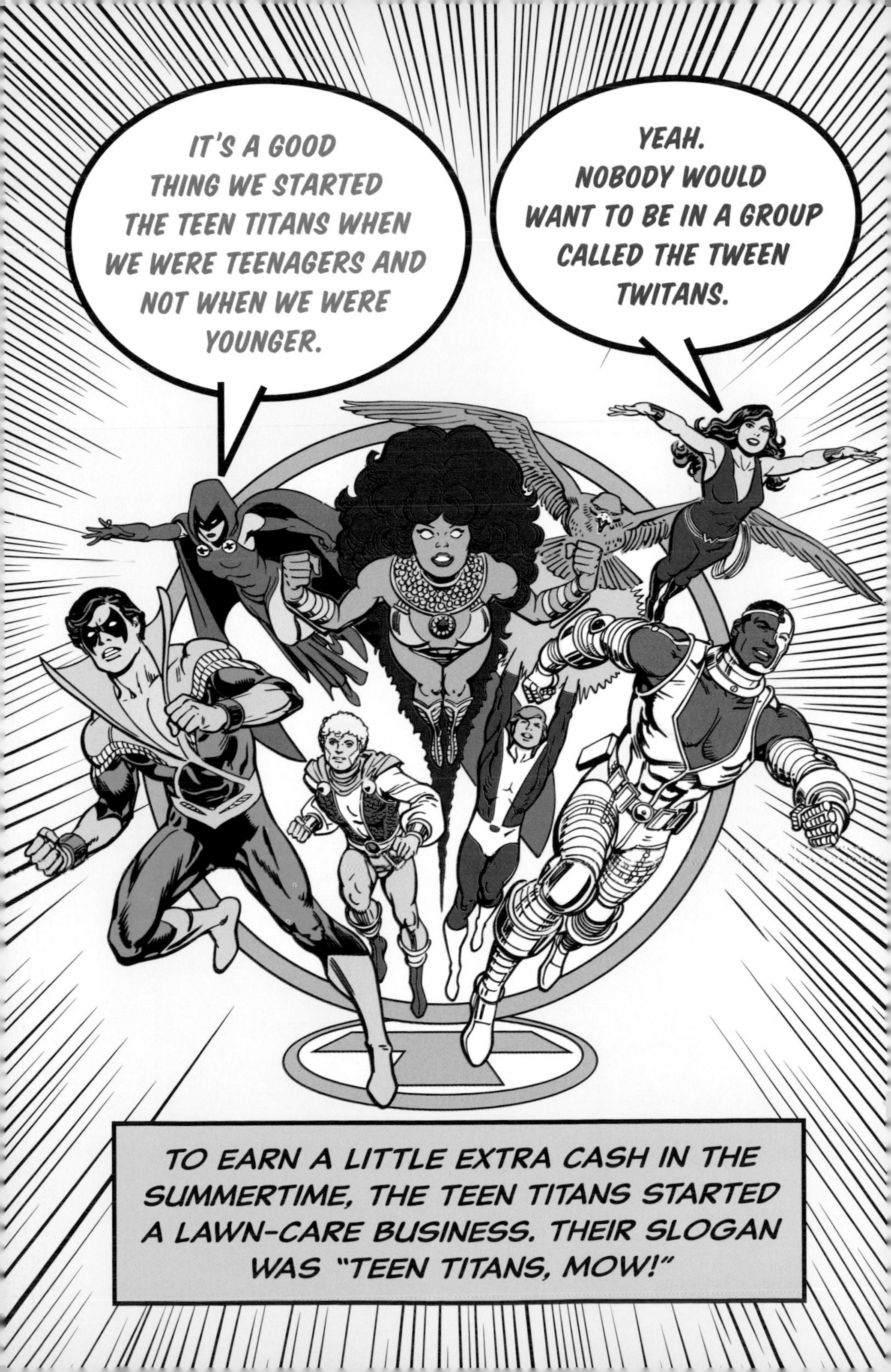
IT'S A GOOD THING WE STARTED THE TEEN TITANS WHEN WE WERE TEENAGERS AND NOT WHEN WE WERE YOUNGER.
YEAH. NOBODY WOULD WANT TO BE IN A GROUP CALLED THE TWEEN TWITANS.
TO EARN A LITTLE EXTRA CASH IN THE SUMMERTIME, THE TEEN TITANS STARTED A LAWN-CARE BUSINESS. THEIR SLOGAN WAS "TEEN TITANS, MOW!"

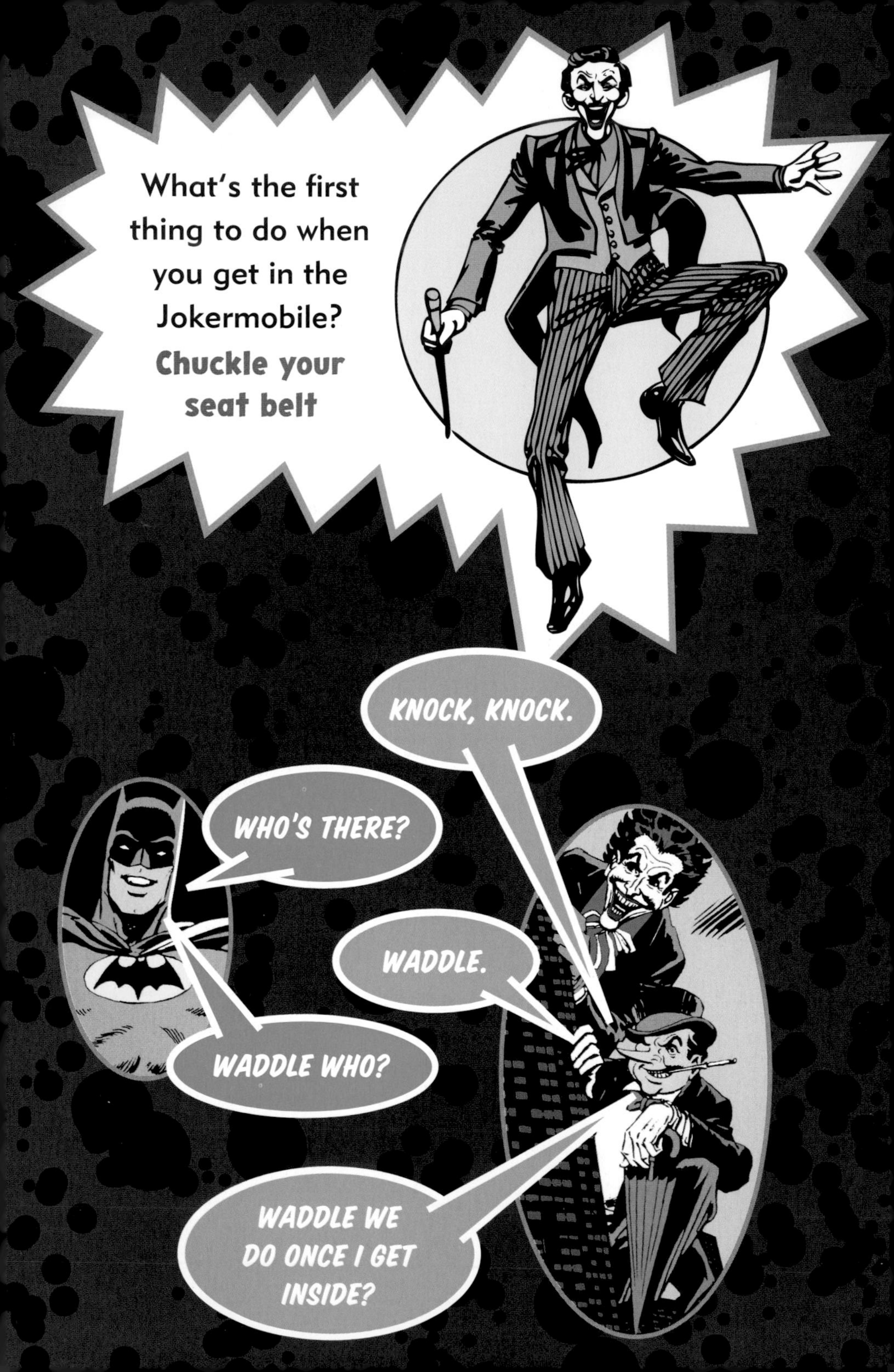
What's the first thing to do when you get in the Jokermobile?
Chuckle your seat belt
KNOCK, KNOCK.
WHO'S THERE?
WADDLE.
WADDLE WHO?
WADDLE WE DO ONCE I GET INSIDE?

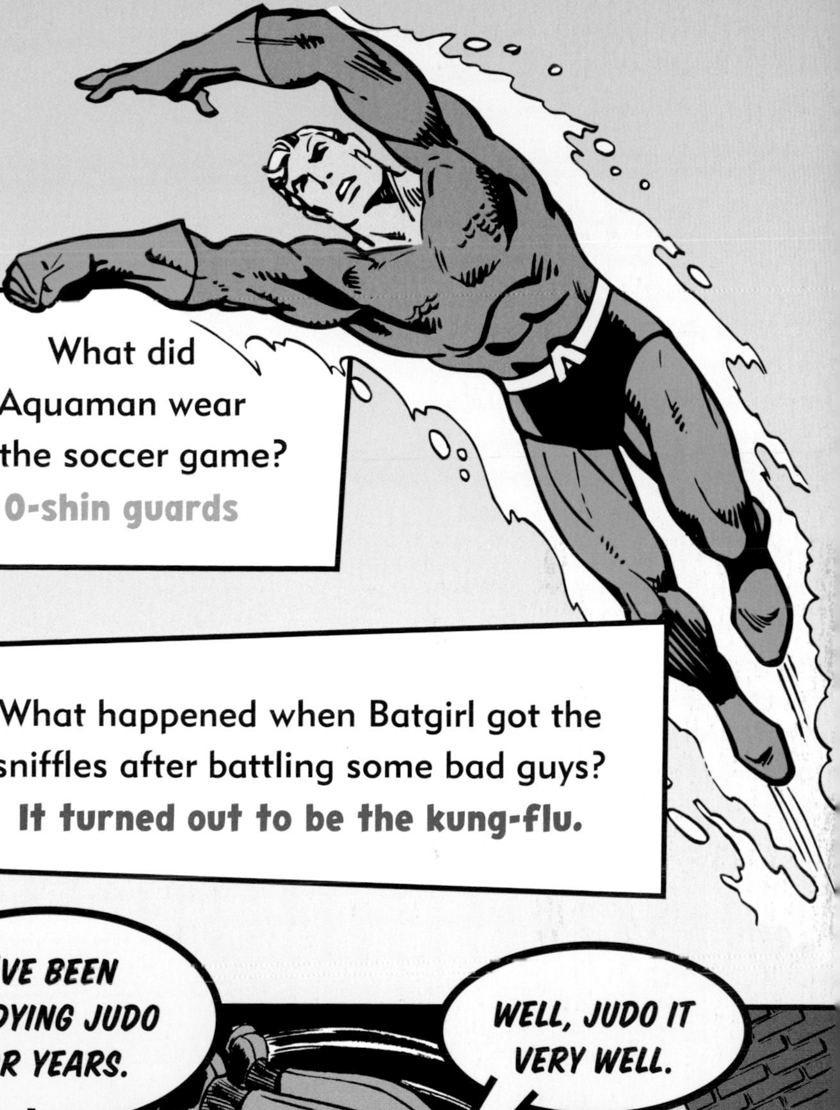

What did Aquaman wear to the soccer game?

O-shin guards

What happened when Batgirl got the sniffles after battling some bad guys?

It turned out to be the kung-flu.

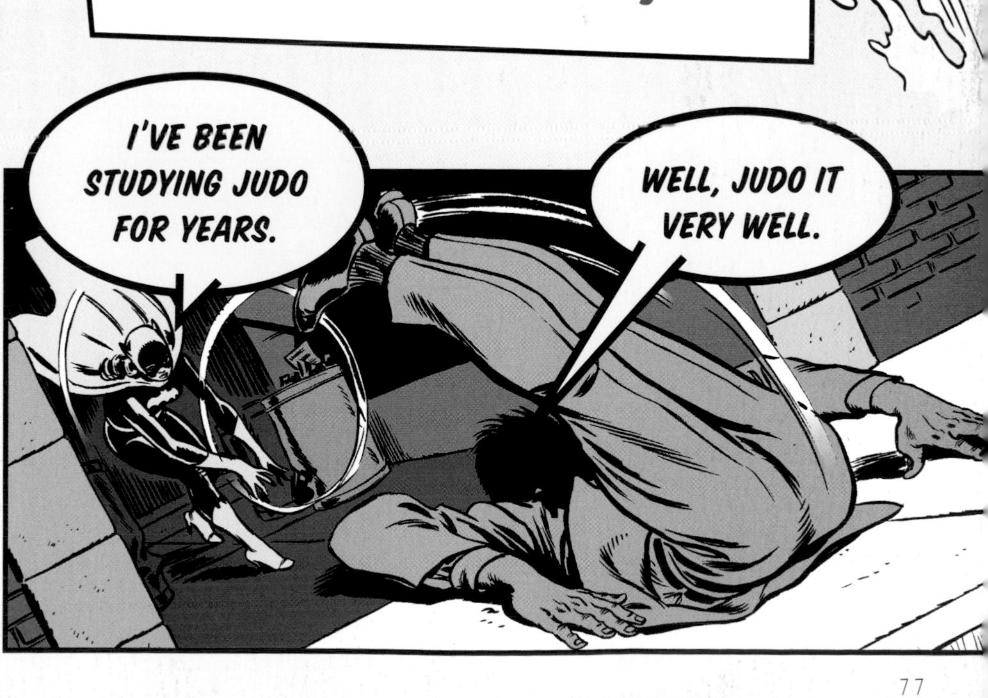
I'VE BEEN STUDYING JUDO FOR YEARS.
WELL, JUDO IT VERY WELL.

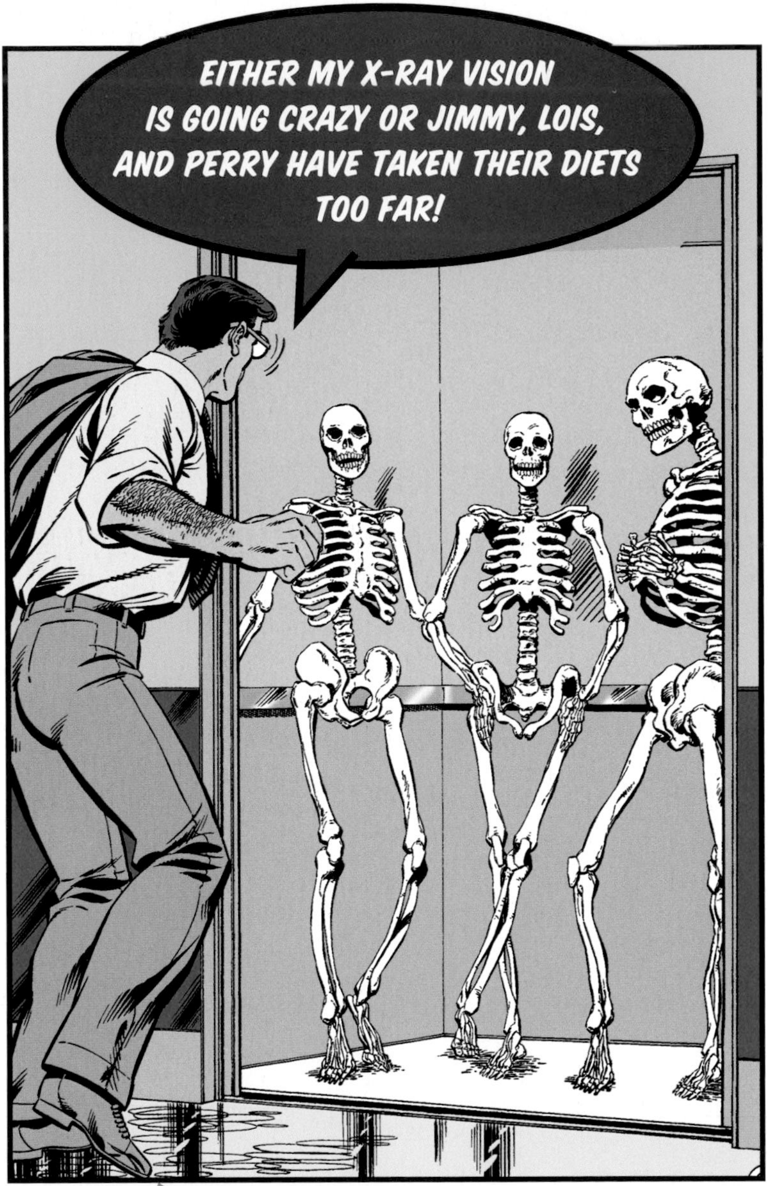
EITHER MY X-RAY VISION IS GOING CRAZY OR JIMMY, LOIS, AND PERRY HAVE TAKEN THEIR DIETS TOO FAR!

When he got a cold, why did Superman leap a tall building in a single bound?

He just wanted to get over it.

HOW SNEAKY IS CATWOMAN?

One Christmas, Catwoman stole the twelfth letter of the alphabet, which is why we call it "No L."

- - - - - - - - - - - - - - - - - -

She could give a banana peel the slip.

- - - - - - - - - - - - - - - - - -

She could steal your socks without taking off your shoes.

- - - - - - - - - - - - - - - - - -

Even her pencils aren't on the straight and narrow.

- - - - - - - - - - - - - - - - - -

You know the story about the guy who tried to steal Christmas, right? Well, Catwoman once stole Feline-oween. What's that? You've never heard of Feline-oween? Now you know why.

- - - - - - - - - - - - - - - - - -

Why don't super heroes have pockets in their tights? So Catwoman can't pick them.

Did you hear about the pet supply shop near the *Daily Planet*? It's called Pet-ropolis.

DID YOU HEAR ABOUT THE NEW DINER NEAR SUPERMAN'S SECRET HIDEOUT? IT'S CALLED THE FORTRESS OF SOLID FOOD.

Did you hear about the new recycling facility in Metropolis? It's called the Daily Can-It.

DID YOU HEAR ABOUT THE NEW SOUP AND PORK RESTAURANT NEAR COMMISSIONER GORDON'S OFFICE? IT'S CALLED BROTH-HAM CITY.

DID YOU HEAR ABOUT THE NEW COFFEE SHOP NEAR WAYNE MANOR? IT'S CALLED FROTH 'EM CITY.

Did you hear about the time that criminals went to Bruce Wayne's house? Batman appeared and turned Wayne Manor into Pain Manor.

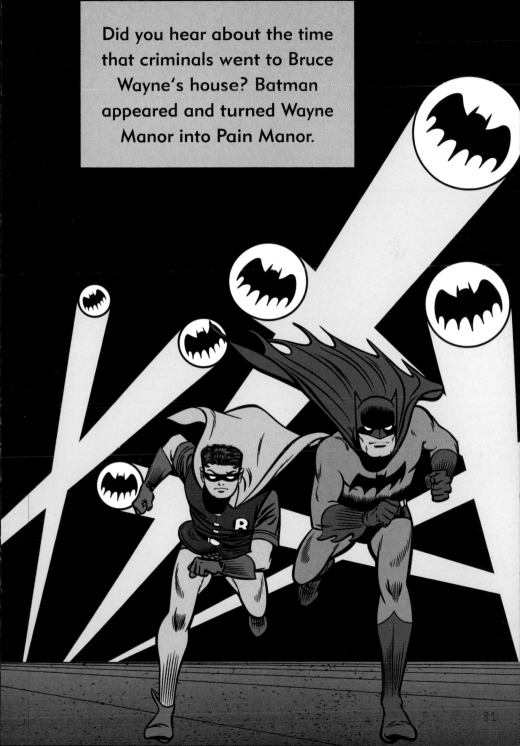

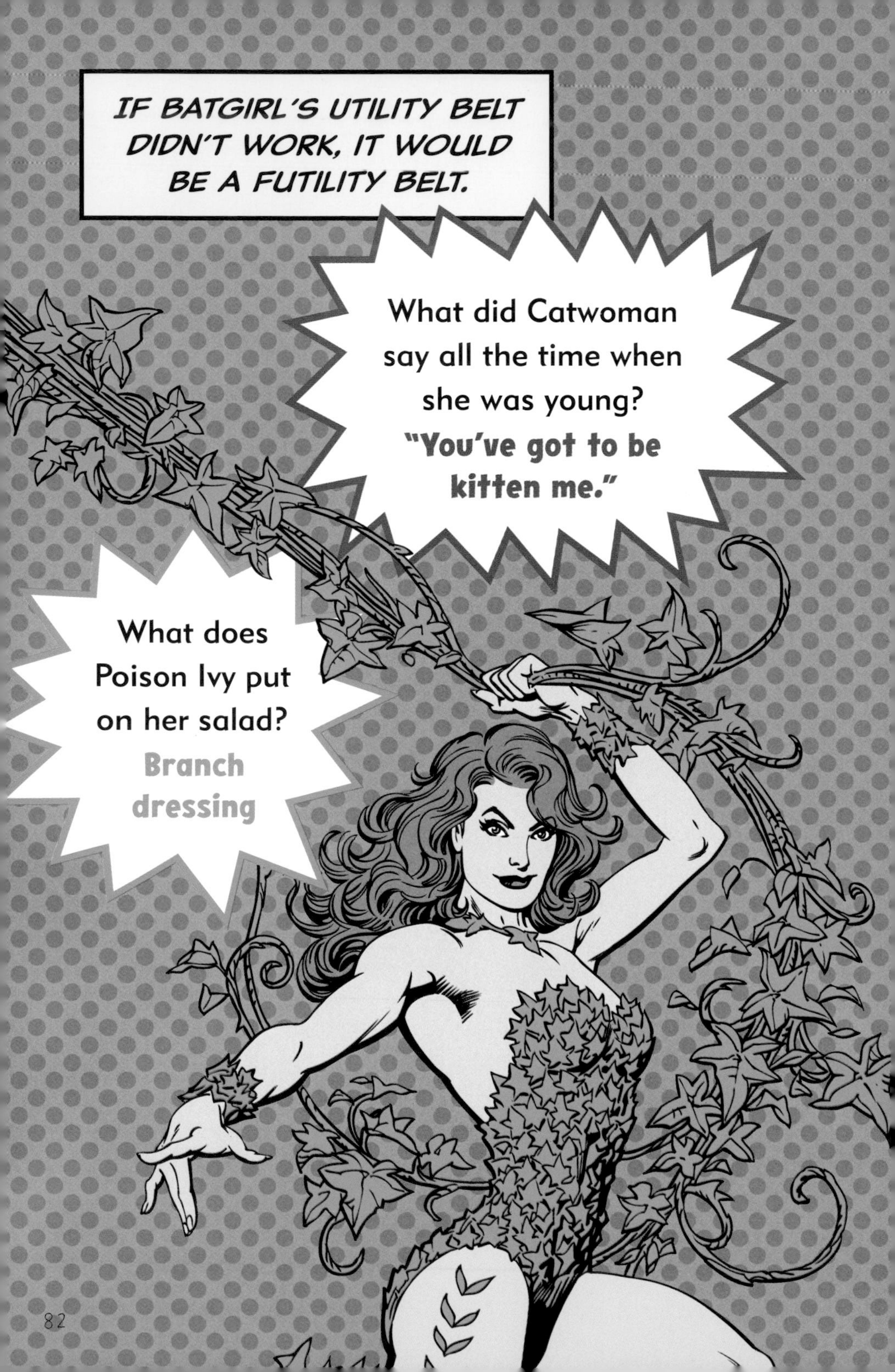
IF BATGIRL'S UTILITY BELT DIDN'T WORK, IT WOULD BE A FUTILITY BELT.
What did Catwoman say all the time when she was young? "You've got to be kitten me."
What does Poison Ivy put on her salad? Branch dressing

Does Captain Cold get stressed-out a lot?
No, he's pretty chill.

Why did Superman go surfing?
To fight for truth, justice, and the American wave

Why is Katana so good at arguing?
She always gets her point across.

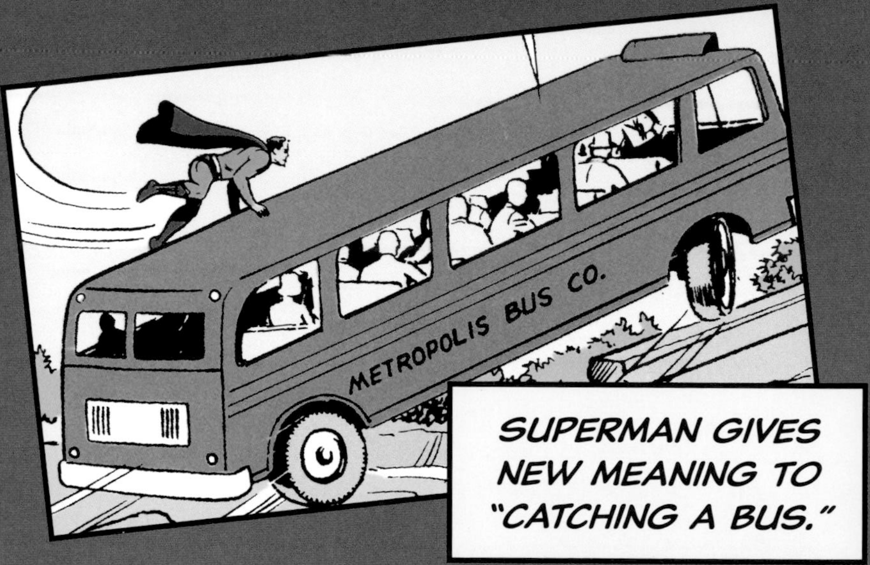
METROPOLIS BUS CO.
SUPERMAN GIVES NEW MEANING TO "CATCHING A BUS."

Why doesn't Hawkgirl eat out with friends?

She always gets stuck with the bill.

Why does Harley Quinn always carry a giant mallet?

You never know when you'll find a giant game of croquet.

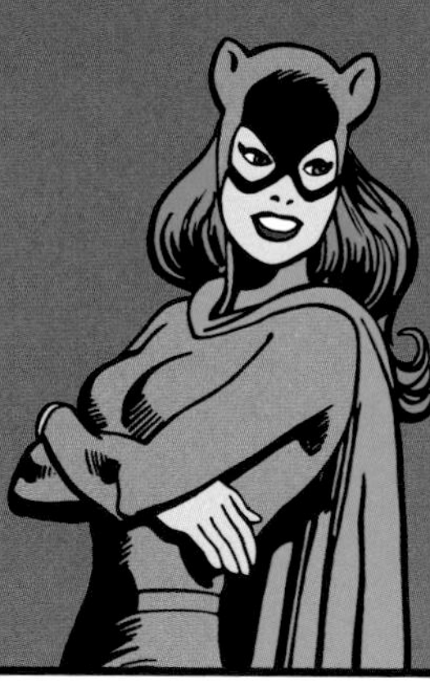

Would Catwoman ever move to another town?

No, she's a Gotham kitty.

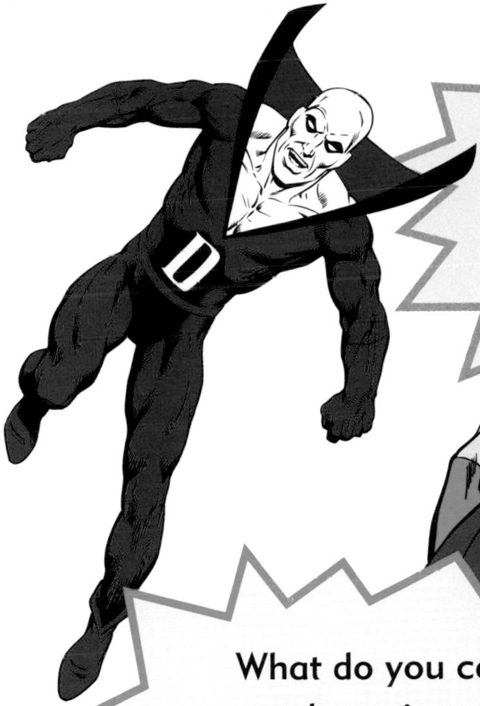

Why did Deadman take cold medicine?

He couldn't stop coffin.

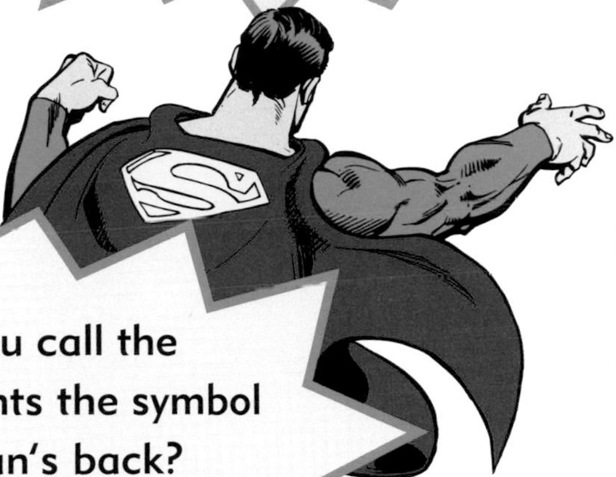

What do you call the person who paints the symbol on Superman's back?

An S-cape artist

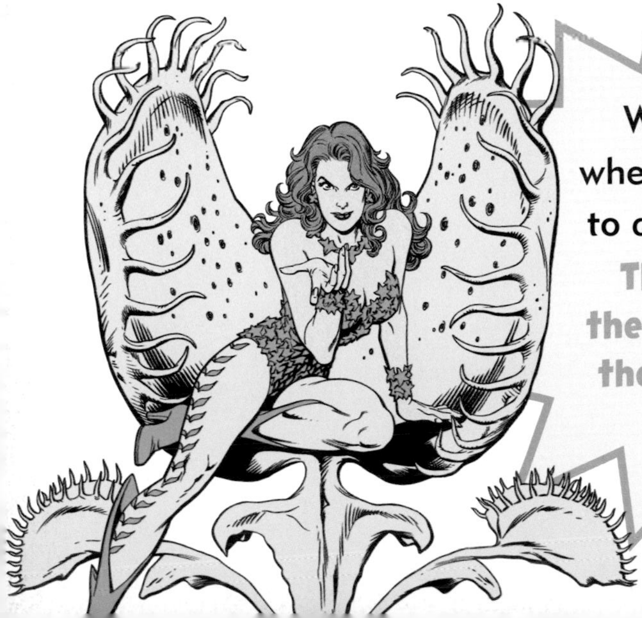

What happened when Poison Ivy went to a baseball game?

The pitcher and the catcher became the itcher and the scratcher.

Does Two-Face like to go to baseball games? **Only if it's a doubleheader.**

Why did Two-Face run from the Caped Crusader? **He was scarred.**

Why did Two-Face buy two sandwiches for lunch? **He couldn't make up his minds.**

Why did Two-Face cross the road? **To get to his other side**

HOW EVIL IS DARKSEID?

He tried out for a play just so he could steal the show.

He helps old ladies across the street, but only halfway.

Santa Claus now has three lists:
Nice, Naughty, and Darkseid.

When he read a book about the extinction of
the dinosaurs, he rooted for the comet.

If he sees someone reading the dictionary, he
starts shouting Z words just to ruin the ending.

Why did
Darkseid put on
flying boots?
To break the law
of gravity

What happens when bad guys break into the Batcave?

It becomes the Splatcave.

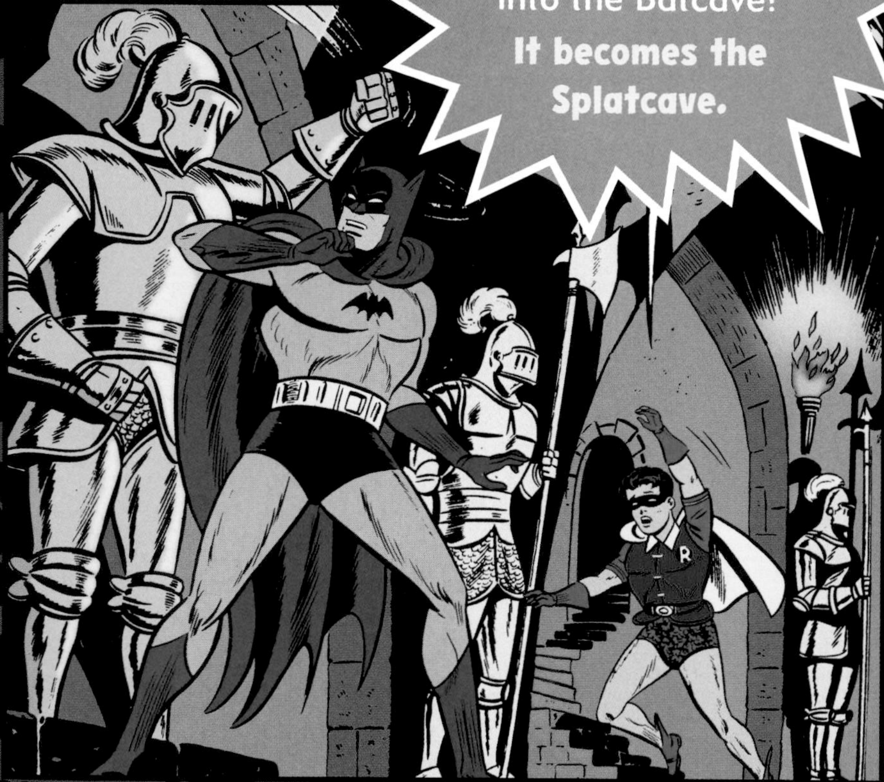

What's Red Tornado's favorite party game?

Twister

What does Batgirl wear to sleep?

Her Dark Knight gown

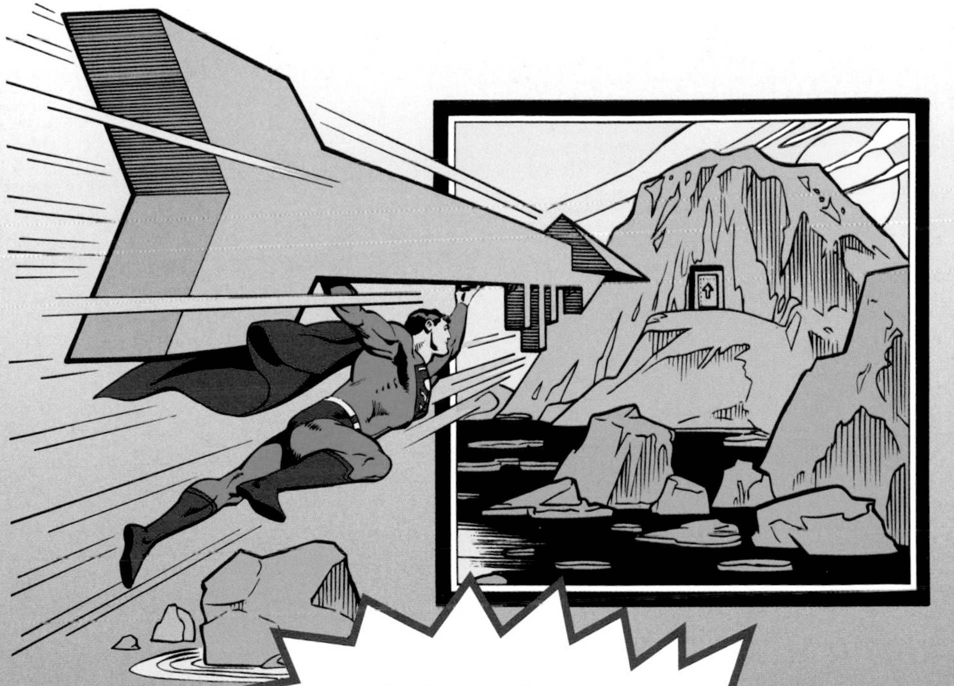

Where does Superman go to play cards by himself?

The Fortress of Solitaire

Why are the citizens of Apokolips so gloomy?

They're always looking on the Darkseid.

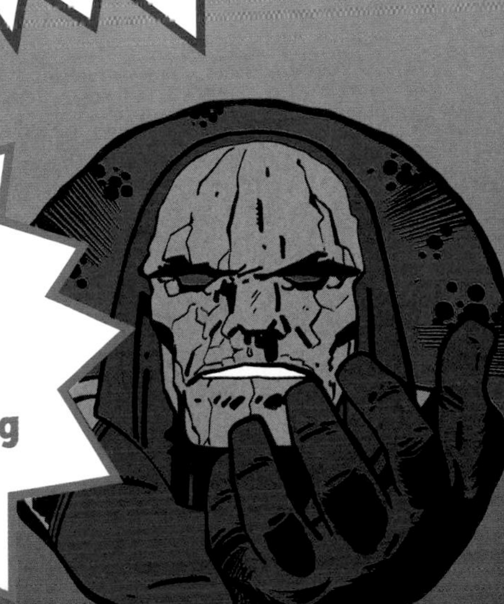

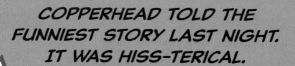

COPPERHEAD TOLD THE FUNNIEST STORY LAST NIGHT. IT WAS HISS-TERICAL.

What does Copperhead do when he gets upset?
He throws a hissy fit.

What was Copperhead's best subject in school?
Hiss-tory

How can you tell Copperhead worries too much about his weight?
His house is covered in scales.

When does Copperhead go to the auto mechanic? When he needs a coil change

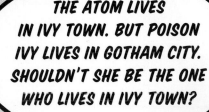

THE ATOM LIVES IN IVY TOWN. BUT POISON IVY LIVES IN GOTHAM CITY. SHOULDN'T SHE BE THE ONE WHO LIVES IN IVY TOWN?

THEN WHERE WOULD THE ATOM LIVE?

SMALLVILLE?

Why are Mirror Master's parents so disappointed that their son is a criminal?
It reflects poorly on them.

Would Green Arrow ever want to visit Robin Hood's forest?
He Sherwood!

What is black and white and goes round and round?
The Penguin, stuck in a revolving door

What's Kara Zor-El's favorite meal of the day?
She's a suppergirl.

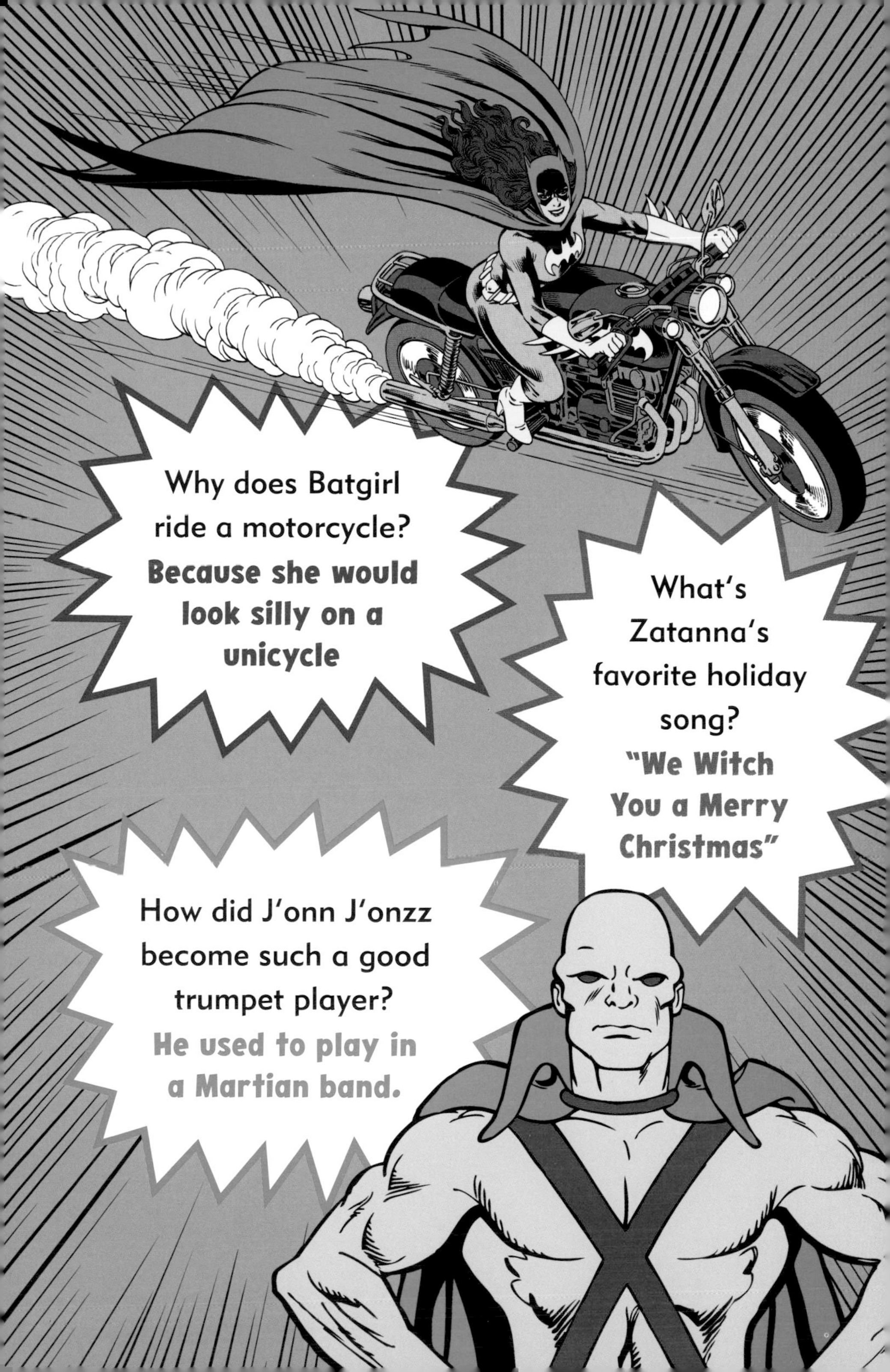
Why does Batgirl ride a motorcycle?
Because she would look silly on a unicycle
What's Zatanna's favorite holiday song?
"We Witch You a Merry Christmas"
How did J'onn J'onzz become such a good trumpet player?
He used to play in a Martian band.

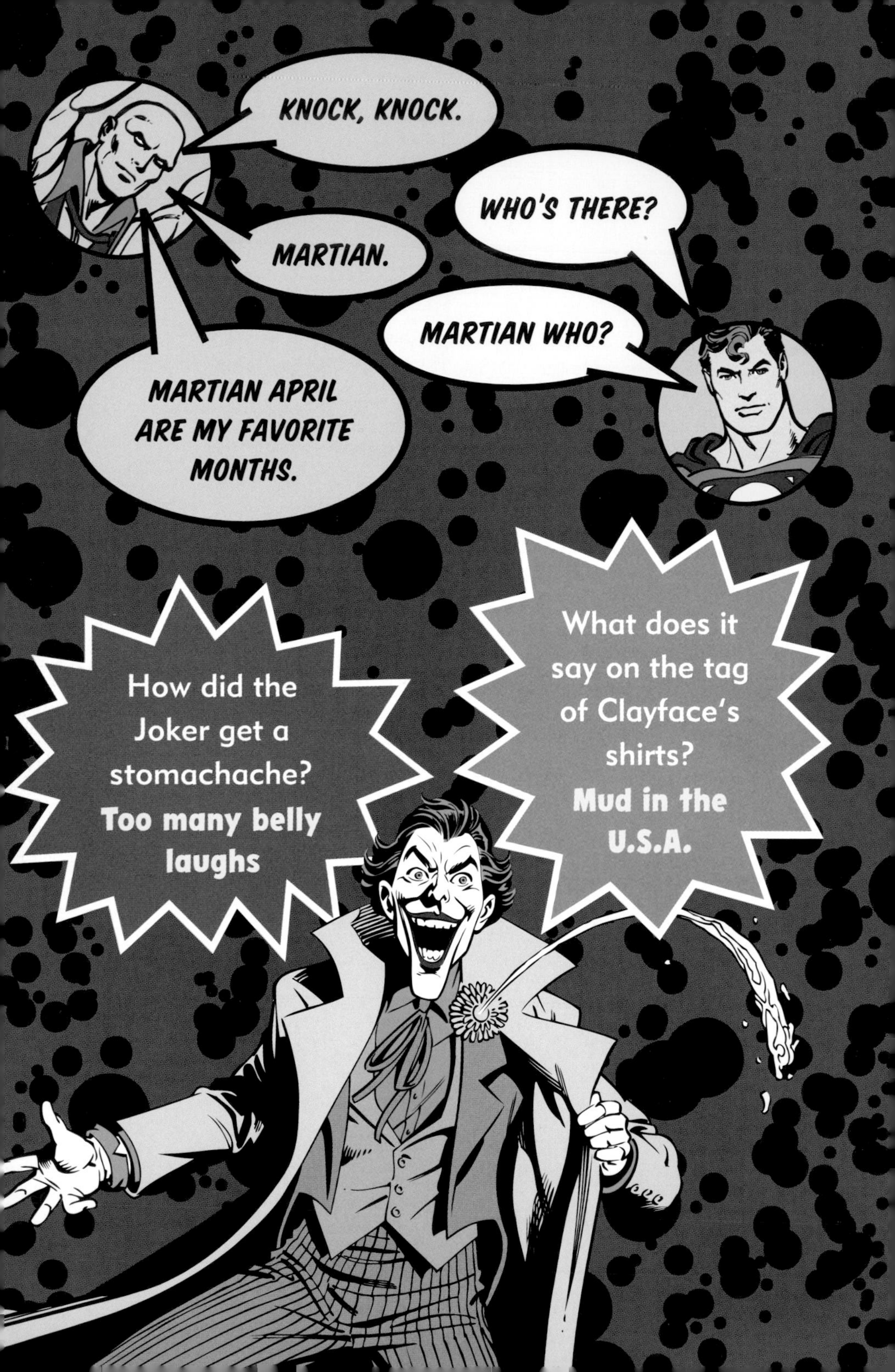

KNOCK, KNOCK.
WHO'S THERE?
MARTIAN.
MARTIAN WHO?
MARTIAN APRIL ARE MY FAVORITE MONTHS.
How did the Joker get a stomachache?
Too many belly laughs
What does it say on the tag of Clayface's shirts?
Mud in the U.S.A.

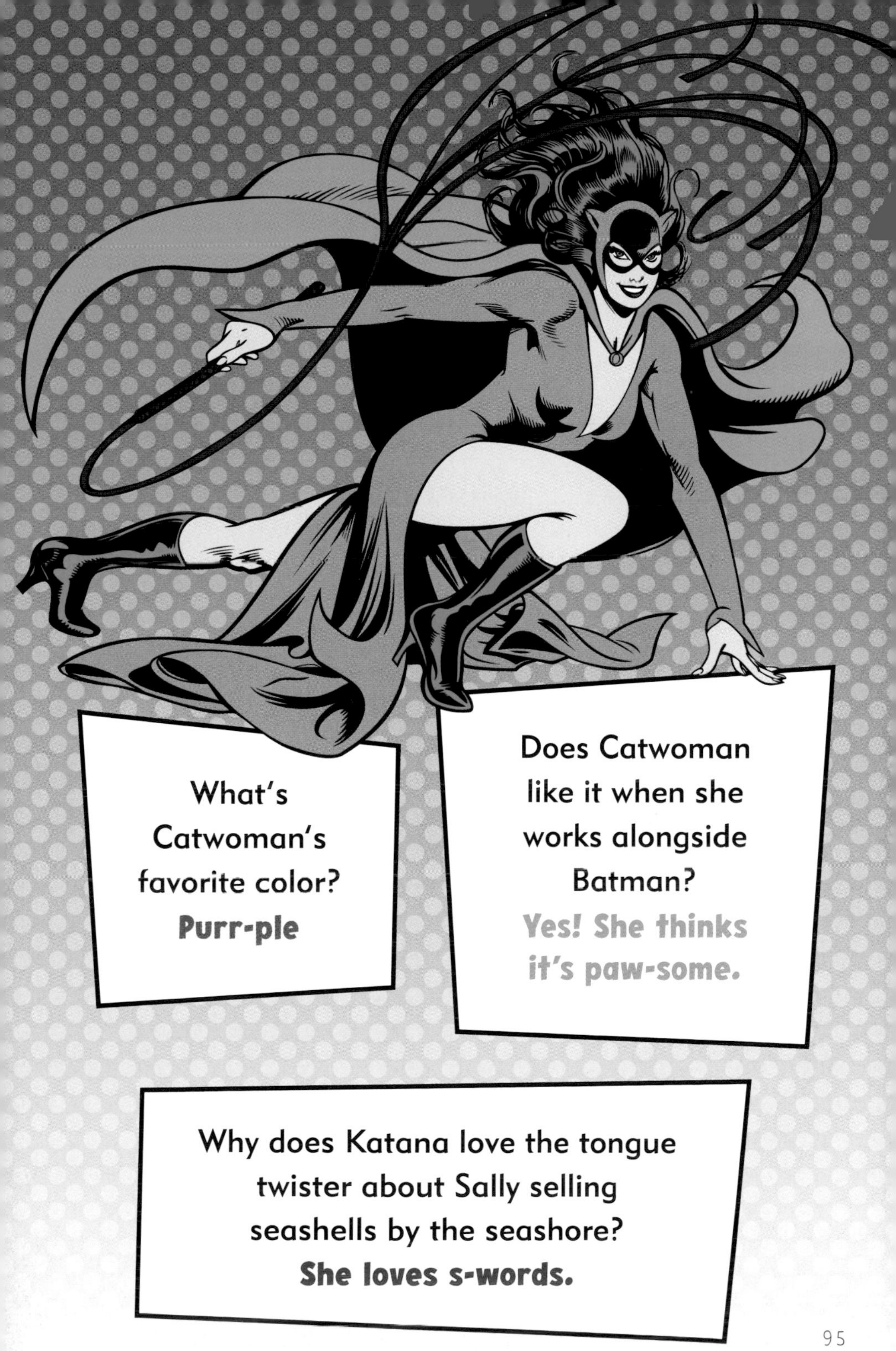

What's
Catwoman's
favorite color?
Purr-ple

Does Catwoman
like it when she
works alongside
Batman?
**Yes! She thinks
it's paw-some.**

Why does Katana love the tongue
twister about Sally selling
seashells by the seashore?
She loves s-words.

What is Bumblebee's favorite condiment?

Honey mustard

SUPERMAN HAS THE MOST SENSITIVE EARS. HE'S A SUPER HEAR-O.

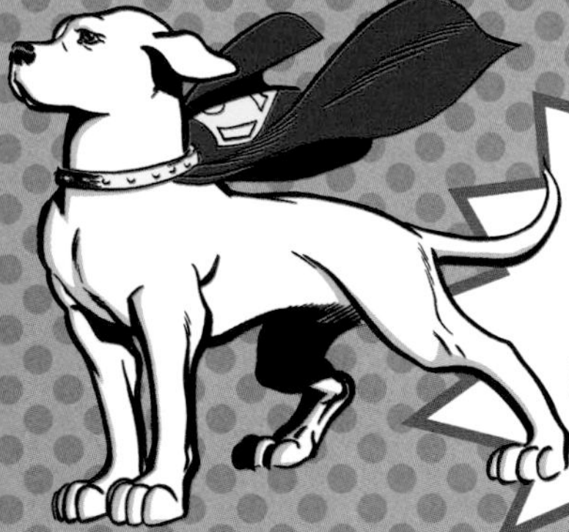

Why are criminals afraid of Krypto?

He can be pretty ruff.

I THOUGHT I WAS AFRAID OF DOGS UNTIL I DOGSAT FOR SUPERMAN. WHO KNEW KRYPTO-NIGHT COULD BE SO MUCH FUN?

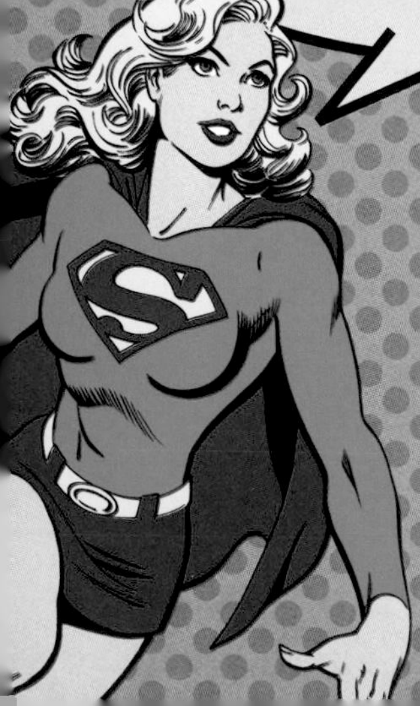

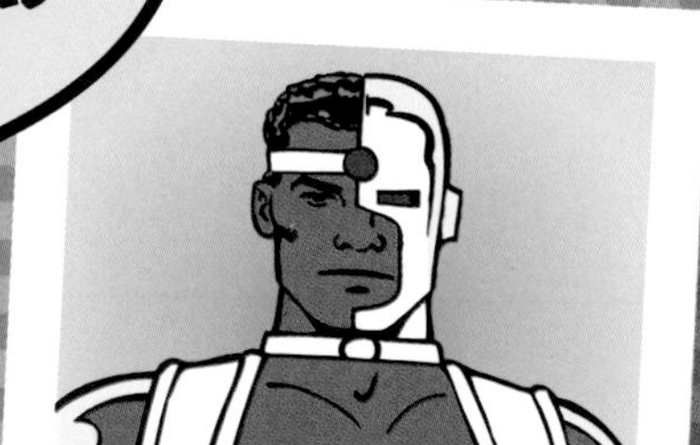

PICTURES OF CYBORG NEVER TURN OUT RIGHT. HE ALWAYS HAS RED EYE.

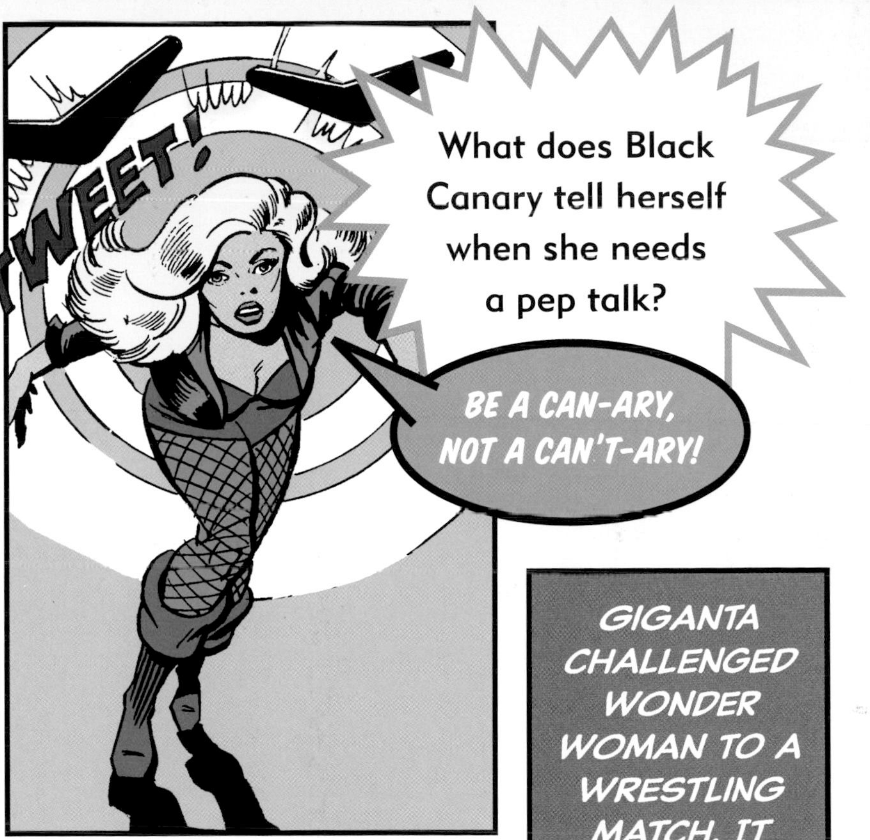
TWEET!
What does Black Canary tell herself when she needs a pep talk?
BE A CAN-ARY, NOT A CAN'T-ARY!

GIGANTA CHALLENGED WONDER WOMAN TO A WRESTLING MATCH. IT WAS A HUGE MISTAKE.

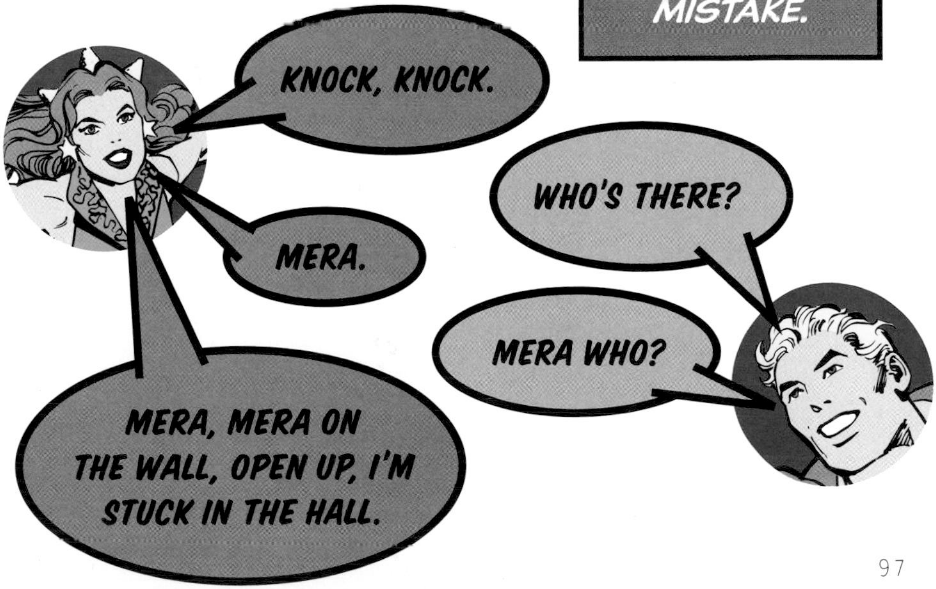
KNOCK, KNOCK.
WHO'S THERE?
MERA.
MERA WHO?
MERA, MERA ON THE WALL, OPEN UP, I'M STUCK IN THE HALL.

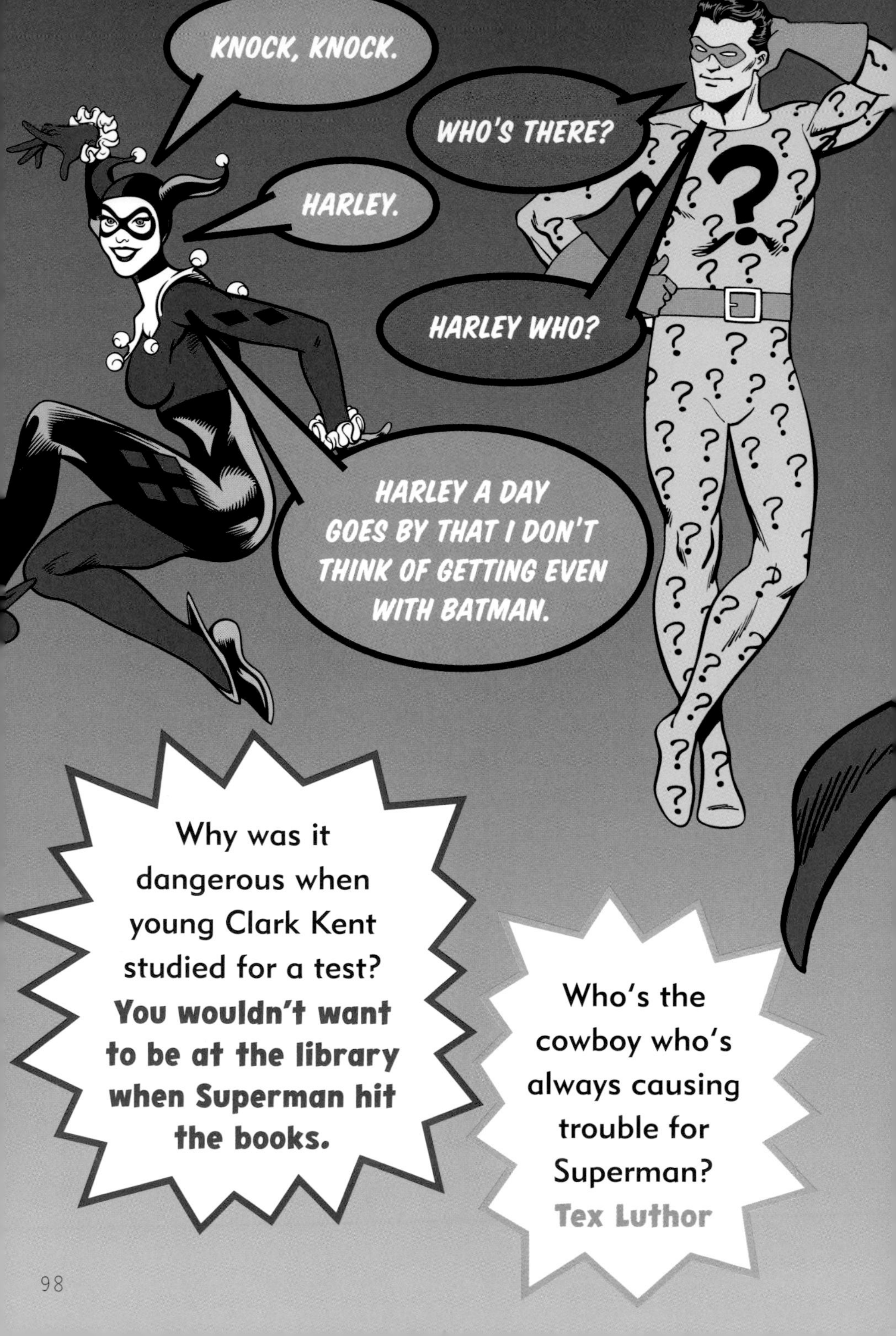
KNOCK, KNOCK.
WHO'S THERE?
HARLEY.
HARLEY WHO?
HARLEY A DAY GOES BY THAT I DON'T THINK OF GETTING EVEN WITH BATMAN.

Why was it dangerous when young Clark Kent studied for a test?
You wouldn't want to be at the library when Superman hit the books.

Who's the cowboy who's always causing trouble for Superman?
Tex Luthor

Why did Giganta cross the road?
She didn't mean to. Her feet are just really big.

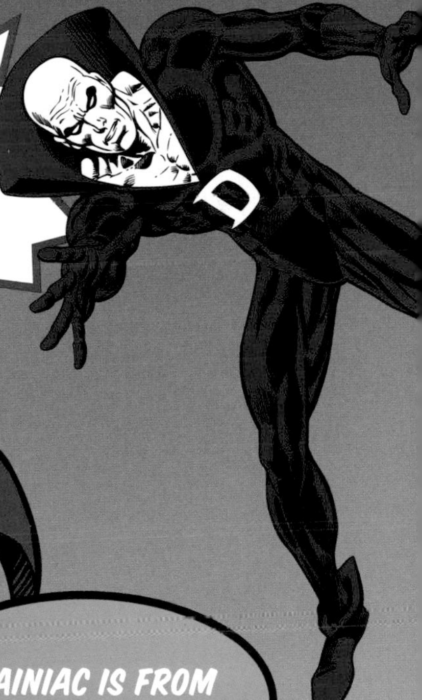

Where will Superman meet up with Deadman?
In the crypt tonight

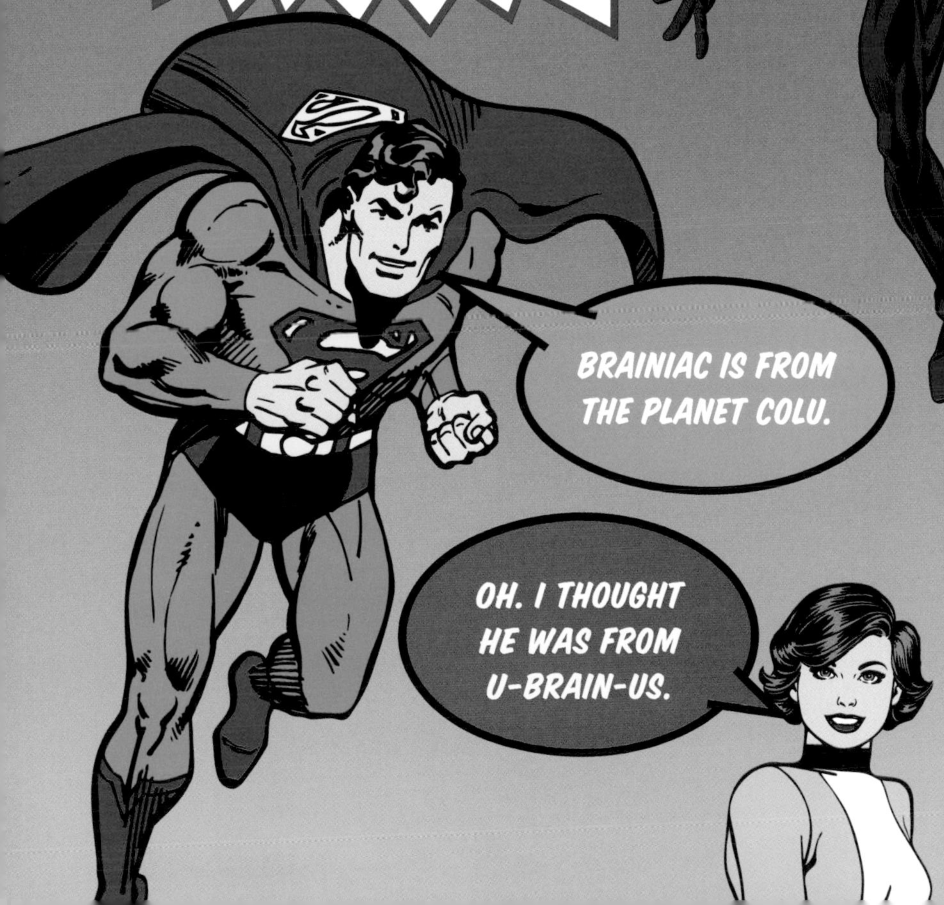

BRAINIAC IS FROM THE PLANET COLU.
OH. I THOUGHT HE WAS FROM U-BRAIN-US.

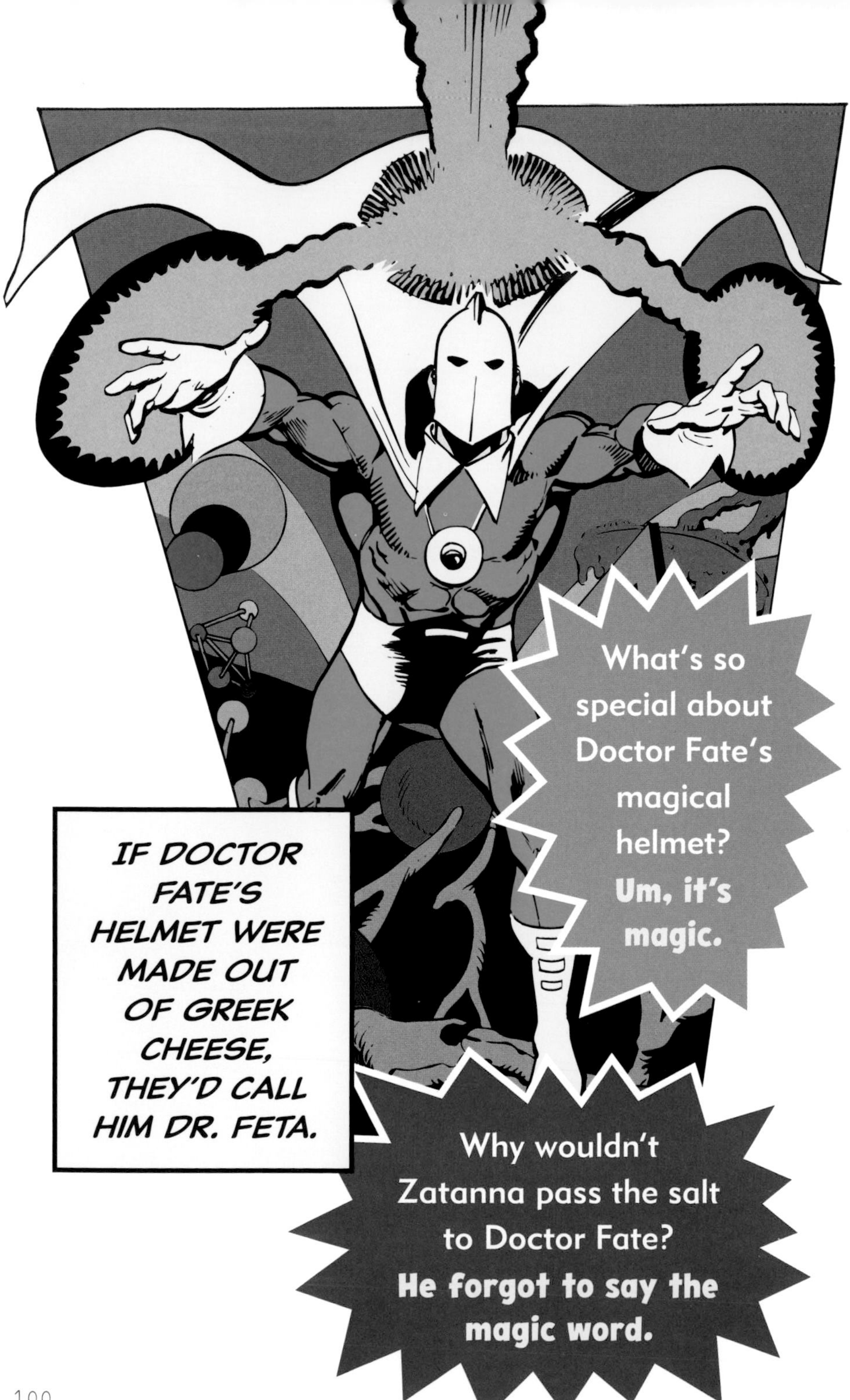
What's so special about Doctor Fate's magical helmet?
Um, it's magic.
IF DOCTOR FATE'S HELMET WERE MADE OUT OF GREEK CHEESE, THEY'D CALL HIM DR. FETA.
Why wouldn't Zatanna pass the salt to Doctor Fate?
He forgot to say the magic word.

In which state does Comet the Super-Horse live?
Mane

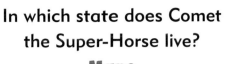

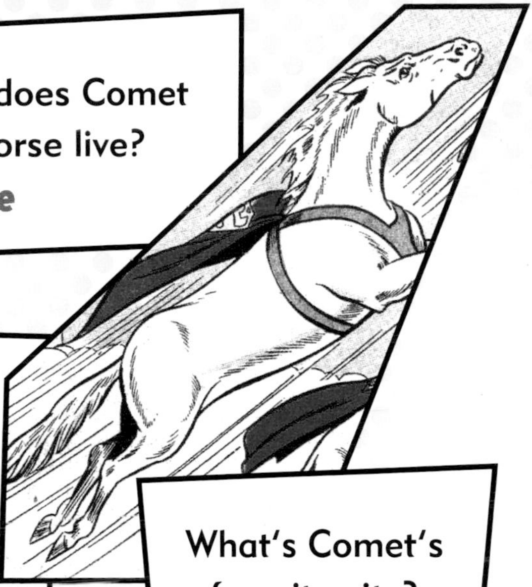

What happened when Comet went for a run in the rain?
He caught a colt.

What's Comet's favorite city?
Filly

What did Mother Goose say when she heard about Superman?
**"Sing a song of Krypton,
A rocket passing Rao.
A little baby Kal-El is tucked inside its prow.
When the ship is opened,
On Earth, he'll be a hero,
Fighting for his weighty wish—
the crime rate down to zero."**

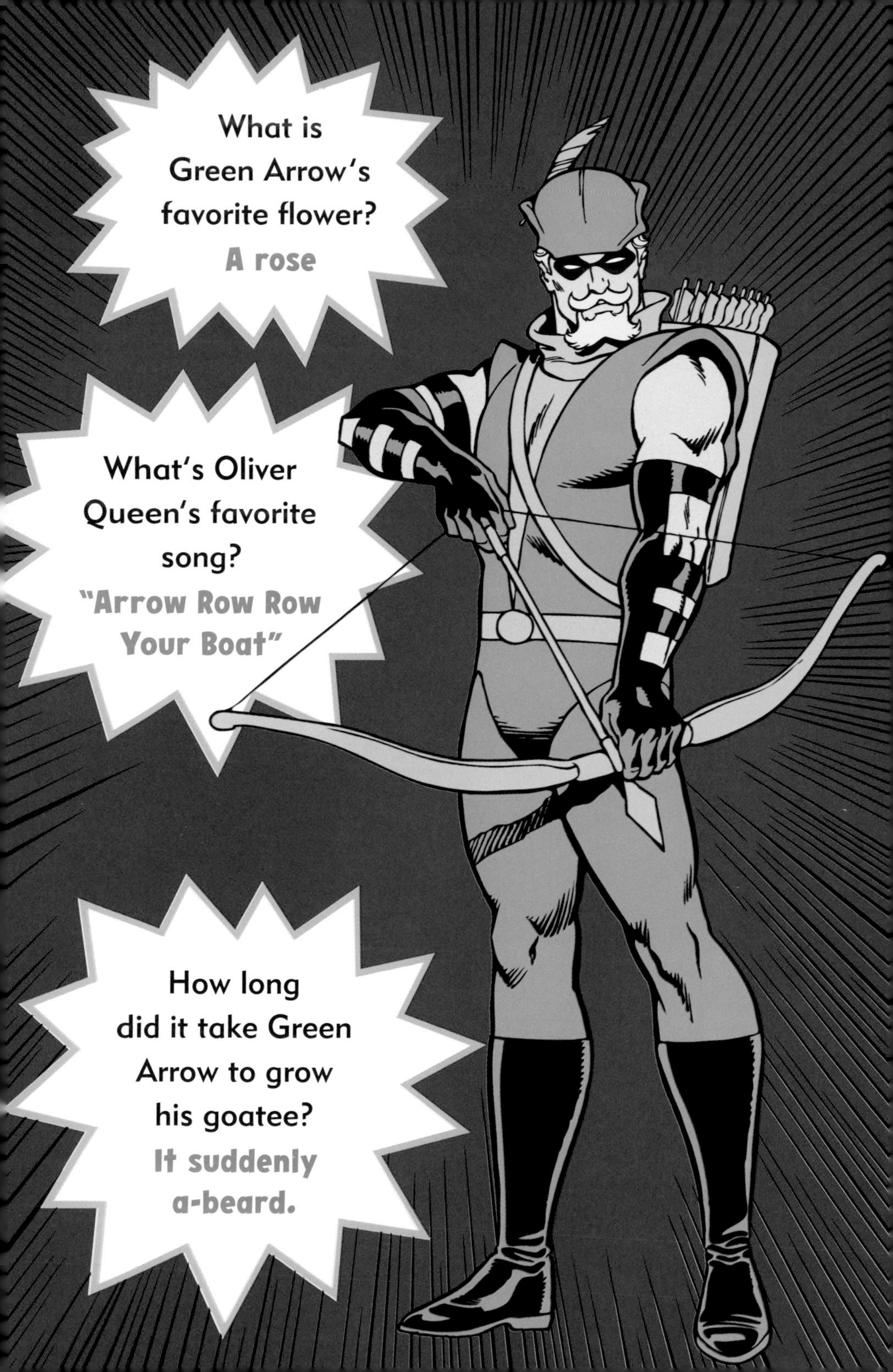
What is Green Arrow's favorite flower? A rose
What's Oliver Queen's favorite song? "Arrow Row Row Your Boat"
How long did it take Green Arrow to grow his goatee? It suddenly a-beard.

What does Green Arrow say when bad guys make fun of his beard?

"Goatees someone else."

What happens when bad guys run from Green Arrow?

They get the point.

What do bad guys do when they see Green Arrow coming?

Quiver

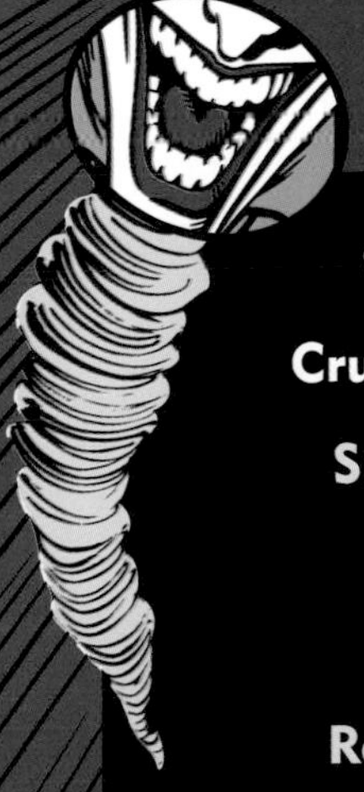

SAY THIS FIVE TIMES FAST!

Crummy criminals clobber crabby creeps.

Sly super heroes save scared civilians.

Martian Manhunter munches mini mint marshmallows.

Raven wrangles wretched wrongdoers.

Loathsome Lex Luthor loudly lectures Lois Lane.

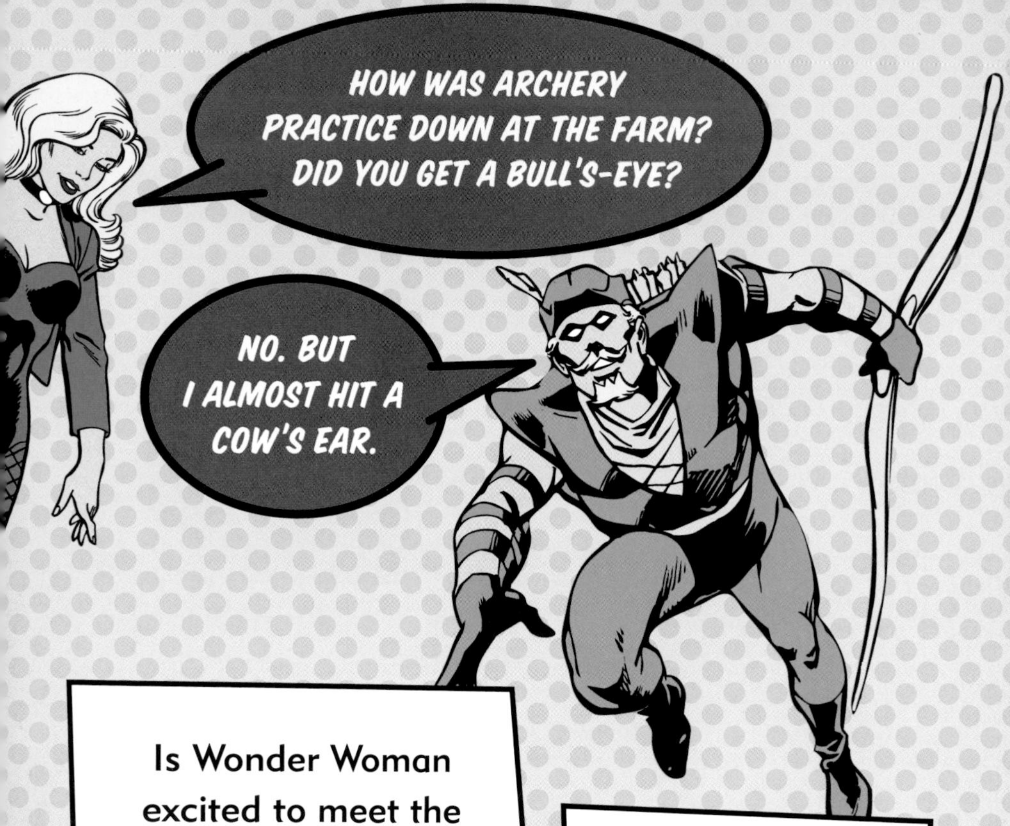
HOW WAS ARCHERY PRACTICE DOWN AT THE FARM? DID YOU GET A BULL'S-EYE?
NO. BUT I ALMOST HIT A COW'S EAR.

Is Wonder Woman excited to meet the president?

Are you kidding? She's Diana meet him.

Did The Flash really read the dinosaur a bedtime story?

Just one veloci-chapter

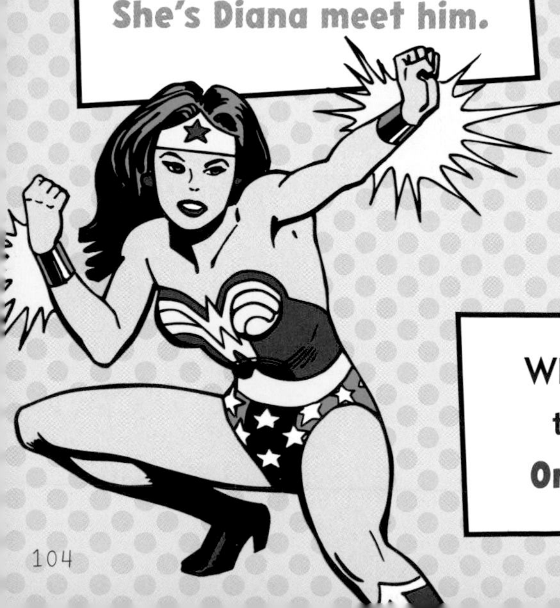

What's the best way to reach Krypto?

On his mobile bone

What happens when Plastic Man gets really excited?

He becomes Enthusiastic Man.

What happens when Plastic Man swings over the pommel horse?

He becomes Gymnastic Man.

What happens when Plastic Man makes a snide remark?

He becomes Sarcastic Man.

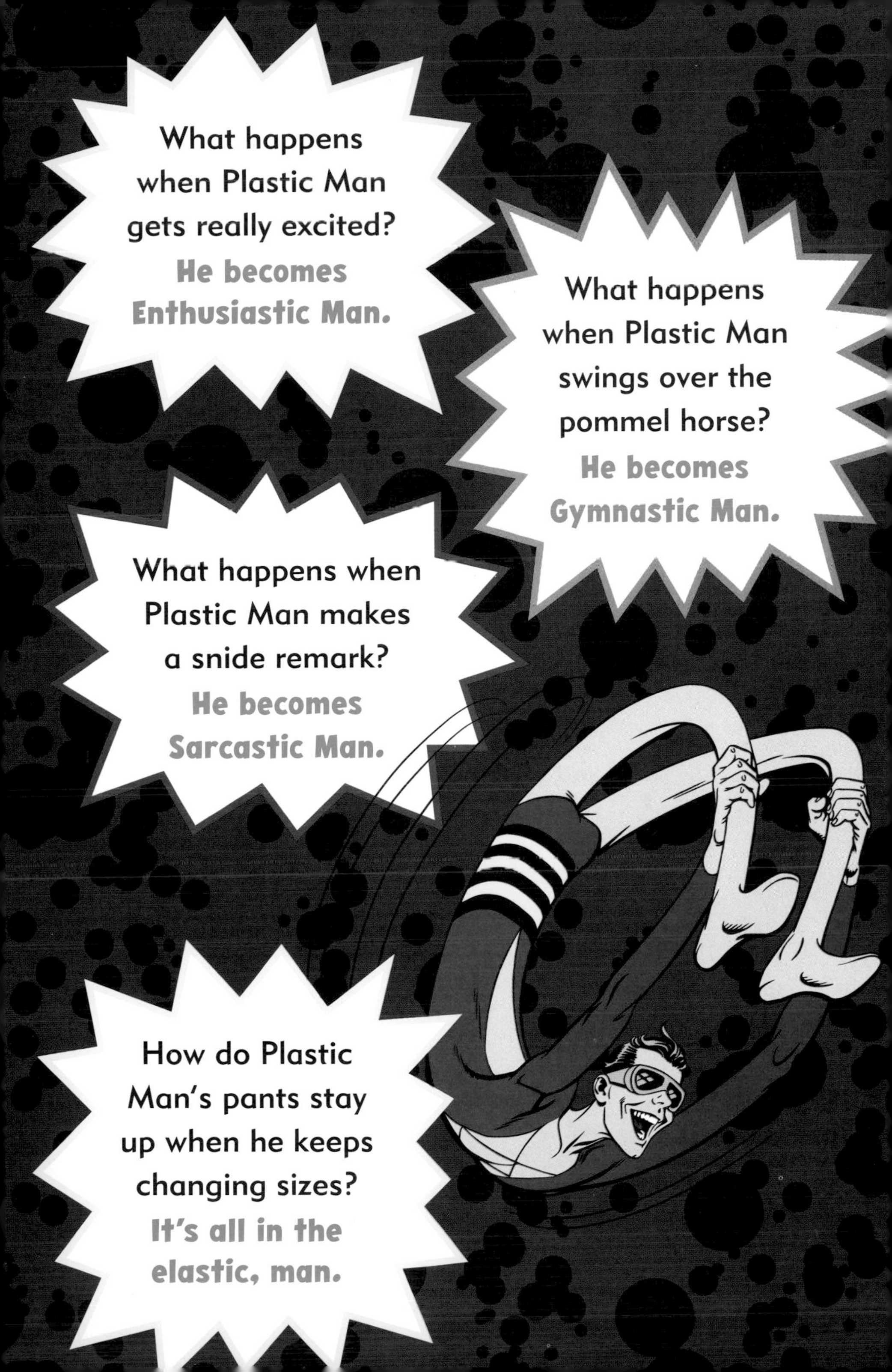

How do Plastic Man's pants stay up when he keeps changing sizes?

It's all in the elastic, man.

DO YOU HAVE A LOT OF LIBRARIES ON MARS?

YES, WE'RE A WELL-READ PLANET.

Which super heroes like to get up the earliest in the morning?  
Pup and Atom!

Harley Quinn tries to hit heroes with her mallet. What does the Joker use?
A comedy club

What happened when Clayface fell asleep in the sun?
He became a hardened criminal.

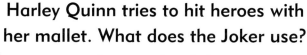

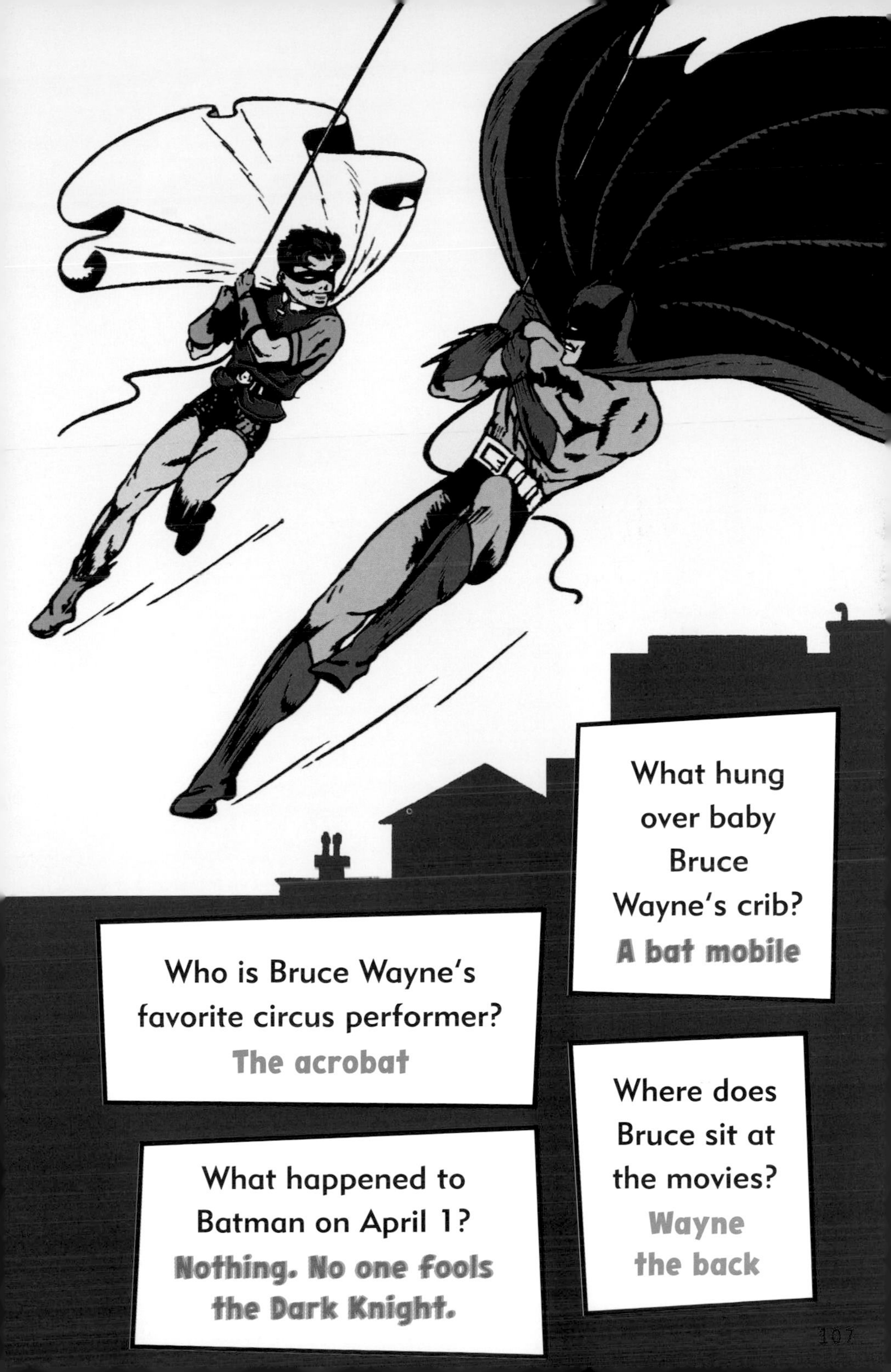

What hung over baby Bruce Wayne's crib?

A bat mobile

Who is Bruce Wayne's favorite circus performer?

The acrobat

Where does Bruce sit at the movies?

Wayne the back

What happened to Batman on April 1?

Nothing. No one fools the Dark Knight.

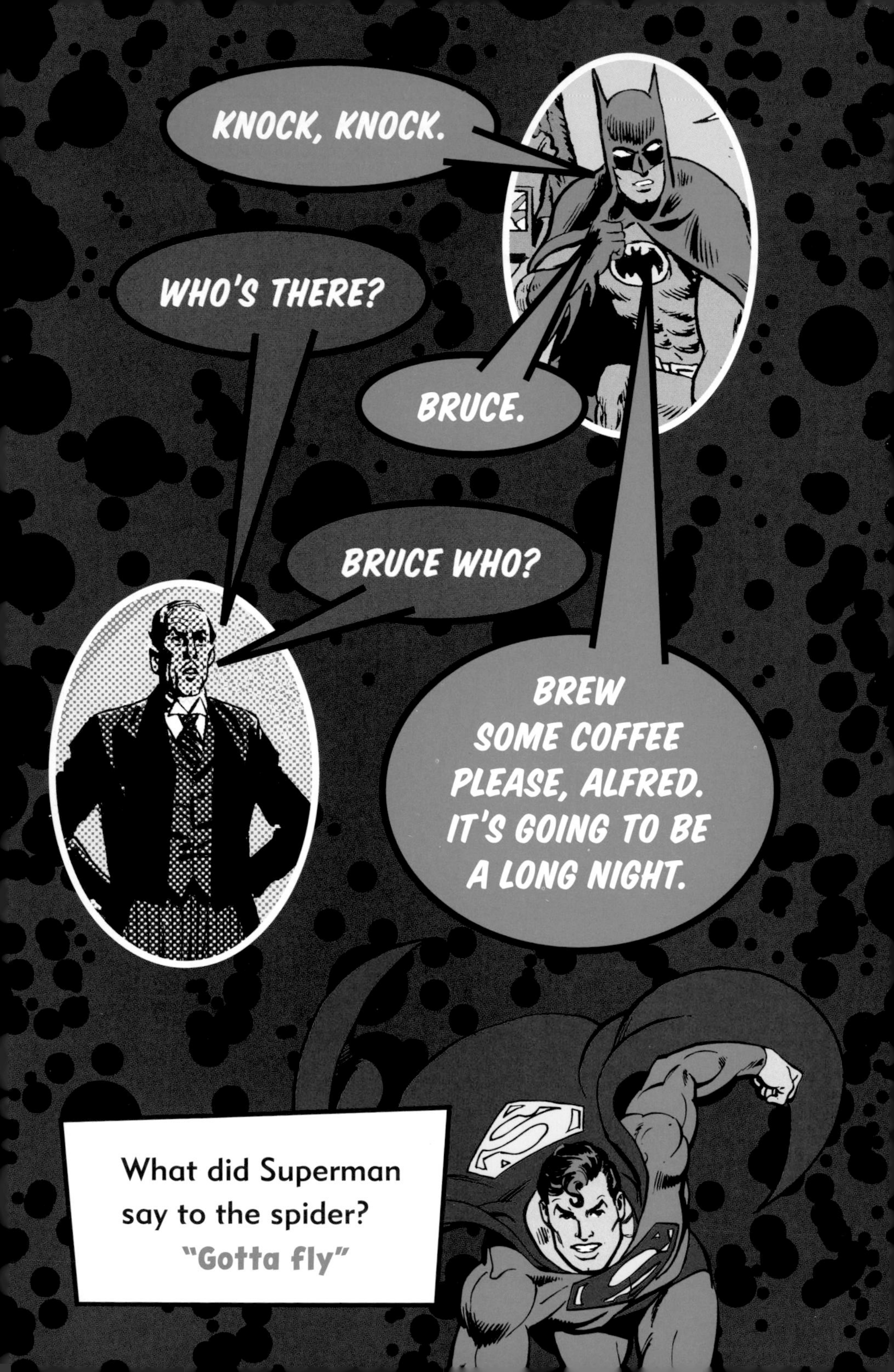
KNOCK, KNOCK.
WHO'S THERE?
BRUCE.
BRUCE WHO?
BREW SOME COFFEE PLEASE, ALFRED. IT'S GOING TO BE A LONG NIGHT.

What did Superman say to the spider?
"Gotta fly"

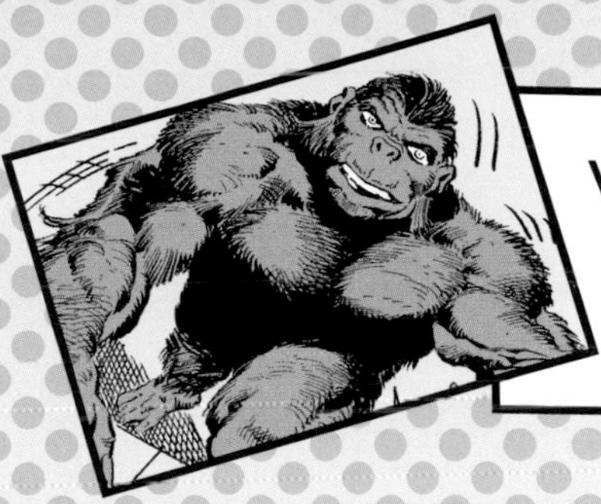

What is Gorilla Grodd's favorite month?

Ape-ril

Why did the Atom have to borrow money to pay for lunch?

He was a little short.

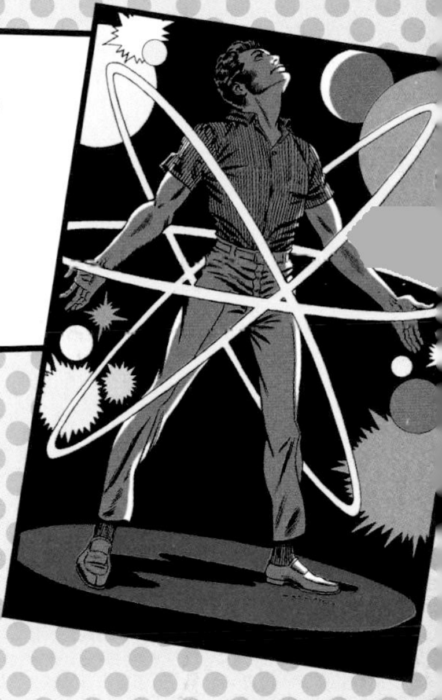

Does Mr. Freeze like cake?

Only the frosting

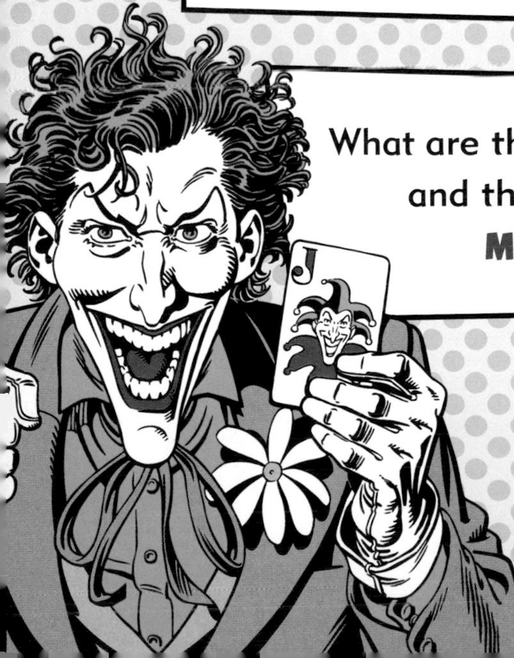

What are the rules when Hawkman and the Joker play cards?

Maces are wild.

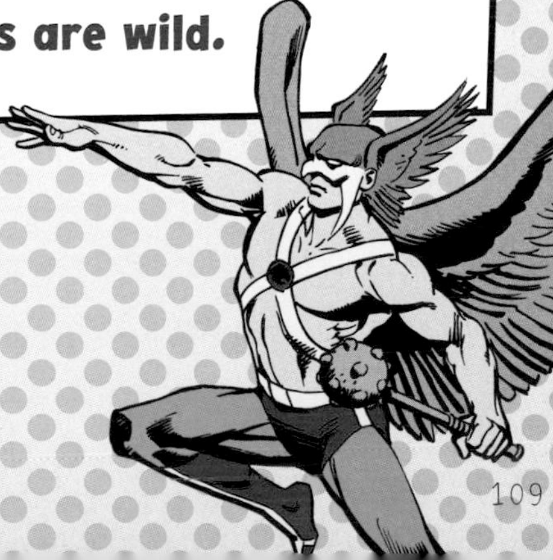

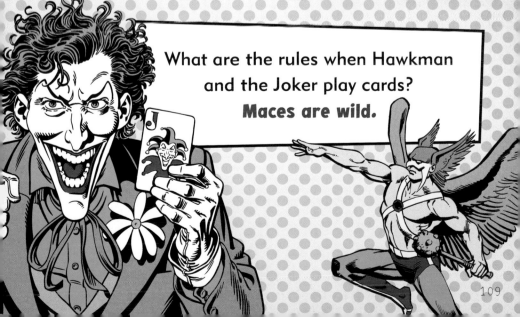

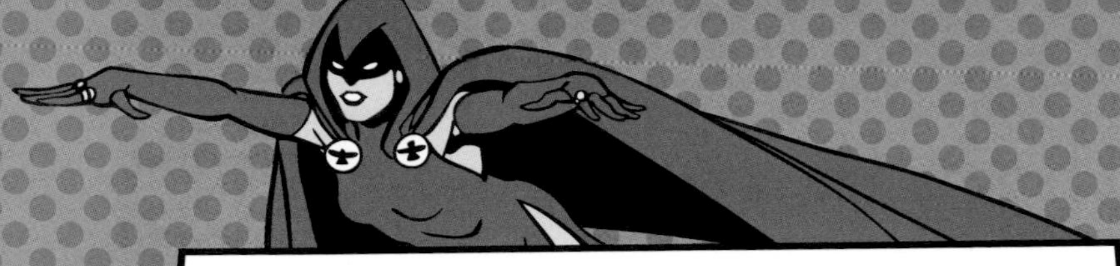

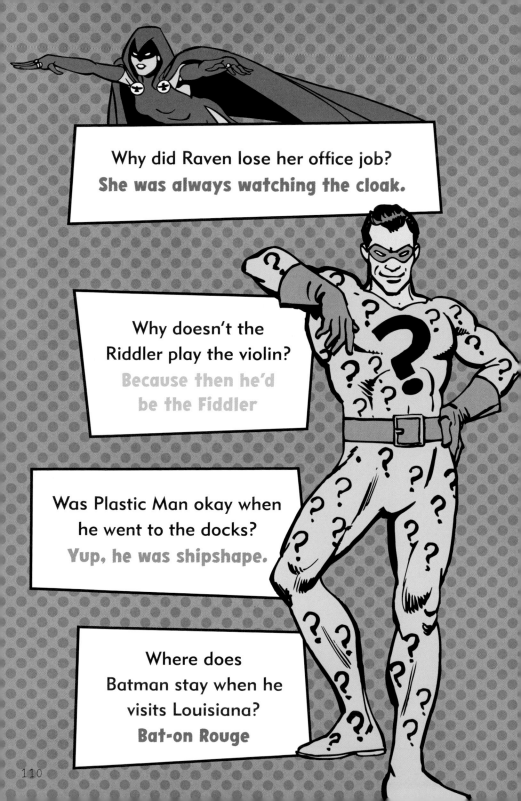

Why did Raven lose her office job?

She was always watching the cloak.

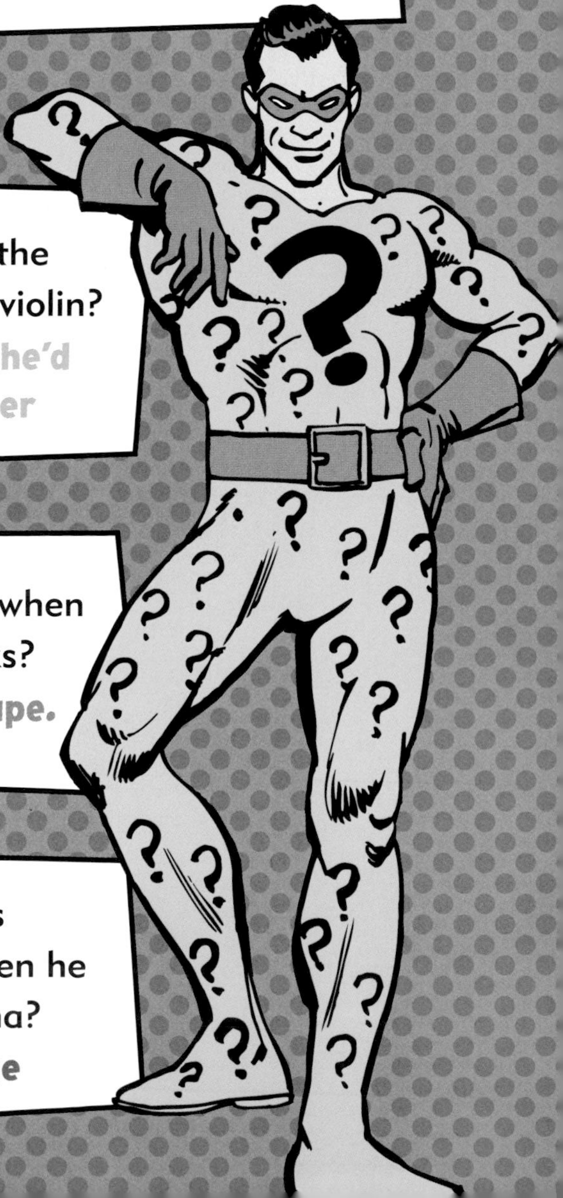

Why doesn't the Riddler play the violin?

Because then he'd be the Fiddler

Was Plastic Man okay when he went to the docks?

Yup, he was shipshape.

Where does Batman stay when he visits Louisiana?

Bat-on Rouge

What time is it when Wonder Woman makes a bad guy tell the truth?
Lass-o'clock

How can you tell Wonder Woman tracked mud into the house?
You see Diana prints.

Where does Two-Face stay when he visits Arizona?
Two-son

Where does Two-Face go when he leaves the country?
Two-nisia

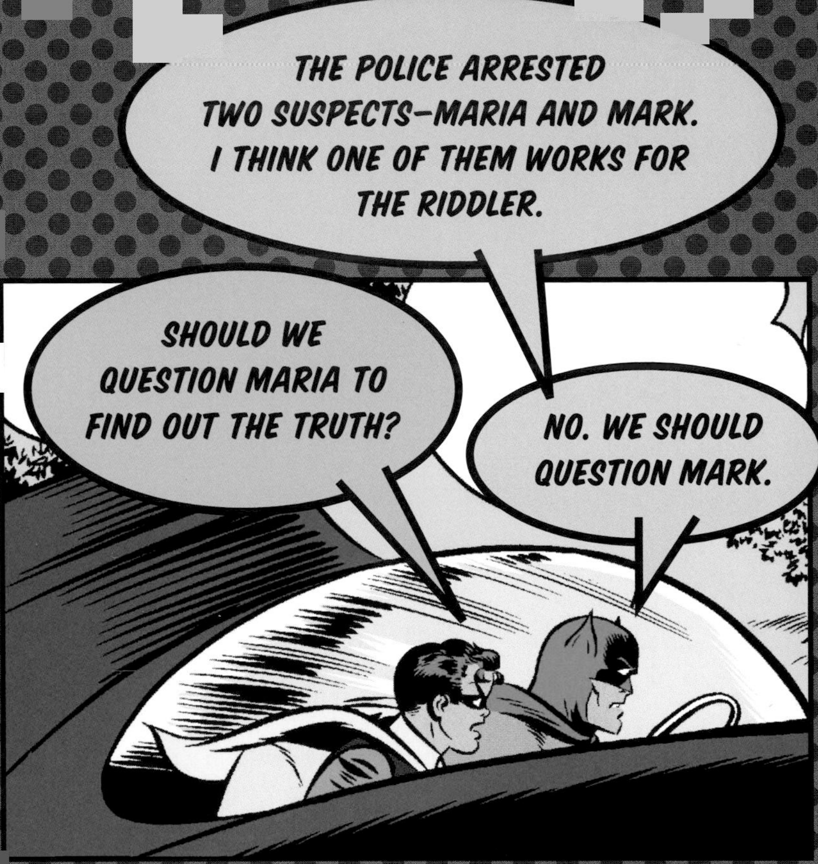
THE POLICE ARRESTED TWO SUSPECTS—MARIA AND MARK. I THINK ONE OF THEM WORKS FOR THE RIDDLER.
SHOULD WE QUESTION MARIA TO FIND OUT THE TRUTH?
NO. WE SHOULD QUESTION MARK.

What's the difference between Hawkman and a parakeet?

Would you let Hawkman perch on your head?

Why do villains hate to battle Blue Beetle?

He really bugs them.

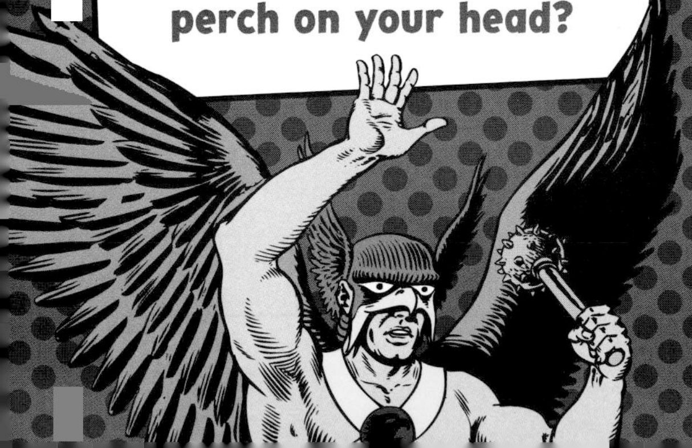

What's
Black Canary's
favorite game?
Hide-and-go-shriek

What's Black
Canary's
favorite color?
Yeller

What's Black
Canary's
favorite dessert?
I scream.

What's Black Canary's
favorite holiday?
Holler-een

113

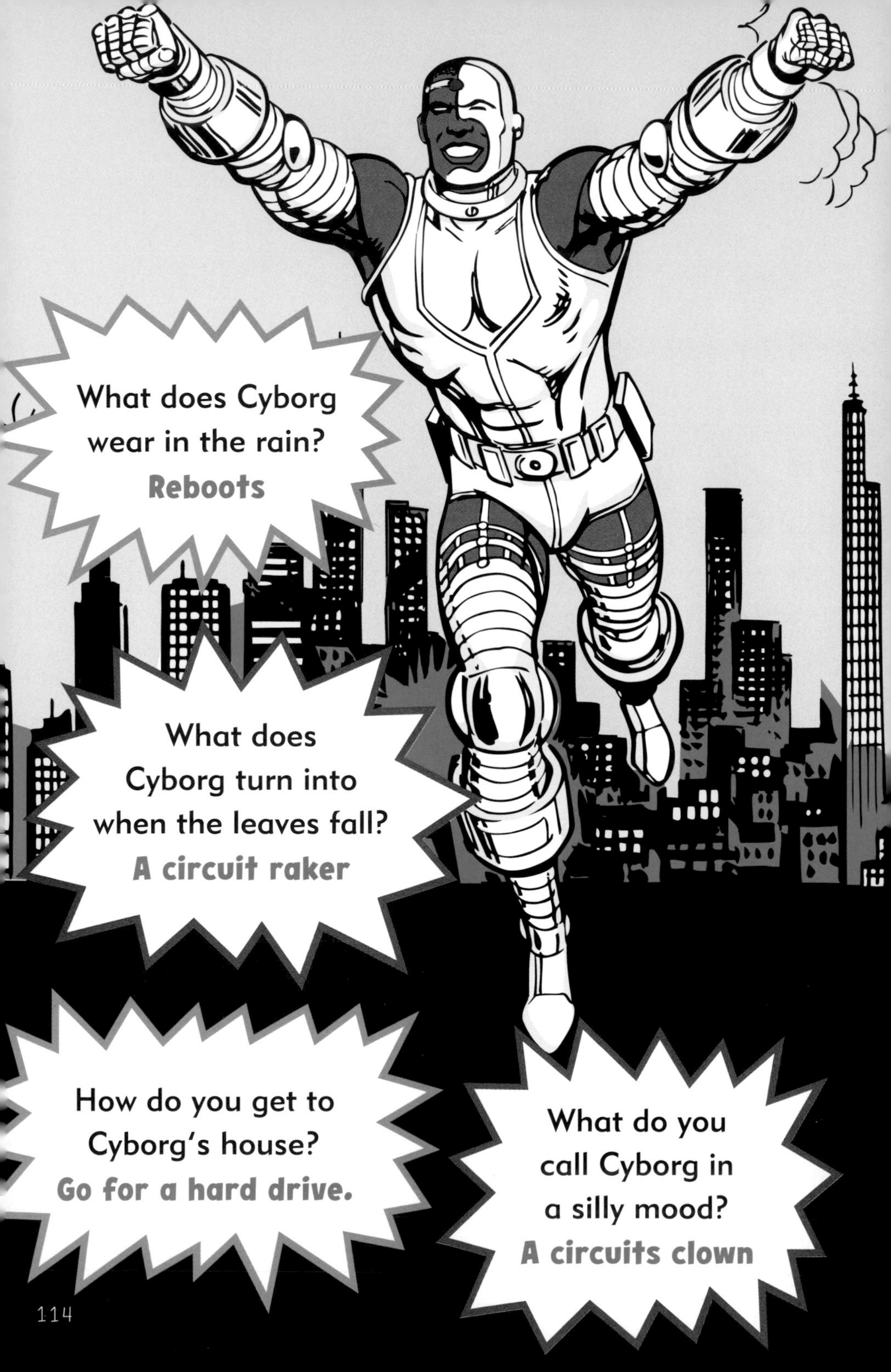
What does Cyborg wear in the rain?
Reboots
What does Cyborg turn into when the leaves fall?
A circuit raker
How do you get to Cyborg's house?
Go for a hard drive.
What do you call Cyborg in a silly mood?
A circuits clown

What do you call Doctor Fate when his muscles ache?
A sore-cerer

What do you call Doctor Fate when he puts up a fence to keep out villains?
Doctor Gate

What do you call Doctor Fate when he scores five goals in one hockey game?
Doctor Skate

Why doesn't Doctor Fate's helmet have a nose?
No nose is good nose.

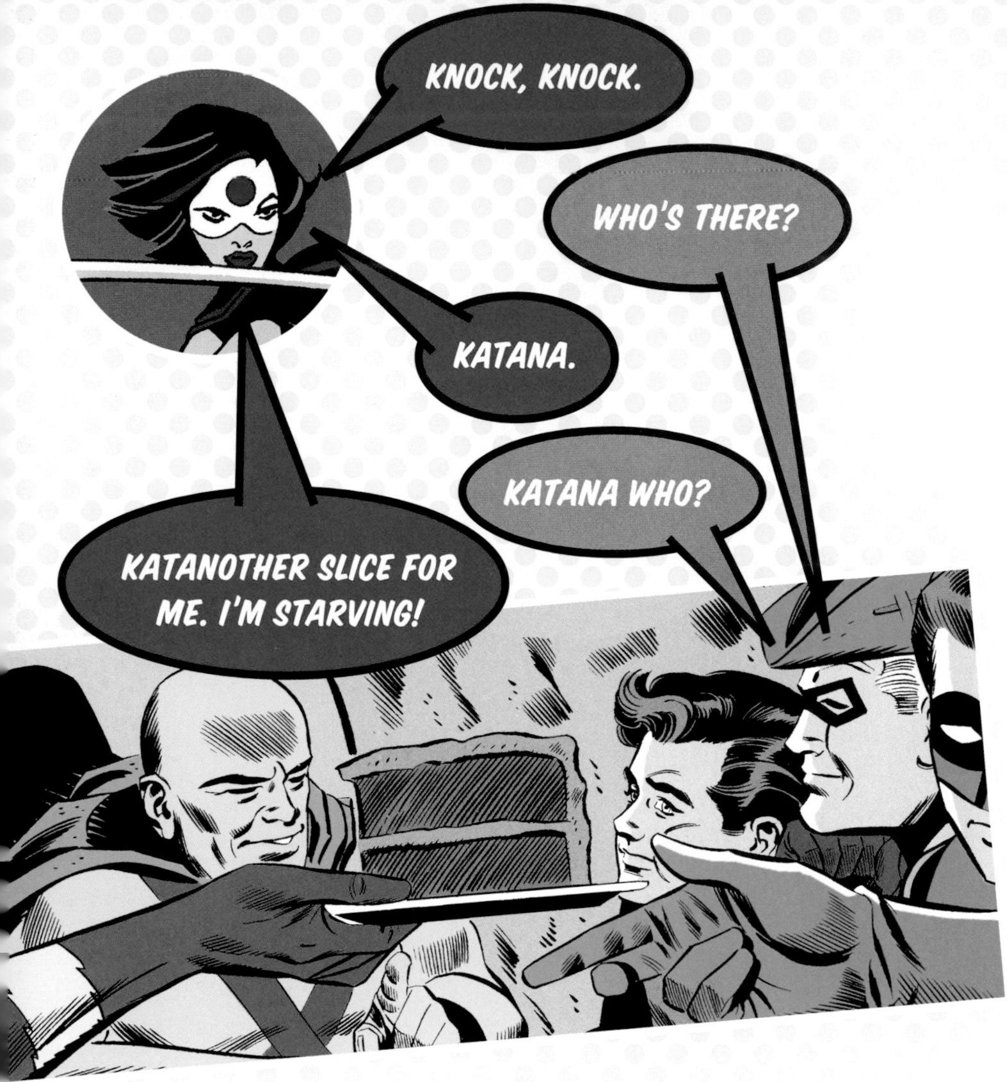

KNOCK, KNOCK.
WHO'S THERE?
KATANA.
KATANA WHO?
KATANOTHER SLICE FOR ME. I'M STARVING!

What do Bumblebee's foes think of her?

They think she's interest-sting.

What happens when Krypto leaves the car by the curb?

He gets a barking ticket.

Why did Grodd marry his wife? **She was the gorilla his dreams.**

What's Grodd's favorite Christmas song? **"Jungle Bells"**

What do the gorillas in Gorilla City drink at breakfast? **Ape-fruit juice**

Grodd is a giant ape. So where does he sit at the movies? **Anywhere he wants**

Can Robin walk
a tightrope?
**Well, it's easier than
walking on a loose one.**

Do Aquaman and Mera have a butler?
No, but sometimes they hire a mer-maid.

What will Mr.
Freeze bring
to the potluck
dinner?
**He'll probably
make some
chilly.**

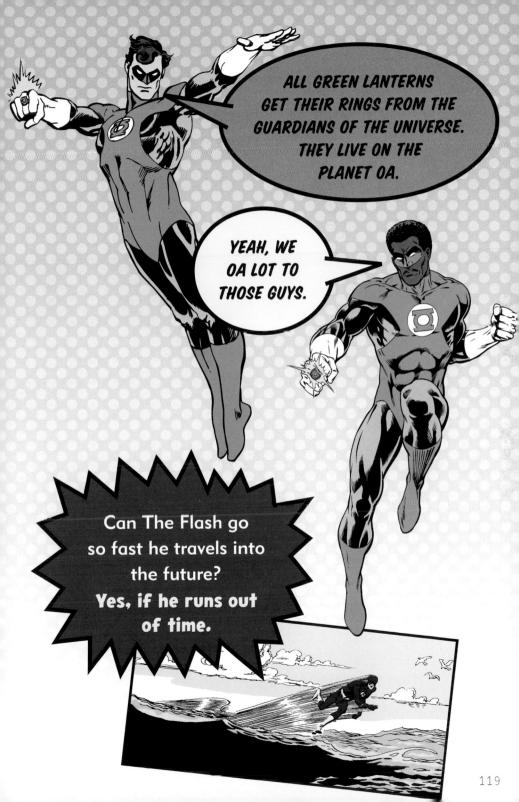

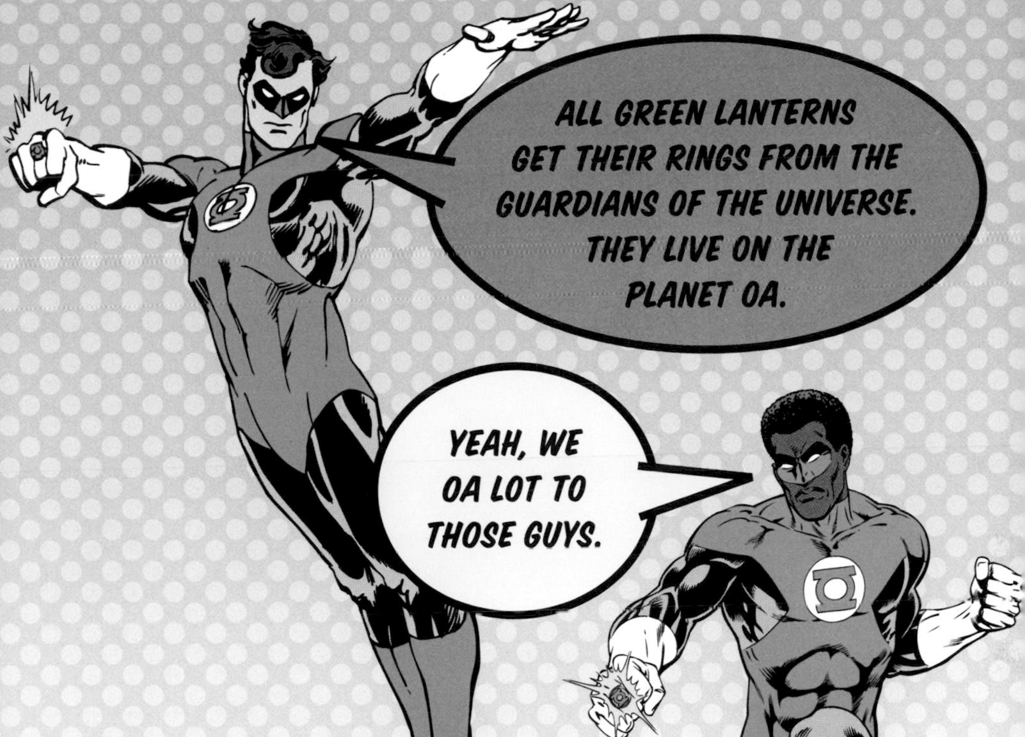
ALL GREEN LANTERNS GET THEIR RINGS FROM THE GUARDIANS OF THE UNIVERSE. THEY LIVE ON THE PLANET OA.
YEAH, WE OA LOT TO THOSE GUYS.

Can The Flash go so fast he travels into the future?

Yes, if he runs out of time.

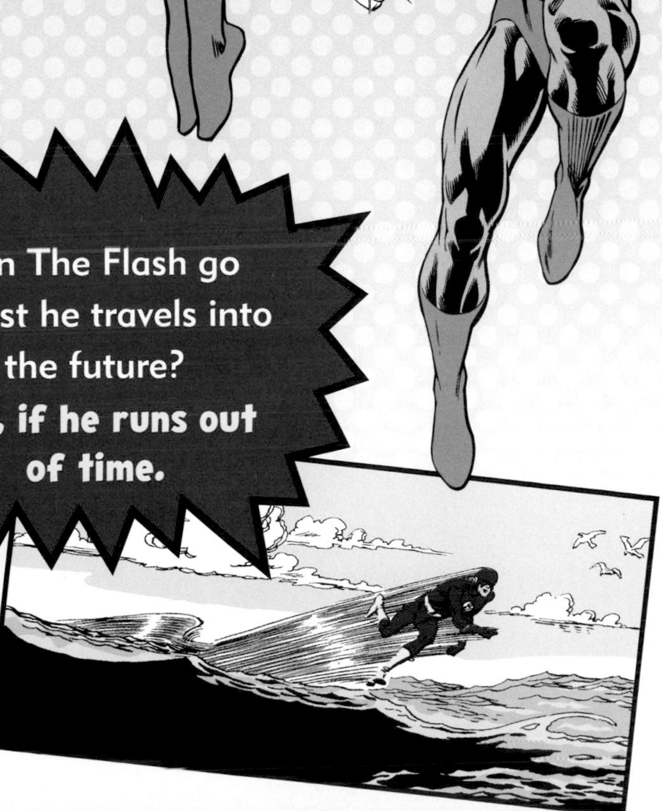

Why did Bumblebee get sent to detention?
Bad beehive-ior

What's Bumblebee's favorite game?
Hive-and-go-seek

Why was Bumblebee asked to leave the ball game?
She tried to sting the national anthem.

What did the villain say when he captured Bumblebee?
"Victory is in the eye of the bee-holder."

What do Bumblebee's friends say when she tells too many jokes?
"Quit pollen my leg."

What would you find outside Bumblebee's front door?

A wel-comb mat

What happened when Bumblebee wore a disguise to catch a criminal in the act?

It was a sting operation.

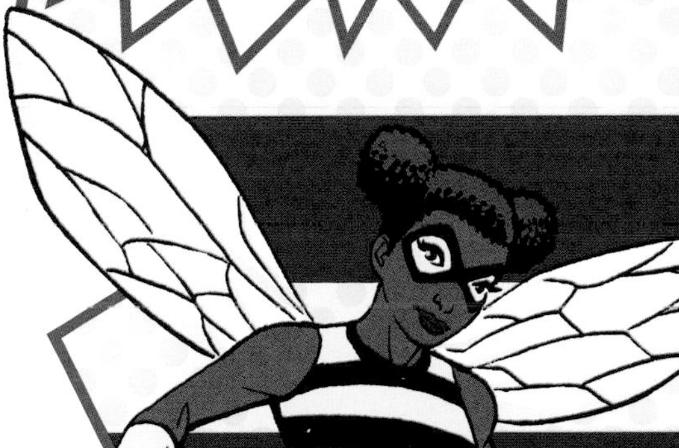

What do you get when you cross Bumblebee with a ghost?

Bumble-BOO!

What's Bumblebee's favorite hairstyle?

The honeycomb-over

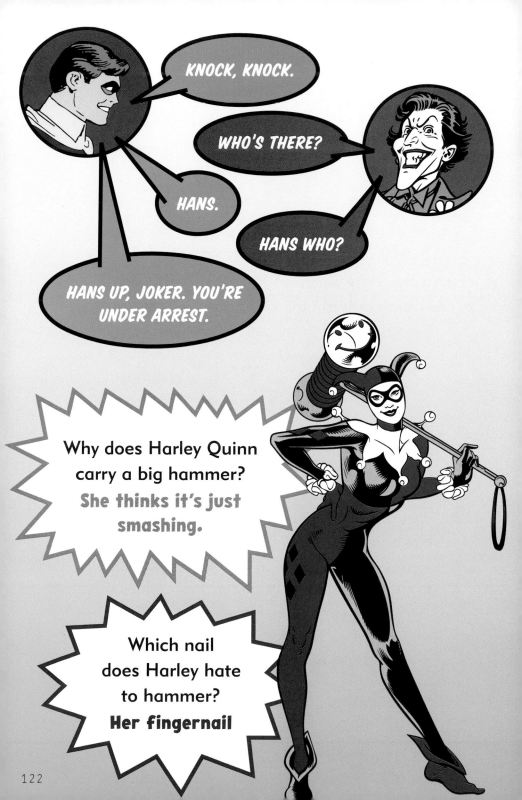

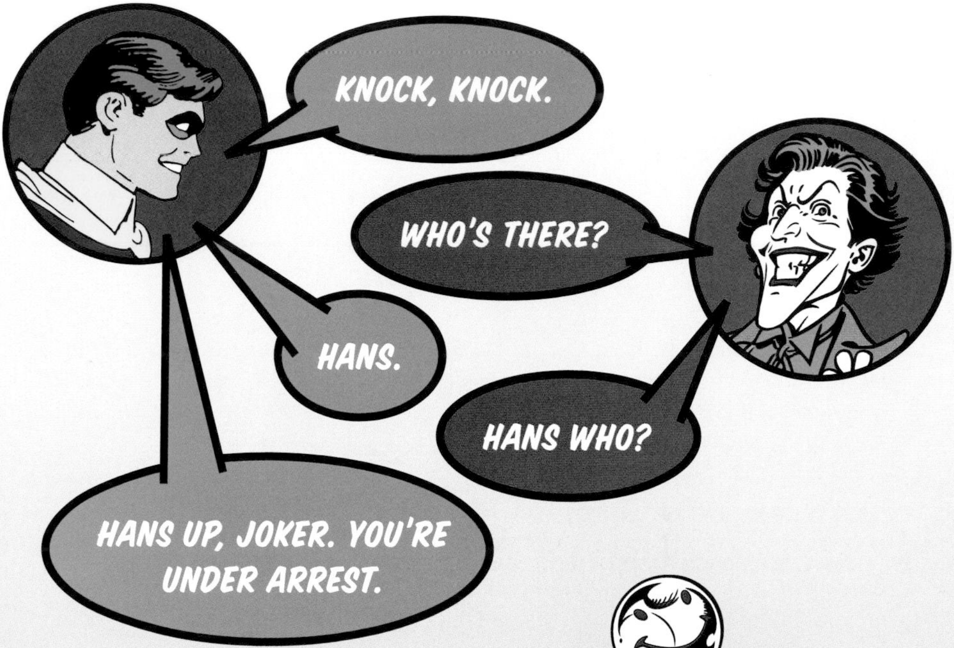
KNOCK, KNOCK.
WHO'S THERE?
HANS.
HANS WHO?
HANS UP, JOKER. YOU'RE UNDER ARREST.

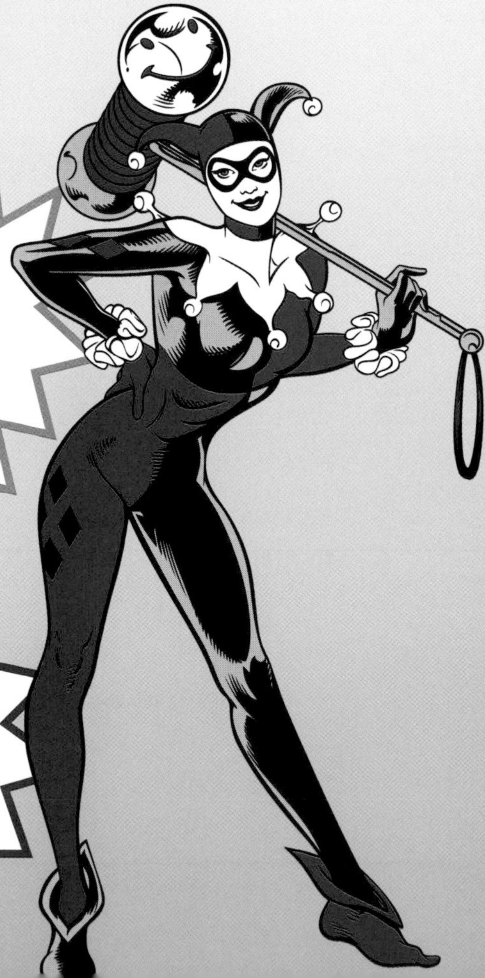

Why does Harley Quinn carry a big hammer?
She thinks it's just smashing.

Which nail does Harley hate to hammer?
Her fingernail

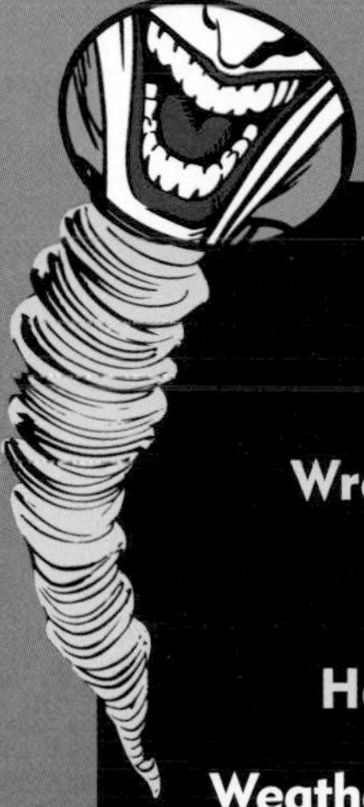

SAY THIS FIVE TIMES FAST!

The Flash's fists fly fast in fights.

Wrecking red wagons really rattles Robin.

Batman bests boastful bullies.

Harley hurls a hefty hammer harmfully.

Weather Wizard whips up whirling winds, worrying Wonder Woman. Whether Weather Wizard wafts wildly or wends westward, Wonder Woman will win.

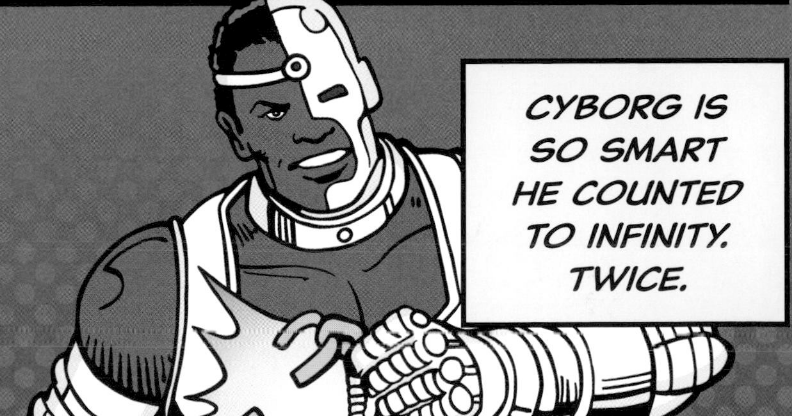

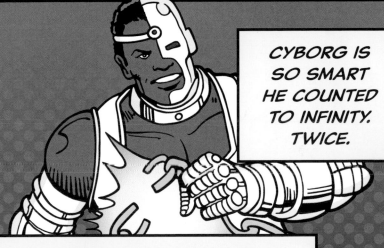

CYBORG IS SO SMART HE COUNTED TO INFINITY. TWICE.

LAST WEEKEND WAS SO SLOW THAT CYBORG WENT FROM SIGH-BORG TO CY-BORED.

Why did Raven eat so much dinner?

She was Raven-ous.

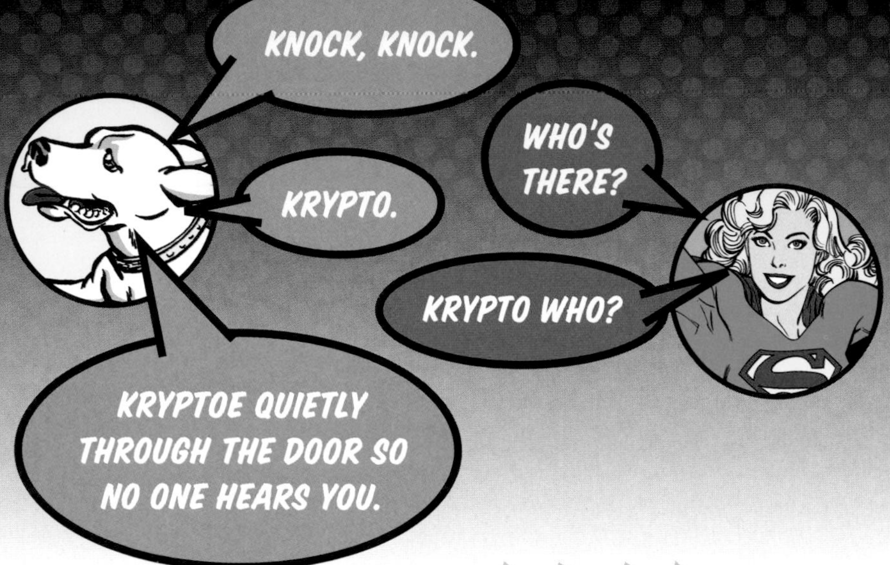
KNOCK, KNOCK.
WHO'S THERE?
KRYPTO.
KRYPTO WHO?
KRYPTOE QUIETLY THROUGH THE DOOR SO NO ONE HEARS YOU.

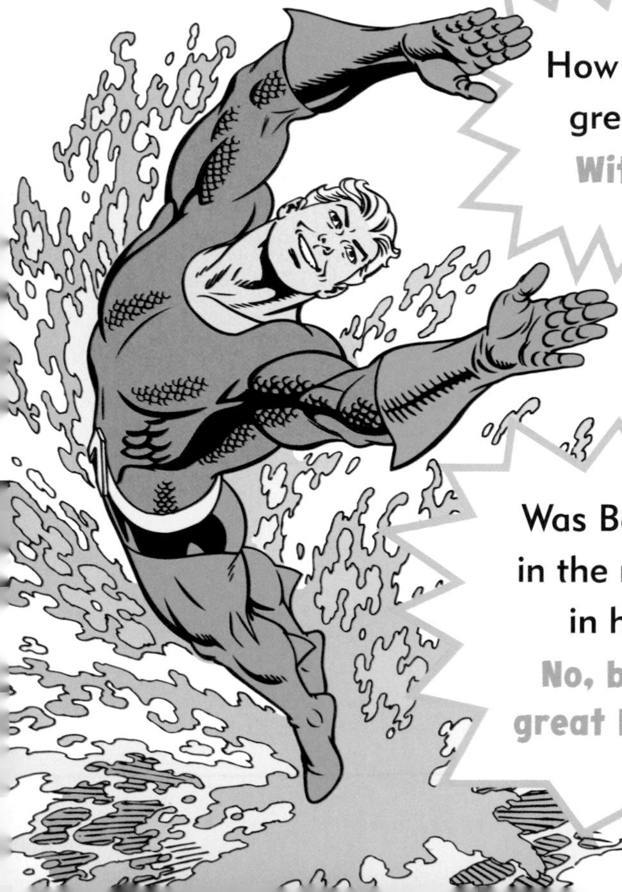

How does Aquaman greet his friends?
With a big wave

Was Barbara Gordon in the marching band in high school?
No, but she was a great bat-on twirler.

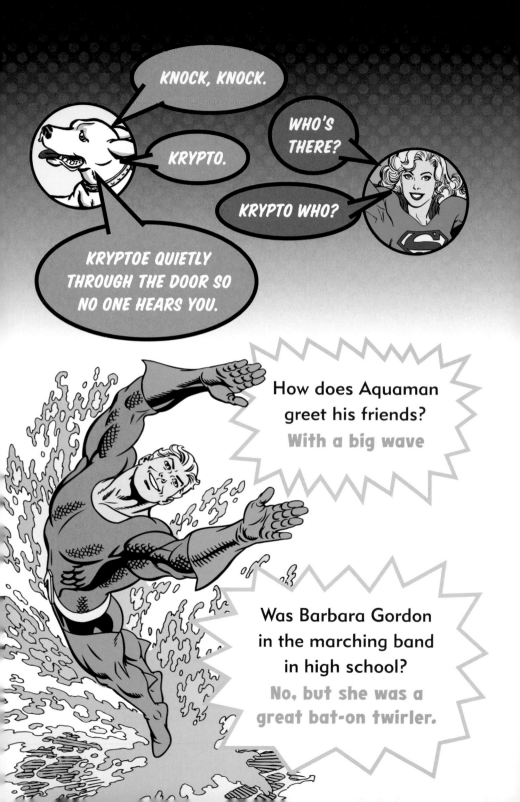

Where does the Atom go to drink a tiny cola?
Mini-soda

What's Red Tornado's favorite state?
Wind-iana

Where did Hawkman and Hawkgirl spend their honeymoon?
In Hawk-waii

What state does Lex Luthor keep his money in?
Dollar-ado

Where did the Joker build his latest hideout?
Lair-izona

Where's Harley Quinn's favorite place to pound things with her hammer?
Ala-BAM-a

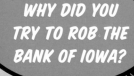

WHY DID YOU TRY TO ROB THE BANK OF IOWA?

IOWA LOT OF MONEY.

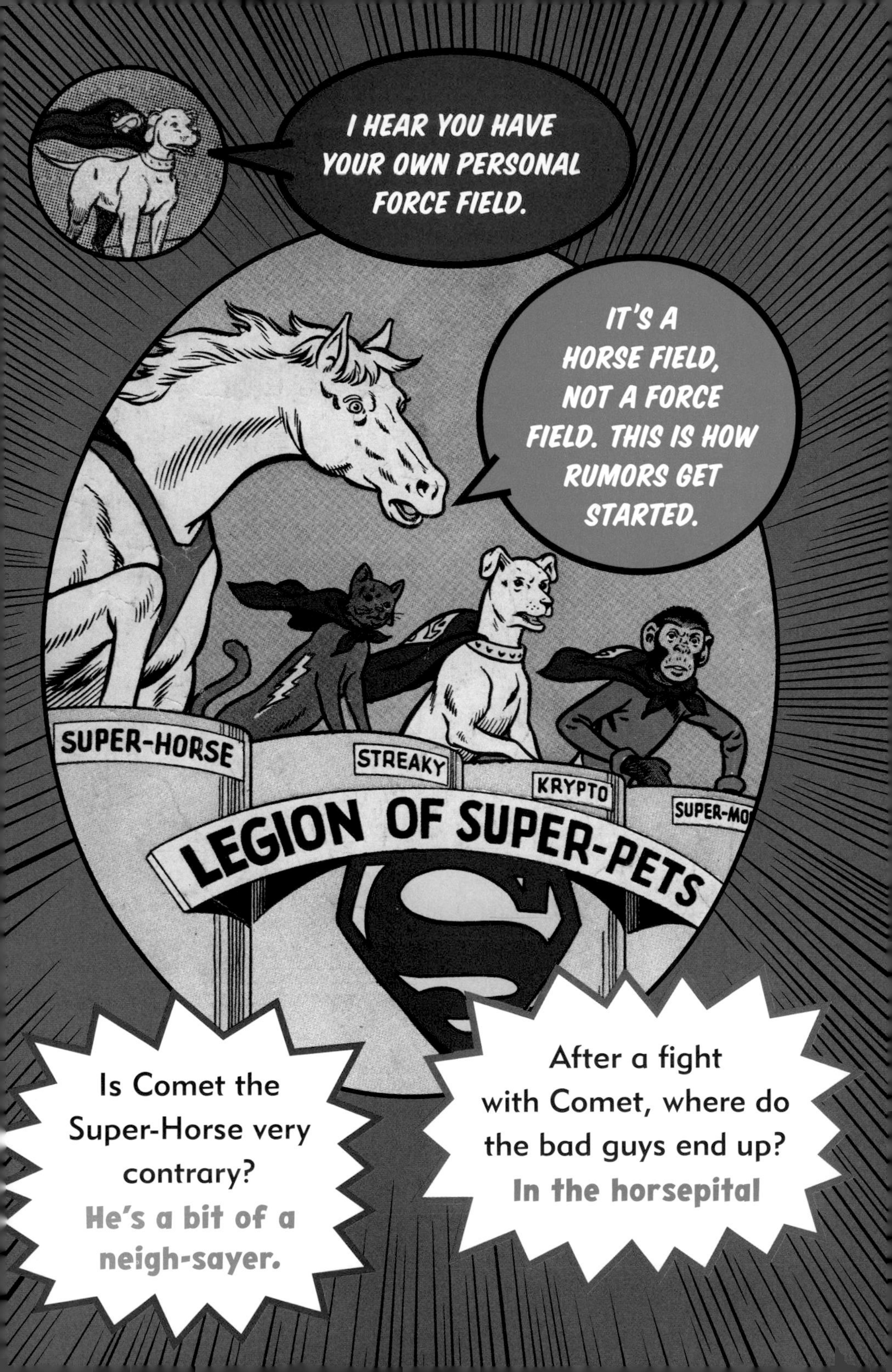
I HEAR YOU HAVE YOUR OWN PERSONAL FORCE FIELD.
IT'S A HORSE FIELD, NOT A FORCE FIELD. THIS IS HOW RUMORS GET STARTED.
SUPER-HORSE
STREAKY
KRYPTO
SUPER-MO
LEGION OF SUPER-PETS
Is Comet the Super-Horse very contrary?
He's a bit of a neigh-sayer.
After a fight with Comet, where do the bad guys end up?
In the horsepital

Why was Comet's voice scratchy when he was younger?

He was a little horse.

How does Comet predict who will win an election?

He reads the gallop polls.

What's Comet the Super-Horse's favorite song?

"The Saddle Hymn of the Republic"

HOW BRAVE IS WONDER WOMAN?

Wonder Woman makes blankets feel secure.

- -

Even her old clothes never get 'fraid.

- -

She always carries a dictionary with her because
she doesn't know the meaning of the word "fear."

- -

Wonder Woman never backs down.
She once beat a statue in a staring contest.

- -

Heights are afraid of her.

- -

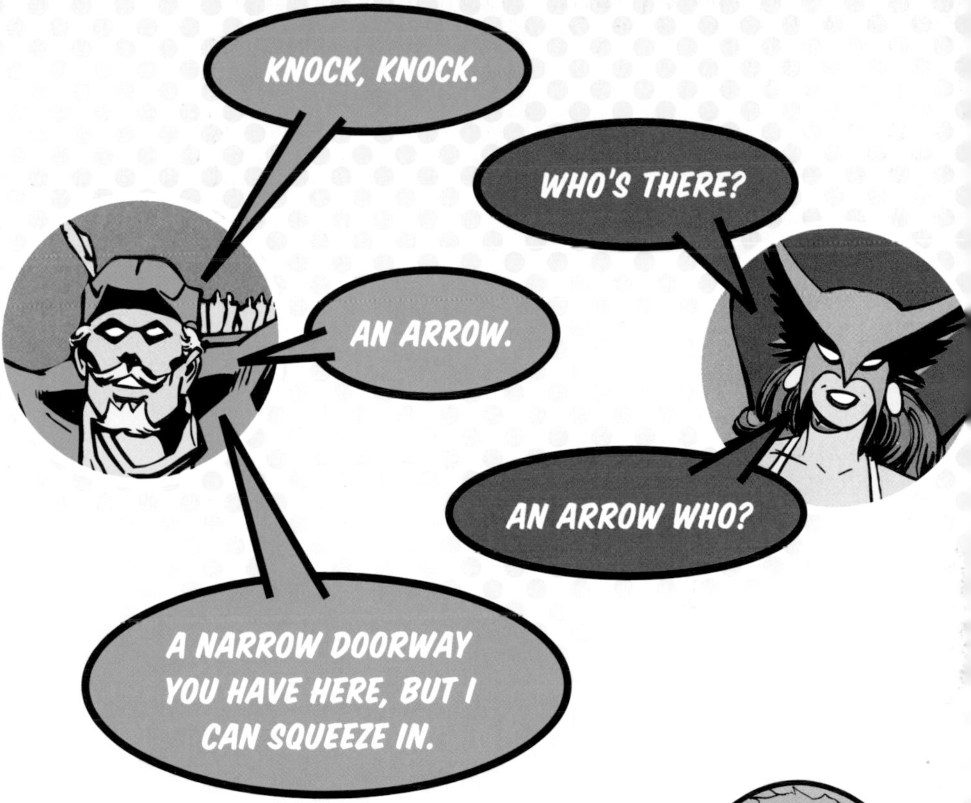
KNOCK, KNOCK.
WHO'S THERE?
AN ARROW.
AN ARROW WHO?
A NARROW DOORWAY YOU HAVE HERE, BUT I CAN SQUEEZE IN.

Why does Commissioner Gordon want to see Batman?

He mustache him a question.

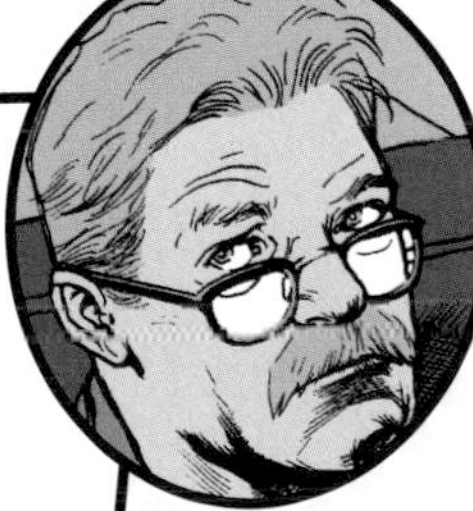

BATMAN GOES ON LOTS OF MISSIONS WITH ROBIN, BUT JIM GORDON IS ALWAYS HIS CO-MISSIONER.

Beast Boy can turn into any animal to fight crime. Usually this works out just fine, but there were a few times when things did not go well . . .

BEAST BOY'S **WORST** TRANSFORMATIONS

He turned into a rabbit to chase a villain, but the villain got away. Beast Boy was hopping mad.

He turned into a mouse. I'd tell you more, but the story is too cheesy.

He turned into a lamb, but he kept falling a-sheep.

He tried to get a job at a circus by turning into an elephant, but he had to work for peanuts.

One Wednesday, he turned into a camel because he heard it was hump day.

He turned into a sparrow, a lark, an eagle, and a wren, but then he decided that was all for the birds.

He turned into an owl, but no one gave a hoot.

He turned into a skunk, which really caused a stink.

He turned into a cow and failed udderly.

He turned into a snake, but that plan didn't have legs.

He turned into a porcupine with no quills, but that was pointless.

He turned into a black-and-white bear, and it was panda-monium.

He turned into a snail, but he was so slow all the slime.

He turned into a sea lion, but it was the sealiest thing he'd ever done.

He turned into a frog, and it was toadally a mistake.

He turned into a big cat, but whenever he talked, people thought he was lion.

What did they call Brainiac when he called customer service?
Complainiac

What did they call Brainiac when he was a construction worker?
Crane-iac

What did they call Brainiac when he tried a career as a wheat farmer?
Grainiac

What did they call Brainiac when he worked as a reporter?
Lois Lane-iac

What did they call Brainiac when he tried a career as a meteorologist?

Rainiac

What did they call Brainiac when he worked as a prop comic?

Zany-act

What did they call Brainiac when he worked as a plumber?

Drainiac

What did they call Brainiac when he volunteered to be a blood donor?

Veiniac

What did they call Brainiac when he was a horse groomer?

Mane-iac

What did they call Brainiac when he set up locomotive tracks all over his house?

Toy trainiac

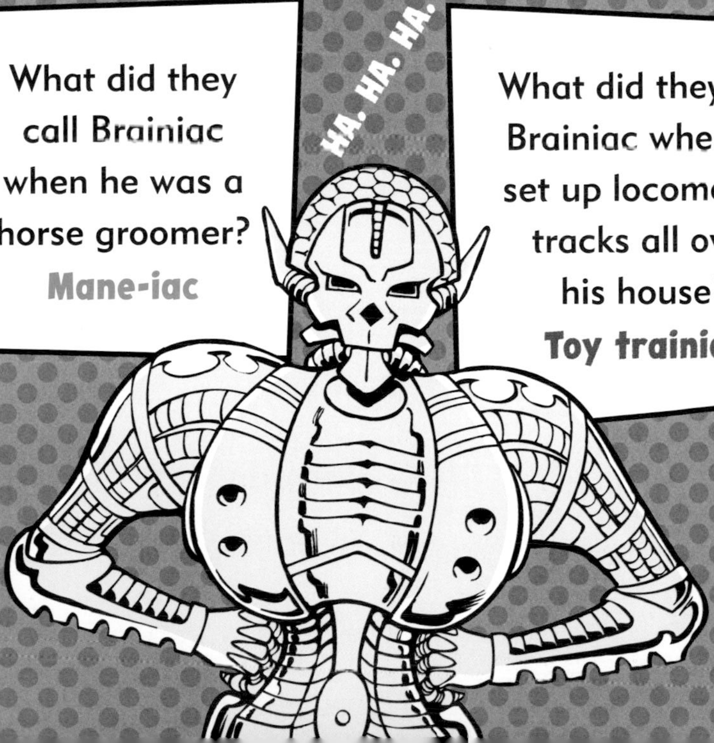
HA. HA. HA.

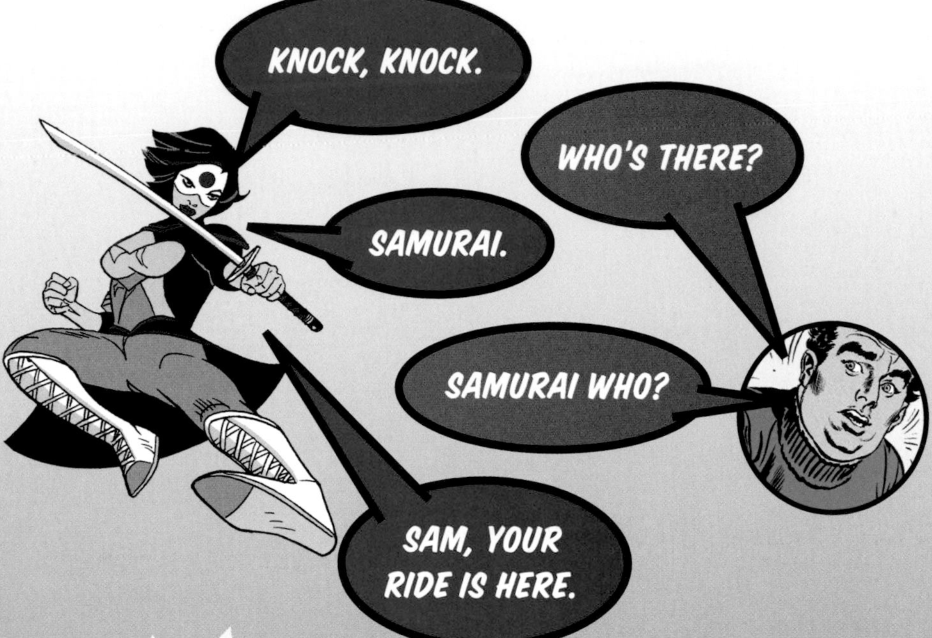
KNOCK, KNOCK.
WHO'S THERE?
SAMURAI.
SAMURAI WHO?
SAM, YOUR RIDE IS HERE.

What's Eclipso's favorite dessert?
Moon pie

What makes Poison Ivy's car go?
Grassoline

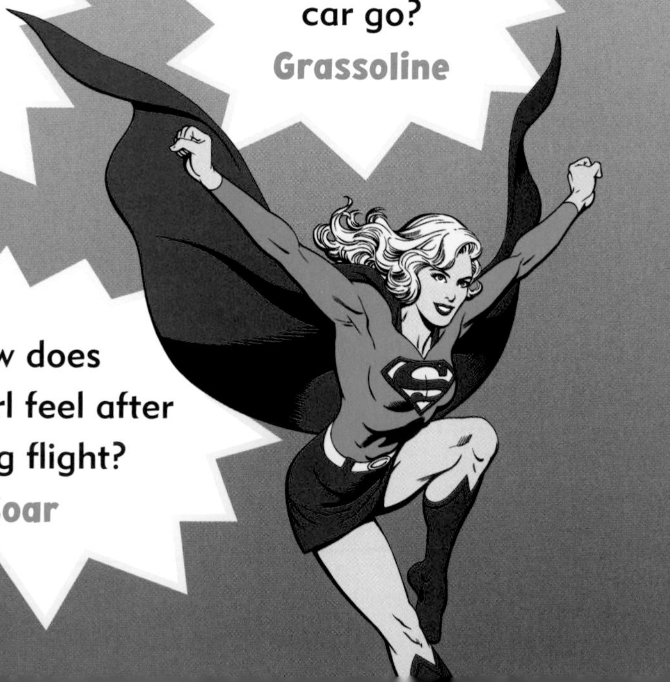

How does Supergirl feel after a long flight?
Soar

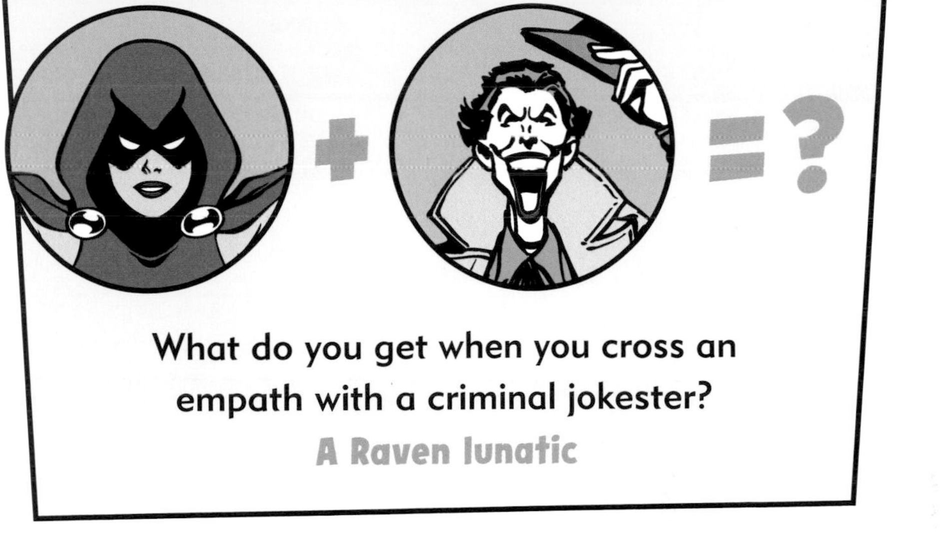

What do you get when you cross an empath with a criminal jokester?

A Raven lunatic

What does the Riddler say when he orders his breakfast at the diner?

"Griddle me this!"

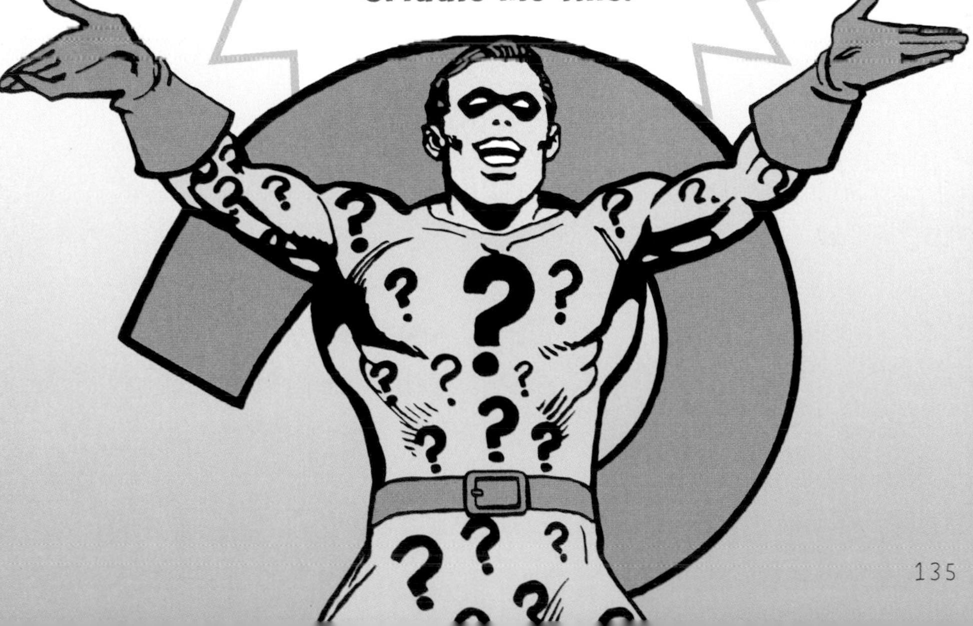

What happens when Captain Cold goes to a football game?

The home team needs to practice de-frost instead of de-fense.

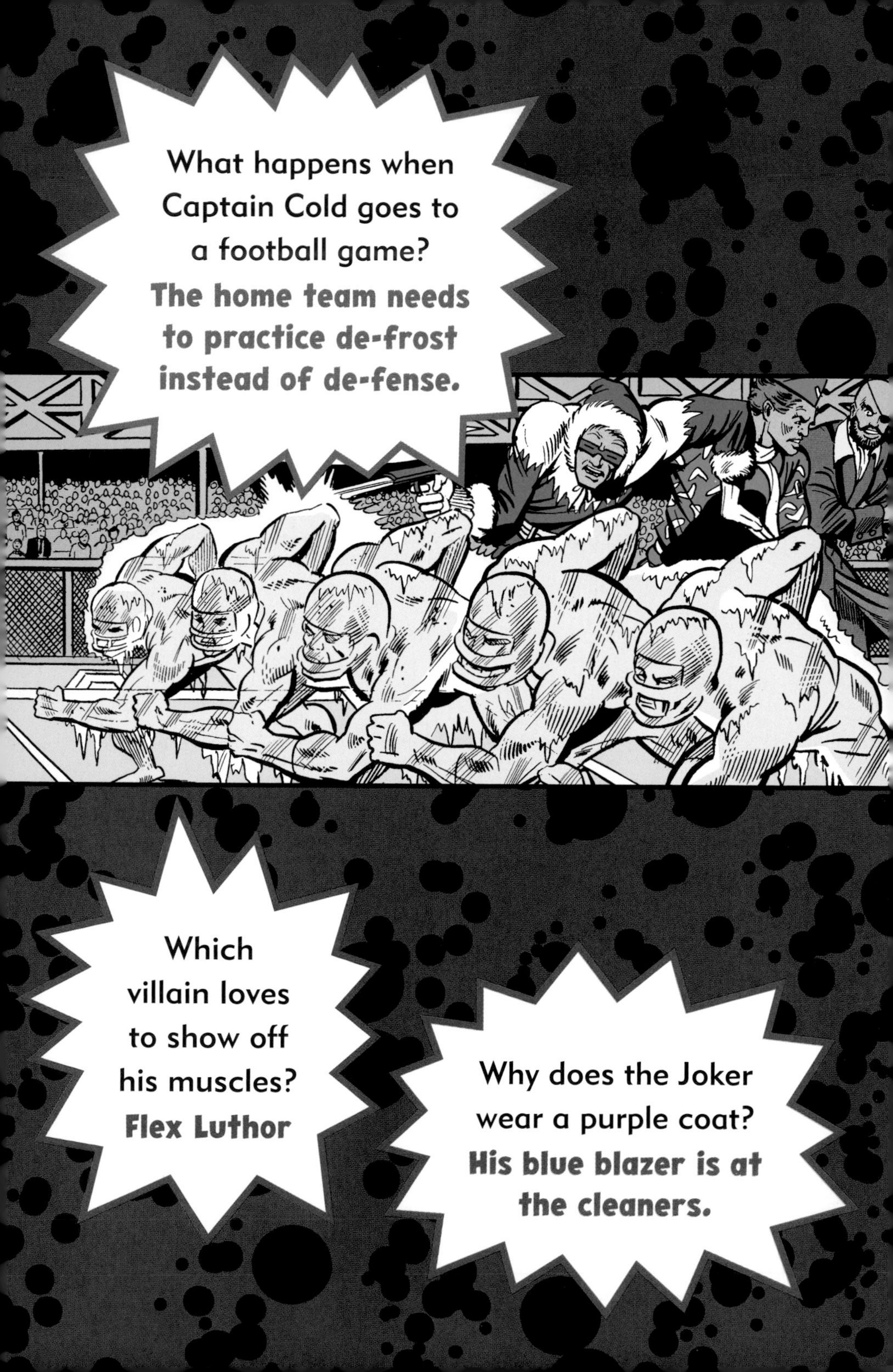

Which villain loves to show off his muscles?

Flex Luthor

Why does the Joker wear a purple coat?

His blue blazer is at the cleaners.

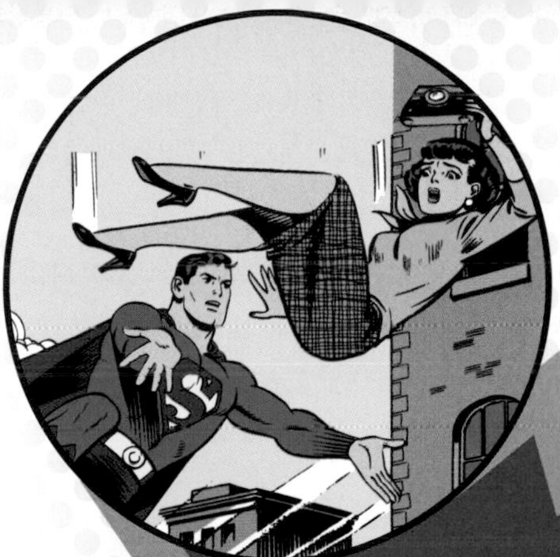

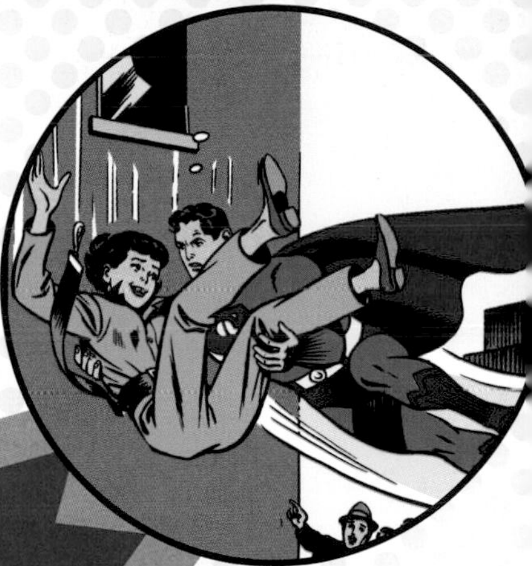

What position does Superman play in baseball?

Catch-her

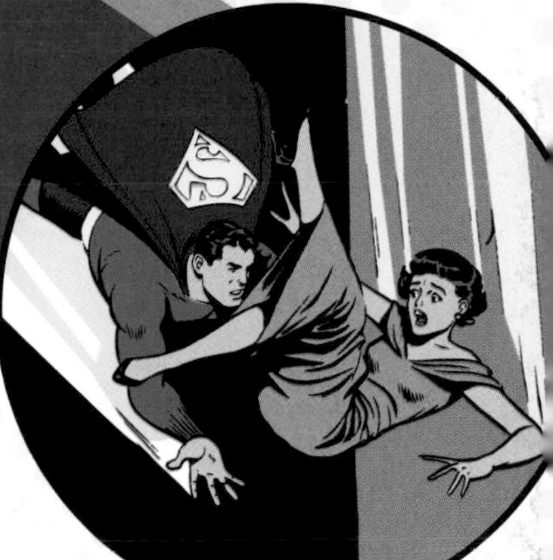

Why did Superman cross the road?

To get to Lois Lane

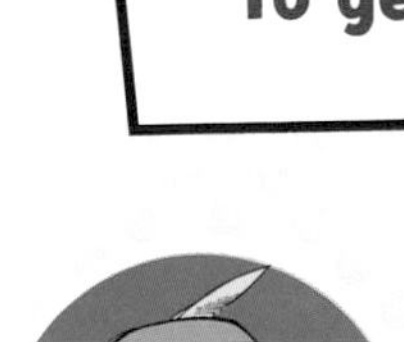

KNOCK, KNOCK.

WHO'S THERE?

OLIVER.

OLIVER WHO?

OLIVER DOORS ARE LOCKED. DO YOU HAVE THE KEY?

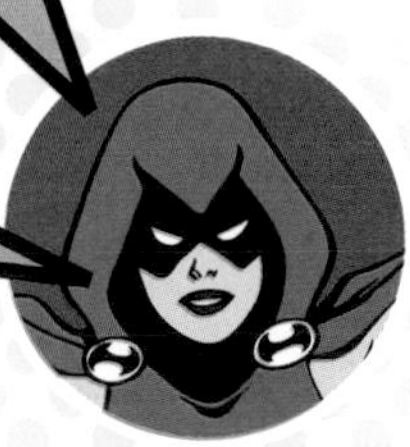

Why does Killer Croc have so many henchmen?
He's a good dele-gator.

Who captured Killer Croc?
An investi-gator

Why is Killer Croc always in charge of the directions?
He's a great navi-gator.

What does Killer Croc do when he doesn't feel like taking the stairs?
He takes the ele-gator.

How did Killer Croc decorate his bathroom?
With rep-tile

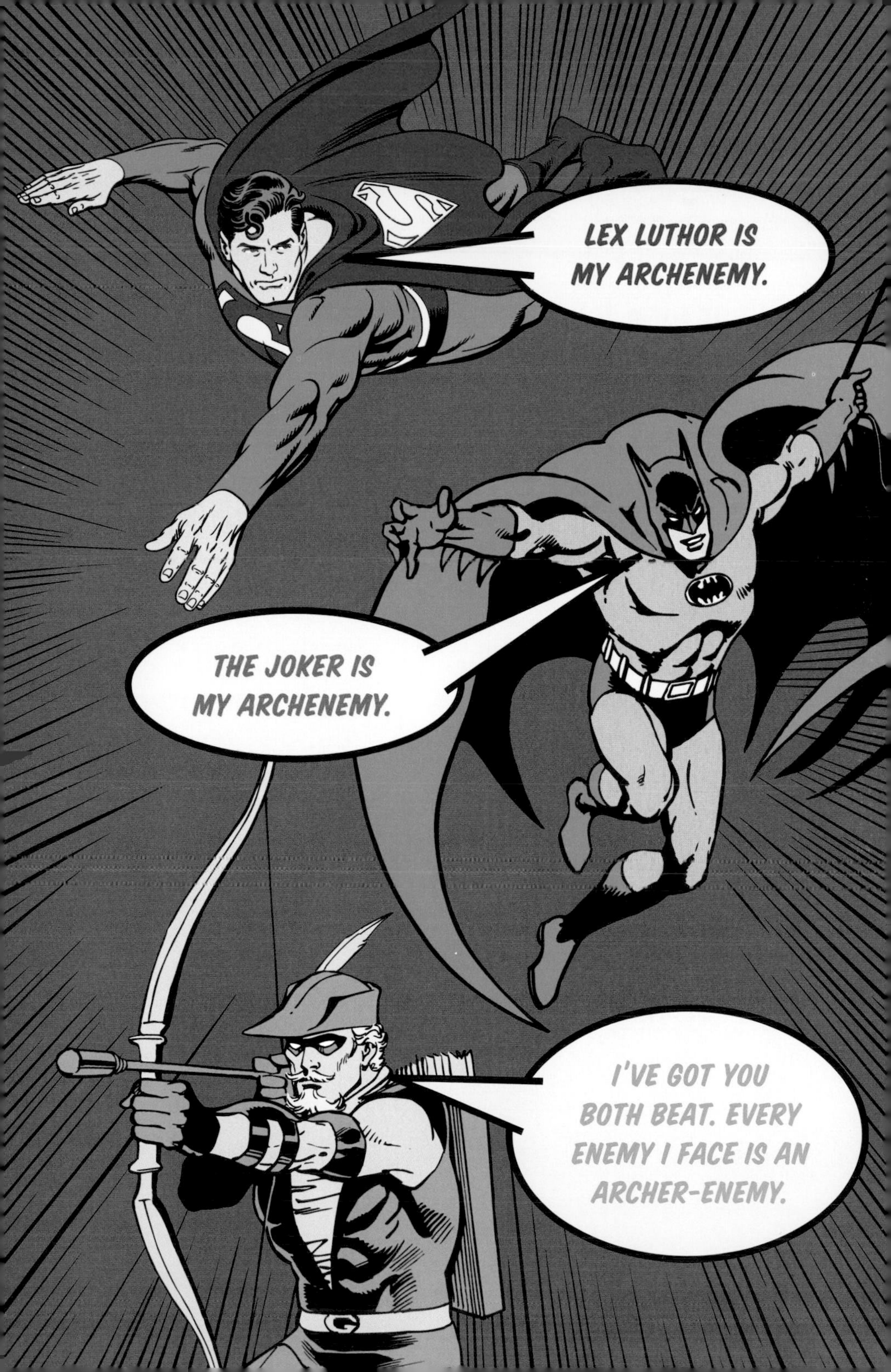
LEX LUTHOR IS MY ARCHENEMY.
THE JOKER IS MY ARCHENEMY.
I'VE GOT YOU BOTH BEAT. EVERY ENEMY I FACE IS AN ARCHER-ENEMY.

What's the Joker's favorite kind of pasta?
Chortle-ini

Will Scarecrow ever stop using his fear gas to commit crimes?
I'm afraid not.

What happened when the giant globe fell off the Daily Planet building?
It became the Daily Plummet.

KNOCK, KNOCK.

WHO'S THERE?

BEN.

BEN WHO?

BEEN LOCKED UP FOR A LONG TIME, AND NOW I AM COMING FOR YOU, BATMAN.

When Billy Batson says "Shazam!" he gets incredible superpowers. What happens when he says "City plan!"?
He builds incredible super-towers.

What does Billy Batson spread on toast?
Sha-jam!

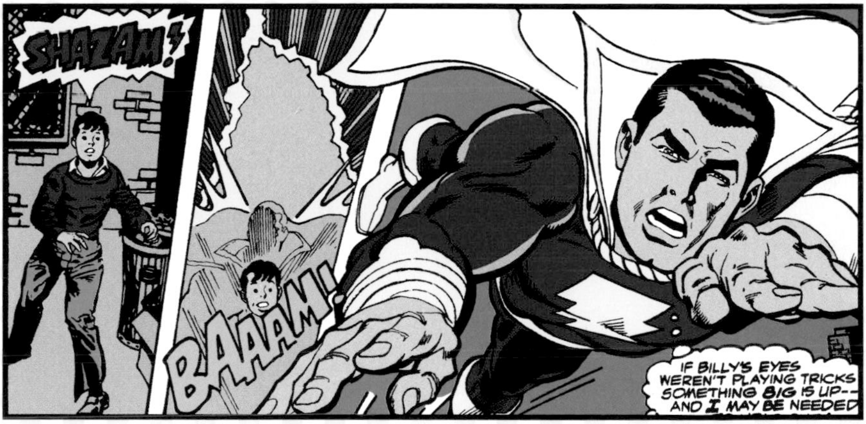
SHAZAM!
BAAAM!
IF BILLY'S EYES WEREN'T PLAYING TRICKS SOMETHING BIG IS UP-- AND I MAY BE NEEDED

Who gets flowers from Billy Batson every May?
Ma-zam!

What does Billy Batson say when he feels sheepish?
"Baa-zam!"

What does Billy Batson say when he wants to be alone?
"Sha-scram!"

What does the Atom get at the drive-thru?
A small fry

What is Aquaman's favorite fruit?
Watermelon

What is Cyborg's favorite food?
Anything from the USB drive-through

What is Superman's favorite sandwich?
A hero

What is Green Arrow's favorite Spanish dish?
Arroz con pollo

What is Comet the Super-Horse's favorite dish to make? **Maca-pony and cheese**

What is Katana's favorite food? **Swordfish**

What is Batman's favorite side dish? **Baked bat-atoes**

What is Batgirl's favorite food? **Anything with a kick**

Why does Wonder Woman bounce bullets off her bracelets? **It's safer than bouncing them off her earrings.**

Why does everyone remember Two-Face? **He's unforget-double.**

What happened when John Stewart, Hal Jordan, and Guy Gardner teamed up to fight crime under the Big Top? **It was a three-ring circus.**

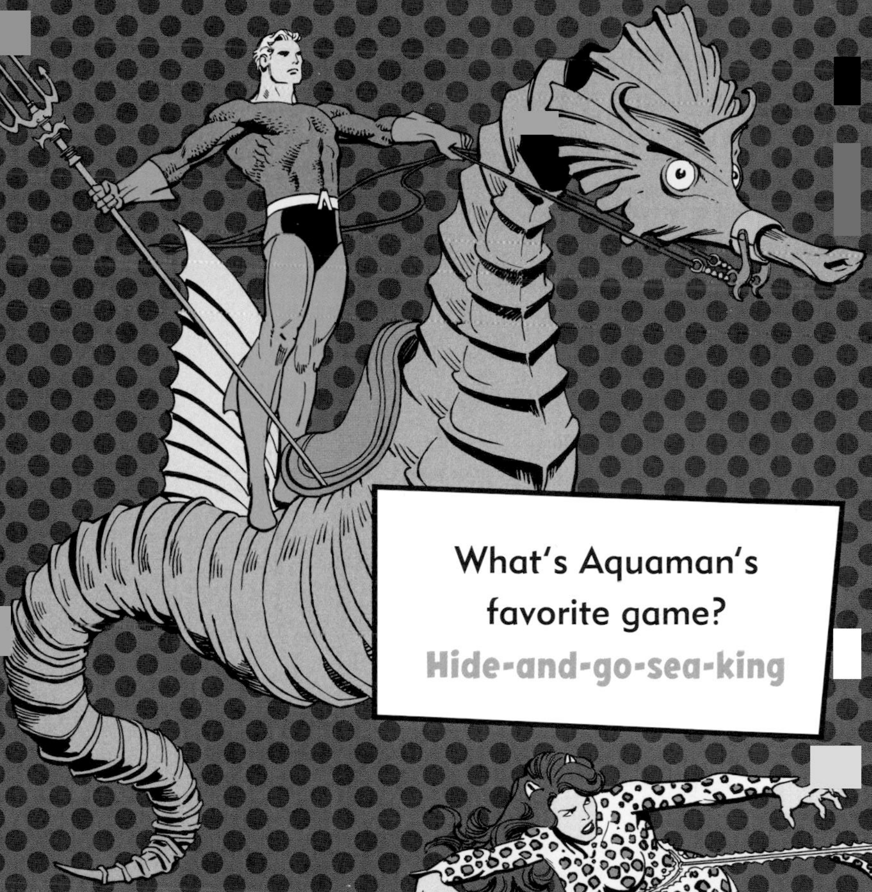

What's Aquaman's favorite game?
Hide-and-go-sea-king

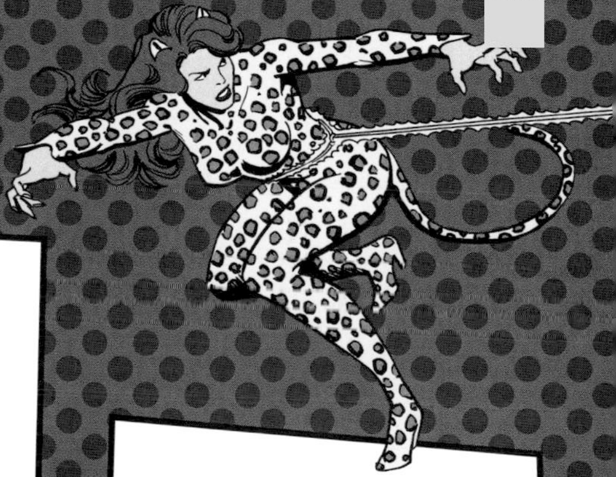

What do you get when you cross the Joker with a cookie?
A snickerdoodle

What happened when Cheetah tried to outrun Wonder Woman's lasso?
They tied.

Why doesn't Catwoman like lemons?
They make her a sourpuss.

Why can't you trust the Joker?
Give him an inch, and he takes a smile.

What's the Joker's favorite ice cream flavor?
Chuckle-at

What is Two-Face's favorite instrument?
The two-ba

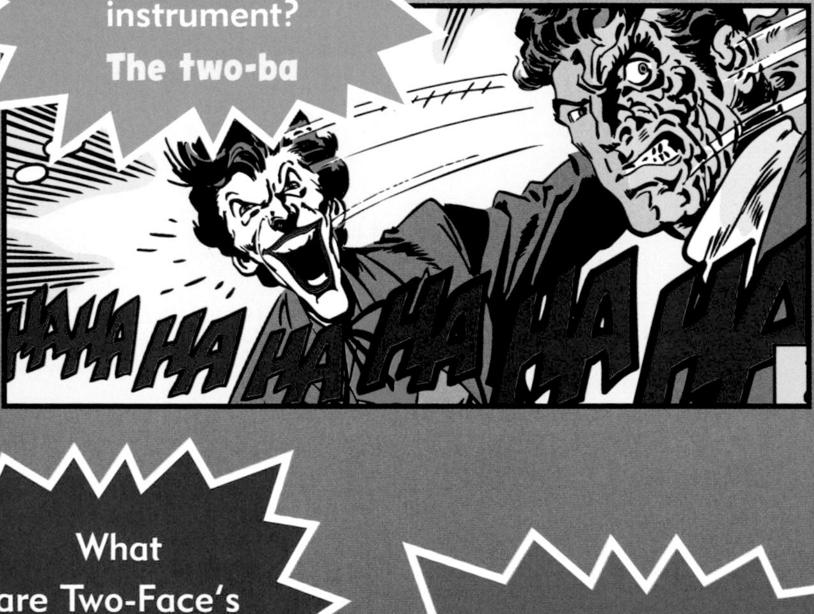
HAHA HA HA HA HA HA HA

What are Two-Face's favorite flowers?
Two-lips

Why doesn't the Joker ever miss a day of work?
He's har-har-hardy.

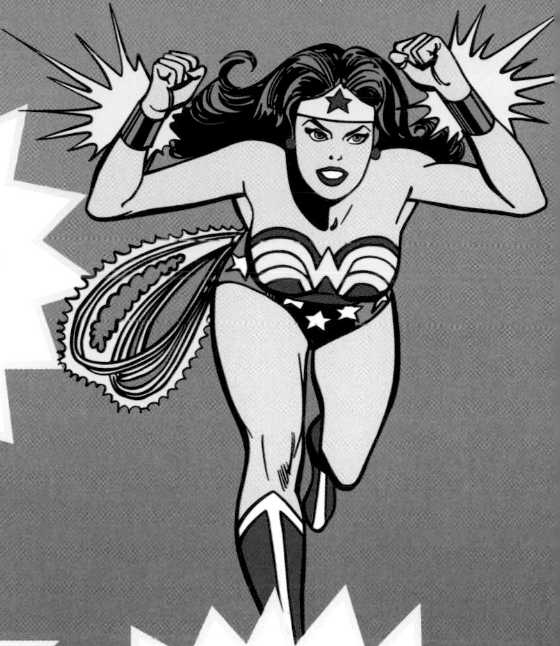

Does Katana get carried away with her weapon?

Sword of

Why did Batman repeat himself?

He had to face Two-Face.

Why did Wonder Woman *not* cross the road?

Wonder Woman isn't chicken.

How strong is Krypto?

He can leap tall buildings in a single hound.

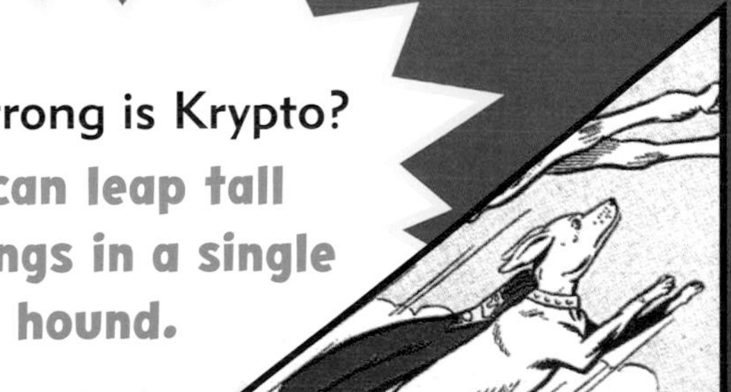

What happens when Diana Prince goes on a really long walk?

Wonder Woman becomes Wander Woman.

What happens when Diana Prince takes a nap?

Wonder Woman becomes Slumber Woman.

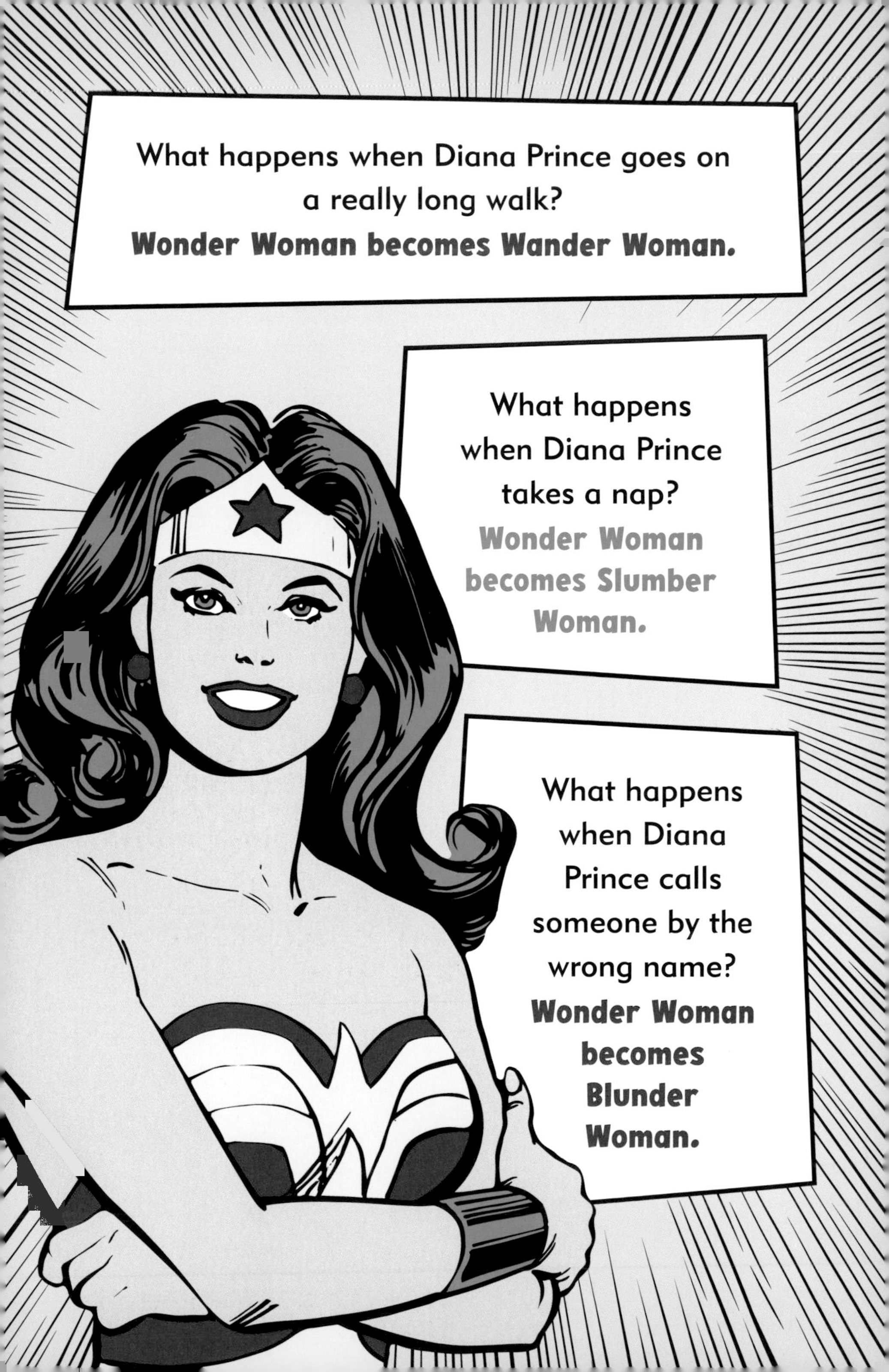

What happens when Diana Prince calls someone by the wrong name?

Wonder Woman becomes Blunder Woman.

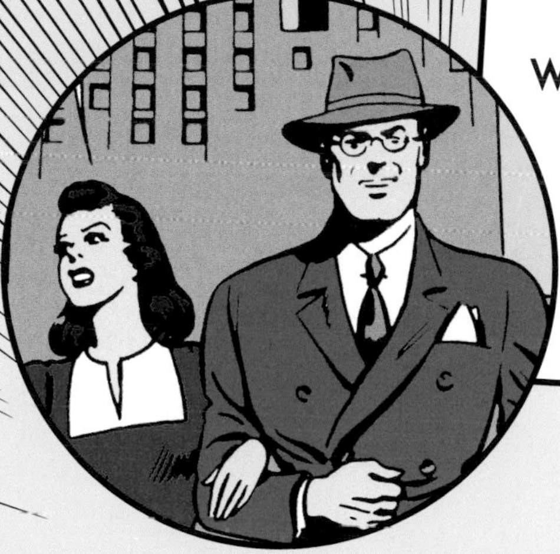

Why does Clark Kent wear a fedora?

Because it makes him look fedorable

How is Batgirl's career as a librarian just like her career catching criminals?

Either way, she likes to book 'em.

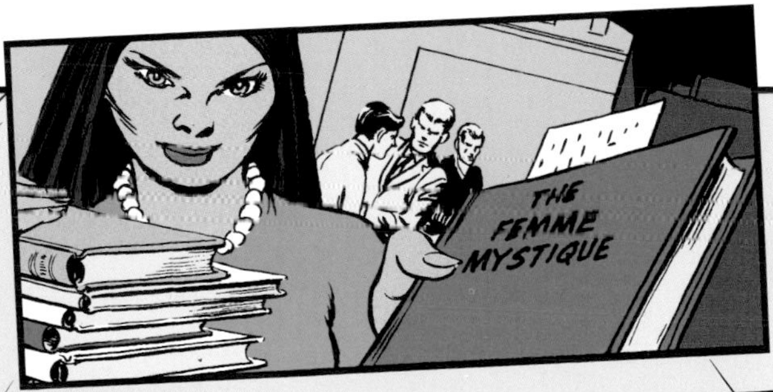
THE FEMME MYSTIQUE

Why did Two-Face get a parking ticket?

He was double-parked.

Why did the Jokermobile get a ticket?

It was trouble-parked.

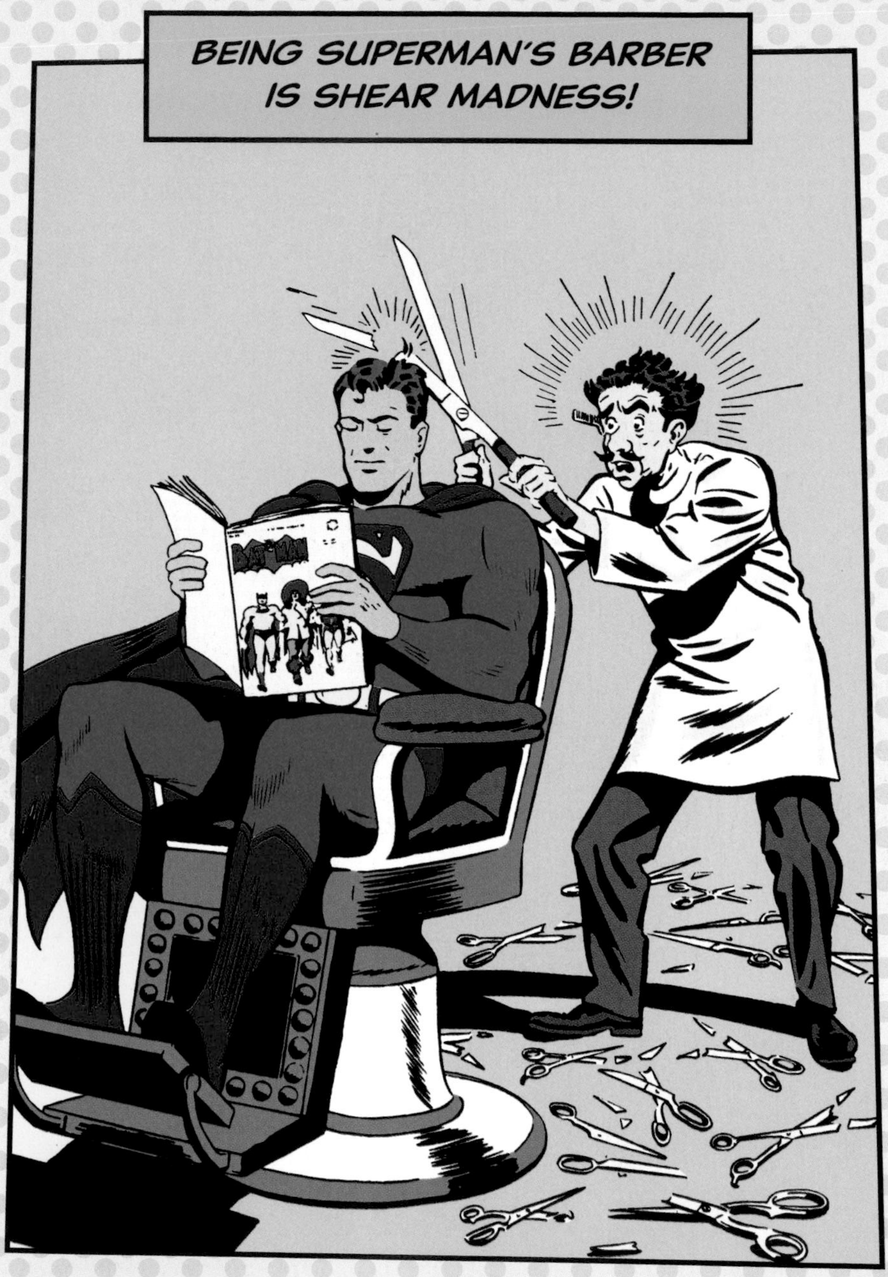
BEING SUPERMAN'S BARBER IS SHEAR MADNESS!

BLACK CANARY, WHY DID YOU USE YOUR CANARY CRY TO BLOW OUT YOUR BIRTHDAY CANDLES?

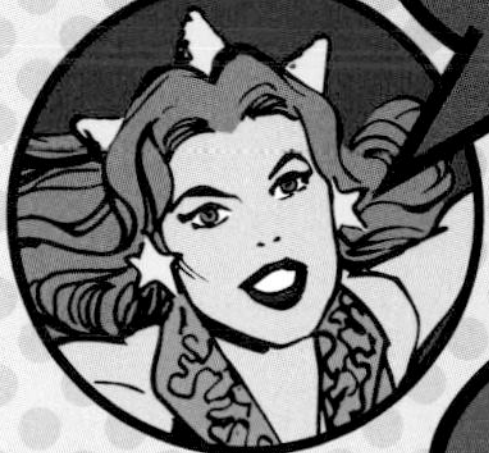

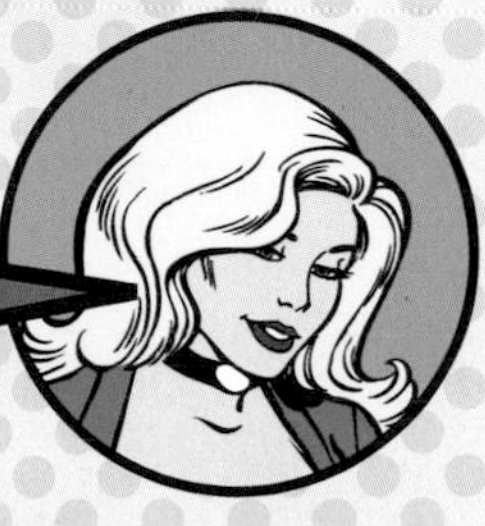

IT'S MY PARTY, AND I'LL CRY IF I WANT TO.

What did Harley Quinn's valentine to the Joker say?

Roses are red,
Ivy is green.
Sugar is sweet,
And, boy, are you mean.

What did the Joker's valentine to Harley Quinn say?

Roses are red.
Kindness is heinous.
Let's cause some trouble.
I love your insaneness.

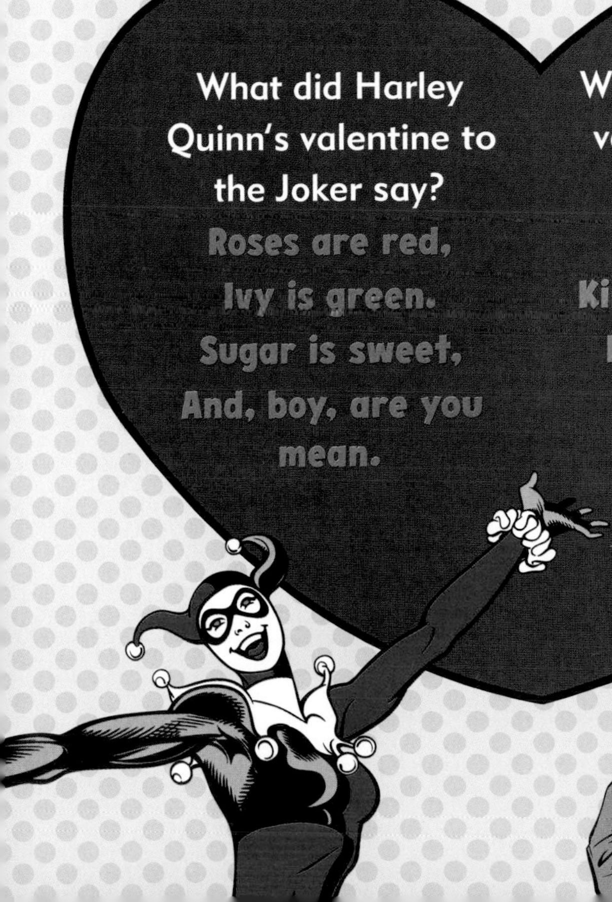

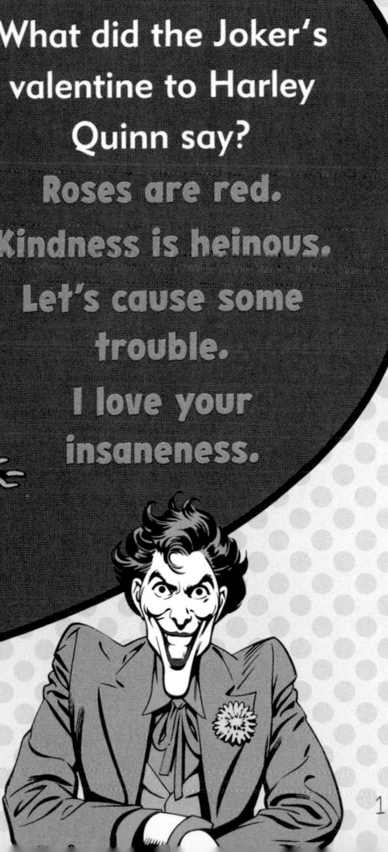

What happened when Superman tripped walking out of the phone booth, got his cape caught on a tree branch, and accidentally melted the mayor's door with his heat vision?

This super hero became a blooper hero.

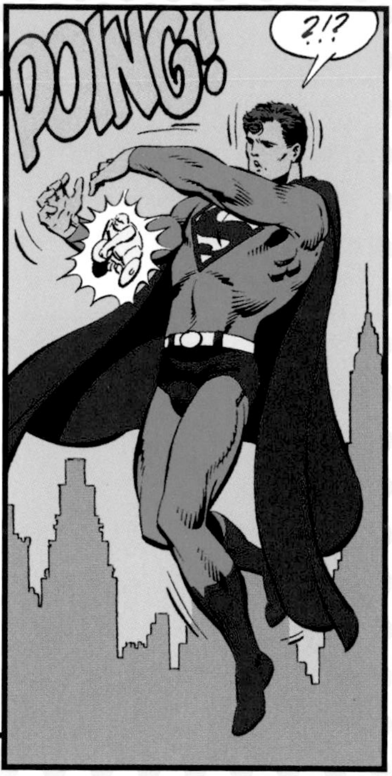
POING!
?!?

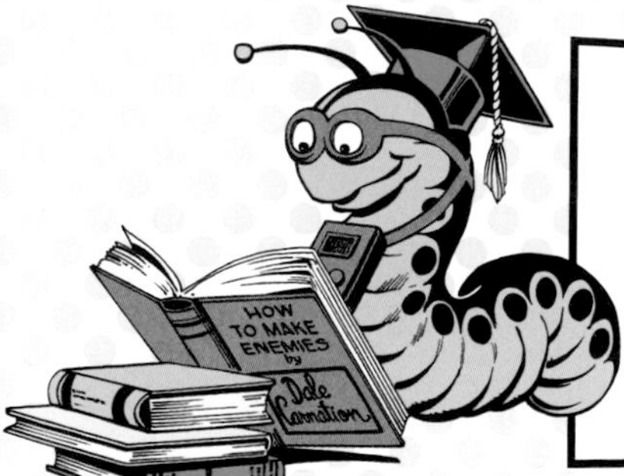
HOW TO MAKE ENEMIES by Dale Carnation

Why did Mr. Mind go into Barbara Gordon's library?

He was a real bookworm.

How come Superman never barbecues?

Once, he accidentally squeezed a bag of charcoal too hard and filled his grill with diamonds.

What's the
Scarecrow's favorite
prehistoric beast?
A terror-dactyl

How does Catwoman
cross the river?
On a catamaran

How did Aquaman
get to the top of the
mountain so quickly?
He took his shell-icopter.

Why did Lex Luthor put
a rabbit on his head?
**It was just another
hare-brained scheme.**

What happened when Mr. Freeze attacked Titans Tower? **It became an iced T.**

What is Eclipso's favorite day of the week? **Moon-day**

What's The Flash's favorite pitch? **A fastball**

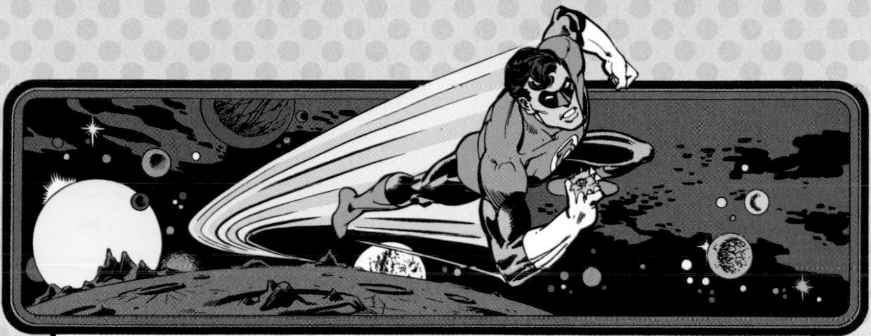

How does Green Lantern start a race?

On your mark, get set, GLOW!

Why did the Joker lose the tennis match?

He guffaw-lted his serve.

Why does Wonder Woman like her friend Etta Candy so much?

Because she's so sweet

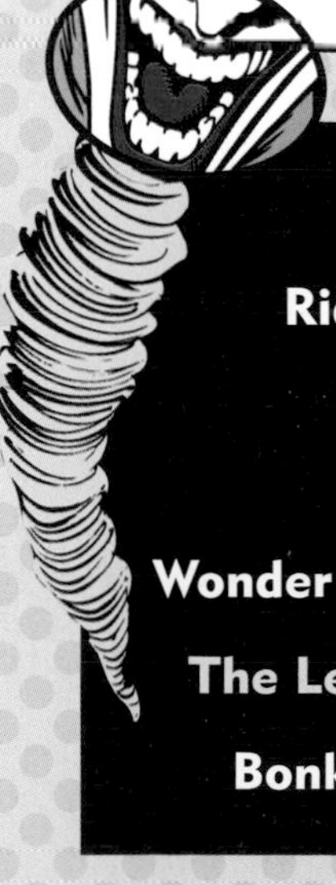

SAY THIS FIVE TIMES FAST!

Riddler's wrapping Robin's ribbon round Raven's reuben wrap.

Kal-El levitated eleven elevators.

Wonder Woman wowed wide-eyed window washers.

The League left lettuce leaves on Luthor's lawn.

Bonkers! Batman's Batarang's been burgled.

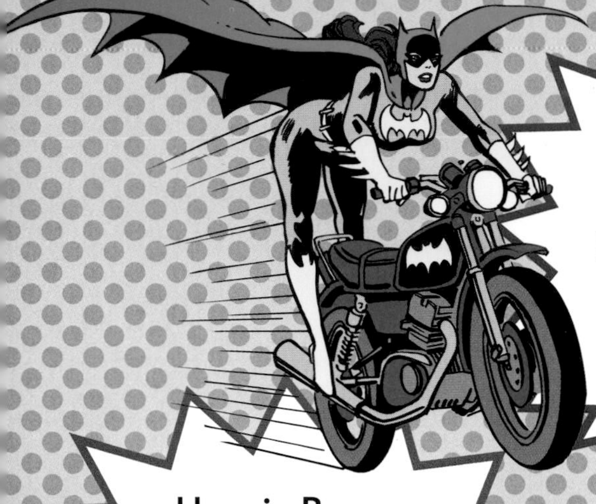

Why couldn't Batgirl get to the Batcave on time?

Her motorcycle was two-tired.

How is Bruce Wayne's house different from Arkham Asylum?

Wayne Manor is a sane manor.

Why is Batman actually like a thief?

Because he rarely goes anywhere without Robin

KNOCK, KNOCK.

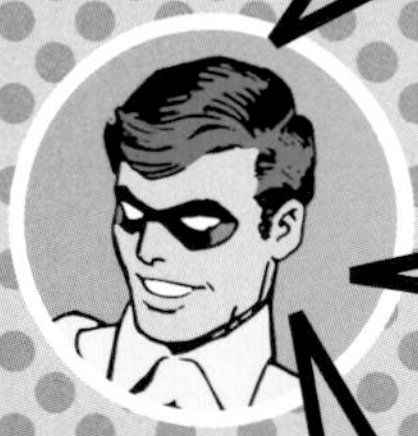

WHO'S THERE?

WOO.

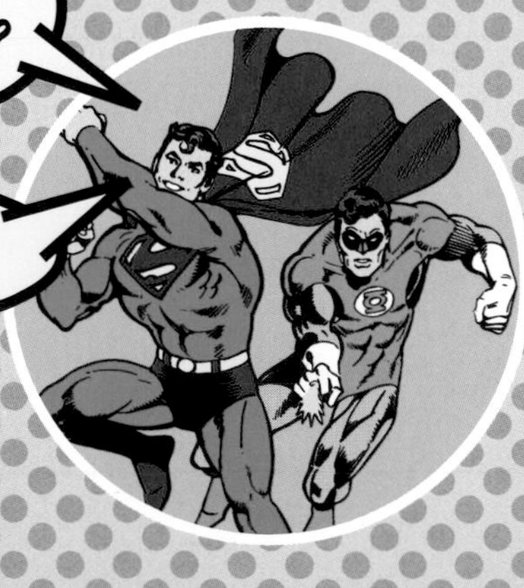

WOO WHO?

DON'T CHEER YET, WE'RE NOT DONE SAVING THE DAY!

What happened when the Joker tried to spray Batman with his trick flower?

It was a sneer miss.

What does Batman do when the Joker starts throwing cards?

He deals with it.

Why does the Joker throw cards?

He likes to give you a hand.

Why does the Joker wear purple?

So he can commit violet crimes.

What's the Joker's favorite Christmas tune?

"Deck the Halls"

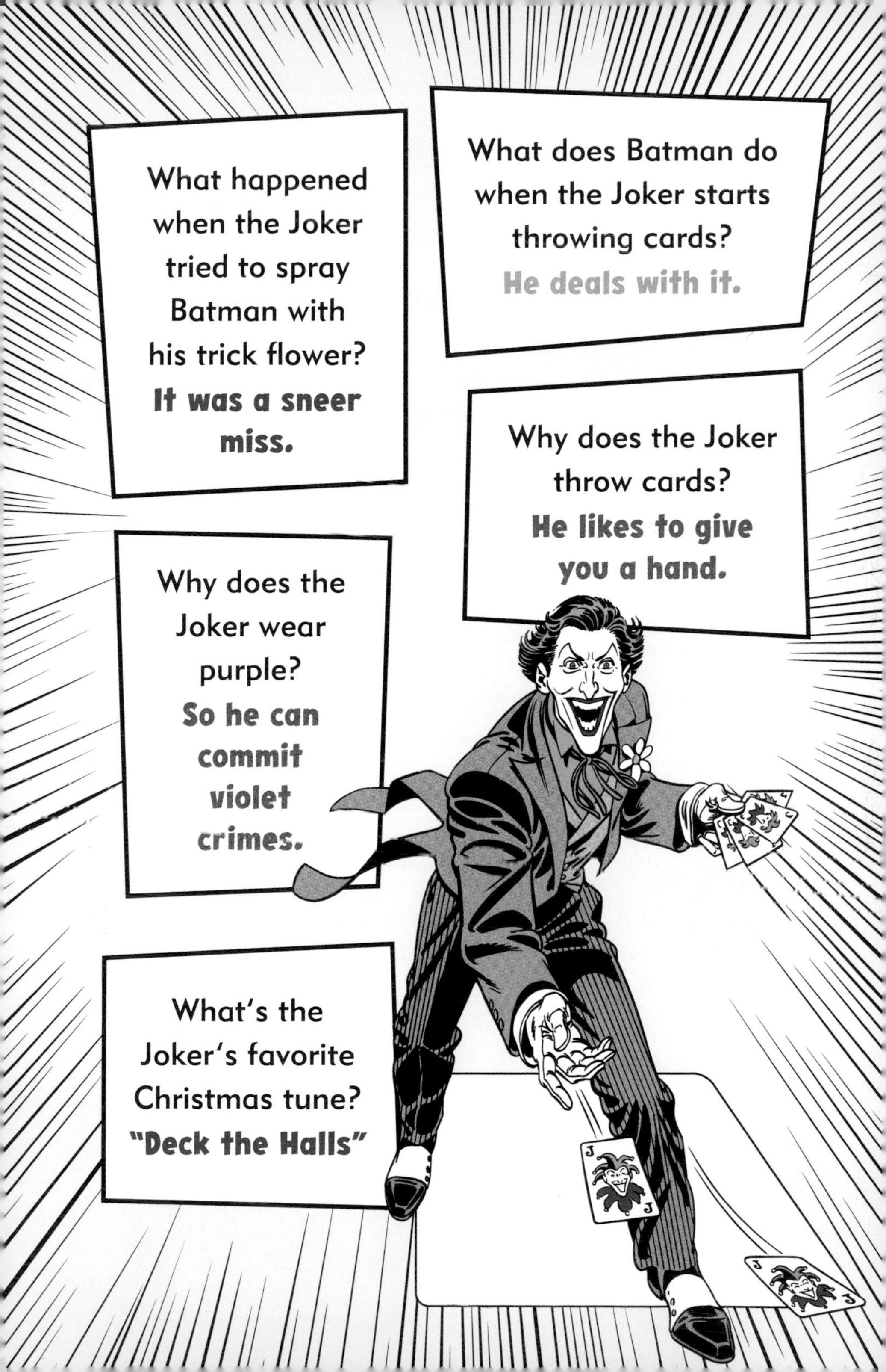

Why didn't the crook answer his phone after Wonder Woman caught him?

He was all tied up.

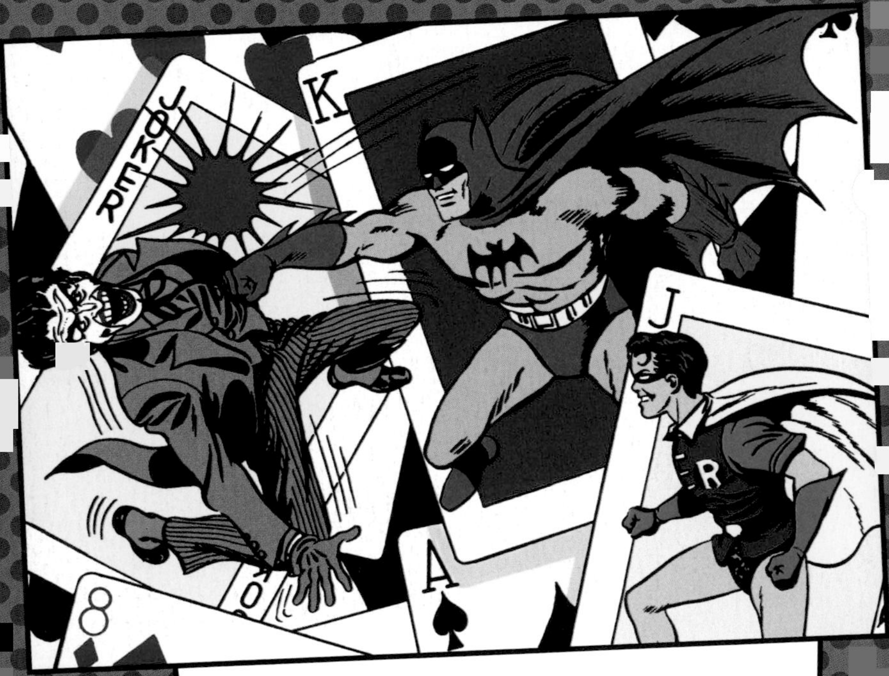
JOKER

What's the only part of the Joker's jokes that Batman likes?

The punch line

Why won't the Joker play cards with Wonder Woman's archenemy?

She's a cheetah.

Why is it a bad idea to joke around with Katana?
She has a cutting sense of humor.

What do you call Katana when she forgets where she left her blade?
A sword loser

What does Shazam! wear beneath his costume?
Thunderwear

What did Shazam! use to make his costume?
A lightning bolt of fabric

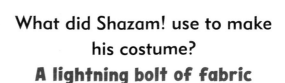

HOW RICH IS LEX LUTHOR?

Banks asked him to stop leaving money with them because they couldn't get the vault doors shut.

- -

He's never been to a car wash. If his limousine gets dirty, he just buys a new one.

- -

He once bought an island with the loose change he found in his couch.

- -

The credit limit on his Mastercard is "the sky."

- -

He's the only person who knows whose face is on the quadrillion dollar bill.

- -

His bank accounts don't just earn interest, they earn fascination.

- -

What does Catwoman do when she spots a stray kitten?

Whisker away

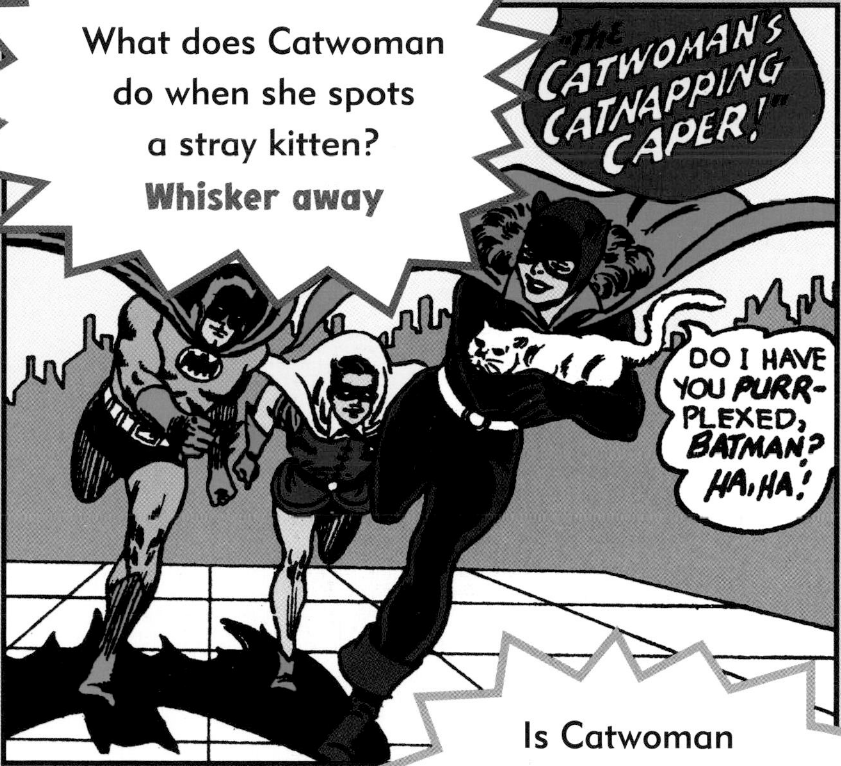
"THE CATWOMAN'S CATNAPPING CAPER!"
DO I HAVE YOU PURR-PLEXED, BATMAN? HA, HA!

Is Catwoman very outdoorsy?

Yes. She likes to climb meowtains.

What does The Flash put on his burgers?

You'll-never-ketchup

What is Catwoman's favorite mountain range?

The Catskills

Does Batgirl ever hesitate to stop a criminal?

She never bats an eye.

Why did Batman cross the road?

To get to the other sidekick

JACK WAS NIMBLE, JACK WAS QUICK, BUT JACK COULDN'T DODGE A BATGIRL KICK!

What happens when The Flash can't go for a run?

His energy gets all bottled up.

How is Superman different from a pig? **The Man of Steel doesn't squeal!**

When the members of the Justice League play poker, who hands out the cards? **Superman. The Man of Steel likes to deal.**

Would Superman ever dye his hair? **No! The Man of Steel keeps it real!**

WHEN SUPERMAN SAYS HE'LL GIVE YOU A LIFT, HE REALLY MEANS IT.

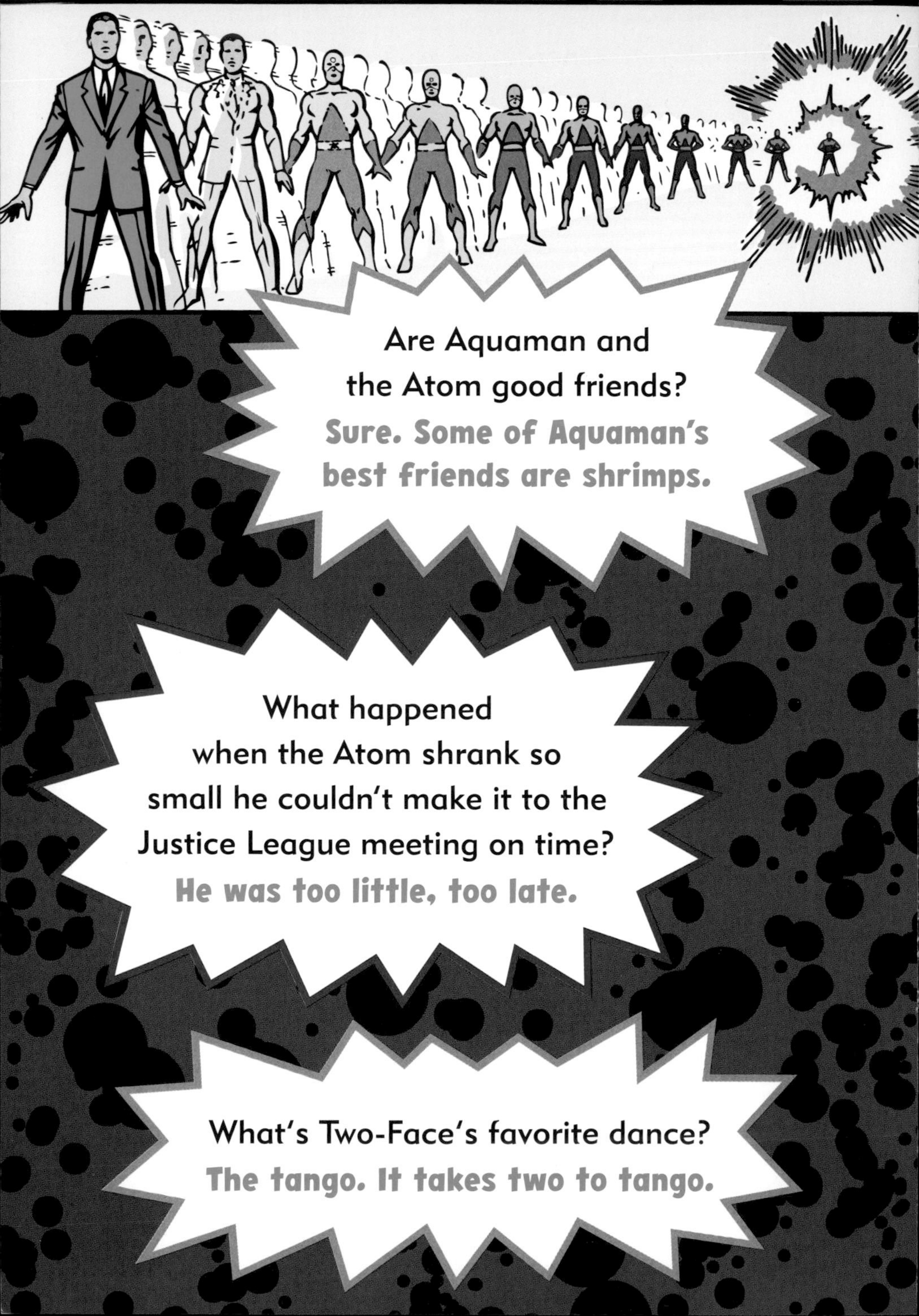

Are Aquaman and
the Atom good friends?
Sure. Some of Aquaman's best friends are shrimps.

What happened
when the Atom shrank so
small he couldn't make it to the
Justice League meeting on time?
He was too little, too late.

What's Two-Face's favorite dance?
The tango. It takes two to tango.

When did French criminals try to kidnap Batman?
On Bat-steal Day

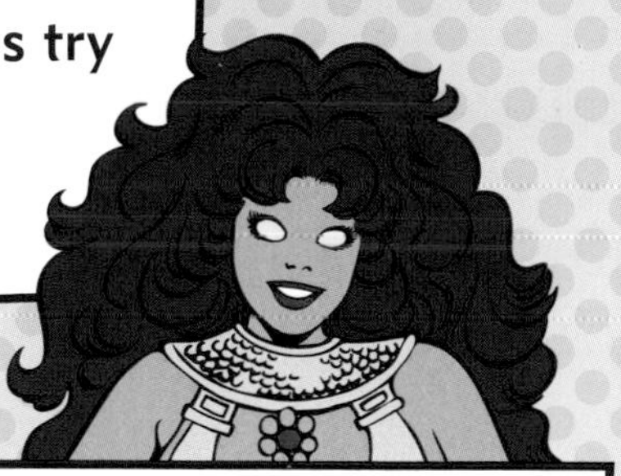

How can you recognize Starfire?
By the twinkle in her eye

Did you hear that Superman transformed the scientific field of radiology?
Yes, he's an X-ray visionary.

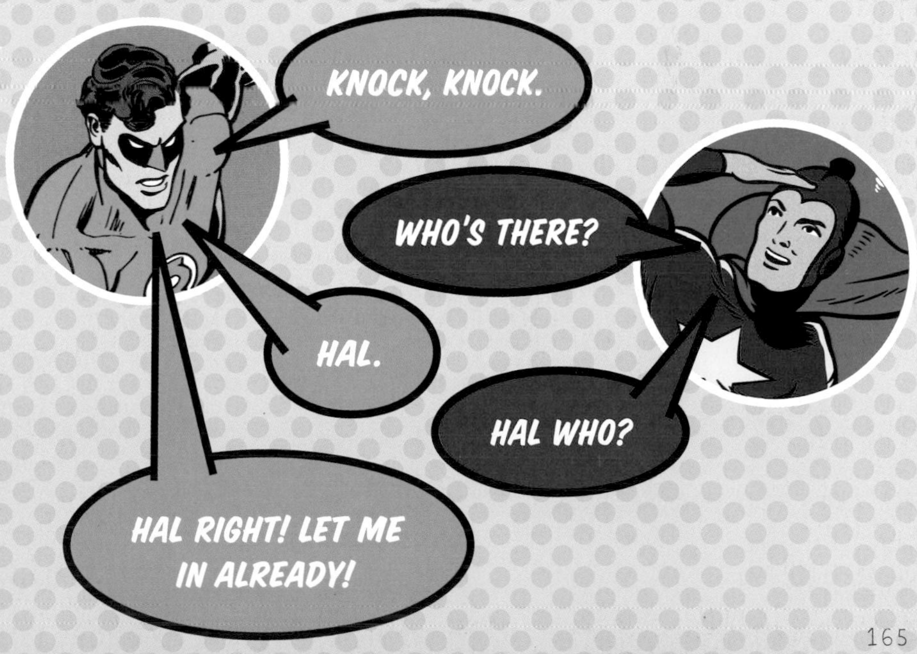
KNOCK, KNOCK.
WHO'S THERE?
HAL.
HAL WHO?
HAL RIGHT! LET ME IN ALREADY!

What did Luthor send to Superman on his phone?
A Lext message

What's Swamp Thing's favorite dessert?
Marsh-mallows

Does Bumblebee have a crush on anybody?
None of your beeswax!

THANKS FOR PUTTING ON YOUR COWL AND COMING TO HELP US.

NO PROBLEM. COWL ME ANYTIME.

How are Lex Luthor and a pastry chef alike?

They're both rolling in dough.

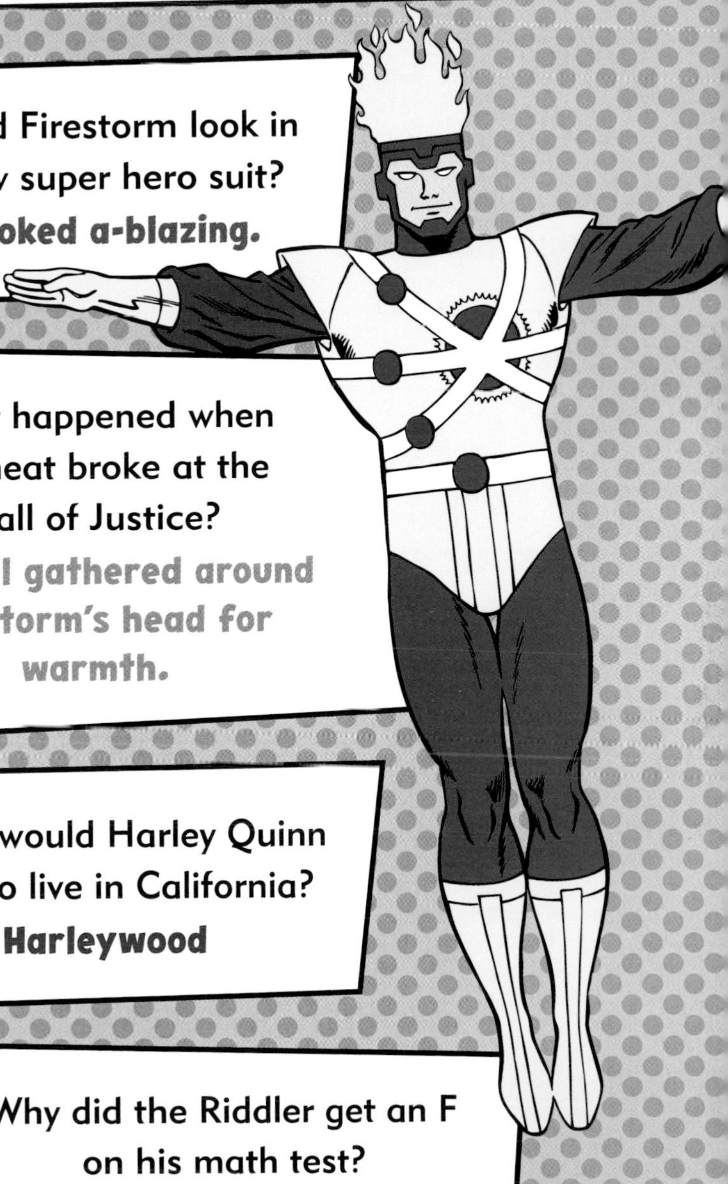

How did Firestorm look in his new super hero suit?

He looked a-blazing.

What happened when the heat broke at the Hall of Justice?

They all gathered around Firestorm's head for warmth.

Where would Harley Quinn want to live in California?

Harleywood

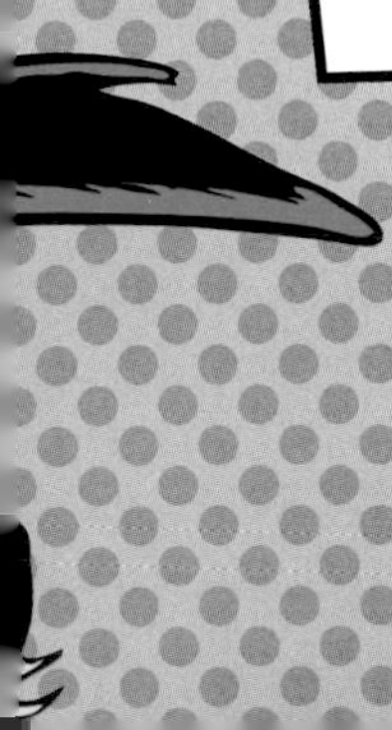

Why did the Riddler get an F on his math test?

It was riddled with errors.

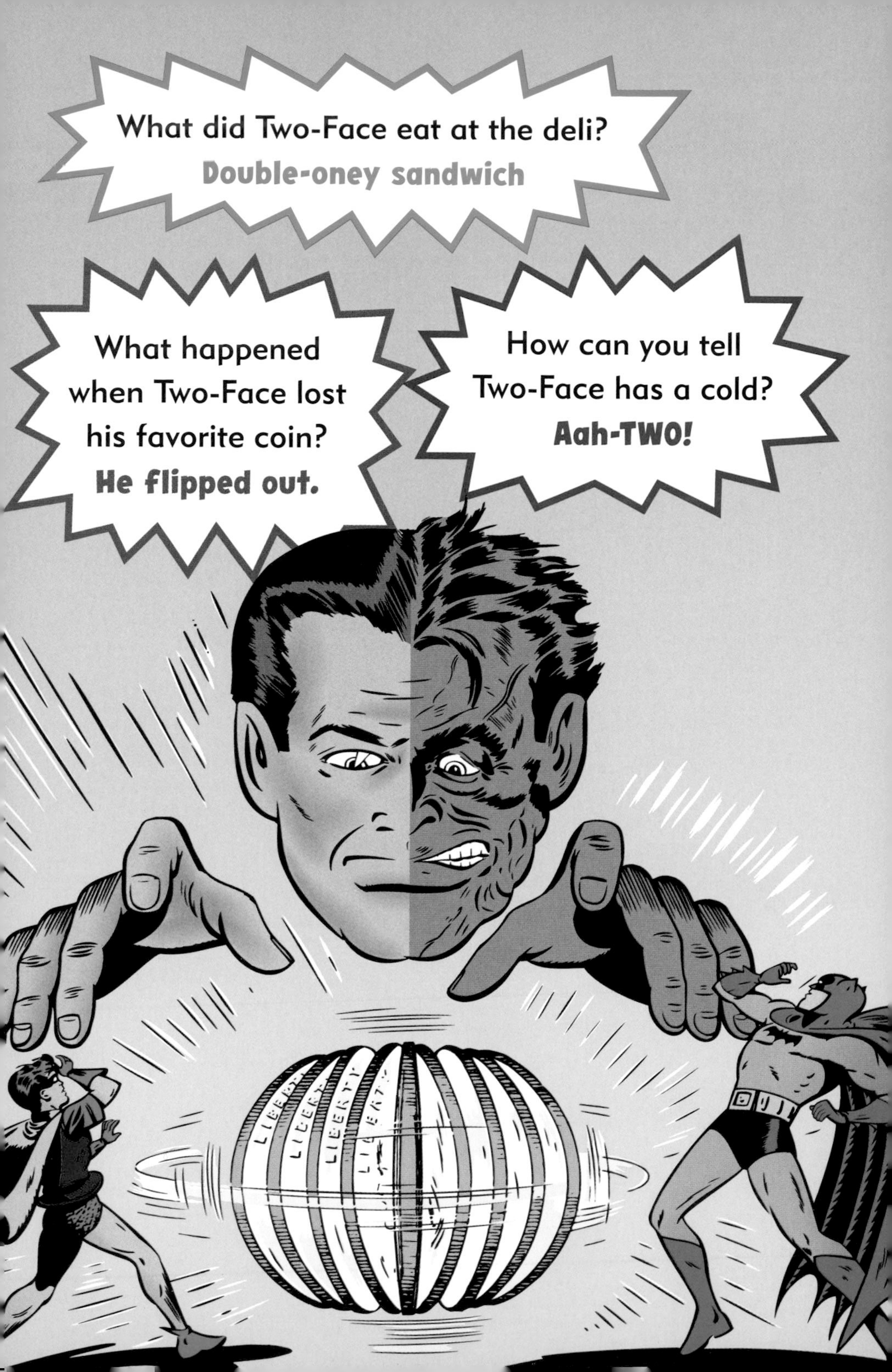
What did Two-Face eat at the deli?
Double-oney sandwich
What happened when Two-Face lost his favorite coin?
He flipped out.
How can you tell Two-Face has a cold?
Aah-TWO!

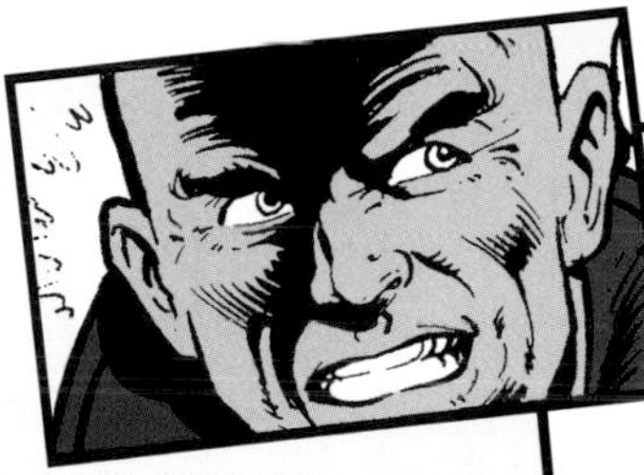

Why did Lex Luthor get angry at his test tubes?
He was a mad scientist.

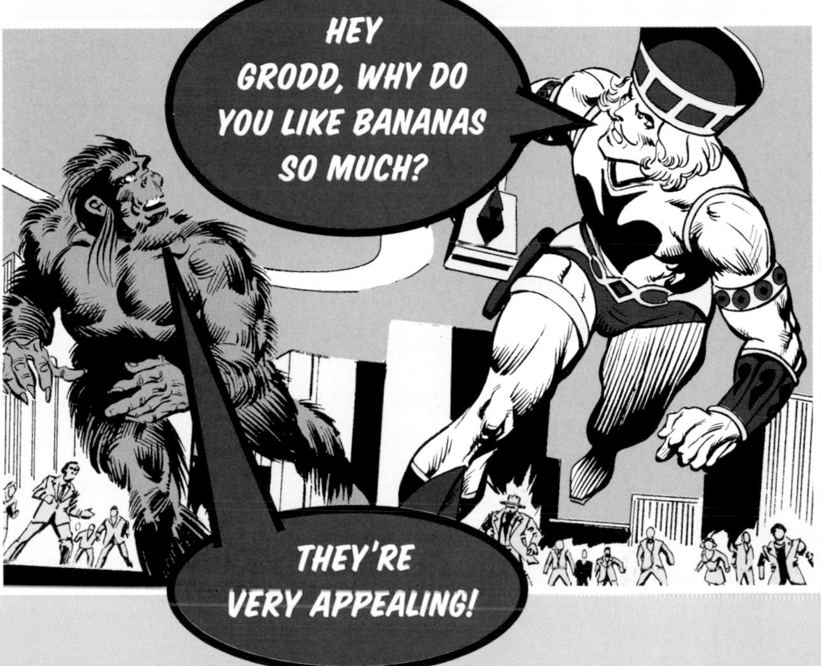
HEY GRODD, WHY DO YOU LIKE BANANAS SO MUCH?
THEY'RE VERY APPEALING!

If Harley Quinn had four identical sisters, what would you call them?
The Harley Quinntuplets

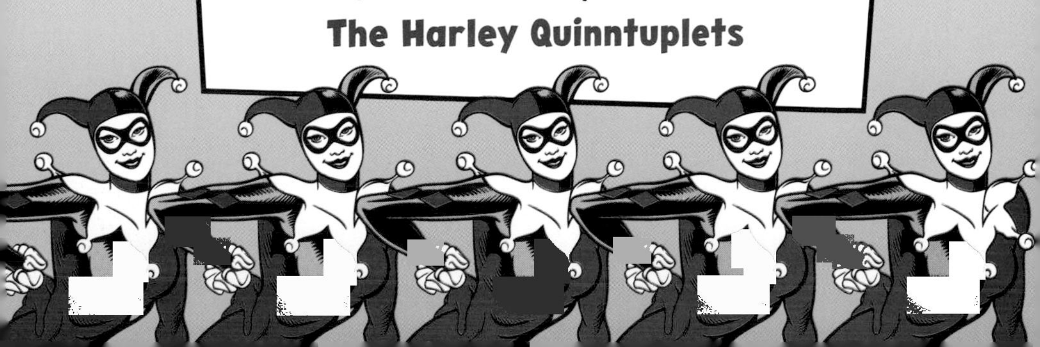

Superman's mail is addressed "Care of the *Daily Planet*." How is Supergirl's mail addressed?

Kara Zor-El, of course.

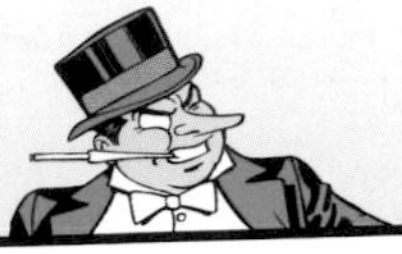

What does the Penguin say when he takes your breakfast order?

"Waddle it be?"

Is Poison Ivy popular in Europe?

Yes, in the germination

Why do most people avoid Poison Ivy?

They make a rash decision.

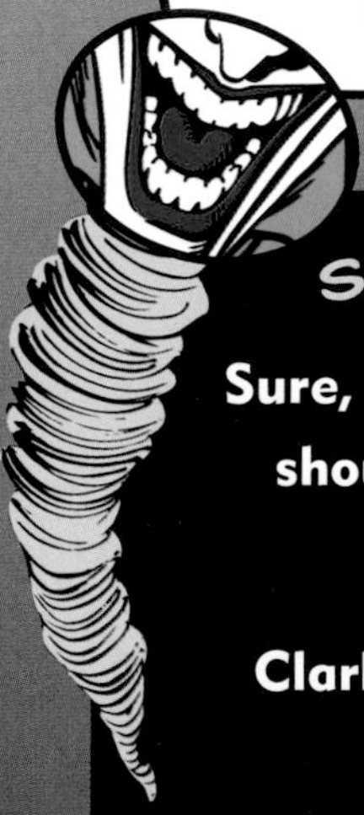

SAY THIS FIVE TIMES FAST!

Sure, Supergirl shocks shouting show-offs—shouldn't she shame the shady sharks?

Joker juggles jiggling jelly rolls.

Clark Kent can't count the cooking clutter covering his counter.

The Penguin plots perilous ploys.

Next, behind his specs, Clark's X-ray eyes inspect Lex's vexing exit.

Why did Kid Flash join the running team?

To make himself a-track-tive

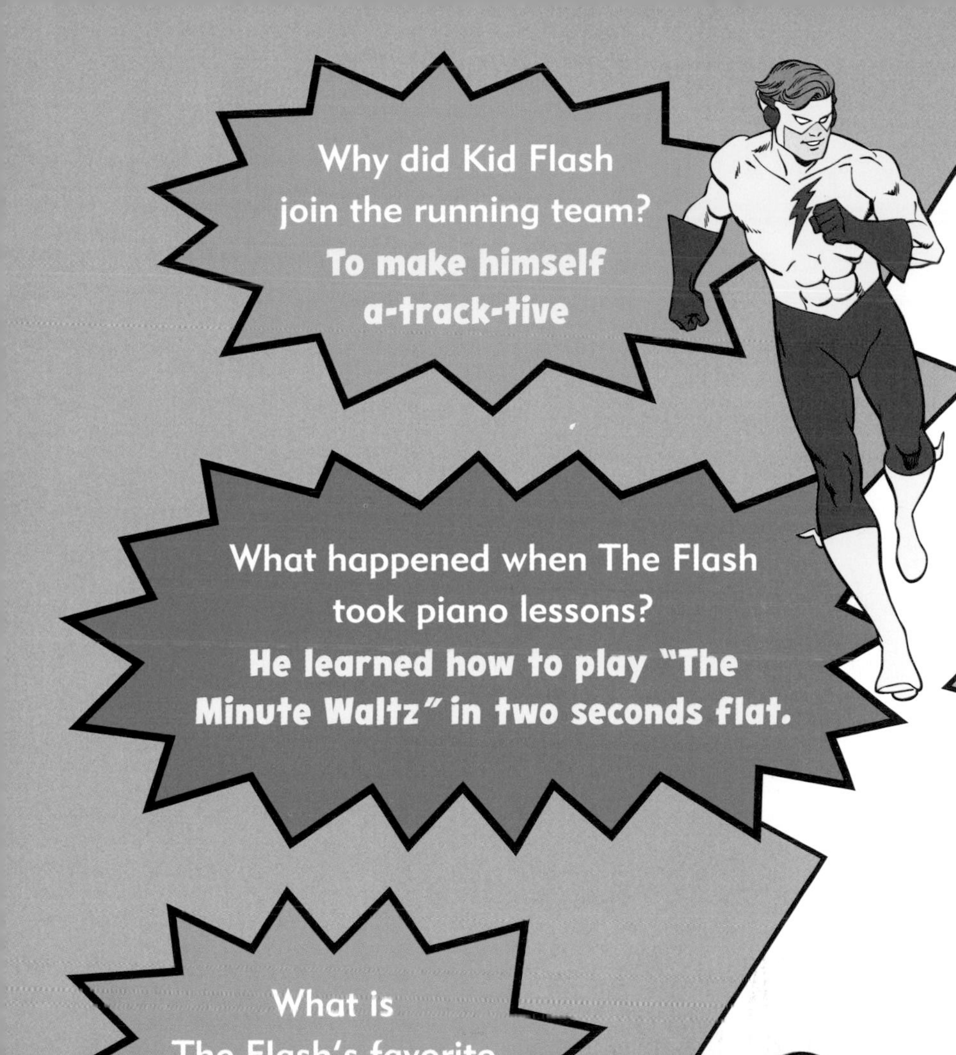

What happened when The Flash took piano lessons?

He learned how to play "The Minute Waltz" in two seconds flat.

What is The Flash's favorite meal of the day?

Breakfast, followed by lunchfast and dinnerfast

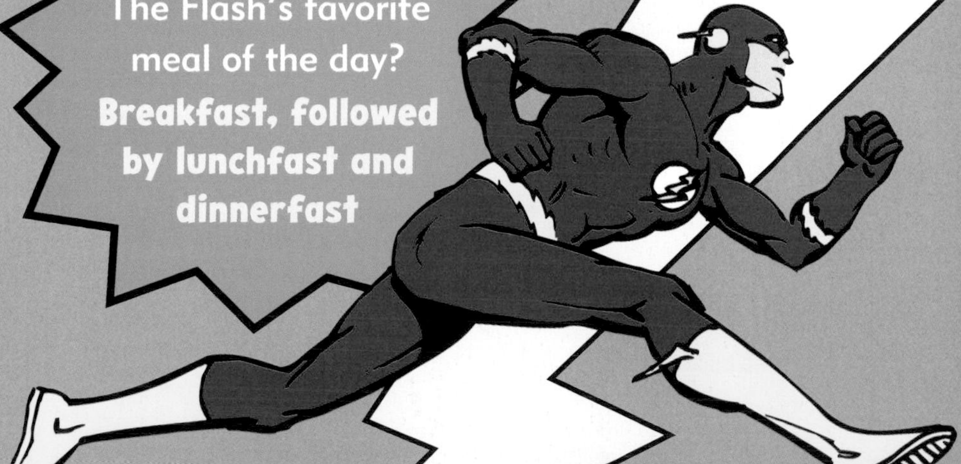

How do criminals feel when they hear Billy Batson say "Shazam!"?
Terribolt

Does Red Tornado get along with the Justice League?
He's their biggest fan.

How did Cyborg feel when he woke up and found that half his body was powered by electricity?
He was shocked.

What do Robin's foes experience?
The agony of de-feet

What's the most important part of the Justice League constitution?
The Bill of Tights

What do you get when The Flash takes a nap?
A runny doze

How many feet does The Flash have to move to go around the world?
Two—his right and his left

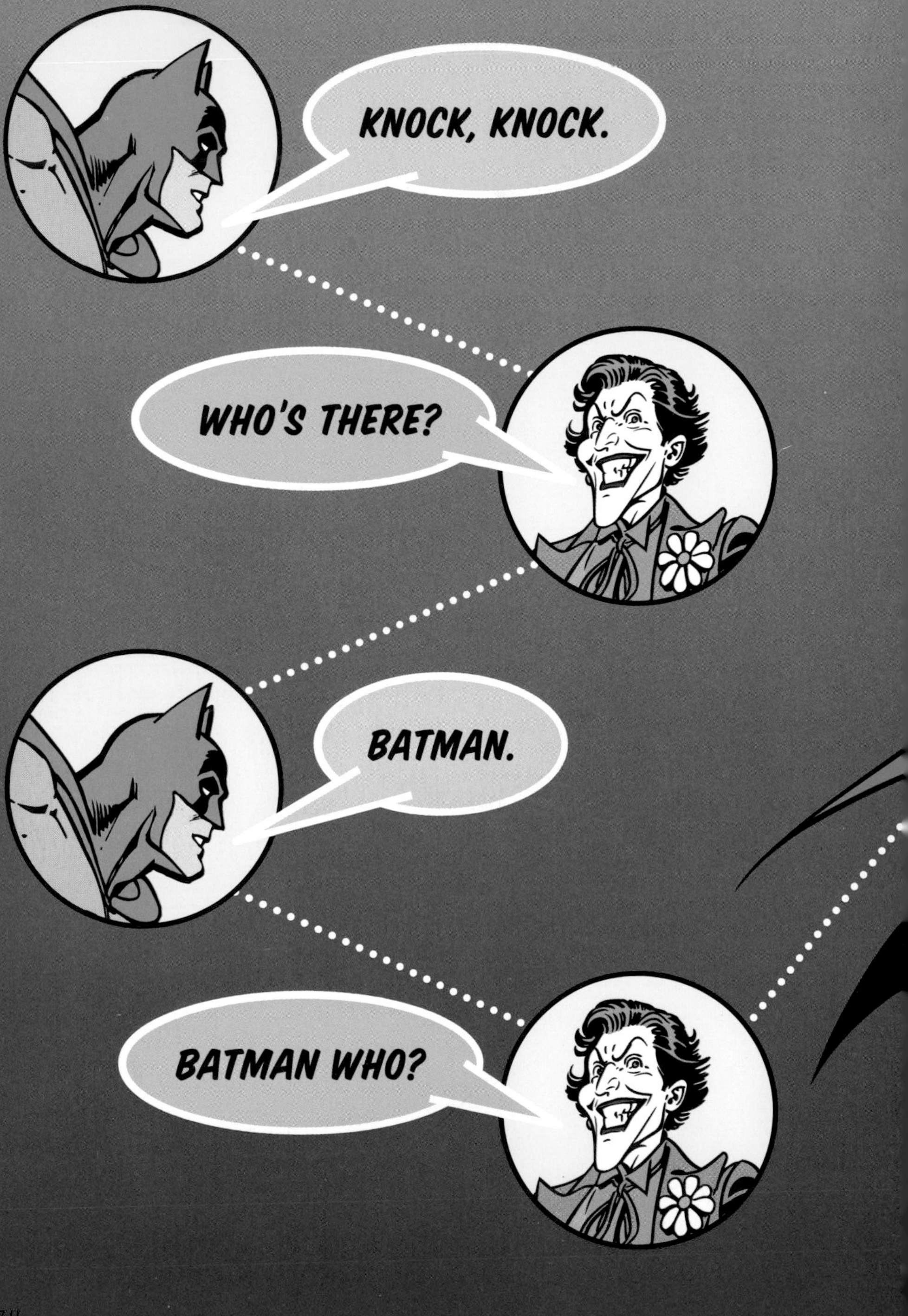
KNOCK, KNOCK.
WHO'S THERE?
BATMAN.
BATMAN WHO?